THE
DECK
OF
OMENS

THE DECK OF OMENS

CHRISTINE LYNN HERMAN

HYPERION

LOS ANGELES   NEW YORK

First Edition, April 2020
10 9 8 7 6 5 4 3 2 1
FAC-020093-20066

Printed in the United States of America

This book is set in Minion Pro/Monotype; Anavio Bold/Fontspring
Designed by Tyler Nevins

Library of Congress Control Number: 2019957854
ISBN 978-1-368-02527-0

Reinforced binding

Visit www.hyperionteens.com

SUSTAINABLE FORESTRY INITIATIVE

Certified Sourcing
www.sfiprogram.org
SFI-00993

Logo Applies to Text Stock Only

For my parents, who taught me
how to fall in love with books

CHAPTER ONE

All the most important moments in May Hawthorne's life had happened beneath the tree in her backyard.

She had come into the world there sixteen years ago; her mother, too stubborn to admit she was in labor until it was too late, gave birth all on her own as night faded into dawn on a blistering summer morning, then drove herself and her newborn daughter to the hospital.

May had touched the Deck of Omens for the first time beneath that tree. Challenged her older brother to see who could swing themselves up into its branches more quickly. Whispered a thousand secrets to the knot in the center of the trunk, forever frozen in the shape of a half-shut eye. When sleep eluded her, she would sneak outside and curl up beneath the hawthorn's gnarled branches on a bed of moss and fallen leaves. Its deep, steady heartbeat never failed to lull her into slumber.

It was the only place in the world where she felt safe, the only place where she didn't have to be someone's daughter or sister to garner attention. And now, after a century and a half of watching over her family, it was gone.

May rested a hand against the hawthorn trunk that had given

her family its name, warm bark turned to red-brown stone, and listened desperately for a heartbeat.

"There's nothing," she said, panic turning her voice raw and scratchy. "It's dead."

"We don't know that for certain." Augusta Hawthorne, May's mother, stepped out from the other side of the tree, her feathery blond hair slicked back from her forehead. She wore black silk pajamas and a matching pair of gloves, her feet shoved hastily into work boots. The weak light of dawn seeped in behind her, turning the dark circles beneath her eyes into cavernous pits.

The tree had called her, just as it had called May. Its cry for help had woken May at the break of dawn, her heart pounding in her chest. Her throat constricted in a silent scream as she shoved her curtains aside and stared out the window. The hawthorn's branches were frozen and stiff instead of swaying softly in the early morning breeze.

The tree had not called to Justin, her older brother. May had found her mother in the backyard, then run to fetch him. But he'd refused to even open his bedroom door, and she'd realized that he did not—could not—care about this the way she did.

Her mother cared, though. They stood in the backyard together, May pretending she didn't see the tears glistening in Augusta Hawthorne's eyes as they both surveyed the hawthorn's frozen corpse.

"We'll have to handle this," she said now. "Just us. No sense in burdening your brother."

And for once, May wasn't angry with her mother for letting Justin off the hook.

When a Hawthorne turned sixteen, they asked the tree to give them access to the powers that were their family's birthright.

These powers enabled them to protect the town of Four Paths from the monster that lurked in the woods in a lifeless prison called the Gray. But Justin had failed his ritual. Which meant there were powers he would never have—and responsibilities he would never bear. Keeping him around to watch them work would only have hurt him more.

It also gave May a chance to show her mother why the tree had chosen her over him in the first place. Because she could handle everything Four Paths threw at her. Even this.

"No one can find out," Augusta continued, staring at the branches. "If the town discovers this attack on our family, the consequences will be catastrophic."

"An attack," May said, the words sour in her mouth. That was the right term for it, but it still felt dangerous to say. Because this attack hadn't come from the monster they were supposed to be defending the town from. It had come from one of their supposed allies, someone she'd once considered a friend.

"This is Harper Carlisle's fault," May whispered. Harper, who was immensely powerful but had never known it—until now. "She got her memories back."

Her mother nodded grimly. "It's the only possibility."

May stared at the hawthorn tree, its corpse turning more red than brown in the light of the rising sun, and thought of the past few weeks. The way the roots that connected Four Paths had split apart and woven themselves back together.

From the moment she flipped over Violet Saunders's card a month ago, a passageway had opened up in her mind, roots tunneling down a path she'd never seen before. One where everything changed. She could have stopped it, let the roots wither. But instead, May had chosen to trust her brother and Isaac, chosen to give Violet Saunders her memories back after Augusta had erased them. She'd believed it had been the right thing to do to keep the town safe.

And Violet *had* kept the town safe—but surely she had realized that Augusta was capable of much more. That she had used her powers against other founders, like Harper. Violet must have figured out how to return Harper's memories, too, leading Harper to seek revenge on the family who had taken them from her. Which meant that what had happened to the hawthorn tree was May's fault. Guilt rose in her stomach, thick and bubbling, as she wondered how long it would take for Augusta to realize what she'd done.

May had been the perfect daughter to Augusta Hawthorne for the last seven years. But Augusta's memory was long, and May knew that she had not forgotten the time before that, when her daughter's attention and adoration was reserved solely for her father. It didn't matter how well May behaved herself now. Augusta would never truly trust her. And if Augusta found out about what she'd done, it would shatter the fragile peace between them—possibly forever.

"How do you think it happened?" May asked, trying to keep her voice calm and methodical.

"The Saunders family," her mother said immediately. May sagged with relief. "I was a fool to think I could change the old Carlisle-Saunders alliance. To be *happy* that June—" She shook her head and pressed a gloved hand to her mouth.

"Okay, so the Saunders family might have given Harper her memories back," May said hastily. She didn't like people paying special attention to her when she was overcome by emotion; she could extend her mother the same courtesy. "What do we do about it? How do we fix this?"

Augusta's face twisted with fury. "If Harper Carlisle is truly the one responsible for this," she said, "we will see to it that she sets this right, and answers for what she's done."

May let the word *we* kindle inside her—a promise. "Yeah. We will."

Augusta nodded approvingly. "You know what you need to do next, I assume."

May sighed, but she inclined her head. It wasn't that she minded using her powers—it was just that Augusta never asked her for any help beyond her abilities. They were the only part of her daughter she seemed to care about. "You want a reading."

"Yes." Augusta gestured toward the hawthorn. "But I want you to do it for the tree itself. Is that possible?"

May stared up at the tree, her heart heavy in her throat. Normally the smaller branches would be bending in the wind, birds chirping from above as they nestled in the copper-and-yellow leaves. But the tree was stiff and still, the wildlife gone. Perhaps they had been scared away; perhaps they had been petrified, too, for May had spent the past three weeks with Harper Carlisle, and she knew by now that Harper had no mercy. Still, May understood that it was not in the branches where the true lifeblood of a tree lay, nor was it in the knot on the trunk or its yellowing leaves.

It was the roots that really mattered.

"I think so." May reached into the pocket of her pink pajama shirt and pulled out the Deck of Omens, then knelt at the base of the tree. "I can do my best."

Augusta's lips pursed, and May knew exactly what her

mother was thinking—that her best was not a guarantee of victory. That it had never truly been good enough. But she sat beside May anyway.

The Deck of Omens was the Hawthorne family's greatest heirloom, crafted by the family's founder, Hetty Hawthorne, from the bark of this very tree. In most hands they were useless, but in May's grip they contained the power of possibility—the ability to gaze into the past and future of a living focal point, assuming she asked the right question. The cards changed over time, evolving with each generation to reflect the town and allow for more accurate readings. The only person May couldn't do a reading for was herself.

May's hands shook as she began to shuffle the deck, searching for the connection that always formed in the back of her mind when she touched the cards, the opening of a pathway that only she could travel down. Lives were complex, twisty things, brimming with a myriad of possibilities. It was her job to follow the pathways most likely to occur, to use the cards as a guide that would cut through any internal turmoil. People, she had learned, were often in deep denial about where they had come from and where they were going.

But it wasn't her job to fix them. It was her job to tell the truth, whether they liked it or not.

For a moment, the pathway resisted her, and panic swelled in May's chest, a bubble that burst a moment later as the familiar feeling coursed through her. May gasped with relief. It was not dead, then, merely hurt, and that meant she could find a way to heal it—she *would* find a way to heal it. Because without this tree her family would be broken; without this tree, she would be nothing at all.

"How can we fix what happened to you?" she asked the stone trunk in front of her, addressing her question directly to the gnarled, half-shut eye. A path unfurled in her mind, and she followed it, images rushing through her brain, as the cards in her hand began to disappear.

During May's first few readings, the images had been overwhelming—people she didn't know, symbols she didn't understand, coming at her so quickly that it was impossible to process them. But she had learned to channel her thoughts and merely let them flow through her, a vessel for the Deck of Omens, for the Hawthorne family. It was almost like watching a slideshow. Now she saw a traffic jam on Main Street, a puddle of strange iridescent liquid, a flash of the Carlisle lake. And then suddenly one image, stronger than all the others: a tree with the bark half melted away. Something *wrong* was stirring in the wreckage of the collapsed trunk. May's heartbeat sped up as a wisp of gray extended outward from the tree like an unfurling hand.

The vision faded, and May was left clutching three cards, the taste of decay in the back of her throat. Things were rising that should have been long buried—bodies and broken promises, betrayed friends and dishonored families.

Across from her, Augusta was staring intently at the cards. "Three seems low for this sort of reading."

"I don't control how many are left. You know that." May pushed down her annoyance at how much Augusta always questioned this, questioned *her*, whenever she did a reading. Screaming would change nothing, and so all she had was this: the satisfaction that nobody else knew what she was thinking.

She inhaled shakily, then laid the cards out on the grass and pressed her palms to the earth, her fingers digging into the loamy soil. May pictured herself grasping the roots that tunneled beneath the ground, roots that had long ago taken up residence in her soul.

Some of the founders' descendants wanted nothing more than a way out of this town, but May Hawthorne had never once considered it.

This was her home. This was her birthright.

And this moment, of dawn breaking, earth on her palms, hope in her heart—this was what she was meant to do.

May reached forward and flipped over the first card.

It was her card. The Seven of Branches. A girl with her arms lifted above her head, her face tipped back toward the sky. Branches wove around her body and rooted themselves in the earth; her fingers elongated into tendrils, leaves budding from the edges.

The card frightened Justin. He'd told her multiple times that he found it unsettling, the way the tree had taken her over. But May saw it differently: the serenity on the girl's face, the peace in her posture. She belonged to the forest, and it belonged to her.

"Interesting," Augusta said softly, across from her.

May tried to understand what the cards were telling her. She rarely pulled her own card in readings that weren't for a family member—but maybe the tree was as good as a family member. Maybe that was why.

She flipped over the second card, and her heart twisted in her chest.

It was the Two of Stones. Harper Carlisle's card. The art showed a single hand breaking through the surface of a lake, a stone visible in its clenched fist.

May's gut had been right. This was her fault, and she had to clean up her mess before it got even worse.

"I think Harper can fix it," she said. "I guess that makes sense."

Augusta's jaw twitched. "I suppose so."

May sank her fingers into the dirt again and thought of the roots, felt the path in her mind unfurl a little further. She could feel the hawthorn more clearly. Another vision—herself, standing in the same place she was kneeling now as the tree changed from stone to bark. And yet it didn't feel like a victory. The vision May had seen a moment ago tugged at her mind, a deeper dread, a bigger problem. Something she needed to solve.

"I don't think my card is just here because I'm doing the reading," she said, frowning.

Augusta raised an eyebrow. "Oh?"

"No." May swallowed. "The tree is asking me for help."

The doubt on her mother's face hurt. "Are you certain?"

"Would you have said that to Justin?"

May hadn't meant to put it so bluntly. She knew from the thinness of Augusta's lips that she would pay for it later somehow, in a privilege taken away or an unpleasant patrol schedule for the next week. But it wasn't fair—it wasn't. That nobody seemed to believe she could be that important. That, deep down, May worried they were right.

"Justin isn't here," Augusta said. "And you still have one card left."

May stared down at the all-seeing eye. It was easier to look at the card than her mother's face. Her hands trembled as rage, hot and heady, swirled within her. Rage for her tree. Rage for her mother, still desperately chasing down the child who could not help her and ignoring the one who could.

Deep in her mind, the pathways spiraled and wound. May felt something unfurling—a path that was *hers*. Thin and spiky, coiling around itself like a tangled knot of possibilities that could not yet be unraveled.

It pulsed in her mind like a beating heart, and for the first time, May reached for it. She grasped at the tendrils and pulled that path into focus, letting the roots worm their way into her mind.

It's mine, she snarled, at the cards, at Four Paths itself. *Whatever happens next belongs to me.*

A surge of energy coursed through her, to the card in her hands. It burned white-hot between her interlaced fingers, tracing the maps of old wounds that had long since faded. It was only her sense of self-control that kept her from crying out.

May felt the path lock into place. Felt the card in her hand vibrate—then shift, until the heat on her palms had faded.

She took a deep breath and opened her eyes. She could feel blood pooling beneath her nostrils and at the rims of her eyes, blurring her vision. When she blinked, crimson splatters appeared on her pajama pants.

"What was *that*?" Augusta said sharply.

May's lie was quiet, easy. "The cards had more to tell me."

But it had been just the opposite. She'd had more to tell the cards—and they had *changed*. They'd *listened to her*.

A Hawthorne shouldn't have been able to do that. But she had.

May flipped over the final card without another word, ready to see her path, ready to accept her future.

And gasped.

Her eyes took in the Crusader—a knight on a horse, reared back to charge, no part of him visible but two fiery eyes beneath his helmet.

Her father's card.

May already knew that when she looked at her mother's face, all she would see was crushing, inevitable disappointment. Augusta would insist it meant nothing, that it was a sign to be ignored.

But May knew better.

Because the Crusader in this context could only mean one thing: She would not be able to fix the hawthorn tree without her father. And if that meant going against Augusta's wishes, so be it.

After all, the Deck of Omens wasn't her mother's to command. It was hers.

CHAPTER TWO

One week later

Harper Carlisle waited for her reckoning with a blade in her hand and a deep, impenetrable dread in her heart.

"You can put that down," Violet Saunders said, the calm in her voice belied by how aggressively she was gripping her cup of coffee. They stood side by side in the backyard of her friend's imposing manor house, staring out at the woods. The treetops on the hill before them shone like a wildfire in the late-afternoon sunlight. "They aren't going to hurt you."

Harper eyed the two figures standing at the bottom of the hill, perhaps twenty feet away, and opted not to lower her sword.

"They're my family," she said. "Of course they're going to hurt me."

This meeting hadn't been her idea. But she had agreed to it when her siblings texted Violet, desperate to see her. Because after a week sequestered in the Saunders manor with nothing to do but stare at creepy taxidermied animals, Harper was sick of hiding.

There were problems she needed to deal with if she ever wanted to leave the safety of Violet's house again. And although she didn't want to talk to them, Seth and Mitzi Carlisle were still the least awful of the conversations she had ahead of her.

Nobody spoke beyond awkward greetings as Harper's siblings shuffled through the back door. Violet shepherded them all to the living room, where Seth and Mitzi sat on the wide leather couch. Harper took a plushy armchair, her residual limb twinging with pain as she surveyed her brother and sister. Her left arm ended just after the elbow, the result of an accident that had happened right after her ritual. When she was particularly frightened or upset, she could still feel the pain in her phantom limb, an invisible left hand aching.

They had both seen better days. Mitzi's long red hair was piled in a messy bun atop her head, her eyeliner smudged at the corners and a zit budding on her chin. Seth was wearing a sweatshirt that read PUBLIC SAFETY HAZARD; it looked more like a statement of fact than a bad joke.

"I brought this," her sister said quietly, shoving a duffel bag onto the coffee table between them. "It's your clothes and makeup and shit."

Harper raised an eyebrow. "You're wearing my black sweater right now."

"I didn't say *all* your clothes." Mitzi was fourteen, and in that moment she sounded it, petulant and frustrated. "You know you don't have to do this, right? You could just come home."

"Mitzi." Seth's voice was low and hoarse. He reached into his pocket, pulled out Harper's phone, and tossed it onto the table beside the duffel bag. "She was so desperate to get away from us that she didn't bring *anything* with her. She's not coming home just because you ask."

Harper stared at the gauntlets her siblings had thrown on the table, her heart heavy. She wanted to give Mitzi skin-care advice and tell Seth to wash his hair. She lowered the sword onto her lap instead. It was the only thing she'd brought with her when she'd shown up here seven days ago—that and a muddy, soaking-wet nightgown that she'd been forced to throw away.

"Seth's right," she said. "I'm not coming home. But it's not because I'm trying to get away from either of you."

Mitzi leaned forward. "Is it . . . ?" Mitzi's voice was soft. "The reason you're not coming back . . . is it because it's true? What the Hawthornes are saying about you?"

Harper's heartbeat hammered in her throat. Violet, who'd remained perfectly silent until now, cleared her throat.

"Careful," Violet said. Orpheus, formerly a house cat and currently Violet's undead companion, leaped into her lap. "You promised not to ask too many questions." It wasn't a threat, not exactly, but Harper's siblings stiffened just the same.

This was why Harper had asked Violet to sit in. Not for physical protection—Harper was more than capable of defending herself if necessary—but because there were things they both knew she was unwilling to talk about. Truths she wasn't ready to tell. This one, though, Harper was okay with.

"It's all right," she said. "You want to see what I can do? You want proof?"

Harper's hand brushed the edge of the neglected fern sitting beside the table. She took a deep breath and *pushed*.

She had not gone to the Hawthorne house the night she got her powers back with the conscious thought of destroying their tree. But when she saw the hawthorn's great branches spreading behind the roof, waving in the wind, she had felt the cumulative rage about everything that had been done to her—her father's hands closing around her neck, the Church of the Four Deities in their dark brown robes, Justin staring at her, a sword pressed against his neck, and, of course, the night that had just come back to her. The night Augusta Hawthorne had taken her powers away before she'd ever gotten the chance to use them.

Violet was obviously the reason her memories were back. Violet had gotten them back herself, after all, and so had Violet's mother; clearly she was the one who had figured out the secret to restoring herself, clearly she was the one who had left Harper that note.

There was so much to sort through. So much to feel. Harper understood now why Justin Hawthorne had behaved strangely toward her these past few weeks—because his mother wasn't the reason she'd lost everything.

He was.

He'd betrayed her the night of her ritual. Sold her out to his mother before she could have the chance to use her newfound powers.

Pushed her into the lake, which had led to the accident that had cost her a hand—and led her straight into the Gray.

Harper had lost sight of herself in that moment, dizzy with longing for everything Justin and his family had taken from her. She'd reached forward, her palm pressing tightly against the trunk, and pushed her anger into it. And when she pulled back and realized that the hawthorn had gone deathly still, she hadn't wanted to reverse it.

This time, the change was smaller, almost gentle. The leaves froze in place, their color fading to red-brown and spiraling down into the dirt, until there was no plant remaining, only stone. But then Harper felt something else: a push to keep going. The stone spread down the side of the fern pot, encroaching toward the floor, and Harper's throat went dry with panic as she realized that she didn't know if she could stop.

Violet's hand landed on her shoulder, wrenching her focus away. Harper exhaled with sharp relief as she realized that the spread of stone had stopped. When she looked up, Mitzi and Seth were both gaping at her.

Her brother spoke first. "Shit."

Mitzi knelt on the floor, examining the plant. When she caught Harper's gaze, her eyes were as round and wide as two full moons. "You have powers?"

Harper's laugh was slightly bitter, slightly manic. "Yeah."

"And you used them..."

"On the family that deserved some retribution," she said. "So, yeah, I left, because I didn't want Augusta Hawthorne to punish any of you for me. Because you deserve to make your own choices instead of being forced to go along with mine."

"Choices?" Mitzi returned to the couch, tugged on her earring—a nervous tic.

Harper sighed. This was the part of the conversation she'd been dreading the most.

"Augusta Hawthorne took my memories of my powers away," she said. "Do you still want to patrol for her, knowing that?"

Mitzi hesitated. "Patrolling is what keeps the town safe."

"Does taking my powers away seem *safe* to you? Maybe if I'd had access to them, fewer people would have died."

"Or maybe you would've turned more than the hawthorn tree to stone." Seth's voice was the most somber Harper had ever heard it.

Her stomach churned with nausea. She'd known it would go this way—but she'd still hoped otherwise.

"Well," she said. "I'm here if you change your minds."

After Harper's siblings had left—Mitzi stomping hastily out the door, Seth moving a little more slowly, eyeing a taxidermied bear head in the corner suspiciously—Violet helped her carry her things up to the room she'd claimed.

"You could have told them the rest of the truth, you know," Violet said as Harper shoved her clothes into a musty old dresser and grabbed her phone. "That might have changed their minds."

Harper looked up from her phone screen. She'd been trying to turn it back on, but the battery was dead. Phantom pain twinged at the end of her residual limb again.

She wasn't just staying with Violet and her mother because she'd turned the hawthorn tree to stone. The real reason she couldn't go home was because her dad had tried to kill her. He couldn't remember it, thanks to Augusta Hawthorne, but she would never forget.

"You saw how it was with them," she said, plugging her phone in to charge. "They wouldn't have believed me anyway. They don't even need Augusta to use her powers on them to be in the Hawthornes' pockets."

Violet's mouth thinned into a sharp line, and Harper could tell she disagreed with her, but to her relief, the other girl didn't push it. Maybe she figured Harper had been through enough for the time being.

"All right," she said. "Hey—I'm meeting Isaac to do some research into the founders this afternoon. Do you want to come? We could use the extra pair of eyes."

"I do *not* want to talk to Isaac Sullivan right now." Harper knew she sounded irritable and petty. She didn't care. She was worn thin enough as it was. "And I can't even leave the house, remember? I'm stuck waiting around until the Hawthornes decide they don't want to kill me."

"You don't usually wait around for someone to give you permission," Violet said, fixing her with a pointed stare. "Why now?"

Harper hesitated.

The truth was that for so long, she'd been ignored. It had felt a lot easier to be bold when she knew no one was watching her. The town's eyes had made her cautious, because she knew that in many ways what happened next would be a kind of first impression. And the Hawthornes' attention had made her most cautious of all.

"You're right. I just don't know how to make the Hawthornes see me as anything but a threat. And we both know what they do to threats."

Violet paused. "I'm not entirely sure it's true that the Hawthornes *do* see you as a threat. Not all of them, anyway."

"Sure they don't."

"No, seriously." Violet hesitated, as if considering something, then exhaled and continued. "You remember when I had my memories taken away by Augusta?"

Harper nodded, unease stirring in her gut. "Of course."

"Well, May's the reason I got them back."

Harper gaped at her. "That's not possible."

May Hawthorne was a perfect blond automaton, an extension of Augusta with shiny teeth and an endless supply of pastel bomber jackets. She was the last person Harper would expect to defy her mother.

But if what Violet was saying was true, then she had, in a major way.

"I know how impossible it sounds," Violet said. "But it's true. There's ... more going on there than you might think."

On the nightstand, Harper's phone had finally come back to life. Blinking on the screen were dozens of unread texts. She didn't have to look at the number to know who most of them were from.

"Maybe you're right." She turned away from Violet to stare at it more closely. If her friend was telling the truth about May, surely it stood to reason that Justin couldn't be as mad at her as she'd imagined. Surely there was some way to work all of this out. "I ... I need to make a call."

* * *

Violet met Isaac Sullivan in the foyer of the town hall that evening, as planned. The familiar echo of her feet on the marble floors agitated her. This was the third time they'd met in the past week, all with the same goal in mind, and she had no reason to believe this excursion would be any more successful than the others.

Unfortunately, the only other idea she'd brought up had just gone to shit.

"The hair's new," Isaac said, detaching himself from the shadowy corners of the foyer like a lanky wraith. He was fond of making dramatic entrances, although he'd been careful to avoid startling Violet after she'd cursed him out the first time he emerged unexpectedly from a dark hallway. "Is it part of an early Halloween costume or something? Because you know Four Paths doesn't celebrate that."

The hair was indeed new. It had taken Violet all afternoon to get from her natural color—a brown so dark it was almost black—to this new one. Bleach, toner, box dye, and one blow-dry later, though, she was finally done.

The result was a bob the bright crimson of a founders' medallion. Of an open wound. Of a rose.

"I'm going to kill a monster," Violet had whispered at her new reflection, letting the words echo through the bathroom, and in that moment, she could almost believe they were true.

Now, staring at Isaac, she felt a little foolish.

"I know," Violet said tersely. The Halloween thing was another Church of the Four Deities holdover—nobody dressed up or trick-or-treated, since it wasn't considered safe. "I just... wanted a change, okay?"

"Fair enough." Isaac frowned into the darkness behind her. "Did you invite Harper?"

"I tried," Violet said, the words sour in her mouth. "She's not interested. The Hawthornes are a bigger problem than the Beast right now, as far as she's concerned."

Violet knew firsthand how dangerous the Beast was. Fighting it was bigger than all their petty disagreements—but she couldn't force Harper to see that. Her friend had already been through enough.

"We could've used another founder's help," Isaac said. Violet nodded. She followed him up the stairs at the back of the foyer and to the locked door in the hallway behind it, one Isaac had somehow managed to get a key to. It led to the founders' archives—the best store of information either of them had been able to find on the history of Four Paths. They'd been meeting here regularly since Isaac had agreed to help her try to kill the Beast.

Violet was grateful that she didn't have to search for answers alone. But it was hard to keep her emotions toward Isaac contained at *grateful*. She hated that she'd wanted some kind of reaction from him—about the hair, about *anything*. When she'd first moved to Four Paths almost two months ago, Violet had mistaken Isaac's basic human decency for romantic affection. She'd been too starved for human connection to know the difference between friendship and a crush. But she knew better now.

Isaac had a crush, all right, but it was a crush reserved entirely for Justin Hawthorne. And it didn't matter that Violet could tell Justin didn't feel the same way—that Justin and Harper were locked in their own messed-up story. It still hurt. Which made her feel pathetic and grumpy and annoyed with herself.

She flipped on the row of harsh fluorescent lights in the founders' archives, blinking at the sudden brightness, and sighed at the familiar piles of papers that loomed in front of them. The portraits of the four founders on the wall across from her watched them intently, something like judgment in their gazes.

"Well, then," she said. "Let's go look at some more useless newspapers."

"Wait." Isaac gestured to the desks in the middle of the room where they'd centralized their research efforts. Violet looked over and saw a stack of materials she didn't recognize—notebooks kind of like the one that had held Stephen Saunders's journals, clearly well-worn and referenced. "I found something new I think you might be interested in."

"What are those?" Violet asked, stepping toward the stack.

"They belonged to the other members of the Church of the Four Deities," Isaac said. "Augusta confiscated them when she took their memories—it's everything she could find about their resurrection of the cult. Meeting times, rituals, goings-on, et cetera."

"And she *gave* them to you?"

"Nah. I stole them from the evidence lockers at the station."

Violet's heartbeat sped up. "Holy shit. These could actually be helpful."

"Wow," Isaac drawled. "That was, like, eighty percent of a compliment."

Violet raised an eyebrow. "Maybe it'll be a hundred percent of a compliment if the Church actually knew how to attack the Beast."

"I break the law for you, and this is the thanks I get?"

"You work for Augusta," Violet said, flipping the first notebook open. The symbol etched into the inside of the cover was all too familiar: a circle with four lines cut into it, extending nearly to the center. "You basically are the law."

"I'm not the Hawthornes' attack dog." Isaac's voice was low but vehement. "You know that, right?"

Violet glanced up at him. He was looking at her a shade too intensely, and she knew that although she'd been mostly teasing, it was important to him that she didn't actually believe what she'd said.

"Yeah, I know."

His jaw loosened, and he nodded once, brusquely. "Good."

Something had been off about Isaac lately—a layer on top of other layers, a problem Violet told herself wasn't hers to try to solve. Besides, if she didn't ask questions, she could still maintain the illusion that she didn't want to know how he'd gotten that scar on his neck—or what had really happened to his family.

"Anyway," Isaac said, a little too quickly, "I already looked at the Church's archives. You can read them all on your own time if you want, but the only interesting stuff is in here."

He pulled a different notebook out of the stack and flipped it open, tapping on the name scrawled on the title page. *Maurice Carlisle.*

"This belonged to Harper's dad."

Isaac nodded. "I wasn't sure how Harper would take it if she was here, honestly. Us rifling through his things. But you said you wanted to kill the Beast—and I don't think we're going to solve a mystery that's plagued this town for a century and a half by playing nice."

"I know we aren't," Violet said quietly. "I don't care. It messed up my family. I want it dead."

"So do I," Isaac said.

"You read these notes already. And you must have found something, or you wouldn't have bothered with all this."

Isaac met her eyes, and she knew she was right.

"Here," he said simply, flipping the notebook open to a bookmarked page. "It's how the Church of the Four Deities planned the ritual they tried to do on your mom. The one to turn her into a vessel for the Beast."

Violet looked down at the page. The words were scratched in messy handwriting.

The Beast has warned us that it cannot survive in corporeal form in Four Paths without a host. If cut off from the Gray for too long, it will wither and die.... We cannot allow this to happen. We must not seal the gate before the transfer of its soul is complete.

Her throat went dry. This was exactly what they'd been looking for: a weakness.

"So if we can draw the Beast out," she said slowly, "the same way the Church did, but cut it off from the Gray..."

"It'll die," Isaac finished.

"How can we close the Gray, though?"

Isaac raised his hands in the air. "My power extends to the Gray, remember? Any portal it opens, I can disintegrate."

Violet winced, remembering how much messing directly with the Gray had seemed to cost Isaac, but nodded.

"Okay," she said. "But that doesn't answer how we would lure it out, does it? We'd need somebody connected to it. Somebody—oh."

Suddenly she was back on the night of that ritual again, staring at her mother's lifeless body lying in the circle of bone. Watching Rosie appear in front of her, in her bedroom, in the Gray, in the spire.

She couldn't do that again. Not willingly. Not when it had taken everything she had just to escape with her life.

"Absolutely not." Violet slammed the book shut. "I refuse to be monster bait."

"You just said you agreed that we couldn't play nice," Isaac said roughly. "And you already drove it out of your head once. I know you can do it again."

"This is different," Violet whispered, thinking of how the Beast had melted the flesh away from Rosie's face, forced her to watch it decay. "I beat it that one time, yeah. But if it comes back, it's not going to let me get away so easily. And we don't even know if this will work. To risk everything like this—it's reckless."

"Maybe it is," Isaac said. "But if you really want it dead, well, this might be our best chance."

"I have to think about this." Violet snatched up the journal and stuffed it in her bag. "Just give me a little time, okay?"

Isaac's face softened. He made no move to get the book back from her, which Violet appreciated.

"All right. But know this: Nobody's ever changed things in Four Paths by pulling a punch. They pay for every victory."

Violet's eyes strayed to the founders on the wall, all solemn, all beautiful, all dead.

"I know," she said, and then she turned and strode out the door.

CHAPTER THREE

Most of Four Paths avoided the depths of the forest, especially at night. But it was the part of town May loved best. She tipped her head back and shook the tension out of her shoulders, listening to the birds chirping in the trees. A yellow moon hung above her head, a waxing gibbous surrounded by a sea of hazy stars.

"I think I just twisted an ankle," grumbled a voice beside her. "This is totally going to mess with my race next week."

The tension returned to May's shoulders immediately. She moved her gaze away from the sky and toward the figure on her right—Justin Hawthorne, her older brother, Four Paths' guilt-ridden golden boy and their mother's undisputed favorite child.

"You'll live," she said tersely. "Stop complaining. You should feel lucky you're back on the patrol schedule at all."

"Yeah, on a trial basis," said Justin.

May thought bitterly that a trial basis was more than Justin deserved considering all the shit he'd put their family through. He'd betrayed their mother and she'd still given him what he wanted.

Justin, it seemed, was impervious to true damage—he would spring right back up again no matter how many times you knocked him down, while May felt sometimes as if she would shatter into tiny pieces if she had to handle one more catastrophe.

"Let's just concentrate on completing the route," May said. He was ruining the way the forest made her feel at night, reminding her of everything she couldn't be. "We need to be on alert. We don't know when or how Dad is coming back."

Mentioning their father was a cheap shot, but it did what May had intended—made Justin tense up, too.

"Are you totally sure you saw him returning?" he asked, not for the first time.

The Hawthorne family did not talk about Ezra Bishop. No one had ever specifically made the rule, but May had followed it anyway—it was an unspoken truth in a sea of other unspoken truths, and May had grown quite good at learning how to veer away from anything that might tip the delicate balance between herself, her mother, and Justin.

But there was no avoiding this. Not anymore. And deep down, May was grateful for it.

Augusta hated May's father, so of course Justin did, too. But May missed him. He was the only person in her life who had ever chosen her over Justin. Who had ever made her feel special. She knew he wasn't perfect—but neither was Augusta.

"I'm certain," she said. "Mom's pretending it isn't happening. But it will. Those cards don't lie."

But they'd changed—changed for May. Justin didn't know that, though. Nobody did. And although Augusta had reacted to the news of her ex-boyfriend returning to town about as well as she'd reacted to her ex-girlfriend returning to town—which is to say she'd firmly refused to talk about it—May knew that the future she had chosen would come to pass.

She trusted the cards. She trusted herself.

"I know," Justin said quietly. "But he left so long ago. I thought maybe this time, he was finally gone for good."

May remembered their father's last day in town. It had begun with a fight, as most days did, but this time, when Augusta had told him to get out, he'd listened.

I'll be back soon, he had told May, planting a kiss on her blond head. She'd clung to his waist, her head buried in the soft leather of his jacket, and wailed like a banshee when Augusta peeled her away. It was the last time she had cried in front of someone else.

Take me with you, she'd asked her father, and Augusta would never forgive her for it.

It had been seven years, long past *soon*, but May still held out hope for his return.

The birdsong had faded away now, and there was only the sound of their footsteps as they crunched through the underbrush.

"He promised he'd come back," May said to Justin.

Justin shrugged, his broad shoulders silhouetted in the moonlight. What little she could make out of his face was frowning. "Yeah, well, he broke every other promise he ever made to us. Why would he have told the truth that time?"

The words flew out before she could stop them. "You're not really one to talk about lies."

Justin scowled in response. "Neither are you, May. Don't think I've forgotten how you sold us out to Mom."

"I didn't sell you out," May said. "I was worried about you. And I apologized for going too far."

She had said some awful things to Justin. She felt bad about that. But she had been tired of tagging along while he dragged people into dangerous situations, and worried that his propensity for playing the hero would only end in tragedy. Isaac cared about Justin far too much to ever call him out, and Augusta indulged him too much to see the truth. May had been the only one to hold him accountable for his decisions—and in the end, it hadn't even mattered.

Justin got to be the hero who helped save the day, and May's hawthorn tree got turned to stone. It wasn't fair.

"I know you said you were sorry," Justin said. "But our mother has been taking peoples' memories away for years, and you don't seem to care about it at all."

"That's not true," May whispered. "I care more than you know."

She had cared enough to give Violet her memories back—but she wasn't Justin. She couldn't just go around flagrantly disregarding her mother's rules and expecting to be welcomed back with open arms. Justin would never understand how hard she had to work to be treated half as well as he was on a bad day. Which was why she hadn't told him about Violet.

Because he wouldn't be impressed. Because he wouldn't understand what a big deal it had been for her to act against Augusta at all.

Justin coughed, grimacing, and turned toward her, jolting her away from her rising fury.

"Holy shit," he said. "Do you smell that?"

May breathed in deeply. She knew the smell of Four Paths' woods well—earth and oak. This time of year it was often tinged with the slight scent of dying leaves.

But May held a hand up to her mouth as a wave of decay washed over her, frowning. Dead leaves didn't smell like this.

Perhaps there was some kind of rotting animal—but no. This was more than that. It was the kind of smell that felt like a tangible thing, like the very air around her was somehow diseased.

"Yeah, I smell it," May said, pulling her flashlight out of her pocket and shining it on the thicket of branches in front of them. Again she noticed how silent it was, but this time she felt a twinge of unease. She should've picked up on the strangeness of that ages ago, but she'd been too busy arguing with Justin. "Something's wrong."

"You think the Gray got someone new?" Justin asked grimly. They both had their flashlights out now. May scanned the clearing around them for any sign of the smell, but there was nothing strange about the nearby forest.

May shook her head. "The bodies . . . they don't smell like anything."

May was deeply disturbed by the corpses that the Gray spat out, but at least she knew what they looked like. She didn't know *what* this was.

She held up her hand, noted the direction the wind was blowing, and pointed into the trees. "It's coming from over there."

"Great." Justin crashed forward through the underbrush with all the subtlety of a steamroller.

"Hey!" May yelled after him, reluctantly following in his wake. "You are literally that dude in the first five minutes of a horror movie right now. I hope you know that."

"We're on patrol," Justin said cheerfully from in front of her. "It's our job to walk into trouble."

May vehemently disagreed with that. Anomalies in the woods were meant to be mapped—she whipped out her phone and placed a pin at their location—and reported to Augusta. But this was classic Justin, breaking the rules, knowing there would always be someone there to catch him if he fell. If the Beast didn't kill him, maybe *she* would.

The ground sloped upward into a small hill. May paused for a brief rest while Justin, always in better shape than her, surged ahead. She was searching her backpack for a water bottle when she heard her name.

"May..." Justin's voice floated through the trees. "I found it."

His tone was too somber to warrant a snippy *I told you this would be disturbing.*

"All right. I'm coming." May clambered uphill and ducked beneath a low-hanging branch, pinching her nose in a futile attempt to block out the smell of decay.

She found Justin standing stiffly in the center of a small clearing, the shaky beam of his flashlight trained on the tree in front of him.

There was something horribly wrong with it. Part of the bark had faded from brown to a dark gray, and rivulets of liquid dripped down the trunk, leaving a slick, oily sheen behind them. The smell that wafted from it was nearly unbearable. May's eyes stung; she tried to blink her tears away, coughing.

May raised her flashlight, shuddering as she traced the spread of gray toward its branches.

"What do you think is happening here?" Justin asked, his voice muffled by the hand he'd clapped over his mouth and nose.

"I don't know," May said. She had been in the Gray just once, the time she had saved Justin from the Beast after he'd failed his ritual. Something about this tree reminded her of the forest she'd seen there, pulsating and alien, branches twisted toward her like clawing hands. But it wasn't the same—although it was damaged, the bark that remained was still unmistakably normal, still part of Four Paths.

She took a picture of it on her phone, then lowered her flashlight to the ground.

Iridescent liquid pooled on the ground below, soaking into the soil. May watched, alarmed, as it slid toward them. She'd never heard of anything like this before, yet it looked oddly familiar.

"We should move," she said, grabbing Justin's arm and yanking him back. "I don't think it's a good idea to touch it."

For once he didn't protest, his expression nervous. "Yeah. Wait—what's that?"

He gestured at the tree, and May swung her phone flashlight forward, a terrible sense of déjà vu washing over her.

She didn't know why it had taken this long for her to recognize it. But now, as she saw the half-melted trunk, harshly illuminated, and watched a tendril of gray emerge, she remembered sitting beneath the hawthorn tree just a few days ago, shuddering at that exact image. Before she could even fully process what it might mean, the gray dissipated, vanishing into the air like a puff of smoke. She shone her flashlight on the tree, on the iridescent trails of liquid still creeping toward them, but all signs of it were gone.

"Shit," she whispered, her grip tightening on Justin's arm. She had seen this coming for them, but that didn't tell her what it was—or how to stop it.

"You saw that too." His voice was raw. "The Gray. You saw it, right?"

May nodded, nausea churning in her stomach. "Let's get out of here. Mom needs to know about this."

They hurried back through the forest, their earlier argument forgotten. Long after the smell faded away, May still felt the touch of decay against her skin, as if rot were seeping into her very pores. And in her mind, that smoke unfurled over and over again, reaching for her.

Isaac Sullivan pressed a hand against the vault in his family's mausoleum that he should have been buried in, the plaque still engraved with his full name, and sighed.

Then he flipped it off.

He didn't particularly enjoy visiting his grave—it was always an unpleasant experience, best done with a stolen six-pack and a friend. But today it had felt necessary, even though he was stone-cold sober and was currently not speaking to the only friend he would have wanted to take here.

"This fucking family," he muttered, the sound of his footsteps echoing off the mausoleum's marble floors as he paced down the row of vaults. "This fucking town."

Most of Four Paths' dead were buried deep underground, their ashes stored in forgotten passageways in the catacombs beneath the town hall. But the founders each had their own wing in the mausoleum's main building. It was red-brown stone and polished marble, dozens of urns tucked away in neat rows of vaults.

Isaac's eyes strayed to the biggest plaque, the one at the top of the room, engraved with the Sullivans' signature dagger.

Richard Sullivan was buried here. His founder. His ancestor.

Isaac had never met him, but it didn't matter—he hated him. For making a deal he didn't understand with a monster he'd never properly seen. For trapping his descendants in a town where people died in awful ways and leaving them to stop it. For giving Isaac the powers that had led to the urns slotted neatly beside his own empty grave.

Guilt churned in his throat and made his eyes water, but Isaac forced himself to look at the plaques on either side of his. Caleb's and Isaiah's. It was the least he could do, considering the fact that two of his older brothers were dead because of him.

Grieving them was a harsh, strange thing, a double-edged knife that caught Isaac unawares each time he thought, perhaps, he'd begun to heal. It had only stopped hurting as much once he stopped trying to stanch the flow of his agony, once he accepted that his grief would always be an open wound.

But then a voice rang out from behind him and gouged it all open again.

"This fucking family, indeed," said Gabriel. "Shit, I hate this place."

Isaac turned around, trying to push down the steady pulse of panic in his chest as he stared at the only brother he had left. Gabriel had towered over Isaac when he'd left four years ago, but a growth spurt had evened the gap between them. They were about the same height now, although Isaac was lanky where Gabriel was broad-shouldered and muscular. Tattoos spilled out from beneath his brother's sleeves and across his forearms, covering the scars Isaac knew lurked beneath them. Isaac studied the ink on the hand closest to him: a skull with a dagger stabbed through the eye socket.

His own scar, a line drawn across his neck, began to throb beneath his high-necked sweater. A souvenir from the last time he and Gabriel had been together.

"You wanted me to meet you here," he said softly, the words echoing off the marble walls. "We didn't have to do this in front of the dead."

"You're wrong," Gabriel said evenly. "This is a family affair."

"Is that why you're here?" Isaac asked angrily. "To make me join them?"

Gabriel sighed. "I'm not going to kill you."

"I find that very difficult to believe."

Looking at Gabriel was like glimpsing a portal to the past. It had happened the first time Isaac had seen his brother a week ago, too, at the Sullivan ruins. Isaac hadn't said a word. His strength to speak had been gone, replaced by the sharp, insistent press of fear. He'd bolted instead, the scenery blurring with a memory he'd pushed down a long time ago, the memory of his fourteenth birthday, the night his family had taken him into the woods behind their home and tried to slit his throat.

He'd run that day, too, staggering through the trees. Crimson had followed in his wake, falling in dark, uneven splotches on the yellow leaves.

Follow the blood, he had grown up hearing. *Follow the blood, and you will find the Sullivans.*

And at last, too late, he had understood why.

He'd lived through that day somehow. And for the past few years, he'd convinced himself he was safe. But now Isaac understood just how wrong he'd been. He'd agreed to meet with Gabriel because he was tired of running. Because at least now he could face his brother, not in chains, but with the full might of their family's power in his blood. But so far, Gabriel hadn't tried to attack him. He genuinely seemed to want to talk. Which was almost worse, because Isaac had made a terrible mistake all those years ago and he deserved to be punished for it.

"Listen," Gabriel said, his voice even. "I'm not here to hurt you. You're my *brother*. I'm here about Mom."

Isaac stiffened. "What about her?"

Maya Sullivan was in a vegetative state at the nearest hospital. Had been for the last three years. Isaac was the only Sullivan who visited her because he was the only one left to do so.

"I don't know if you know this," Gabriel said, "but I've been getting updates of her medical records while I've been gone—"

"I've seen her medical records, too," Isaac said sharply. "And I've seen *her*. Have you ever bothered to visit?"

The shame on his brother's face was answer enough. Isaac felt a sharp twinge of smugness.

"That's not the point," Gabriel said evenly. "Her condition's worsened lately. The doctors recommend that we take her off life support."

Isaac glared at him. "She didn't sign a DNR."

"I know," Gabriel said. "But do you really think she'd want to live like this?"

Isaac flinched. Maybe Gabriel was right, but his mother was the only family he had left who still loved him. It was hard not to hope that as long as she drew breath, there was a chance of her coming back.

Love had always been painful for him, a weapon held to his throat that his family and friends had used to control him. It was an unanswered question, a constant ache in his chest, the distant echoes of memories he wished he could forget. Yet none of that could quash the hope he carried that, one day, he'd be able to care for the people around him and have it feel like victory instead of surrender. That his emotional bonds would make it easier, not harder, to be human.

"You don't know what she would have wanted," he said. "Neither of us do."

"And we'll never find out," Gabriel said. "Which means we need to make the best decision we can with the information we have. We're both legal adults now—we share the power of medical attorney for her. They're not going to do anything without both of our consent."

"Good." Isaac felt his power surging through his veins, building with his anger. His palms itched the way they always did in the moments before an outburst. "Because I say no, and I'm not changing my mind."

"Isaac . . ." Gabriel's voice was thick with warning. "You're not a child anymore. You know these kinds of decisions aren't ever easy, but they're necessary. At least promise me you'll think about it."

Isaac raised a hand in response. The air around him had begun to shimmer, purple and red light collecting around his palm. Gabriel stepped backward slowly.

"You're right," Isaac whispered. "I'm not a kid anymore. Now leave me alone."

He turned away from his brother, his hand closing into a fist, terrified that the tears collecting behind his eyelids would show if he looked at him for a moment longer. When he turned around again, Gabriel was gone, and Isaac's phone was buzzing in his pocket.

He scowled and fished it out, waiting for some kind of manipulative text. But it wasn't from Gabriel—it was from May.

"Oh no," he muttered, staring at the words on the screen. Reluctantly, he typed a response.

A few minutes later, May appeared in the doorway of the mausoleum. She wore her usual disdainful expression and a large amount of pink, but there was something slightly unraveled in the way her nails tapped anxiously against her thigh as she surveyed the vaults of founder remains.

Looking at her was painful, too, but in a different way. She bore too close of a resemblance to her older brother for comfort.

"You were just hanging out...here?" she asked him dubiously as she stepped inside, her heeled boots clicking on the marble floor.

Isaac shrugged. He didn't want to explain Gabriel to her, or to anyone. "You know. Paying my respects."

"Uh-huh." May sat down on the mausoleum's lone bench and gestured for Isaac to join her. "Well, it's private, at least."

Isaac sat beside her, staring at the engraving of the founders' seal carved into the center of the floor. It was a circle with four lines cutting through it, almost but not quite meeting in the middle. Visitors would have thought it was a cross; Isaac knew better.

This town lived in fear of a very different kind of god. Something more monstrous than holy, although for the founders they had been the same thing. Power was power and people would always want it, whether it was dressed up with pretty words and careful manipulation or stripped down to teeth and claws.

"Well?" he said, a little more sharply than he intended. He was still thinking about Gabriel. But he hadn't wanted to wait—with the Hawthornes, he'd learned, it was best to move quickly. "What did you want to talk about?"

"I need your help." May launched into the story of the diseased tree she'd seen and its potential link to the Gray. "We need to get rid of this problem before the rest of the town finds out about it."

But as May continued to speak, Isaac's own voice rang through his head, broken and hoarse, the words he'd said to Justin just a few weeks ago. *I'll do whatever you want because your happiness trumps my misery.*

It had been incredibly difficult for him to confess his feelings to Justin when he knew they were unrequited. But that was the only way Isaac could think of to cut himself off.

For too long, Isaac had thought it better—safer—to follow the Hawthornes instead of carve out his own path. He knew now that it was a toxic pattern, one that he was trying hard to break. But it wasn't proving easy.

All Isaac had done by answering May's text so quickly was give in to temptation. It didn't matter that he was in the middle of handling his own problems. The instinct to push them aside for the Hawthornes was too strong to ignore.

But Isaac had his own plans now. His research with Violet. His troubles with Gabriel. All of them belonged to him, and they were *his* story. He would not abandon them just to protect another family—a family that had always asked for far too much.

"I'm sorry," he said, rising to his feet. "I'm not doing damage control for you. Not this time."

May gaped at him. "What? But, Isaac, this could be incredibly dangerous."

"Then your family will handle it," he said roughly. "That's your job, right?"

It felt good to say no. To walk away and push open the doors to the mausoleum, to squint in the afternoon sunlight as he walked across the town square toward his home. It felt like freedom.

CHAPTER FOUR

Harper's first breath of fresh, clean forest air was a revelation. She'd been cooped up for so long in the musty interior of the Saunders manor, she'd almost forgotten what the outside world felt like. A knot in her chest loosened as the spires of the house disappeared behind the trees, orange leaves drifting from the latticework of branches above her head.

She was as ready for this as she was ever going to be. She'd chosen her outfit carefully: comfortable boots, a denim jacket with the left sleeve tied under her residual limb, and a midi-length skirt. Her sword was tucked in a scabbard at her waist. Plus, her eyeliner was perfect. All of it felt like armor.

And none of it mattered the moment she stepped onto the track behind Four Paths High School.

The asphalt below her feet was coated in dead leaves that had yet to be swept away. School was out for the day and cross-country didn't have practice that day, but Justin Hawthorne had stuck around anyway.

Mostly, kids used the rusty bleachers beside the track for the space under them—to gossip or hook up or smoke. Today, though, Justin sat alone, a half-drunk water bottle beside him. Strands of blond hair clung to his forehead; his posture was hunched and frustrated. It had taken them a few days to arrange this meeting; Justin was being watched now, and so was she. This was the only time they'd both been able to manage.

Harper saw him notice her, his eyes widening with something a bit like fear and a bit like hope. There was no point in saying hello. They were far beyond pleasantries.

"I know what you did to me," she said, the words ringing out across the field. Again, she thought of his betrayal the night she'd lost her powers, grabbed that rage in her mind and held it as tightly as she could. "What do you have to say for yourself?"

"I never wanted you to forget." He stood up, closed most of the distance between them in a few long strides. They stood at the exact spot where the forest met the track, roots bubbling beneath the asphalt. "But I hope you know that as soon as I could, Harper, I found a way for you to remember. I hope that counts for something."

"I—*what*?" Harper said, frowning at him. "It was Violet. *Violet* gave me my memories back."

Justin's face fell. "I assumed . . . When you asked to meet, I thought that meant you knew."

"Knew *what*?"

"It was me." Justin's voice trembled, but his face was utterly resolute. Bile rose in Harper's throat.

Justin was a very good liar, but she didn't think he was lying. Not this time.

She'd never once considered Justin was the one behind this, because her memories of him were damning. Memories where he ruined her life. There was no way he'd want her to have those back; no sense in him making it possible. Harper thought about his behavior over the past few weeks. His guilt, the way he'd apologized for hurting her all those years ago. She'd thought it was all an act, a way to hurt her more than he already had.

The Hawthornes had tried to keep her in the dark because they had been frightened of what she could do. Made her a prisoner in her own mind for three years, taken advantage of her inability to see the truth in order to spread their lies. But if Justin was telling the truth, then he had turned on his own family—the one thing she'd never truly believed he could do—to help her.

"You should've told me," she whispered. The world was wobbly and new, as if it had been reborn around her. She felt guilty, and then felt furious that Justin had managed to make her feel guilty at all. He had saved her and damned her; he had hurt her and healed her. Harper felt the collective weight of those things all at once, an onslaught of emotion that made her want to weep from sheer frustration. It wasn't fair that all her best and worst moments should come from the same person.

"I know." Justin kicked at the asphalt with the toe of his sneaker. "I'm sorry I wasn't brave enough to help you sooner. I'm sorry I listened to Augusta so much. I'm sorry you had to spend years alone, believing you were powerless. You deserved better."

Harper was suddenly, dangerously close to tears. "Thank you."

"I know you'll never forgive me," Justin continued. "And I know you have no reason to believe I'm not still hiding things from you."

But Harper *did* believe him. Because she could remember that night now. What had really happened. She'd been terrified when Augusta Hawthorne had attacked her, and she'd lashed out, not understanding her powers. Justin had acted to protect his mother. And she hadn't forgiven him, that much was true, but she understood why he'd pushed her into the lake, into the Gray. He hadn't known how badly it would hurt her. He hadn't known what she would have done to his mother.

Harper didn't know what she would have done, either. She knew now what it was like to feel Augusta's flesh begin to harden beneath her grasp, to see the fear rising in the sheriff's eyes. It had been terrifying. But it had felt necessary, too. People like Augusta Hawthorne did not listen to reason—they only yielded to fear.

And Augusta Hawthorne had been afraid of her, a fourteen-year-old girl. She still was. Harper wondered what scared Augusta more: the fact that she was more powerful than her, or the fact that, despite all she'd done to keep him away, her son wouldn't leave Harper alone. The thought sent a thrill running through her chest. All Harper had wanted for the past three years was to be powerful, and now she was.

She had come here to use that power.

She wanted her own life again, one that wasn't spent hiding inside the Saunders manor. Justin could help her do that. She just had to play this right.

"You hurt me," she said evenly. "I'm not pretending you didn't. And I'm not promising forgiveness. But I know that what I did to your family's tree wasn't fair. I want to find a way to work all of this out without anybody else getting hurt."

"Perfect." The voice did not belong to Justin. It was smooth and crisp, each syllable carefully enunciated. "You're willing to cooperate, then."

May Hawthorne stepped out from the forest behind her brother, the Deck of Omens clutched in one hand. The sunlight turned her ash-blond hair nearly white, illuminated the medallion that hung at the neck beneath her champagne-colored silken blazer.

"May?" Justin's voice was raw. "What are you doing here?"

Betrayal surged through Harper, hot and sharp. She'd been a fool to think that she could arrange a meeting with a Hawthorne. She stumbled backward, into the safety of the trees.

"You promised to come alone," she said, swiveling her head to glare at Justin.

"I did." He looked helplessly at May, then at Harper. "Please, you have to believe me, I didn't know she was there."

Harper hesitated. Justin looked genuinely distraught. But then, she'd just been thinking about what a good liar he was. "So you expect me to believe she was spying on us?"

"Yeah! Because she was!"

"With good reason, apparently." May shook her head, eyeing Harper with visible mistrust. "You attacked our tree. A direct provocation isn't something we can just ignore. You're lucky we haven't formally declared war."

"May," Justin said. "You can't just throw around a word like *war*—"

"She already did," Harper said. "Look, May, you should just leave. Justin and I were doing a fine job of figuring this out on our own. You're only making things worse."

"I'm not going anywhere." May crossed her arms. "Justin's not very good at critical thinking when it comes to you."

"Hey!" Justin glared at her.

But Harper, staring at May, realized that *she* was the one with the upper hand here. Because Violet might not have told her about Justin, but she still knew May had turned on her mother, too.

"I know what you did to help Violet," she said softly, enjoying the unease flickering across May's face. "You're not the perfect Hawthorne they all think you are."

"You don't know *anything* about me," May said roughly.

"I know your family made my life a living hell for *years*. And I know that I was still willing to try to compromise with you—but since you clearly think so little of me, I'm not so willing anymore."

May advanced toward her, that unease morphing into rage. Justin grabbed her arm, but she shrugged it away.

"Hey," he said uselessly. "You *really* shouldn't fight each other—"

But it was a bit late for that.

Harper had only seconds left before May would be upon her. The weight of her scabbard was comforting, made her glad she'd come here ready for a fight. But the truth was, she didn't need a sword anymore to make someone regret attacking her.

She reached for the tree nearest to her, laid her palm flat against it, and *pushed* with all of her collective rage.

The stone spread across the trunk immediately, stiffening the wood and turning it red-brown. But it didn't stop there. Birds scattered, alarmed, as the stone spread across the forest floor, rustling beneath the leaves and snaking up the trees nearby. Harper could feel her power radiating through all of her, not just her hand; she was suddenly dizzy with it, her stomach churning with the knowledge that this was *her*; she was doing this. She tried to remove her hand from the trunk, satisfied by the sight of May frozen to the spot, staring apprehensively at the stone spreading toward her. But her palm was glued to the tree.

Power was still surging through her, stronger now, *too* strong, and Harper gasped for control, at last wresting her hand away.

She shuddered, swaying, but was determined not to show any weakness.

"I'm leaving," she said coldly, doing her best to look formidable. "Don't come any closer."

She held it together for as long as she could, hustling through the forest until she was long out of earshot. Then she tumbled to the ground and retched. Nothing came up, but she still felt ill, her body convulsing with exhaustion. Harper groaned, wiped her mouth, and turned—to see that, of course, Justin Hawthorne had followed her.

"Shit," she hissed, rising to her feet. "Your sister was right about your critical thinking. Don't you ever listen?"

He stepped forward, his face grim. "You're shaking. Let me help you—"

"As if I could trust you after what just happened." She glanced around, waiting for May to emerge, but Justin shook his head.

"She's not following us this time. I promise. Harper—"

She swayed, and Justin's arm swept around her back, carefully lowering her to the forest floor and resting her against a tree trunk. His hands were gentle against the fabric of her jean jacket, and for a moment he was close enough for her to see the tiny freckles on his nose, the softness in his eyes. Then he pulled back, and she was left thinking about the way he'd smelled, like soap and woodsmoke, and how deeply annoying it was that she liked it.

He procured his water bottle and she sipped from it, glaring at him. How dare he be kind and helpful after she'd just threatened to turn him to stone.

"You don't know how to use them, do you?" he asked. "Your powers."

Harper fought the urge to fling the rest of the water bottle in his face. "Would you like another demonstration?"

"Hey." Justin crouched beside her. "I didn't mean that as an attack. More . . . an observation. Most founders get training after their rituals. You never did."

"And your point is?" Harper said crankily.

"My point is that I don't think you know how to fix the hawthorn tree. That's why you were so willing to scare May off."

"So what if I don't?" Harper scowled.

"So . . . what if you could learn? My mother would happily give you lessons."

Harper raised an eyebrow. "I am *not* taking lessons from your *mother*."

"I'll keep her under control," Justin said quickly. "I may not have powers, but she'll listen to me. And if she's training you, you won't be considered a threat to my family anymore."

Harper hesitated. It sounded absolutely bizarre, the idea that she could possibly have anything to learn from the woman who'd destroyed her whole life. But Justin was right that it would make things safe for her. There was a catch here, though; there had to be. With the Hawthornes, there always was. And it didn't take her long to figure it out.

"You want your tree back," she said flatly. "That's why you're offering your family's help."

Justin nodded. "It's a small price to pay for control," he said.

But it wasn't just about control. It was about the Hawthornes controlling *her*. Harper didn't trust them, didn't trust any of this. Unfortunately, she wasn't sure she had any better options.

And there was that part of her that still kindled when she thought of him. A foolish, terrible part of her that was impossible to completely ignore.

"I'll think about it," she said slowly, and got to her feet.

May had stormed straight home from her encounter with Harper Carlisle, determined to make her mother understand why this was a potential threat. Why May deserved to be listened to.

Unfortunately, Justin had managed to worm his way in first. He'd called Augusta and told her whatever poisoned, twisted version of the truth best suited him. Which meant that May had returned to a furious parent who was pacing outside the reading room, collecting her thoughts before she came inside to yell at them.

May wanted to scream. She wanted blood under her nails and dirt on her fingers. She wanted to reach across her family's scarred wooden table in the reading room and rip the smug smile off her brother's face.

Instead, she forced the emotion out of her voice until there was only ice left.

"You gave Harper her memories back," May said to Justin. It was not a question. "She turned our tree to stone, and you're still crawling back to her."

Justin flinched. "My personal life is none of your business."

"It is when it leads to a direct attack on our entire family," May said, shaking her head.

"What our mother did was *wrong*," Justin said hoarsely. "I wanted to fix her mistake. Isn't that what you wanted to do with Violet?"

He gave her a pointed look, and panic swept over her. She'd

hoped that he had missed Harper's allusions to what she had done during their argument, but clearly he hadn't.

The door creaked open before May could respond, and Augusta swept in, her gigantic mastiffs trailing behind her. Brutus's black jowls quivered as he let out a sharp, accusatory bark in her direction, and May felt a stab of hurt. Even the dogs were pissed at her.

She turned to Augusta, horror dawning on her as she saw the disappointment in her mother's gaze—directed not at Justin, but at her.

"You told her," she breathed, rounding on her brother. "You *told her*—"

"Enough yelling," Augusta said calmly, sitting beside both of them. "Yes, May, your brother told me that it seems there's some kind of rumor going around that you were the reason behind Violet's memories returning. Is that true?"

Faced with direct confrontation, there was nothing May could do but nod, ashamed.

Augusta's jaw twitched. "Very well. Yet again, you've both deceived me. Justin—you're grounded, effective immediately. No cross-country. No parties. And certainly no patrols."

Justin tensed, but he nodded. "And what about Harper potentially joining us?" he asked, jutting out his chin.

"Juniper Saunders and I will be meeting shortly to discuss the situation. You are invited to participate, if you wish. Now." Her gaze turned toward May. "Leave. I need to talk to your sister."

This was barely a punishment, May realized. Justin was getting rewarded for his transgressions, as per usual, while she was about to be eviscerated for hers.

She met her mother's eyes and waited for the ax to fall.

"Oh, May." Augusta's face was so similar to May's, and yet May still struggled to read it—she had mastered control of it long before May was even born. "The future of this town has rested on my shoulders for a long time. Soon it will rest on yours, and I need to know you're capable of holding it all together."

May heard the unspoken doubt behind those words. It was the same undercurrent of distrust that ran between her and Augusta constantly, because she would never be her mother's first choice, and neither of them would ever forget it.

"I *am* capable," May said, exhausted.

"You didn't tell me you could override my powers." The words were soft, dangerous. "Why?"

May hesitated. There were so many reasons why she'd kept her ability a secret, and none of them felt safe to say aloud.

"I wasn't sure I could," she said at last. "Violet was . . . a test. And after everything that happened with her, I wasn't sure how you'd react to the news that I was behind it."

This was a blatant lie. May *knew* her mother would react poorly to news of what she could do, because it would make her a threat to Augusta. Because she'd spent her entire life seeing how her mother dealt with threats. Because already, it felt like anything she did would be scrutinized and punished, and she did not want to give her mother any more reasons to watch her closely.

Her palms itched, and she was reminded yet again that her mother could never know what she'd done to change the future— or the secret that lurked beneath all her others, in the wounds on her hands that had long since faded away.

"I'm concerned about you, May," Augusta said. "You're

fixating on this corruption you insist you saw in the forest and on Harper instead of focusing on patrol and damage control after the Church of the Four Deities incident."

"What do you mean, *insist I saw*?" May's stomach churned with unease.

"I sent deputies to the location you and Justin showed me. There was no evidence whatsoever of what you two claimed to have seen."

"I have photos—"

"Enough." Augusta's voice left no room for a rebuttal. "I need some time to come up with the proper punishment for your deception. But for now, I want you to simply follow orders. Go on your patrols. No side missions—and no questioning. Understood?"

The word felt like a stone in May's throat. "Understood."

Back in her bedroom, May collapsed onto her pristine white bedsheets and released a strangled yell into her pillow.

"You're all alone," she whispered, curling into a ball on the bed. She hated how broken it sounded, how true it was.

No matter how hard she tried to be Augusta's perfect daughter, she would mess it up. She would never make her mother happy.

Which meant she had nothing left to protect anymore. Nothing left to lose.

May sniffled and rolled over on her side, an idea coalescing in her mind.

Then she scrambled off the bed and tugged out the lowest drawer of her vanity, sliding away a false bottom. After her father had left, her mother had eradicated every trace of him she could find. The small box May had hidden in her vanity contained the few items she'd saved from Augusta's purge.

Several photographs—her father hadn't liked pictures, but May had managed to save a couple of faded snapshots of his blond hair and thin-rimmed glasses. A heavy silver watch. A folded flannel shirt, musty now, although May imagined that some remnant of her father's whiskey-and-oak smell still clung to it.

And—scribbled in pen on a yellowed scrap of paper—a phone number.

Her father had pressed it into her hand the day he'd left, and she had kept it all these years, waiting for him to reach out.

She was done waiting.

May fumbled for her phone and dialed the number.

CHAPTER FIVE

Violet's life had changed tremendously in the past few months, but at least one thing had remained the same: Sitting down at the piano brought her automatic comfort. She'd been working on a composition, a piece that was turning from experimental scales and chord progressions into the first clumsy movement of a piano sonata. She didn't know if it was any good, but she was enjoying working at it anyway. Composing meant flexing her pianist's muscles in a way she'd never used them before, and it was incredibly reaffirming to create something that belonged entirely to *her*.

It was good to have a distraction. Because she didn't want to think about the plan Isaac had proposed to her—or how quickly she had shot it down. Violet played a C-sharp minor chord, enjoying the satisfying way it rang out through the music room, then absently added a harmony with her left hand.

"Are you still working on that new piece?" Her mother's voice was hesitant. "It sounds...interesting."

Violet snorted and turned. Juniper Saunders stood behind her, wearing her reading glasses and an expression of gentle bewilderment.

"It sounds bad, you mean," she said.

"It absolutely does not!"

"You're protesting too much," said Violet, raising an eyebrow. Orpheus slunk out from behind her mother, his ears twitching. She could have sworn the gray tabby cat looked relieved that she had stopped playing. "It's okay. You don't have to cheer me on when I suck—I know you don't like the hair, either."

"First of all, I'm your mother, and therefore I support you in all hair-dyeing and musical endeavors, because at least they're not you running around in the woods in mortal danger," Juniper said dryly. "And I would like to remind you that being seventeen and teaching yourself to compose is no small feat, nor were you ever going to master it overnight."

Violet was slowly but surely getting used to this new version of her mother, one who sought out her daughter's company instead of avoiding it, one who seemed determined to make them a two-person family. They weren't going to master all that stuff overnight, either, but at least they were both trying.

"I guess you're right," she said. "I just...hate this. I wish I could be good at it right away."

Juniper sighed and reached down to scoop up Orpheus, stroking his head between his twitching ears. "Life doesn't work like that." Her brow furrowed, and she gestured to the couch. "Sit? We need to talk about something."

Violet sat, staring out the window at the forest sloping down the hill behind the house. Four Paths wore October well. The leaves hanging from the chestnut oaks had turned into rich reds and golds that her sister, Rosie, would have loved to paint, and the air had grown crisp with the promise of frost.

"Let me guess," she said quietly. "Harper?"

Her mother hesitated. "Have you heard what happened?"

"You mean besides the tree?"

Juniper sighed. "Yes. I received an interesting call from Augusta Hawthorne this afternoon."

She detailed what had happened behind the school—the display of power Harper had shown. The fact that she still hadn't come back, even though the sun was setting.

"I thought you might know where she is," she finished.

But Violet shook her head, suddenly concerned. "She's not answering my texts."

"Well. She might answer your texts if you tell her that Augusta Hawthorne wants to meet with her to discuss a deal."

Violet gaped at her. "A *deal*? What kind of deal?"

"Harper needs training," Juniper said calmly. "She's powerful, but unpredictable, and the Hawthornes wish to rectify their earlier mistakes by formally inviting her to join them and hone her talents."

"They just want her to fix their problems the same way Isaac does," Violet muttered.

"But the thing is, the Hawthornes aren't the only people who could train Harper."

Suddenly Violet understood.

"You want me to convince her not to take Augusta's deal. You want her to stay with us."

Juniper nodded. "Our family has a chance to take this town back, Violet. The Hawthornes have done nothing but lie and put this town in danger. If we play this right, we can change things."

Violet hesitated, unease pooling in her stomach. Her mother was right that the Hawthornes could not be trusted with the fate of Four Paths. They'd taken half the town's memories away, including hers and her mother's. People had died under their watch. The Gray had grown stronger. But something about this still felt wrong.

"I'm not going to force Harper into anything," she said, knotting her hands together in her lap. "She deserves the chance to make her own decision about what's best for her."

"Do you really think this choice is hers?" Juniper shot her a pointed look. "Justin Hawthorne is laying it on thick, I'm sure, trying to sway her to his side."

"Justin's not a bad person." Violet frowned at her mother. "I'm your daughter, not your tool. And Harper isn't your tool, either."

"Of course she isn't," Juniper said. "I'm just concerned that Augusta has some sort of personal vendetta here, especially considering our history."

"Your history," Violet echoed.

They hadn't talked about this, but Violet had seen the way the two women looked at each other when Juniper got her memories back, and a whole lot had started to make sense. She'd been waiting ever since to see if it was something Juniper was ready to talk about.

Violet had been doing a lot of waiting lately, she realized. For Isaac to open up to her. For Harper to cool down. It was starting to make her antsy.

"Yes," Juniper said. "Augusta Hawthorne and I dated back in high school."

"I sort of guessed," Violet said. "You know you could've told me, right?"

There was a vulnerability on her mother's face that Violet

had never seen before, but she recognized it all the same. She'd seen it in the mirror.

"I always told myself I would talk to you and Rosie about my sexuality, but . . . it was hard for me to do. People weren't as open when I was growing up as they are now."

"Yeah," Violet said. "I get that."

The only person she had ever come out to was Rosie, and she'd always felt like that had barely counted. Because Rosie had come out to her first, and she'd been delighted to show Violet her favorite queer musicians and TV shows and books that had helped her figure out her own sexuality.

She knew that whatever she and her mother could give each other would be different. But she saw, suddenly, that this was something they could share, that she had been so lonely without realizing it. And Violet wanted there to be someone, somewhere, who knew the truth about her.

So she took a deep breath and looked Juniper in the eyes. Her mother's face was backlit in gold and orange, and Violet realized that she looked anxious, too, that no matter how old you were or how many times you'd done it, coming out was scary. It was weirdly comforting to know that they were *both* frightened about the same thing.

"Thank you for telling me," Violet said softly. "And, Mom? Um. Me too."

Juniper's eyes went wide. "Violet—are you saying—"

"Yeah. I mean, I've never dated anyone, period. But I'm bi. And one day, I'd like to date *someone*."

Juniper leaned forward and took both of Violet's hands in hers. Her grip was firm and reassuring.

"I love you," she said hoarsely. "And I'm so glad you trusted me enough to tell me. I know neither of us is very good at this kind of thing, but I promise, you can always talk to me about whoever you might want to date, and I'll always support you."

Violet let out a soft snort and tried not to think about Isaac's dark curls. "There's nobody to talk about."

"Well, if that ever changes, I'm here." Juniper paused, then added, "Honestly, Violet, I'm glad to see you making so many new friends. I've never seen you tolerate such a large group of people before."

"You mean the group of people who all hate each other right now?"

Juniper paused, guilt crossing her face. She pulled her hands away from Violet's. "I didn't mean to drive a wedge between you and your friends, you know. I just . . . I failed my family all those years ago, when I ran away from Four Paths. This is my second chance, and I can't fail again."

"I understand that. But if you handle this the same way Augusta does, you're no better than her."

"You're right." Juniper shook her head; the words were hesitant in her mouth, and Violet knew they both weren't used to talking like this. Like they were mother and daughter, but something else, too. Mutual survivors—the only ones left to carry on their family name . . . and to shoulder all their family trauma. "I was wrong to try to use you to get to Harper, and I'm sorry."

"Thank you," Violet said, and meant it. "I'll do my best to talk to Harper about this meeting, but I can't guarantee anything."

Violet twisted a red lock of hair around her finger. No, her mother wasn't wrong that the Hawthornes did not deserve to have Harper on their side. But Violet wasn't sure her family could do a much better job running the town than they had.

That wasn't the problem here—the problem was, as long as the Beast existed, the founding families would never stop fighting. And they were too caught up in their own petty struggles to see the bigger picture.

She'd been too scared before. Too concerned about the ghosts she'd see if she said yes to Isaac's plan, the cost of failure if things went wrong.

But now Violet was ready. Now, at last, she understood that reckless gleam behind Isaac's eyes.

Isaac watched the sunset from the edge of an all-too-familiar clearing, squinting miserably into the forest as he waited for Violet to show up.

It was early October, and the trees had started to show it. The forest was alive in the way things could only be when they knew they were dying, every leaf shot through with color, drifting through the air with points outstretched like it was trying to touch the sky one last time before being crushed into the dirt. He had always thought the autumn leaves were at their most beautiful in their final days, as if reminding the world that they should be mourned once they drifted to the ground.

Violet emerged from the trees. Her gray tabby cat loped at her side, his yellow eyes gleaming in the twilight. The red yarn tied around his ear matched her new hair color.

"You're sure you can handle this?" he asked when she was close enough to hear him.

It shouldn't have surprised him that Violet initially had been so unwilling to re-create what had surely been one of the worst moments of her life. But Isaac had been surprised anyway.

Violet was cranky and cynical, but more than anything else, she was brave. He'd seen that time and again as they dealt with the Church of the Four Deities, as she went head-to-head with Augusta Hawthorne and the Beast. The idea that she could be hitting her breaking point unnerved him.

So when she rolled her eyes at him in response and said, "Of course I can handle it. What, are *you* scared now?" he couldn't hold back a grin.

"Nah," he said. "I'm not scared."

She raised a still-dark-brown eyebrow. "This is a weird time to be smiling."

"That's my monster-killing face."

"Uh-huh."

Together, they stepped gingerly into the clearing where, just a few weeks ago, the Church of the Four Deities had tried to free the Beast from the Gray by allowing it to possess Juniper Saunders's body. Isaac's last memories of this place were pure chaos. Church members being escorted away by the Four Paths police force. The circle of bones they'd created being roped off by deputies. Blue and red lights flashing everywhere, illuminating the relief in Justin Hawthorne's eyes.

Isaac remembered it so well not just because of the ritual, but because of a moment that had happened after, when Justin stopped him on the way back to the Hawthornes' pickup truck and squeezed his shoulder.

"Thanks," he'd said, voice gruff and low. "We'd all be dead without you."

And Isaac had known then that if he didn't learn how to say no to Justin, he would spend the rest of his life craving those tiny moments of gratitude. So he'd decided to stop it for good. Even though it would mean telling Justin the truth about his feelings. Even though it would hurt almost as much as his ritual had.

"Isn't it so messed up that they can't remember what they did here?" Violet's voice floated through the clearing, anchoring him back in reality. "The Church, I mean. Augusta's power is terrifying."

Isaac shook his head and trained his gaze on her bright red hair. "I asked Augusta to help me forget, once," he said quietly. "She told me no."

Violet turned her head sharply, but there was no accusation on her face—only understanding.

"So did my mother," she said. "That's why she couldn't remember what was going on here. That's why she almost died. I promise you, whatever you wanted taken away—it wouldn't have helped."

Isaac let out a long, shuddering breath as a gust of wind whipped through the clearing, rustling the leaves of the chestnut oaks. It was a beautiful night, clear enough to see the shine of the half-moon above them reflected in Violet's dark, solemn eyes.

"I know. But I wanted it to be easier. Even though I knew it was the weak thing to do."

"There's nothing weak about wanting to skip a step. To heal faster. To erase something terrible." Violet stepped toward him, her voice gentle. "I wanted Rosie back so badly, it almost cost me my life. But I'm learning how to live without her, even though it's hard."

Isaac nodded, tears stinging the back of his throat, and turned away. Working with the Hawthornes, it had always felt as if he were the one putting everything on the line for them. Risking his life over and over again for their reputation, their safety, their comfort.

But Violet was risking just as much as he was to be here. More, maybe. It was new for him to feel another person making room for him the way he'd always been taught to make room for someone else.

"Um. Let's get started," he said gruffly, kneeling in the grass and gesturing to an outline in the dirt. It was the founders' symbol, the circle with four lines spearing through it, nearly meeting in the center. "This is where they did the ritual."

The police had done a reasonable job clearing the bones away, but fragments of ivory still shone beneath the glow of his phone's flashlight. Unease prickled down his spine as Violet knelt beside him, her brow furrowing. Her cat lurked behind them, his tail twitching.

"The Church did the ritual by singing outside the circle. But if we want to lure the Beast here, I should probably be inside it. Like my mom was."

Isaac swallowed hard. "Then I'm going inside, too. I can open the Gray for you."

Violet sighed and stood up, her toes poised at the edge of the circle. "When I teamed up with you, I really thought you'd help me figure out something logical and reasonable—"

"Do you have a better plan?"

She rolled her eyes and stepped over the circle's edge. "Obviously I don't."

They stared at each other nervously, but nothing happened. So after another moment, Isaac stepped over the line and joined her. Violet's cat waited outside. Isaac figured Orpheus was the only smart one here.

Everything felt normal. So normal that as they sat down on the grass, Isaac spared a moment to wonder if this would even work at all.

"Okay," Violet muttered, pulling out her phone. Isaac did the same. They'd gotten the song lyrics from the Church's confiscated papers, and the picture he'd taken of the words made his chest feel tight with worry. "I can't sing for shit, you've been warned—"

"I actually can," said Isaac, feeling a little self-conscious.

Violet glared at him. "Of *course* you can."

"What's that supposed to mean?"

"Nothing." She cleared her throat. "On three?"

He nodded. "One, two—"

Sinners who were led astray,
Wandered through the woods one day,
Stumbled right into the Gray,
Never to return.
Hear the lies our gods will tell,
The prison the Four wove so well,
But listen to us when we say:
Branches and stones, daggers and bones,
Will meet their judgment day.

At first, their voices were awkward and strained. But Violet had warned him that the Church had chanted the lullaby again and again, so when they finished, they merely started it over, their voices unsure and cautious in the night. Isaac did not know when he realized something had changed, only that it had. The words were no longer voluntary; they poured from his throat like water, smooth and clear, blending with Violet's voice until it felt as if something else were singing through them both.

The founders' symbol around them began to glimmer, the fragments of ivory oozing iridescent liquid. Isaac had never seen anything like this before, and it made his voice falter slightly, his heartbeat speed up. He watched uneasily as the liquid ran through the grooves of the dirt lines, carrying with it a choking scent of decay. Isaac raised his hands, still singing, and concentrated.

The air around his hands grew warm as he summoned his power, light fragmenting across the entire clearing. His power always hurt. Made a dull ache rise beneath his skin, turned him flushed and feverish. Use it for long enough, push it hard enough, and he'd pass out. But Isaac was used to the pain.

He set his jaw, curled his fingers in the air, and tore a hole in the world.

It didn't always work, opening the Gray. But it did this time. Isaac held his hands out, widening the gap, as mist poured into the circle. He'd opened it on his left so both he and Violet could stare through it, and as the fog thickened and their singing continued, he sensed her stiffening beside him.

The entire circle seemed to shift around them, and Isaac had the sense that they had been flung through the door he'd opened. There was no Four Paths anymore, just grayscale, the iridescence still oozing ever closer. Around them, trees crowded into his peripheral vision, their branches undulating grotesquely, and the sky was an undying, staticky white.

They stared at each other, no longer singing. Violet's face was grim. They hadn't just called the Gray—they'd gone inside it. He'd expected this to happen after what Violet had described, but that didn't make it any less unnerving. Humans weren't supposed to be here; that was impossible to forget.

"It's here," Violet whispered, the words ringing out through the circle a moment after her lips moved. Isaac shuddered. He'd never entered the Gray for longer than a few seconds, and already every bit of him wanted to leave. He didn't belong here.

He was opening his mouth to ask Violet how she knew the Beast was close when a voice spun around the edges of his mind, cruel and cold. It hissed, tinny and hollow, and Isaac gritted his teeth against the sound. The fog around him began to thicken, until it had become a humanoid form that Isaac recognized all too well.

"You need to leave," Maya Sullivan whispered. She wore a hospital gown that could not quite hide the ritual scars snaking across her shoulders. Tubing wound around her arms and legs, puncturing her flesh. "Now."

Isaac had steeled himself for the possibility that the Beast would show him some sort of vision designed to throw him off. But it was still hard to look at his mother like this: awake but trapped by the medical devices that kept her alive, her face animated with fear. It sent a chill through his entire body, a bone-deep fear that took him back to his fourteenth birthday. He could hear the faint sounds of his brothers screaming. A memory, he told himself—it was just a memory.

Beside him, Violet looked confused. "Who is that? I don't understand."

"It's a trick," Isaac whispered. "You know it's a trick."

He forced himself to look away. There was nothing the monster could show him that was worse than the images that played in his own mind every night as he tried to sleep. The knife. Blood dripping onto the leaves. The smell of charred flesh, the distant sound of screaming.

"*Run,*" his mother hissed, her hand outstretched, fright contorting her features, and then a gust of wind rushed through the Gray, blowing her away into smoke.

The smell washed over them again, decay so strong it nearly made Isaac gag. He had just enough time to remember what others had told him about the Gray—that there was no smell in there at all—before he felt something twining around his legs.

He glanced down and gaped. The iridescent liquid from the founders' symbol had become roots, and they'd snaked forward, viscous and oily, to wrap around his thighs. Isaac summoned his power and gripped the roots, shuddering at the way they felt against his palms—warm and soft as human flesh, almost like he was touching someone else's hand. He concentrated as best he could and burned the roots away. But they grew back faster than he could destroy them, encasing the tips of his boots in bark. He shook them off and stumbled backward.

"Isaac!" Violet's voice was shrill and panicked. He glanced up and saw her struggling to kick more roots away. Tears snaked down her cheeks, the same iridescent gray as the liquid that pooled around them. "Get us out of here!"

He'd never seen anything like this before. Never even heard of it. But he didn't need to see more to know that if they stayed here for much longer, they would die.

He summoned all his strength, wincing, and sent the biggest shock wave he could manage through the roots, disintegrating most of them into ash. Then he reached upward and tried to rip the air open again, gasping—but as it opened wide, instead of relief, he felt something else.

Dread.

The world around him faded. Fog engulfed him like a second skin, and suddenly, he was gone.

Isaac floated, ephemeral, in a sea of static. His body was frozen; when he glanced down, he saw that he had turned as smoky and transparent as the vision of his mother. Roots twined around his arms and legs, crawling toward his nostrils, his ears, the corners of his eyes. They burrowed through his hair like centipedes, hooking around the edges of his mouth and pulling it open as they tried to snake down his throat.

Everywhere they touched hurt like nothing he had ever known. He could feel himself decaying, knew that when the roots finished growing over him there would be nothing left of him but bones.

And then something smacked against his cheek, *hard*, and his eyes fluttered open.

Above him was the familiar half-moon in Four Paths' night sky. Violet's face appeared in his field of vision a moment later, tendrils of red hair framing her small round face.

"That better be you in there," she whispered. "That better not be the Beast."

"My eyes are way prettier than the Beast's," Isaac said, coughing.

She broke into a relieved grin that made something warm flare up in his chest. "There you are."

Isaac hauled himself up on his hands, the side of his face stinging. He could feel blood trickling down his cheek. "Did you . . . did you just *punch* me?"

"Not exactly." She lifted her hand up to display the wriggling, sluglike remnants of a root. Just the sight of it dissolving in her fingers made him want to retch.

"It was trying to go under your skin," she said matter-of-factly. "I yanked it out."

"But the Gray," Isaac said, gesturing weakly at the forest behind her. "How did we escape?"

"You opened the portal and immediately collapsed." Violet shrugged. "You're tall, but it was still pretty easy to drag you out."

Now that he was no longer in immediate mortal danger, Isaac could feel a whole new host of aches and pains. He inspected himself, wincing; there were freshly singed holes in his jeans, and that strange iridescent liquid had dried into a hardened scab on his arm. He scratched it off and shuddered.

Isaac didn't know what any of this meant—the way Maya had told him to run, that vision he'd had, this new weapon the Beast seemed all too adept at wielding. He just knew that none of it was good.

He saw now how reckless and foolish both of them had been. If they were going to kill the Beast, it would take a lot more than this.

"I don't think our plan worked," he said softly.

Beside him, Violet winced. "No. I don't think it did."

CHAPTER SIX

Harper had, technically, agreed to this meeting. But it was still hard for her to suppress the urge to get up from the Saunderses' kitchen table and run.

It was an uncomfortable group of people who had come together to argue about her: Juniper and Violet in one corner, Justin and Augusta in the other. Harper was already tired of this, and no one had even broached the subject of her powers yet. Instead, Juniper and Augusta had argued over the quality of the coffee, while Justin and Violet made strangely hostile eye contact with each other across the room. As if Harper was beholden to any of them besides herself.

Violet had been somewhere the night before. Harper had heard her come home in the wee hours of the morning, when she was lying in bed thinking instead of sleeping, heard her curse and slam the bathroom door and run the shower for far longer than was necessary. Harper hadn't asked, and Violet hadn't offered any explanation. She'd been too busy trying to figure out what she wanted out of this meeting. Unfortunately, she still didn't know.

"Things in town are worsening," Augusta Hawthorne said grimly from across the table. "We understand why trusting us is a difficult proposition. But if you formally become part of our patrol roster, you would strengthen our forces. You would save lives."

"The sheriff lies." Juniper's voice, from the opposite end of the table, was sharp. "She lied about your memories, to both you and your family. We're perfectly capable of training you, too, and if you lend your power to us, we can change the problems plaguing Four Paths for good. We can protect the town far better than Augusta has."

Augusta's nostrils flared, her gloved hand clenching her coffee cup, but she said nothing.

They were all sucking up to her, Harper realized. It was absurd. Two months ago, the Hawthornes didn't care if she lived or died, and now they were begging for her help. She imagined Justin on his knees and felt a pleasant twinge of satisfaction. She could make him do that, if she wanted. She could make them grovel for her—and maybe she should.

"What about the hawthorn tree?" she asked softly. "May seemed pretty upset about it."

Augusta's face twitched. "She is, and so I thought it best that May not be included in this discussion, due to her ... rash actions the other day. But I assume that, should we become your allies, you will join us in our quest to preserve our power by restoring the tree—and we, of course, would be willing to forgive such an indiscretion if you prove your dedication to assisting us."

"You can't trust them," Juniper said, her eyes narrowing.

Augusta stared at her. "This is a civil affair, June."

"I *am* being civil, August."

Harper did not know what to say to either of them. All she knew was that she didn't want to let Four Paths twist her the way it had so clearly twisted both of them. It had turned her own father into a monster, turned her friends' parents bitter and angry.

She wanted to believe it wasn't too late for her, but she worried it already was. She'd attacked the Hawthornes. She'd estranged herself from her family. And now here she sat at a crossroads, unable to find her own voice even as the others around her grew louder and more agitated.

"Mother." Justin's tone was pointed. "You promised to stay calm."

Augusta shot her son a glare. "Don't push me."

"You're not listening to me either, Mom," Violet said quietly, from the other side of the table. "We're trying to prevent a war here, not start one."

"We have always been at war with one another, Violet." Juniper looked deeply sad as she stared Augusta down. "Our powers aren't meant to be shared."

Violet groaned. "You're all missing the point."

"And what point *is* that?" Augusta asked. "That you sheltered a fugitive?"

Violet didn't miss a beat. "That you lied to our entire town?"

"Enough!"

The voice came from somewhere deep inside her—the same place her powers surged from, the same place that had helped her wake up before dawn each morning to practice swordplay, the same place that had allowed her to spend four days in the Gray and survive.

It stopped the rest of them midsentence, turned all eyes to her. Harper pushed back her chair and stood up, her heart thumping in her chest.

She knew now what she wanted: the same thing she'd wanted

before she'd gotten her powers back. Before her dad had ensnared her in his reckless plot. Before Justin Hawthorne had wormed his way back into her life.

She wanted to get out of this town and never look back.

But it was not as simple as running away. Her siblings—Seth and Mitzi, Brett and Nora, her baby brother Olly—all of them deserved to grow up somewhere safe. So she would have to make it that way, a town that would never hurt her family the way it had hurt her. If she left Four Paths with no loose ends, it would never have any reason to pull her back.

"I choose both of you," Harper said calmly. "And I also choose neither of you. Sheriff Hawthorne, I want your training. You took my memories and sent me into the Gray because you knew I was powerful. So teach me how to use that power, but know that I'll only use it for the town—not for *you*. And Juniper, if you'll have me, I'd like to keep staying here for now and train with you as well. You both have things to teach me, and you both have reasons to use me—which means I might as well use you back. I want to help keep this town safe. I want to fix the hawthorn tree. But I'm not fighting for either of you—I'm fighting for myself."

The two women looked at each other, both still frowning. But Harper didn't care about them. She cared about the small nod Violet shot her across the table. And she cared about the smile stealing across Justin's face, like a secret he knew he shouldn't be telling.

"I think," Justin said, trying and failing to contain his grin, "Harper makes an excellent point."

"I agree," Violet said primly.

Juniper's lips twitched. "I suppose it is your choice."

Augusta's mouth was a hard-edged line, but when Justin nudged her with his elbow, she spoke. "Fine."

And Harper felt victory course through her as Justin herded his mother away from the table and toward the Saunders manor's front door.

Ezra Bishop hadn't changed at all in the seven years since May had seen him last. He had the same graying blond hair, curling gently where it met his ears. The same dusting of stubble on his cheeks. The same lupine, sharply angled face, which was now turned toward her, assessing her like a puzzle he'd been trying to solve from behind his wire-rimmed glasses.

They'd exchanged awkward hellos at the entrance to the restaurant—a pizza place May had found a thirty-minute drive away from Four Paths, far enough that nobody would recognize either of them. Since then, they'd attempted small talk that had lapsed into an uncomfortable silence, May stirring too many sugar packets into her coffee, Ezra simply watching her. She wasn't sure what either of them was waiting for. She was starting to wonder with every second that passed if this had all been a terrible idea.

"I'll confess, I'm not quite sure how to do this," he said at last, from across the red-and-white-checkered tablecloth. "I wasn't sure I'd ever see you again."

His words were casual, but May could feel the undercurrent of despair in them.

"Funny," she said. "Since the last time I saw you, you promised to come back."

He winced. "I know. And I assure you, I had every intention of keeping that promise."

"So what changed?"

Ezra wrapped a large, square hand around his own coffee cup, looking uncomfortable. "I was told that if I came back, I wouldn't be wanted."

May didn't have to ask who had told him such a thing.

"Of course she said that to you," she said sharply. "Why on earth did you believe it?"

The words rang out a bit too loudly across the mostly empty restaurant. The only other patrons—an older couple with matching baseball caps—turned their heads.

"You and Justin were very young when I left," Ezra said, lowering his voice. "It was painful, but I knew that when I was around your mother, we brought out the worst in each other. It didn't seem healthy for you both to see us acting like that. So as the years passed, I grew convinced it would be best for us all if I left the three of you alone."

"You mean you gave up," May said hollowly. This wasn't the father she remembered—this sad, quiet man who was looking at her now with shame in his eyes.

"Yes," he said heavily. "I suppose I did."

May hadn't anticipated this, but it made a strange sort of sense. Ezra had left town for good because Augusta had finally driven him away. But Augusta had made a critical mistake: She hadn't considered how May would feel, or what she'd want.

May reached into her purse and pulled out one of the old photographs she'd kept in her box. It was the only one she had of just the two of them. She was maybe four or five, wearing pink overalls and a gap-toothed grin. Ezra's hands were wrapped around her waist, lifting her up so she could grasp the bottom branches of the hawthorn tree.

She slid the picture onto the table and tapped her father's smiling face.

"Maybe you gave up," she said. "But I didn't."

For a moment, there was silence. Ezra stared at the photograph, and May did not let herself breathe, did not let herself hope. Then Ezra smiled in a way that May had almost forgotten—teeth bared and wide, a smile identical to Justin's creasing in his cheeks.

It was a smile that meant the man she'd come here to find was still in there.

"You said you needed my help," he said slowly, and May nodded, hope flaring in her chest.

She had contacted Ezra for reasons beyond simply wanting to reconnect. He'd been a PhD student at Syracuse University, doing research for a dissertation on local theological movements, when he'd met Augusta Hawthorne during her undergrad years. She didn't know how he'd wormed the truth about Four Paths out of her mother, only that he'd become just as fascinated with the town as the founders were. One of her most prominent childhood memories was Ezra's multiyear attempt to catalog the founders' archives in the town hall.

"I don't know if you abandoned your research when you left," she said. "But there's something dangerous happening in Four Paths, and if you're willing to brave Mom's wrath, I think you might be able to help me stop it."

Ezra leaned forward as she explained the corruption she'd seen to him, detailing the strangeness of it, the way it had disappeared, and her determination to get to the bottom of it. His face was alight with interest.

"I know you're scared to come back," she finished. "But I really do need help. So what do you say?"

Their waitress appeared at the table, sliding two slices of pizza toward them before silently backing away. Ezra eyed the half-congealed cheese before him with distrust before meeting her gaze. His gaze was thoughtful and solemn.

"All right," he said. "I'll help you."

May nodded, satisfaction flickering through her. "Good."

She tried not to think about the other reason she wanted him to come back. The secret she'd kept for a long time, about just how much Ezra had uncovered during his research. He could help her understand exactly what she'd done beneath the hawthorn tree. He could help her figure out this new dimension to her power.

Her palms itched again as she thought of her long-healed scars, of blood and bark and the scent of earth. She lifted her coffee cup to her mouth and downed the sludgy, sickly sweet liquid inside.

PART TWO

THE THREE OF DAGGERS

CHAPTER SEVEN

Isaac couldn't stop thinking about his family. The Sullivans always haunted him, but seeing the Beast imitate his mother had dredged up an endless well of memories. Her image had reminded him of the way she'd protected him on his ritual day, the sacrifices she had made to try to keep him safe. It was why Gabriel's insistence that they let her go had offended him so much—she'd done everything in her power to save his life. He would do the same for her. His focus drifted as he floated through another day at Four Paths High School, distracting him even further from the backlog of homework piling up in his room and the tests he'd forgotten to study for.

His teachers generally went pretty easy on the founder kids— it was the only possible explanation for Justin's solid B average, considering Isaac had never seen him crack a textbook—but Isaac could feel himself slipping even by their lenient standards.

There was also the issue of the whispers. People had stared at Isaac a lot over the last few years thanks to all the rumors his ritual had set in motion, but lately those stares had been... pointed. Isaac was used to the town acting hostile toward him. This felt different—he just didn't understand how.

He was determined to focus, to put his family out of his

mind. And that was going just fine until he walked into the high school courtyard during lunch and saw Gabriel leaning against the concrete wall, scrolling through his phone.

Isaac's stomach lurched. He wanted it to be the Beast again, or his own imagination. But he knew it wasn't.

"What are you doing here?" he asked, closing the distance between them. His gaze darted to the other students milling around. He didn't want to draw any unnecessary attention to this, but surely someone would figure out what was going on before long. And if news of another Sullivan in town got around, well . . . Isaac didn't know what would happen, but he knew he wouldn't like it.

Gabriel looked up from his phone, his face utterly impassive. "I *am* an alumnus, you know."

Isaac scowled at him. "You're still trespassing."

"I have a visitor pass," Gabriel said mildly. He slid his phone into his pocket. The tattoo on his inner forearm—a wolf—bared its teeth at Isaac. "Also, people have been reporting suspicious activity in a woods clearing where a recent police investigation took place. The people at the Pathways Inn had a lot to say about it last night. There are quite a lot of rumors about us founders now, did you know that?"

Isaac froze, his heart thumping in his chest. So *this* was why Gabriel was here: to talk to him about the ritual he and Violet had tried to do.

"I . . ." he began, unsure what to even say. "I was trying . . ."

"I told you not to come out here." The voice was so loud, Isaac was sure it was addressing him. But when he turned he saw that Cal Gonzales, one of Justin's track friends, was standing at the other end of the courtyard, speaking very loudly.

Beside him, the clear target of his ire, was Justin Hawthorne.

Isaac had walked through many hallways with Justin over the years. He knew how people reacted to his friend: a mixture of awe and friendship that he'd never managed to earn for himself. Today though, Cal was staring at Justin with obvious disdain. Isaac looked around at the rest of the courtyard: Their expressions matched his.

Unease coursed through his stomach. He'd known things had worsened at school for Justin after the truth about his lack of powers had spread, but he hadn't realized it had gotten this bad.

"Hey." Justin's voice sounded strained. Isaac had never seen him alone like this: no friends beside him, no powers to shield him, just a backpack and a feigned smile. "Just trying to eat lunch, man."

"Not with us." Cal gestured to the people clustering behind him—the rest of the cross-country team. People Isaac had heard his friend talk about for years with so much respect, so much care.

Justin's gaze flicked across the courtyard, meeting Isaac's, then widening a bit as it caught on Gabriel. But he said nothing to them. The expression on Justin's face hit Isaac like a bullet. Not because he looked angry, but because he looked resigned.

Isaac's temper roared in his ears. He could make everyone in this courtyard kneel if he wanted to—force them to apologize. Force them to admit that they had no idea the pressure the founders were under, the lengths Justin had gone to in order to protect them. His power was already tugging at him, begging him to use it. It would be so *easy* to let it loose.

But Gabriel was watching. Everyone was watching. So he used his words instead.

"Cal," he said. The boy turned toward him, the disdain on his face changing into something else entirely. That same look Isaac had been noticing more and more often. "He's eating with me."

The track team murmured uncomfortably. Cal stepped back, raised his hands slightly.

"If you say so," he said. "I don't want any trouble. Not with you."

Justin walked over to him reluctantly, shoulders tense, jaw clenched. Isaac caught his eye, and they walked out of the courtyard together, Gabriel trailing behind.

"Why—" he began softly, but Justin shook his head.

"Don't." His voice was gruff and low. "They used to listen to me. Now they listen to you."

He stalked off then, and Isaac sagged backward in the hallway, struggling to remember how to breathe.

He wished he hadn't understood Justin's words. But he did. He had assumed that after news of Justin's deception got out, the rest of the town would automatically distrust all the other founders alongside him. But that wasn't true. They were punishing Justin, and that look they were giving Isaac—that look was *respect*.

It was a look that terrified him, because he knew he'd done nothing to deserve it. If the person the town felt safest turning to was a Sullivan, they really were all in trouble.

"Things sure have changed around here," Gabriel said, and Isaac jolted. He'd half forgotten that his brother was behind them, but at least Gabriel looked distressed, too. "What *happened* while I was gone? Why are they being so hard on the Hawthornes?"

"He doesn't have powers. The town found out," Isaac said

shortly. His breath was still coming a shade too quickly. "Honestly, the founders' track record just isn't what it used to be."

Gabriel's brow furrowed. And then he said the last thing Isaac expected.

"So let me help," he said. "I'm a founder, too. I know you're involved with whatever happened in the forest—"

"No." The word flew out of Isaac's mouth before he could even think about it.

He couldn't trust Gabriel. Not with his failures, not with *anything.*

Because every time Isaac looked at Gabriel, he saw his older brother standing over his chained-up body, holding a knife to his neck, ambivalence in his eyes.

Harper stood beneath the tree she had turned to stone, guilt churning through her stomach. It was a cloudy fall afternoon, but the sun still shone brightly enough to illuminate the stiff, unmoving branches. It was red-brown stone all the way from the top of the tree's gnarled branches to the place where the trunk sank into the soil.

She knew exactly why Augusta Hawthorne had arranged for her to come here for her first training session. It was meant to destabilize her, to give Augusta justification for whatever she was about to put Harper through. Harper was determined not to let it get to her.

"You're late." Augusta appeared in the Hawthorne house's back doorway, her lips pursed into an annoyed grimace. Her mastiffs loped into position behind her a moment later. They were bigger than Harper remembered; on two legs, they would easily have been taller than she was. Another show of force. Another not-so-subtle reminder that while Harper had successfully stood up to Augusta and Juniper, neither of these women were pleased about it. "I said three thirty."

Harper pulled her phone out of her pocket. It was 3:31. Annoyance built in her throat, but she forced it down. She would not let Augusta rattle her—not visibly, anyway.

"It won't happen again," she said smoothly.

Augusta inclined her head in a sharp nod. "Good." She wore black from head to toe, her hands ensconced in their usual leather gloves. A trench coat fell to her ankles, the tails flapping slightly in the breeze as she made her way across the lawn, her dogs trailing behind her. Harper had known Augusta Hawthorne her entire life, but that was not enough to overcome the sheer presence she exuded. Something about her demanded focus. Harper had thought for ages that it was a Hawthorne thing, but when she'd seen it in her siblings after they passed their rituals, she'd realized the truth.

It was a founder thing. They all knew how to be watched— something Harper had yet to learn.

"Before we begin," Augusta said, locking eyes with her, "there are a few things we must cover. Firstly, I'm well aware you do not trust me. I do not expect you to, not yet. But I *do* require your respect. Can you do that?"

Harper's throat was tight, but she nodded. There was no world in which she would ever trust Augusta Hawthorne, but she'd always respected her. Even when she'd hated her.

"Good." Augusta's voice was as chilly and brisk as a fall breeze. "Secondly, I want you to be aware of what we're facing here. Four Paths is in a time of turmoil right now, and the town needs all of our strength to steady it after what happened with the Church of the Four Deities—we're still feeling those aftershocks. Something strange occurred the night before you agreed to train with us, at the place where the Church attempted their ritual."

She drew out her phone and showed Harper a series of photos. Harper stared, frowning, at the iridescent liquid oozing through the lines of the founders' symbol, the deep grooves in the dirt.

The night before she'd agreed to train with them. That was the night Violet had been out late.

"Do you know what that is?" she asked Augusta.

Augusta shook her head. "Something new," she said sharply. "Something dangerous. Which means there's no more time to waste."

At first, Harper just exercised. Stretches, which Augusta modified for Harper's residual limb; lunges, a quick jog around the yard. Harper was sweating and glad she'd worn workout clothes by the time they were done. After forty-five minutes of physical labor, Harper chugged most of a bottle of water, then sank to her knees beneath the tree she'd turned into a statue, panting. The branches above her head shone in the light of the setting sun.

"Now that we've dealt with the basics"—Augusta's boots appeared a foot away from Harper's knees, crunching across the desiccated autumn leaves—"let's discuss your powers."

Harper tipped up her head. Augusta's face was impassive, but Harper wondered if her mind was full of the same memories Harper was now replaying. The night Harper had gripped her arm and tried to turn her to stone. The night she'd fallen into the lake. The night her life as she knew it had changed forever.

"All right," Harper said, starting to get to her feet, but to her surprise Augusta shook her head.

"No, I'll join you." She lowered herself into the leaves, crossed her black leather boots, and placed her gloved hands primly on her knees. Harper wasn't sure she'd ever actually been eye to eye with Augusta Hawthorne before. She'd expected the woman's gaze to be even more piercing up close, but it was softer instead. The setting sun deepened the crow's feet around her eyes, set her feathery blond pixie cut ablaze, and it occurred to Harper that this woman had watched this town crumble in her grasp, that she held the very weight of the forest itself on her shoulders.

"What happens when you turn something to stone?" Augusta said mildly. "Describe your technique."

Harper hesitated. "It's like . . . I push," she said, extending her palm. "And it sort of flows from there."

"Localized in the hand, naturally," Augusta said, her brow furrowing. "Sounds as if the power comes when you call, so what's the problem?"

"I don't know when to stop." The words tumbled out of her, shameful and soft. Harper had always thought she'd excel as a founder if only she had powers, that the meticulous control she'd put into her weapons training would be easily applicable. She'd even judged Isaac for his inability to keep his powers in check. But now she was out of control, just like him.

Maybe she would have learned if Augusta had given her a chance instead of cutting her off. Maybe fewer people would have died in the Gray. The knowledge of how unfair it was surged through Harper's chest, and she knew that Violet would have let it take her over, stood up and stormed out.

But Harper wasn't Violet. She knew Augusta had wronged her—and she knew, just as well, that she could not change the Hawthornes' betrayal. But it didn't mean there was nothing to learn from the sheriff. So again she stayed silent, and to her surprise, Augusta's face creased not with derision, but sympathy.

"I had the same problem when I first came into my powers," she said, almost gently.

"Really?" Harper asked, surprised.

"It is extremely unpleasant," Augusta continued, rather stiffly, as if the very words made her uncomfortable, "to feel as if you are merely a vessel instead of the one in control."

Harper's surprise deepened. She hated being used. She'd hated it when her father had done it, when Augusta and Juniper had tried to do it. But most of all, she hated that the power she had waited her entire life to have felt like it was just using her, too.

"Yes," she said, trying not to show how much it meant to her that someone else felt that way, too. "It is. So how do I stop it?"

"Well, the difficult thing is that you *are* a vessel. All of us are. That is what our rituals do—they make us proper receptacles for power. Which means you must learn how to tame it before it tames you. You're good with a sword, yes?"

Harper nodded. "Very good, thank you."

Augusta's lips twitched. If Harper hadn't known better, she'd have said the older woman was amused.

"Think of your power as a blade, then. One you must wield internally. Hone it in your mind. Call upon it with clear intention. Set boundaries, and do not allow it to surpass them."

This all made sense to Harper—too much sense, almost. It seemed so simple.

"I see," she said slowly, and then: "I want to try it."

"I thought you might." She gestured to the leaves scattered on the ground. "Perhaps you can begin with one of them. Turn something small to stone. See if you can stop."

Harper's heart thudded in her chest as she lifted a browning leaf into the air. She twirled it in her fingers, thinking of Augusta's words—*Call upon it with clear intention*—and pictured the leaf transforming to stone, just that leaf, nothing else. Then she pushed her power into it, exhaling. Immediately, stone spread from the tips of her fingers, rushing up the leaf's stem and engulfing it in reddish-brown.

"There," she said, setting the thin piece of stone down gently on the grass.

Augusta gave her a sharp, approving nod.

Harper was about to smile when she felt something course through her again, another wave of power. She slammed her palm against the ground and shuddered as a wave of stone rippled out from between her fingers, this one spreading across the ground. Augusta scrambled hastily out of the way as it rushed toward her.

When the surge of power faded, Harper was left staring at a swathe of stone leaves and grass before her, extending perhaps five feet outward from where her hand had struck the ground. She felt dizzy and disoriented again. Her residual limb ached as her frustration deepened, phantom pain twinging through a left hand that no longer existed.

It hadn't worked. Of *course* it hadn't worked. Harper hated that she was disappointed. She rose cautiously to her feet, the world still spinning, and braced herself for whatever insult Augusta Hawthorne was about to hurl her way.

But instead, Augusta was staring at the damage Harper had done, an unreadable expression on her face.

"Hmm," she said. "Perhaps asking you to work on this here was unwise. We'll try your lake next time."

"*My* lake?" Harper asked, trying not to sound dubious. "It doesn't belong to me."

"Yes, it does." Augusta gestured to the tree behind her. "The founders' rituals might be different, but they are all based around specific places. The Saunderses' attic. Your lake. Our tree. The Sullivans'..." She trailed off, shook her head. "The point is, place *matters* in Four Paths. It puts you in tune with the bargain you made and enables you to focus. Why do you think we hold the Founders' Day ceremony on the seal?"

"I've never really thought about it," Harper said honestly.

"Because that's where the founders sacrificed themselves for the Beast," Augusta said. "It is an important place for us all."

Harper had never known that. There was a lot she didn't know, she realized, guilt rising in her. Maybe the Hawthornes had deserved to have their focal point taken away, but she wasn't sure the town deserved to lose so many of its defenses. Before she had her powers, she had seen the stark reality of what it was like to live in Four Paths, to put your safety in other people's hands.

Revenge on Justin's family had seemed so simple. But Harper knew she could not just consider her own feelings about the Hawthornes anymore. She held the power she had always craved in her small palm; she could not justify misusing it. That would make her no better than her father. No better than Augusta.

"What would happen," she asked quietly, "if all of those places were destroyed?"

Augusta froze. Her gloved hands twitched ever so slightly as she stared at the pile of stone leaves Harper had created.

"I don't think any of us would like to find out," she said finally. "That's why it's so important that you gain control of your powers. And when you *do* gain control, I hope for all of our sakes that you use your power wisely."

CHAPTER EIGHT

May stared grimly at the leaf in her gloved hand, then held it up to the sunlight, squinting. The foliage around her blazed orange and crimson, a perfect Saturday morning in the heart of autumn, but May knew all that was a lie. Beneath their bark, any of these trees could be succumbing to the same disease that she had seen a few weeks ago in the forest, rotting them from the inside out.

"You see it," she said, turning to her father. "Don't you?"

Ezra nodded grimly as May's stomach churned. The sunlight illuminated the exact places where the oak leaf's natural rusty orange faded into splotchy gray, the oily sheen of its veins. Liquid dripped from the stem, gray and viscous, but May's gloves shielded it from direct contact with her skin. It didn't shield the smell from her nose, though.

They were standing in the clearing where the Church of the Four Deities had done their ritual. After their meeting outside of town, May had been able to use her extensive knowledge of Augusta's schedule to successfully smuggle her father into Four Paths.

She was glad she had—now she wasn't the only witness to this slow-motion train wreck.

Iridescent veins spiderwebbed across the tree in front of

her, gray bleeding out from them in patches. The layer of bark between the veins had thinned, glimmering with a fleshy sheen. May could see more veins sliding beneath it, moving toward the heart of the tree. She'd touched the bark with her glove and been disturbed by the way it felt—even through the thin fabric, it was soft and warm, almost like human skin.

"These are the same symptoms I saw in the forest," she said, releasing the leaf and letting it flutter to the ground. "And they're getting worse."

Beside her, Ezra studied the tree, his mouth set in a thin, worried line, and pushed his glasses up on the bridge of his nose. He'd been antsy since she escorted him back into town. She didn't blame him. If Augusta figured out he was here before May could prove she'd called him back for a good reason, she shuddered to think what would happen to both of them.

"You saw fog emanating from the tree before, correct?" he asked, turning toward her.

She nodded. "It looked like an opening, sort of. To the Gray. But I don't see anything like that now."

"Interesting." Ezra walked around the tree, studying it carefully. "There are usually only two possibilities for the Gray opening: the Beast is nearby, or a Sullivan has opened a portal. These symptoms, however, are different. Finding their source requires a return to the beginning of everything—to the founders themselves."

May's eyes widened. "You've heard of this before?"

"Maybe." Ezra's brow furrowed. "There's very little information about what Four Paths was like before the founders locked the Beast in the Gray. But when it roamed wild, it supposedly caused havoc much like this."

He pulled out a tablet from inside his jacket pocket and swiped through it. "After our conversation, I dug back into my research archives on this town," he said, handing the screen to May. "This appears to line up with what we're experiencing here."

May stared at the screen, her mouth agape. It was a scan of a drawing, meticulously detailed and sharply rendered—a tree with the center of the trunk carved out, liquid dripping from the edges of the hole. Veins just like the ones in front of them curved around the bark.

She knew that art style, even though it was ink, not paint. She would have known it anywhere.

"Hetty Hawthorne drew this." It wasn't a question.

Ezra nodded grimly. "It depicts a sort of plague that the uncaged Beast appeared to unleash in its wake."

May's stomach lurched. "It isn't free, though. It can't be free."

"No, it isn't," Ezra said quickly. "Things would be quite different if it was. But from what you've told me, Four Paths' condition has declined significantly since I left town. The line between the Gray and our reality has grown thin. Four Paths may be heading toward a breaking point."

"A breaking point?" May asked. "You mean like the Beast escaping?"

"Maybe. This rotting tree is just the beginning of what the original founders faced at the hands of the Beast. If it does escape, this corruption will eat this town whole. If we're lucky, it'll stop at Four Paths—but if we're not, it'll spread farther."

"We have to stop this," she whispered, shoving the tablet back into her father's hands. "How can we stop this?"

Ezra tucked it into his coat once more. He was calmer than she could comprehend—but then, this was not his town. He was here because she'd asked him to be. She was here because she had no other choice.

"Do you remember when you were younger?" Ezra asked. "That ritual you did?"

The forest seemed to blur suddenly around May, the colors and the iridescence bleeding together, and she realized those were tears.

It had been real. Those memories—he knew it had happened, too. He *knew*.

Her voice, when she spoke, no longer sounded like it belonged to her. "Yes."

The first time he'd cut her palms and asked her to give her blood to the tree, May threw up afterward. The second time, she cried. But the third time, she walked away feeling unbreakable.

The lines on her palms had long since faded away, but the memories hadn't, nor had that strange, persistent itch on her hands. And when the hawthorn tree did not bow to Justin all those years later, she wondered in the back of her mind if it was because it knew her blood instead of his.

"I always told you that ritual would be important someday." Ezra's face was solemn.

May swallowed, her palms itching, the forest still danger-ously woozy. "What did you do to me?"

"The Gray has been threatening to overpower the founders for a long time, May." His voice was gentle. "I knew that if we wanted to have any chance of fighting the Beast, really fighting it, the founders needed to be stronger. I read about the original ritual the founders did for power. I thought it might tip the bal-ance if a founder did it again, but Augusta refused. Said it was too risky."

"But you did it anyway."

He nodded. "Because you asked me to."

May's heart was beating so fast, it hurt. She wobbled, then swayed, her father's hand steadying her and guiding her to a seat on the forest floor. It was true that she'd asked. She'd talked to him about her ritual—about how scared she was of failing it. About how she knew Justin would do well, but she wanted to prove herself, too.

What if we could guarantee that you would pass it? he'd asked her. And she'd jumped at that chance.

It was why she could not hate her father. Because he had given her the power she had always wanted. Because he had seen in her the things Augusta couldn't, or wouldn't. Because he'd been *right*.

"The ritual worked," she murmured, thinking of all her futures laid out before her, of grabbing the one she wanted and yanking it into place. "I'm stronger than I should be."

Ezra knelt beside her, and there was that smile again, big and wide and proud.

"That's not true," he said. "You're as strong as you deserve to be."

Gratitude surged through her. She grinned and turned to thank him—and saw, from her new vantage point, a pair of sneakers twitching behind the nearest tree.

"Dad," she whispered, extending a shaking finger.

She didn't remember standing, or moving, but she knew the moment she recognized the face of the person lying before her. It was a white boy in Justin's grade—Henrik Dougan.

His face was ashen, his eyes open and staring blankly at the clouds above. She would have thought him dead if not for the way his body was twitching ever so slightly. May's mind churned as she noted the pack of cigarettes spilled on the ground beside him. This was a popular smoking spot—but clearly, he'd been interrupted.

"Hey," she said, bending toward him. "Are you all right?"

As if her words had awakened something inside Henrik, a shudder roared through him, starting in his neck and extending down his spine. He jerked, his limbs flailing wildly, and May saw them then: roots, writhing across the skin of his forearms, gray and slimy, wriggling like slugs as they burrowed *beneath the flesh*.

She recoiled, nausea rising in her throat.

"I was worried about this," Ezra said grimly from beside her. "It's spreading faster than I thought it would."

"The corruption?" May rounded on him. "This is the corruption?"

He nodded, and May blanched.

She'd noticed how this disease could hurt the forest. Never had she thought of how it could hurt the people who lived in it, too—people she was supposed to be protecting.

Her stomach lurched, and she turned to her father, the last words she'd ever expected to finish this meeting with already falling from her lips.

"I have to call my mother."

The sheriff's station was deserted. Isaac's spine prickled as he walked down the sterile main hallway, his footsteps muffled by the stained linoleum. Above him, the fluorescent lights hummed and buzzed, flickering slightly. A phone went off behind one of the identical metal doors, its bleating, plaintive ringtone cutting sharply through the silence. Nobody picked it up.

He knew where he was going—the clinic—but he wasn't prepared for what was waiting behind the door. All he knew was that there had been some kind of accident. May and Violet had both contacted him about this, which meant it was clearly an emergency.

Juniper Saunders answered his knock on the clinic door, her hair pulled back in a ponytail, the skin around her dark eyes creased with worry.

"Good, you're here," she said. Behind her, he noticed Augusta Hawthorne. He'd thought they hated each other—or at least, that they couldn't get along. If they were here together, something was really, truly wrong.

He pushed past her and gaped.

The smell hit him first, musky and unmistakably familiar: decay, the same thing he'd smelled during his botched ritual with Violet. The clinic was dark and claustrophobic, the only window shuttered, the fluorescents dimmed. Justin, May, Violet, and Harper sat grimly beside the far wall, staring intently at the boy lying in front of them, his forearms and thighs strapped down to the cot beneath him. Isaac crossed the room, his stomach twisting as he recognized Henrik. His classmate—one of the people he was supposed to be protecting.

Henrik's thin T-shirt was soaked through with sweat, and his body twitched beneath the restraints in small, rhythmic shudders. The smell was nearly unbearable; Isaac pressed his sleeve against his mouth and nose in a desperate attempt to stop it. Henrik's eyes were closed, and the veins on both his arms stood out starkly against his pale skin, gleaming iridescent in the dim light. The skin itself had gone gray around the veins and spread outward, new patterns etching ridges into his forearms and down to his wrists. They looked uncomfortably like tree bark.

Isaac had never seen the Gray do something like this before. The bodies it left behind were always dead and always twisted nearly in half. They smelled like nothing, and their eyes were bleach-white. It had been that way for as long as he could remember.

"What happened to him?" he whispered.

"May found him on patrol." Justin's voice was hoarse. Isaac knew that things were still strange between them, especially in light of what had happened at lunch the other day, but in that moment he didn't really care. "Mom evacuated the station before she brought him back. She didn't want anyone else to see this."

"But he's not dead," Isaac said slowly, avoiding the word *yet*.

"No, he isn't," May said sharply. "It looks worse than it is— his vitals are pretty normal. But he seems to be in and out of consciousness."

Isaac's stomach churned. "Why would the Gray leave him alive?"

Something squirmed beneath the skin at Henrik's neck, drawing Isaac's focus. He watched, horrified, as it crawled up toward his jaw; a moment later, Henrik's breathing changed, becoming rough and labored. A small moan escaped his parted lips. Isaac knew what it was: a root. Just like the one that had tried to burrow into his cheek.

"Where did you find him?" he asked May, even though deep down he already knew the answer.

"The clearing where the Church did their ritual," she said.

Isaac stumbled, bile rising in his throat. Justin was at his side a moment later, steadying him.

"Here," he said gently, handing him a water bottle. Isaac recognized it from the half-dozen cross-country meets he'd willingly gone to just to watch Justin run. He took a swig and hastily wiped his mouth. When he looked up again, Violet's gaze was waiting for his. He saw the guilt there, the same guilt he felt.

There was no hiding from this: Henrik's illness was their fault. Violet hadn't wanted to do that ritual again. He should have listened to her, but he'd been reckless instead, and an innocent person was suffering as a result.

Isaac swallowed, trying to think. He had to fix this before it got worse. And he had an idea of how to do that. A painful idea, but a good one all the same.

"I think I know someone who might be able to help Henrik," he said quietly, addressing all of them. Augusta and Juniper turned, both eyeing him with confusion. "As I'm sure most of you have realized by now, my brother's back."

Nobody looked particularly surprised.

"I'm aware," Augusta said calmly. "We've already reached out to him about rejoining the patrol schedule, but he said it would upset you too much."

There was an accusatory note in her voice that Isaac didn't appreciate. Still, he soldiered on.

"His power," he said slowly, "is uniquely suited to this situation."

Isaac's own powers came from an energy field he could tap into with his palms. When activated, it could disintegrate anything—including the border between Four Paths and the Gray. Gabriel also summoned an energy field, but his power helped everyone he touched instead of hurting them. His healing couldn't work miracles, but it could accelerate a body's natural ability to mend itself. It was possible he'd be able to give Henrik's immune system the boost it needed to fight this disease off.

"You think he'll come here?" Augusta asked.

He nodded, flipped his phone open to text him.

Isaac was the kind of Sullivan who broke things. Gabriel was the kind of Sullivan who fixed them, and Isaac *hated* it. But his pride wasn't worth the possibility of another death on his hands.

It took less than a half hour for Gabriel to arrive. Nobody spoke much while they waited; there was nothing to say. Gabriel's entrance, however, changed all that. From the moment he entered the clinic, the air around him felt slightly charged. Isaac watched Gabriel greet the adults and nod at the other founders. Watched him walk to the cot where Henrik lay, still twitching slightly, and survey him intently.

"Do you think you can heal him?"

Isaac didn't even realize the words were his own until Gabriel looked up from across the cot, and suddenly they were both younger, Isaac holding out his bloodied arm, scraped from a tree branch, and asking Gabriel that same question.

Do you think you can heal me?

Gabriel's jaw twitched. "Depends. How long has he been sick?"

"We don't know," Isaac said. "He was brought here about an hour ago, though."

"And has it gotten worse?"

Isaac shrugged. "Nothing's changed, so I don't think so."

Gabriel studied Henrik. "I haven't used my powers in a long time," he said. "But I can try."

Gabriel knelt beside the cot and clasped Henrik's hand in his. When he exhaled, long and slow, a familiar shimmer appeared around his fingers. Isaac forced down a stab of jealousy.

Henrik groaned, and Isaac's focus moved back to him, watching with alarm as the boy's eyes snapped open. They were flat and lifeless. His mouth opened; a tinny, hollow noise came out. As one, the room recoiled.

"He's possessed," Isaac murmured, horrified. Just like Violet had been.

Gabriel looked disarmed for a moment, but then he took a deep breath and his face contorted with focus. The air around the cot rippled, and then gold and green began to dance through the air around Gabriel's hand. His neck tattoos seemed to writhe as the light danced and hummed. The light extended up the boy's arm until it covered the entire area that had turned gray.

Henrik twitched just once, his hand jerking where it was touching Gabriel's, and then fell perfectly still. Isaac would have worried if not for the steady rise and fall of his chest. The light intensified, and a wave of heat washed across the room. Isaac squinted into it and gaped.

Henrik's skin was changing—the gray receding, the iridescence in his veins dulling. His eyes flickered back and forth between lifeless and his familiar warm brown, his body contorting on the cot. Gabriel reached forward and pushed on the wriggling *thing* beneath his skin, and a moment later, a gush of oily fluid spurted out of Henrik's arm, clouding the room with the smell of decay. Gabriel lifted his hand, and Isaac felt a stab of recognition.

He'd been right.

Clenched between his brother's fingers, wriggling gruesomely, was a root just like the one Violet had gouged out of his cheek.

"What the *fuck*," Gabriel muttered, staring at it with obvious horror.

Isaac opened his mouth to warn him—but not fast enough.

The root curled around Gabriel's fingers, clenching, reaching. Then it burrowed beneath his skin in the blink of an eye. Gabriel jerked backward, a wordless yell of panic emitting from his throat.

Isaac didn't think about it—he just moved, his hand darting forward and wrapping around Gabriel's wrist. He yanked his brother around, his heart jolting at the panic blooming in Gabriel's eyes.

"I can fix this," he said. "But it's going to hurt."

Gabriel exhaled sharply through his nostrils. "Hurry, then."

Isaac laid his brother's hand down on the night table beside the cot, bracing his wrist with one hand. He could feel Gabriel's panic radiating off him—although his brother was doing his best to stay calm, Isaac knew better. Around them, the rest of the room was utterly still.

Isaac breathed in and summoned his power. Light radiated from his right palm, purple and red, swirling and pulsating across his fingers. The moment his fingers touched Gabriel's hand, his brother began to scream.

Isaac's stomach churned as the flesh burned away, the smell of it mingling with the decay already in the air. Gabriel was in agony before him, his face bathed in the light of Isaac's power. Isaac wondered if this was how he'd looked to Gabriel when he'd lowered the knife to his neck: Helpless. Terrified.

He had Gabriel at his mercy, he realized. He could take whatever revenge on him he wanted—he could relinquish his grasp and leave him to fight this disease on his own, or he could keep his power burning long past the point where the root was eradicated, until all that was left of his brother was a pile of ashes on the ground.

But no matter what the rest of the town thought about him, Isaac Sullivan was no monster.

He grabbed the wriggling root and crushed it in his palm, his power burning it to ashes.

"Done," he said, stepping away, the light fading. Gabriel collapsed to his knees, staring wordlessly at the blood pooling in his palm. "You good?"

Gabriel stared up at him, shuddering. "Why did you help me?" he asked hoarsely, swaying slightly. Blood slid in rivulets down his wrist and dripped between his fingers, spotting the floor with crimson.

Isaac's stomach clenched as he realized that gray was spreading across his brother's outstretched palm. He'd failed. Already it had spread; already it was growing—but *no.*

The gray started receding, Gabriel's flesh reverting slowly back to normal.

"It doesn't work on us," he breathed, locking eyes with Isaac.

Isaac frowned at him. "How do you know that?"

"I can feel it," Gabriel said. He reached out and grabbed Henrik's arm again. Immediately, another root burrowed beneath the outer flesh of his hand. He bit back a curse but waved Isaac away, holding out his shaking palm for the entire room to see. Harper was the first to walk forward, her eyes alight with curiosity. Violet and May were close behind.

They watched in stone-cold silence as the root wriggled

uselessly beneath his flesh. A small patch of gray splotched across his palm but faded out again, as quickly as it had arrived. Soon, that root had dissolved, too.

"I don't know if it's because of my powers, or because I'm a founder," Gabriel said.

But Isaac knew in his gut that it was a founder thing. When the roots had attacked him, they hadn't hurt him like Henrik, either. For a moment, sure, he'd been plunged into that strange white hellscape. But then he'd come back.

Isaac stepped back as Juniper Saunders procured a roll of gauze and helped Gabriel bandage his palm. He'd been so determined to assuage his own guilt that he'd protected someone who didn't actually need it. But his powers were clearly useless here.

So were Gabriel's, though. That much was clear as his gaze returned to Henrik's body. The oily liquid that had spurted from his arm was already congealing, and the familiar form of another root wriggled beneath his wrist. The gray engulfing his hands hadn't changed, and his open eyes were flat and lifeless again, that strange hissing noise emitting softly from his throat.

It was the Beast in there, not Henrik. Isaac didn't know what that kind of possession would do to a non-founder, but he was certain it wasn't good.

"How much time does he have?" Violet asked, and Isaac realized that she was talking to Gabriel.

"It's...strange." Gabriel's voice was solemn. "The disease seems to move in several stages. At first, there's an initial assault that tries to get under the skin, literally. It infected him pretty deeply, to the point where Isaac would have to mutilate half his body to get the roots out. But when I touched him, I could sense that the spread had stopped. That's why there's been no change in his symptoms. The corruption's goal, at least for now, is to keep its host alive."

"Do you think it just wanted to possess him?" Violet asked.

"Maybe." Gabriel's brow furrowed. "He needs further observation by a professional before anything like that can be determined, though."

"You're being very technical about this," Augusta said. "Were you pre-med?"

Gabriel looked at her, surprised. "I was, yeah. This is my gap year."

"Then you're the most qualified founder we have who can monitor the spread of this disease. How do you feel about heading up the clinic until we get this sorted out?"

Isaac tensed. But he'd brought Gabriel here. He'd known that would mean pulling him into the center of the action. This was an inevitable consequence.

"I'm not sure you're giving me a choice, Ms. Hawthorne."

"Sheriff Hawthorne," Augusta said briskly. "And no, I'm not."

Gabriel shrugged. "I mean . . . If it'll help, I'm in."

"All right, then." Augusta's voice was a dangerous kind of calm. "We need precautionary measures now. A warning to stay out of the woods at all times—a permanent curfew except for those patrolling. This cannot be allowed to spread any further while we search for a cure."

"What about Henrik's family?" Justin asked.

"They'll be briefed on the situation, of course," Juniper said, casting Augusta a warning glance. "If you want us to work with you, you'll need to do this without your powers. I need that promise from you."

Augusta bristled, but nodded in acquiescence. "Fine. But none of this information leaves this room—understood?"

"Understood." Their voices were soft but obedient, and Isaac stumbled out of the clinic, fleeing from the smell of death and from the brother he still somehow wanted to save.

CHAPTER NINE

Henrik Dougan was the first to fall ill, but two more cases were reported over the next few days—people with roots burrowing beneath their skin, turning their bodies gray and iridescent. Their minds taken over by a monster.

News broke like a tidal wave across the town, sweeping every founder into its wake. Violet knew firsthand how possession by the Beast felt, and she expected nothing but hostility from the town once word of it got around. But that wasn't what happened. She noticed it for the first time when Alina Storey stopped her in the hallway the day after Henrik was admitted to the clinic, her voice low. Violet technically knew who the girl was—she was the mayor's daughter—but they'd barely spoken.

"Hey," Alina said, a little breathlessly. "Is it true that the Sullivans are putting their blood feud behind them to try and help the people getting sick?"

Violet shrugged uncomfortably. Four Paths High School was so ordinary; it felt utterly surreal to get this kind of question here. It was pretty brazen, curious where she'd been expecting fear or even hatred. "Why don't you ask Isaac yourself?"

"As if he'd talk about it to us," Alina said, waving a dismissive hand in the air. "Everybody knows all of you are super secretive."

"Then why ask *me*?"

"Because you're new."

"That doesn't mean I'll talk," Violet said firmly, and she headed off. But it was far from the last question she got over the next few days. Her classmates wanted to know if Harper had her powers back. If she'd really helped defeat that "insurgency group" that Violet quickly realized was how Augusta had explained away the Church. And even when her classmates gave up on her answering them, they still watched her—not with mistrust, but with something closer to excitement.

Somehow, some way, the town expected her to protect them. Violet didn't know how to tell them that it was only through her foolishness that they were in danger at all.

Nearly a week after Henrik had fallen ill, she stood in the clearing where she and Isaac had opened the Gray and stared hopelessly at the corrupted trees in front of her.

"It's getting worse," she said grimly to her patrol partners—Harper and May.

Beside her, Harper nodded in agreement. The smell was disgusting, but that was just the beginning of their problems. Iridescent gray liquid oozed steadily from the founders' seal toward the trees around it. The trees looked terrible, veins spiraling around their bark and down their branches. The Carlisles had tried to block off the area with stone bells, but it had done nothing at all.

It was mid-October now, and the girls were dressed for true fall, Violet in a faux-leather jacket, Harper in an oversize green parka and a beanie pulled tight over her dark curls. May looked perfectly pulled together as per usual in a quilted pink vest and fluffy cream-colored earmuffs.

"That's why we're here," she said, her voice high and crisp. "We need to keep track of its advancement."

"I know why we're here," Violet said, more sharply than she'd intended. That was the guilt talking, but knowing why she was being harsh didn't make her feel better. "You don't have to treat us like infants just because we're new to this patrol."

"Well, you weren't exactly the most *willing* patrol partners," May said dryly. "No offense."

Since the corruption had spread, Juniper and Augusta had made a patrol schedule together that was supposed to combine experienced and inexperienced founders and minimize danger by sending them out in larger groups. Which was how the three of them had wound up together.

Violet had no good reason to protest it. Technically, she knew she should feel good about this alliance—it had the potential to actually help solve this ever-mounting problem. But she'd already caused so much trouble with the Church and the Beast, and she hated the idea that, once again, everyone else would have to rally to fix something she had broken.

"We're here, aren't we?" Harper said as they picked their way through the clearing, staring more closely at the trees. Her hand was constantly hovering over the scabbard at her waist. Dusk had muted the world around them, brushing deep blues and purples over the trees in the final fading light of the sunset. "Not that I can really see much. Why is your mother so determined to do these patrols at night?"

"It's easier to clean up messes in the dark," May said, her voice strained. "It does mess with your sleep, though. I recommend bringing coffee next time—it'll make the next day less horrible."

Harper snorted. "Is that why Justin takes so many naps in class?"

May laughed, a sound that seemed utterly out of place in front of the decaying trees. "No, he's just bored. And he knows there isn't a teacher in this town who would dare to fail him. Well, *knew*, I guess."

Her voice faltered, and Violet thought about how much the town's attitude had changed, not just toward Violet but toward Justin, too. The trust extended to her and the other founders, whether deserved or not, was deliberately being kept away from the town's former golden boy. He was glared at, whispered about, sometimes even jeered at. Harper had told her that his birthday was coming up, something that had basically been a local holiday the year before and was now clearly a massive source of shame for him. Violet felt for him, for all of them.

To be a founder, it seemed, was to fit whatever role the rest of the town had decided you would play or be discarded completely.

"Ah, *shit*." Violet turned and saw Harper shining her flashlight onto a bit of nearby tree trunk. Something was growing from the gleaming, fleshy bark: thin silver strands clumped together. "Is that *hair*?"

"I think so." Violet's stomach churned. She didn't understand how she'd managed to do this, to unleash something that was twisted and disgusting even by Four Paths' low standards.

"Oh, gross," May mumbled from beside her, her face ashen.

"Something has to be causing this," Harper said. "If the Gray keeps opening and infecting our world like this, in a way the Beast has never done before, there has to be a source point. Some event that started it."

Violet shifted uncomfortably. She'd hated keeping this from Harper, and she knew that May had clear ties and allegiances that were more important than any bond between the two of them. Harper had been nothing but a good friend to her, and May had given Violet her memories back when she'd had no obligation to do so.

They deserved to know what was happening here before it went any further.

"Harper..." she started. "I have to tell you something. Oh, screw it, both of you. You should both know."

Once she started talking, it was surprisingly easy to let the words spill out. About the ritual she and Isaac had done about a week and a half ago. How the corruption had clearly emerged from that, how it was her fault *again* that the entire town was in trouble.

"So I think it's us," she finished. "I think we started it, and I feel so useless, because my power can't even help this time."

And when she was done, May said the last thing she was expecting.

"You didn't start the corruption," she said softly.

Violet's head spun. All she could manage was "What?"

"Maybe you spread it, that I don't know," May said. "But you didn't start it. Justin and I found the corruption around two weeks ago. When Augusta came back to look at it with her deputies, she insisted it was gone, and she wouldn't take it seriously. But now it's back. Which means you couldn't have summoned it."

Her relief was immense, titanic; she did not know how to say thank you, and so she settled for a smile instead—one that faded as May's story sank in.

"You didn't tell us about it," Harper said slowly.

May shrugged. "We weren't really getting along at the time. It's not as if Violet told us, either."

"That's true." Violet stared at the trees, distress prickling in her chest as she realized that while this absolved her of culpability, it didn't actually solve anything.

She stepped forward, eyeing the hair growing from the trees with disgust.

"Get back!" Harper's voice rang out a moment too late as a branch fell from the drooping tree. Pain tore down Violet's shoulder, throwing her off-balance. She could feel where the branch had gouged through her jacket, biting into her flesh.

Her body hit the ground a moment later with a *thud* that sent tremors running through her injured shoulder. Her wound throbbed; she could feel a root wriggling beneath the skin and dissolving. It was an awful feeling, like a tiny ball of fire extinguishing inside her arm.

"Are you okay?" Harper was there, kneeling beside her. May joined her a moment later.

Violet forced herself to catch her breath. "Yeah. It hurt my shoulder, though."

May helped her to her feet. "We should look at the wound."

Violet nodded, still feeling disoriented as she shrugged her arm out of her jacket. She didn't think she was corrupted, but she could feel something different all the same.

A feeling was unfolding in the back of her mind, in the same place the Beast permanently resided. A *tether*, spinning out from her and . . . into the trees. Was this how the possession started? It hadn't felt like this when she was dealing with Rosie's apparition, but she felt a stab of panic anyway.

"You're okay," Harper said as May shone a flashlight on the wound. "The gray is already almost gone."

"So we really are immune," Violet murmured.

"I'm still disinfecting it, even if it looks fine." May riffled around in her small white backpack and pulled out a first-aid kit, ignoring Violet's protests and curses as she swabbed the wound with peroxide.

"That hurt almost as much as the corruption did," Violet said, scowling as she shrugged her coat back on.

"Don't be a baby," May shot back.

"Hey!" Harper's voice was alarmed. Violet turned her flashlight beam and saw that the branches above them were moving again, coiling and uncoiling above their heads. That tether unfurled in her mind once more—a tugging, a connection. Just like the one she felt from Orpheus. "We need to get out of here."

"Wait," Violet whispered. She had an idea. A terrible idea. She grabbed that tether in her mind and yanked on it.

"Stop," she said slowly, extending her hands.

The effect was immediate. The branches around them began to slow. Violet could feel them in her mind, strings that she could coil around her hands and yank in whatever direction she wanted.

"Stop," she murmured again, pulling them taut. And just like that, the branches did as she had asked. She knew this wasn't the same kind of control she had over Orpheus, but when she was right here, when she was focused—they would listen to her, at least a little bit.

Not possession, then. Not possession at all.

"How did you do that?" Harper's voice was about an octave too high.

Violet's words came out shaky. "I have no idea."

"Your power raises and bonds with the dead." May's voice rang through the clearing, laced with a new respect. "I suppose that's extended to the trees, somehow—perhaps the way the corruption is changing them has turned them into something you can control."

"It isn't perfect," Violet said slowly. She could already feel the tethers unwinding; grasping for a new connection wasn't working. "We still need to go—I won't be able to hold them for too long."

"But you can train it," Harper said. "You can use this to help us. We're both weapons now, Violet."

The truth of those words coursed through Violet as they retreated back into the night.

Four Paths might be dying. But Violet had seen death before, let it engulf her, let it transform her. And she was ready to use everything she'd learned to keep that death from spreading any further.

She didn't know if any of them could be the hero Four Paths seemed to want so desperately, now that they knew it could not be Justin Hawthorne. But at least she could do something to slow the spread of the corruption.

At least it wasn't her fault.

May sat on a bench, her stomach churning. She'd just come from the clinic, where the three victims of the corruption lay still and suffering on their cots. The nurses who normally staffed it were back, but Gabriel Sullivan had stayed, too, monitoring their vitals with his powers alongside the nurses who did the same with their machines.

They weren't getting worse, at least. After the disease's initial infection, it seemed to slow down, keeping its victims' bodies trapped in torment without destroying them. But they weren't getting better, either. Their minds were not their own—instead, they were in thrall to the Beast, flat eyes tracking her every move and hissing whispers following her around the room.

For now, Four Paths actually seemed to trust the founders— the ones with powers, anyway. Gabriel returning to town and assisting with the clinic was helping stave off questions, but it wouldn't last forever. May knew they weren't beating back the corruption fast enough. Violet's powers had helped a little bit, but May's initial rush of hope that she could be a serious asset was mostly quashed. She could not reverse the corruption, only override the trees' instincts to attack for small, precious allot- ments of time, while Harper couldn't get control of her abilities at all. Isaac had been trying to disintegrate the damage, but it was growing faster than he could destroy it.

This corruption was a match that would light the pile of tinder her family had built, and if they could not stop it, soon enough they would all burn. Which was why she was so anxious to talk to her father about how they might put an end to it.

Ezra Bishop had been off on a research trip for the last few days, gathering his old study materials from his office in Syracuse and transporting them to the motel room he'd booked in Four Paths. Now that he was back in town, he and May had arranged to meet again.

She was hoping that he'd found something in his research materials that could help them, because May herself was at a loss. Usually it was enough to work through ideas in her own mind, but this problem felt bigger than her. She was starting to understand that this was part of why she'd contacted her father: because, as much as she hated to admit it, she was lonely.

She'd had friends who weren't founders when she was younger, but they had all faded out the older she became, the more she realized how different her life would have to be from theirs. Yet even among the other founders, May knew she was the odd one out. Seth and Mitzi Carlisle kept to themselves, insular and careful, while Violet and Harper had found each other almost instantly. They'd only been friends for a few months, but their bond seemed inevitable and unbreakable in a way May had never felt in her own life. And although Justin and Isaac had made her feel included for a little while, she'd soon understood that she was merely tagging along, always a step behind, never their first priority.

Ezra was the only person who'd ever put May first. Who'd seen what she was capable of. Who actually *listened* to her. Which was why she was waiting for him behind the library while her mother was holding a deputy meeting at the sheriff's station.

He appeared, eyes crinkled as he gazed into the sun. The disquiet in May's chest shrank to a dull murmur as he adjusted his glasses and peered at her.

"I've found something," he said matter-of-factly, not bothering with greetings. "It's not ideal. Destruction looms."

"You sound like an ancient prophet or something," May said, frowning at him.

Ezra's face tightened for a moment, but the expression was gone before May could ask about it, replaced by a gentle chuckle. "I'm a college professor, May. Forgive my occasional grandiosity."

"It's fine," May said. "But what *discovery* is this?"

"I need to show you," Ezra said, twisting his hands together. "Are you up for a walk in the forest?"

"Of course."

"Splendid."

"Where are we going?" May asked as she rose to her feet.

"The Sullivan ruins," Ezra answered mildly as they walked into the woods together. May hadn't been there in years, since the house had mysteriously collapsed in the dead of night. Nobody said anything, but everybody knew it was Isaac. "The family's small now, I've heard, but also quite powerful. Especially the youngest boy."

"Isaac's powerful, sure, but it tortures him." The words came out harsh, but May didn't care. Even here, she couldn't get away from the other founders. "He hates what he can do."

"That's a price often paid for strength," Ezra said. "I believe it takes an exceptionally sound mind to manage the burden the Beast places upon you when you draw on its power."

"It's not a burden," May said sharply. "It's an honor."

"You can be honest, May. I watched your mother struggle for years. I know that your powers can be both at once."

May hesitated. "Maybe sometimes they feel like a burden. But it's a burden I'm happy to carry, as long as I can help keep Four Paths safe."

"Of course," Ezra said as they stepped deeper into the trees. They were in a part of the forest that the corruption had yet to really touch, but even without the familiar smell and sights of the disease, May was still on edge.

Soon, they'd reached the edge of the Sullivan ruins. Nobody was foolish enough to venture here—a few had come to gawk in the early days after its destruction, but Isaac had made sure they were too frightened to ever return. Ezra didn't know about any of this, of course, so he led them toward what had once been the backyard with no hesitation.

"Here it is," he said grimly, as the familiar smell of decay washed over them. He grabbed a bandanna from inside his coat and tied it around the lower half of his face. May was glad to see he was protecting himself—the corruption couldn't hurt her, but it *could* hurt him.

"I heard reports of strange smoke trails rising over the trees and came to investigate. This is what I found." His voice was muffled through the fabric.

May's heart stuttered in her chest as she struggled to process the sight in front of her. Cracked in half and sloped diagonally along the ground was a red-brown slab of stone, far away from the rest of the ruins. Twining around it were roots, dozens of them, iridescent veins shining. She knew where they were: at the Sullivans' ritual site. But the altar, an ugly reminder of that family's history, did not distress her nearly as much as the trees that loomed around it.

Hair hung from their branches in matted gray clumps, like the corrupted trees she'd seen on patrol with Harper and Violet. But there was something new about these. Something descended from the branches, buds made of strange gray petals that each folded inward to a glimmering, iridescent point. They were large and ungainly, each one at least six inches long, and the petals were long and skinny, twined together in a way that felt grotesquely familiar.

May stepped closer, nausea welling up in her as she realized what they reminded her of: human hands, the five fingers elongated and fused together. Her eyes roamed across the clearing, counting—there were nearly a dozen.

"What *are* they?" she whispered, turning around.

"Some sort of growth," Ezra said, his voice muffled through the bandanna. He gestured to the tree closest to the altar. May watched, horrified, as a wisp of gray smoke leaked out of the tip and dissipated into the air, iridescent flecks swirling in the autumn sunshine.

"It's spreading the corruption," she gasped.

Ezra nodded grimly. "I believe so. While doing my research, I discovered more oblique references to the corruption we're dealing with now. It would seem that what the founders trapped in the Gray was not just the Beast—it was the powers it possessed when it was roaming Four Paths, and those powers are leaking outward through the Gray and into town, hurting us."

"But they don't hurt the founders," May said.

"I've noticed that, and I have a theory. I believe it's because you are, essentially, already corrupted."

May raised an eyebrow. "Excuse me?"

"It's the equivalent of a vaccination," Ezra said. "You've already been exposed to the pathogen in a contained environment when you completed your ritual with the Beast. The rest of the town, however, has not, and therefore they remain highly susceptible."

"But what about a founder who failed their ritual?" she asked slowly, thinking of Justin.

Ezra hesitated. "If they were still exposed to it and survived... that theoretically means they could still be immune."

May thought about this. Direct contact with the Beast leading to a later immunity *would* include Justin, but she was still a little concerned about the possibility of contamination.

"Either way, you don't have immunity," May said. "So be careful, okay?"

"Don't worry," Ezra said, gesturing to his gloves, his steel-toed boots, the bandanna. May realized that he had as little skin exposed as possible without wearing a hazmat suit. "It spreads through direct contact—for now."

"For now?"

"These growths concern me," Ezra said frankly. "The corruption comes from the Gray, so when it opens, it emerges in its raw form, which seems to dissipate fairly quickly on its own. But when it finds a host to infect, it clings to it, festering and growing, turning its victims into vessels for the Beast. That's how it spreads: Hosts come into direct contact with other hosts, which allows you to monitor and halt the spread with relative ease as we search for a cure. But these growths seem as though they emit a constant stream of raw corruption—as if they've taken it *from* the Gray and channeled it into Four Paths. They're still dissipating fairly quickly, but if they spread, it will be immeasurably more difficult to stop the corruption. People will potentially be infected simply by getting too close and breathing it in."

May struggled to let the true magnitude of this sink in. If these buds bloomed, it would be impossible to stop the corruption from spreading more quickly. All their containment efforts would be for nothing. The thought made her want to rip each of the buds off with her bare hands and stomp on them, but she couldn't do something that rash. Maybe all that would do was release it earlier.

"You're familiar with the other founders' powers, yes?" Ezra asked. May nodded. "I believe a team-up of the Saunders girl, the

Carlisle who can petrify things, and the Sullivan destruction is our best chance to stop this. Their powers are uniquely suited to this situation."

A flash of jealousy hit May. She was almost as useless as Justin when faced with such practical, easily applicable powers.

But they can't do what you can, a voice whispered in the back of May's mind.

Her powers were her responsibility. Her birthright. Her *gift*. What good was that gift if she could not use that to protect anyone?

"Their powers aren't the only ones that might be able to help here," May said slowly.

Ezra turned toward her. "Oh?"

May took a deep breath. "You know a lot about the Hawthornes. Do you . . . Do you know anything about a Hawthorne who could change the future?"

Ezra's face transformed, and he stepped toward her.

"May," he said softly, "do you have something to tell me?"

There was no going back if she told him the truth. He would be the only person in the world who knew what she had done. What she was capable of.

But he deserved to know. So May banished her last bit of doubt, and as the words spilled from her, a plan formed in her mind. She'd changed the future to get her father back. Maybe she could change it again—to make sure they defeated the corruption.

"Do you think it's possible?" she asked him.

"Potentially. But you'll have to talk to someone who knows more than I do about your family's powers." He looked at her pointedly.

May's stomach churned. "Do I have to?"

"I would do it myself, but I sincerely doubt our meeting would be productive."

"Don't," May said hastily. "It's fine. I'll do it."

Beside her, one of the buds began to twitch, like a hand about to unfurl. May swallowed down her nausea and left the clearing behind.

CHAPTER TEN

The founders' seal looked like an opening eye, glowing reddish-brown in the light of the sunrise. Harper's stomach clenched as she stood at the edge of the town square, staring at it.

She'd been thinking. About what Augusta Hawthorne had told her regarding sacred places in the town. About the corruption's spread. All that thinking had led to an idea. A dangerous idea, but Harper had a feeling it would actually work.

"I can't believe you got me up this early." Violet's red hair was sticking up in the back, her eyes swollen with sleep. She clutched her coffee thermos like it was made of gold.

"I told you that you could stay home."

"You *knew* I wouldn't."

"I did." Harper hesitated. There was one thing hanging between them that she wanted to fix. It had been bothering her since their patrol. "The corruption. I didn't realize you were blaming yourself for it. I . . . I wish you'd told me what you and Isaac did a little earlier."

Violet flinched, then seemed to deflate slightly, her head bowing. "I wanted to tell you," she said. "But you didn't seem to care what me and Isaac were up to. And with all you have going on, I felt like I couldn't ask you for help—like I had to handle this one by myself."

"We're friends," Harper said. "I don't want you to feel like you can't talk to me about something, or ask me for help. You don't have to keep secrets from me."

Violet's eyes widened. Harper couldn't read the expression on her face.

"It's easy to say that, but we all have secrets," she said. "And I'm so scared of hurting any more people. When I thought the corruption was my fault, I couldn't handle the guilt. I still feel it—this sense that I got to Four Paths and everything went off the rails."

Harper hadn't known Violet for all that long, but she understood implicitly the deep fear that lurked within her. She'd seen it before when Violet talked about her father, her aunt, her sister. Harper had never lost someone she cared about the way Violet had. But she saw in that moment how it could make Violet worry that any mistake might cost her someone else.

"Four Paths was off the rails long before you got here," Harper said. "The Church of the Four Deities wasn't your fault. Neither was Augusta's bullshit. All you did was take all the messed-up stuff and yank it out into the open, and honestly, I like it better there. It means people can't hide anymore."

"You won't like it quite as much when we all get eviscerated by the Beast," Violet said, but her tone was much lighter.

Harper tried to sound nonchalant. "Saves me the trouble of eviscerating Justin myself."

A smile tugged at the corner of Violet's mouth. "That's a strange way of saying *flirting*."

Harper's stomach twisted. "He gave me my memories back. Did you know that?"

"I know. I—I *knew*." The words were loaded, and Harper understood. *We all have secrets.*

"You didn't tell me," she whispered.

"No." Violet's words were careful. Harper could tell she'd put a lot of thought into this. "I told Justin that if he didn't give you the memories back, I would. He asked me to give him a chance to right the wrong of betraying you—so I did."

"Of course he wanted to do it himself," Harper said, overwhelmed. "Look, you talk about us, and you say we're flirting, but—is that even what we're doing? He makes these ridiculous grand gestures that are really complicated, and it makes it impossible for me to think about him normally."

"None of our lives are normal," Violet said. "Potential dating lives included, I guess."

Harper hesitated. Justin was one of the things that tethered her here most—a loose end that she had no idea how to resolve. Her siblings could be protected, but this—this was something else entirely. "I'm worried that I'm almost obligated to see our romantic relationship through because of everything that's happened to us."

"You're not obligated to feel anything," Violet said sharply.

"I know that," Harper said. "But I also know that he's chosen to tell the town the truth about his powers at least partially because of me. He's trying so hard to grow up—he's doing everything that I thought he wasn't capable of."

"It's great that he's trying to be better, but you should only date him if you want to. Not because you feel that you need to help him, or change him, or save him. *You* come first, okay?"

Harper opened her mouth, then shut it. "That was pretty nuanced dating advice for someone who's never dated anybody *and* was forced to wake up at five a.m."

"I'm an excellent friend. Cherish me."

Harper snorted and elbowed her, sloshing Violet's coffee thermos and earning a yell of disapproval.

Isaac Sullivan appeared on the front steps of the town hall a moment later, eyeing them both with slight trepidation. He was the real reason why Harper had invited Violet here—because she knew there was a far better chance he'd show up if it wasn't just her. And she needed him for her terrible plan to work.

It was a plan that was deceptively simple: Go into the Gray. She had survived there far longer than anyone else in town, which meant she had the best shot of anybody of getting out. And this time, she had a mission: Try to find a source point for the corruption. She knew, as did Violet, that there was a possibility it would accelerate the spread of the disease or lead to some sort of retaliation from the Beast. But they had no leads, no ideas for how to cure it. They had to try everything they could.

Which had meant contacting the last person in Four Paths she'd ever expected to get any help from: Isaac Sullivan. The last time the three of them had hung out, they'd been chasing down her little sister in the forest on the night of the equinox. Somehow, this was just as stressful.

"You're sure you want to do this?" he asked her now as they stood in front of the founders' seal. "You might not come out. Also, someone might see us."

"That's a risk I'm willing to take," Harper said. It was why she'd chosen the break of dawn. As for the location—that was all Augusta's doing. She'd heard about corruption spreading at

the Sullivan house, and she had the stirrings of a theory building in her. Something about the corruption having source points.
Going into the Gray from the seal would help her figure that out.

"She said she can handle it," Violet said. "I trust her."

Isaac still looked skeptical. "Last chance to back out, Carlisle."
He lifted his hands palms-out and spread them wide. The air
around them began to hum and ripple, light refracting off the
tree trunks at the edge of the clearing.

"I won't," Harper said calmly.

The world split open a second later, and tendrils of gray
oozed out from the rip Isaac had created, growing stronger.

"We have to be careful here," Isaac said, gesturing at the gray.
"I can't keep this open." Harper understood—they were creating
a gateway to the corruption. It couldn't hurt them, but it *could*
potentially hurt someone else.

"Reopen it in an hour," she said. "If I'm not there, don't come
looking for me."

"I absolutely *will* come looking for you," Violet said sharply.
"Don't be ridiculous."

Harper bit back a laugh. "Then I guess I'd better be there."

"Yes! You'd better!"

Harper smiled and patted the scabbard strapped to her waist.
"You know I can protect myself."

"I know you can," Violet said.

Then she stepped back, and Harper stepped forward, and the
moment the first wisp of fog brushed against her skin, the world
around her disappeared.

This was the Gray, for Harper: tendrils of white mist swirling
around her, opening before her like a tunnel, or maybe a throat;

a tinny sound in her ears, hollow and tuneless, whirling around her in words she could *almost* understand, and a smell that felt familiar, a mixture of the wood chips in her father's workshop and the loamy dirt at the side of the riverbank.

When the fog dissolved a heartbeat later, she was standing in the center of Four Paths as it had been a hundred and fifty years ago. Although it looked different, she knew her bearings from the town hall. It lacked the spire, but the stained-glass windows were still there, shaded in grayscale and backlit by the weak light.

The biggest difference was the seal itself: It was ringed by trees, gray chestnut oaks with too-still branches and strangely patterned trunks. In the center of the founders' symbol was a stump, gnarled and ancient, the roots cracking through the stone and burrowing beneath it. But although Harper scrutinized the copse of oak trees carefully, she saw no signs of iridescence.

Harper walked slowly down Main Street, where, instead of storefronts, there were only a few log buildings and a dirt road. In the field where the mausoleum stood now was a graveyard, thin crosses and headstones tilting to the side. And all around them stretched the woods. Harper had always thought in the present day that the woods looked like they were about to take over the town, but now she could see how much had been cleared away. The chestnut oaks were everywhere. In the middle of the street, on either side of the town hall, their branches twining above the gravestones, roots snaking across the dirt road.

She watched the dark, oily tree trunks pulsate, shuddering slightly as she realized that they were all moving in rhythm with one another like a great, grotesque heartbeat.

From the way Violet had talked about the Gray, from her own fragmented memories of the time she'd spent there, Harper had thought it would be a hostile place. Instead it simply felt empty, like a dollhouse whose owner had grown out of it.

Well, fine. Harper was looking for trouble. And if it wouldn't come to her, she would find it all by herself. She pulled the sword out of her scabbard and set off into the thick of the woods, letting her lifetime in Four Paths guide her through this strange terrain.

Her first sign that something was off was the smell. It reminded her of burnt hair and spoiled meat, harsh and unnervingly sweet, the same rotting stench that emanated from the corrupted trees in Four Paths.

Harper's heartbeat sped up, and she kept walking, the ground softening beneath her sneakers. When she glanced down at the ground, she saw shimmering pools of iridescence waiting for her. She threaded her way through them, following them until she broke through the tree line to the Carlisle lake.

And gasped.

Instead of water, it was filled to the brim with that same gray, oily, iridescent liquid. It was not a still thing, this shadow lake; it rippled and shivered, creating waves that crested and sloshed at the edge of the lakebed, mere inches away from Harper's sneakers. This close, the smell of it was overpowering. Harper pulled the neck of her sweatshirt over the bottom half of her face and tried not to gag.

The trees around the lake had changed, too. They had grown together, braided branches and trunks, like a massive fence. And they were dying. The trunks were paper-thin and shot through with veins, iridescent and shiny. Buds shaped like bunched fingers hung from their branches, wisps of smoke drifting aimlessly from their tips. Harper's stomach churned as the smell hit her, so strong it was almost a tangible thing.

She had been right. The corruption had worsened at the heart of Sullivan territory, and it was disastrous here, too, at her family's ritual site. She needed to map this farther, check out the Saunders manor and the Hawthorne tree.

The thinning bark of the tree nearest to her shifted, the side bulging out for a moment, as if the tree were an egg about to hatch. One of the buds brushed against her arm, soft and tender as her own flesh. Harper gasped and stumbled away from the branch. She could see the outline of hands pressing against the insides of the mutated tree trunk. Fear stirred in her chest, and a voice stirred with it, tinny and hollow.

Two of Stones, it whispered, thin and fragile as a fleeting breeze. *Interesting.*

She turned away from the tree.

And there, at the edge of the Carlisle lake, was Justin Hawthorne.

Justin couldn't be here. This was not a place for him, without powers, without the strength she knew she'd always possessed. Yet here he was, smiling and blond, dressed in the same jeans and T-shirt she'd last seen him in.

And then she met his eyes—flat and lifeless—and she understood. Something stirred in her chest that throbbed like a heartbeat and ached like a wound. She blinked, gray filling her vision, then let the tear roll down her cheek. She should've been scared. But she had never feared anything more than not knowing, and now she *knew*. Now she *saw*.

It didn't look much like a monster. But maybe that was the point.

"You're the Beast," she said, brandishing her sword—for

whatever good that would do her. The words rang out a moment later, a little shakier than she was proud of.

Its smile widened. It looked wrong on Justin's face—hard-edged and cruel, the smile of the boy she'd wanted him to be because it would make him easier to hate instead of the boy he really was, well-meaning but malleable, torn miserably between whatever he'd convinced himself he owed to her and his duty to his family.

The Beast had taunted Violet with Rosie. Now it was taunting her with *him*.

Very good, it said, its lips moving, although the words still rang out inside Harper's head. *You shouldn't be here, little stone.*

"You're corrupting this town," Harper said hoarsely. Something was bubbling up in her throat; she thought it might be blood but she didn't look away. If she was going to die here, it would not be with her back turned. "And we're going to stop you."

The Beast raised its hands in plaintive surrender, such a human gesture that it made Harper ill to watch.

I'm sick, just like your town.

The words were sent so vehemently into her mind that Harper coughed violently, blood dotting her sweatshirt. Except it didn't look like blood. It looked exactly like the same gray, oily liquid at the Beast's feet.

"But you're possessing people," she said, stepping forward. "What do you mean, you're sick? How could this be anything but you?"

I am trying to find a way out, the Beast snarled. *Look around. Why would I do this to the only place I have left?*

And then it was gone, and Harper felt the world around her

dissolving. She whirled around, brandishing her sword, as Four Paths rushed around her once again.

When she gasped in another breath, she was still standing beside the lake, but it looked normal this time. Harper scoured the trees beside it for the glimmers of corruption, but found none. She sighed with relief and traipsed back through the forest.

She found Isaac and Violet back at the founders' seal, both staring anxiously at the place where she had disappeared. At the sight of her approach, Violet rushed up to her.

"You're okay!" Violet's voice was light with relief. "You're— you saw something in there, didn't you?"

Harper nodded, exhausted. "Yeah."

"Did you find what you were looking for?" Isaac asked.

Harper hesitated. She'd thought about this the whole walk back. Maybe it was a trick, but she didn't think so.

"I don't think this corruption comes from the Beast," she said softly. "I think it's hurting it just as much as it's hurting us."

She explained as best she could to Violet and Isaac, watching both their faces pale at the descriptions of what she'd seen. And on the excruciating walk back to the Saunders manor, all she could think of was the Beast's face laid over Justin's, until she could not quite remember whose smile was whose.

CHAPTER ELEVEN

The burned-out husk of the place Isaac had called home until he was fourteen had begun to return to nature. Gabriel had asked Isaac to meet him there once he got off his shift at the clinic—he'd had an idea, he said, about how they might be able to find some more answers about the corruption. Violet had told him the corruption wasn't his fault, but he knew they both wanted to fix it anyway, so he'd invited her here to help with whatever this was before heading to Justin's birthday party that evening. But he'd beat them to the ruins he'd made, which was unfortunate. It meant he had time to stew, time to *remember*.

Underbrush crackled beneath Isaac's boots as he retraced the route he'd done every day after getting home from school: through the front archway, now two crumbled stone pillars, into the kitchen, where the old fridge was turned onto its side, blackened with dirt and moss. He paused at the edge of the downstairs den—while all the bedrooms were long destroyed, turned into ashes and smoke, there were still too many remnants of the room his brothers had claimed as their own.

Weeds grew thickly here, twining around the legs of a maroon couch that had been split open; rotted stuffing spilled out from the sides like entrails. Isaac walked closer to it, a thousand memories tugging at every piece of him. His brothers laughing, his brothers fighting, his brothers dead, dead, dead—

"It must have been quite an undertaking."

Isaac turned around. Gabriel was standing in the place where the archway over the front doors had once been, waiting for him. "Destroying our house like this," Gabriel continued. "I'm shocked it didn't kill you."

"Disappointing for you, I'm sure," Isaac said dryly. "Then you'd be free to murder our mother all by yourself."

Gabriel's face tightened.

"I don't need to argue about Mom like this," he said. "I made my case."

"And I made mine. She's all the family we have left."

"It's not her in there," Gabriel said softly. "You know that."

"You're talking about her like she's one of your corrupted patients."

"My patients are still themselves when the Beast isn't tormenting them," Gabriel said grimly. "Our mother . . ."

Isaac wanted to hit him. "I'm not talking about this anymore."

"Fine." A beat of uneasy silence passed between them, and then Gabriel spoke again. "I want you to know that I don't want you dead, even as a joke. Look at this." He shrugged out of his jacket and gestured to the tattoo that spilled across his shoulder behind his thin black tank top: four blades tangled together, roots winding around their hilts. "It's a family tattoo."

"Let me guess," he said, unwilling to think about the fact that Gabriel had chosen to include him even after everything that had passed between them. Four of them, together, like they weren't all just as destroyed as the house they'd once lived in. "You told the artist to make one of the daggers a little longer so you could tell girls it was yours?"

Gabriel's smile widened into something more genuine, and Isaac saw a flash of the people they had both been, before everything, standing in this same room when it was a home instead of a ruin. "You're still a smartass, huh?"

Isaac raised an eyebrow. "That wasn't a no."

Gabriel turned his head to the side, clearly suppressing a laugh. Isaac realized how much he looked like Caleb now, stocky and broad-shouldered, dark curls clipped short along his head, stubble dotting his jawline in a way that Isaac was trying to work on.

"Sorry I'm late." The voice was Violet's. Isaac turned to see her at the edge of the trees, her cat trailing at her heels. She was dressed simply in a pair of loose-fitting jeans and a fleece-lined corduroy jacket, and she looked exhausted, her red hair pulled back in a thin ponytail at the nape of her neck. At the sight of Gabriel the tiredness on her face disappeared, replaced by a far more alert stare.

"I don't think we were formally introduced," she said slowly. "You're Gabriel Sullivan."

"And you're the daughter of that Saunders lady who ran away."

Violet shrugged, the shadow of a smirk dancing around her lips. "Seems like you and my mother had running away and crawling back in common."

"Fair enough." Gabriel jerked a head toward Orpheus. "The hell is that thing?"

"*He* is my companion," said Violet, frowning. "He goes where I go."

Orpheus yawned in Gabriel's general direction, then walked up to Isaac and rubbed his head against his leg. Isaac leaned down to pet him, grinning as Orpheus licked his palm with a sandpapery tongue.

"I think he's getting used to me," he said, scratching behind the cat's ears. Animals did not particularly care for Isaac, but this one seemed to be different. Maybe the cat liked him because they were both supposed to be dead.

Violet's voice sounded a little strained, almost like she was embarrassed. "Um. Yeah. Anyway—the corruption is particularly bad back there. I know we're immune, but I still suggest we be careful."

"How are your relief efforts going?" Gabriel asked. "Isaac, does your power help? Maybe you should do something about the yard."

"Not as well as it should," Isaac said, tensing. He was not in the mood for a demonstration, and he *certainly* wouldn't be doing it in his backyard. The altar was back there. It was the only part of his home he hadn't disintegrated, because he wasn't ready to face it. Besides, if he disintegrated the trees, the corruption would simply creep back from the ashes like a cockroach that refused to be squashed.

"What about you?" Gabriel asked, turning to Violet. "Half the clinic is talking about how you can possess the trees."

"I wish that's what I could do," Violet said, shaking her head. "I move branches and roots out of the way—like an override, not a command."

"We're all doing our best." Isaac was not about to watch his friend be criticized when Gabriel couldn't heal anybody, either.

"That's why we're working together, right? To try to find a way to fix it, because our powers aren't enough."

"Right," Violet agreed, nodding. "But why did you want us to meet you *here*?"

"Great question." Gabriel swung his backpack off his shoulder and pulled out a shovel, tossing it onto the ground like a challenge. "The Sullivan archives are right under our feet. We're here to dig for answers."

"Sullivan archives?" Isaac echoed slowly. He'd never heard of such a thing.

"Our family history," Gabriel said. "We kept all of our records in the cellar, in a place Mom and all our uncles called the archive room."

"We have a cellar?"

"They wouldn't have shown you," Gabriel said. "I wasn't even supposed to know about it."

Isaac pushed down a thread of hurt and tried to focus on the positive here. *The Sullivan archives.* The thought was intoxicating. It was possible it held the kind of answers the town archives never had. It was possible they could find a way to face the impossible task that lay before them.

Or maybe he'd destroyed it when he'd torn the house down, just like he'd destroyed everything else.

Isaac pushed the thought away. "Why did you only just remember this now?" he asked Gabriel.

"Honestly? I just didn't think it would be helpful. But May Hawthorne was in the clinic yesterday, talking about how she thinks the corruption isn't new. She thinks it's something old that the original founders had to deal with."

"Where did she get that idea?" Violet asked.

"Probably her mother," Isaac said. Augusta knew more about Four Paths than anyone, but it wasn't information she liked to share. Maybe she'd decided to give some of it to May. "So you think, if the original founders had to deal with it, these archives might have some information on *how*?"

"Exactly." Gabriel gestured at the ruins before them. They were in the rubble where the kitchen had once been, beside the fallen fridge. Bits of metal fixtures gleamed dully in the dirt around them. "We need to proceed carefully—I have no idea what your powers will do to the ground, Isaac—so for now, shovels only."

It took twenty minutes before their shovels hit something metal. The three of them reached down to scrape the remaining dirt away, and there in the middle of the ground, tarnished but still intact, was a trapdoor.

It had been there this entire time, Isaac realized, whenever he skulked to the ruins to stare at them and wish things had gone some other way, whenever he'd asked himself questions about his family that he had no idea how to answer. But that was how it always was in Four Paths. Answers were buried somewhere. You just had to know where to look—and be ready to face the consequences of whatever you found.

Nerves stirred in his stomach. Maybe the cellar had caved in. Or maybe the truths hidden inside it would make Isaac wish he'd crushed it all to rubble. Either way, though, there was no turning back now.

"All right," Gabriel said, reaching down and inspecting the padlock. "Still in pretty good shape. Either of you know how to pick locks?"

Violet shook her head. So did Isaac.

"Figures," Gabriel muttered. His gaze met Isaac's. "Do you think you can disintegrate this?"

Isaac shrugged, swallowing hard. "Only one way to find out. Stand back."

He knelt, spread out his palms and pressed them to the cold, dirty metal of the door. And let go.

In the first few months after his ritual, controlling his power had been harder. Isaac had woken in the middle of the night in a cold sweat, his sheets turned to ash beneath his palms. By now, Isaac had mostly clawed his way to control, but it still wasn't perfect. Handling his power was a war he could not win. He could only hope to lose as few battles as possible.

As his ability roared to life, eating a hole in the center of the door that immediately spread outward, he concentrated on keeping the bubble around his hands as small as possible. The power wanted more, like it always did; it begged to be unleashed on the rubble, on the room below—but he yanked it back.

"All right," he said, breathing heavily as he gazed down at the hole he'd left behind. The daylight illuminated dusty stone steps. "Let's go."

Isaac's first thought as he stepped into the founders' archive room was that he had been here before. Stone walls and high ceilings, an echoing floor, and a series of drawers pushed into the walls reminded him uncomfortably of the mausoleum. He wouldn't have been surprised to find that both places had the same architect. Gabriel handed them flashlights, and Isaac walked slowly through the room, holding his light above his head, eyes peeled for anything more dangerous than a cobweb.

"Isaac," Violet murmured from beside him. "Look at this."

Isaac turned. Her light illuminated a mosaic stretching along the far wall: a tree, of course, laden with green, leafy branches. Violet looked ethereal in the glow of the light bouncing off the artwork, as if the forest itself had birthed her and sent her to Four Paths, instead of a shiny car and a series of family tragedies.

She had shaken all of them up, Isaac realized. Given Harper her memories back, knocked May completely off-kilter, asked Justin to grow into the man he was attempting to be. Isaac was not sure exactly what she had done to him. But just a few months ago, he would never have been able to set boundaries with the Hawthornes. Would never have been able to handle Gabriel without combusting.

Violet's brow furrowed, her gaze turning toward him, and Isaac looked hastily away, eyeing the artwork more intensely than was perhaps necessary. He was immediately drawn to the center of the tree trunk, where a real dagger had been set into the artwork, designed to look as if it were stabbing into the wood.

"This is pretty fancy for a cellar," he said grimly.

Violet nodded, a smile flickering across her face. "I thought the same thing when I found my family's secret attic."

Isaac shook his head. "Why do we even have the town archives if every family decided to hide their good shit away?"

"Because Four Paths has a secrecy problem?"

"A secrecy problem and no other issues at all," Isaac drawled, feeling gratified when Violet laughed.

From across the room, Gabriel beckoned them forward. He stood beneath the drawers themselves. As Isaac came closer, he saw another dagger set into the wall above them.

"Hopefully the contents are still okay," Violet said.

This close, Isaac could see that the drawers were labeled with tiny plaques, starting from *1990–2010* and going all the way back to *1840*. He reached for the oldest drawer and tugged on it, but it wouldn't give. The tiny keyhole beneath the plaque was locked. Isaac sighed in frustration.

Beside him, Violet looked thoughtful. "Do you think you can burn through it?"

"It's worth a shot."

Isaac placed his palm against the stone, but as his power surged through him, concentrated on the door, something stopped him—hitting him like a blow to his sternum. He doubled over, gasping with pain.

"Shit," he wheezed.

"You all right?" Violet asked.

Isaac nodded, wincing. "Just... not doing that again."

"Fair enough," Violet said, starting forward. "I guess we just have to try them all."

The three of them set about tugging on the drawers. Isaac felt more foolish with every handle he pulled, and he was just about to give up when one opened—the drawer labeled *1920–1945*. Inside were a bunch of neatly slotted file folders crammed with books and papers. Not perfect, Isaac knew, but it was a start. They each grabbed a folder and crouched on the floor.

Isaac's was full of photographs. Dozens of them, slotted neatly into an album, scrawled handwriting below telling a story he'd never dreamed of being able to access.

The photos were faded and blurry, sepia-toned and grim, with unsmiling Sullivans facing out of each and every one. Below was a date and a name, and sometimes, a tantalizing bit of information. Several looked like army photos; from their death dates, Isaac ascertained that the draft had reached Four Paths during World War II the same way it had reached everyone else in the USA.

Otto Sullivan, he read, *healer and combat medic, 1910–1944, marked missing during D-Day.*

"Hey, did you know about this?" he said softly, in Gabriel's general direction. "That we had a healer who became a doctor?"

Gabriel nodded without looking at him, buried in his own folder. "That's part of why I wanted to do it, you know? We don't just destroy things. We can make them better."

"*You* can," Isaac corrected him, staring at his own hands.

He could not deny that it had been so much easier to sort through the archives with Violet, looking for the Saunders history, than it was to look for his own. So much simpler when it wasn't pictures of your family, when you weren't the one learning about everything you had destroyed.

In his peripheral vision, he saw Violet stiffen.

"What?" he asked, turning. "Did you find something?"

She stared down at a yellowed letter and shook her head. "No."

Violet was lying. Isaac could see the unease in her stiffened shoulder blades, the same sharp-jawed defenses as Juniper Saunders sliding across her face. But as her gaze flicked between him and Gabriel, he understood. She wasn't lying to *him.*

"All right," he said slowly, returning to the archives. Later, they would talk this out. Later he would figure out what it was, exactly, that Violet did not want his brother to see.

He flipped to a page in the photo album—and frowned.

It began with a black-and-white baby photo. An adorable infant in a frilly outfit, then a solemn toddler, sitting on her mother's lap, a bow in her hair, her thumb shoved in her mouth.

He traced the photos of the same person's life, wondering why there were so many. Every other photo was a group picture or a formal portrait, but this was oddly modern, a clear expense for a family who had lived when cameras were still rare instead of something everyone carried in their pockets at all times.

There was no name beneath the photos of the girl, only captions—*first birthday, grade school graduation*—as she grew into a grinning young teenager with her hair tied back in a kerchief and a jumpsuit with the sleeves rolled up. *First day of work on the war effort,* that one read.

He hit the bottom of the page, and there it was: a formal portrait this time, where the girl stared straight into the camera, her mouth quirked into a small smile.

Sarah Sullivan, it said. *March 2, 1930—March 2, 1944.*

And then beneath it, a single letter in scarlet ink that had been blotched and blotted by the ink: S.

S for *sacrifice.*

Blood roared in Isaac's ears. His hands began to shake as the room around him went out of focus. Suddenly he was struggling and screaming, his wrists chafing against the chains, everything red with panic in the firelight. There was the glint of a dagger and no mercy in Gabriel's eyes, nothing but grim determination. And there was the thought that had echoed in Isaac's mind, clear as a siren:

You're going to die here.

A week and a half after Isaac's ritual, Gabriel left town—the final Sullivan to go, save for one. That night, Isaac snuck out of the guest bedroom window and walked through the woods, retracing the steps he would've known with his eyes closed until he reached his family's home. There were still bandages on his neck from his ritual. The wound throbbed as he walked, pulsing in time with his heartbeat.

He'd walked through the Sullivan mansion room by room—through the kitchen, up the stairs, down the hall, through his old bedroom. Until at last he had stood in the foyer once more, beneath the great stone archway. Gabriel's medallion was tucked into his pocket. He'd come to after his ritual with it lying on the ground beside him, cracked in half. Isaac had ripped it off in the struggle. Now he looped it around his wrist. Because he had passed his ritual. Because he was a true Sullivan now.

Because he needed a reminder of exactly what that meant.

He still remembered how it had felt to press his hand against that great stone archway and call the power within him to life. The wall had quivered beneath him, and Isaac had reached deep inside himself, called on every ounce of pain and heartbreak. The way it had felt to watch his powers spiral out of control. The panic on his brothers' faces, the way his family had turned on one another, his blood, dripping onto the leaves.

The sound the archway made when it tumbled to the ground was the sweetest thing Isaac had ever heard, and as the house fell around him, disintegrating into ash, he wished that he could burn his memories away as easily as he'd destroyed his home.

He wished for that again now, a thousand times over, but the memories would not retreat. Instead they swirled around him, begging for release, and it was all he could do to slam the photo album shut and shove it back in the box. He could not lose it in front of Gabriel and Violet. That would only prove he was just as out of control and irresponsible as he had been the night he destroyed his family.

"Hey," Violet said from beside him, and he realized that his hands were trembling. "Are you all right?"

"Of course." Isaac's voice sounded strange even to him. "I'm fine."

He wasn't, but he forced himself to flip through the rest of the archives, eyes blankly scanning over every page. The world swam around him, blood rushing in his ears. His heartbeat was too fast and his brain was stuffed with cotton, filtering everything around him through a muffled, blurry lens.

He hadn't hurt anyone, and that was what mattered.

You're hurting yourself, said a voice that sounded suspiciously like Violet's. He pushed it aside.

And so Isaac hovered just outside reality for hours, until the ruins were far away and he was back in his own apartment, staring blankly at the ceiling and wondering why he had forgotten how to breathe. Wondering if he would ever remember how to settle back into his own skin.

Catching Augusta Hawthorne at the right moment was no small feat. May spent a full day biding her time. She had a lifetime of experience watching her mother's temper ebb and flow, figuring out exactly when to ask Augusta for permission or forgiveness in order to maximize her reward and minimize her punishment. But the building tensions in Four Paths had made finding that kind of opening exponentially more difficult.

She got her chance on the afternoon of Justin's birthday party. Her mother arrived home from work early that day in a strangely good mood, something May realized could be attributed to Juniper Saunders's new cooperation with their efforts to contain the spread of the corruption. May watched carefully as Augusta poured herself a whiskey on the rocks and situated herself on the front porch, the dogs napping at her feet. She was the most relaxed May had seen her in days.

Part of May felt bad for what she was about to ask her. She knew it would stress her out again. But it was too important to avoid. She needed to know more about her new power if she had any real hope of changing the future to take the corruption away, and Ezra had made it clear that her mother was the only person in town who might actually be able to tell her something helpful. So she walked out onto the porch and gave Augusta her best impression of a carefree smile.

"You've been working late so much these days," she said. "It must be nice to have one normal day."

"I'm not finished," Augusta said, swirling the amber liquid in her glass. "I'll be back at the station tonight. I just wanted to take a few hours' rest."

"Oh." Already, they were off to a less than encouraging start. "Well, I was wondering if there was anything more I could do to be helping with the patrol efforts?"

Augusta set her drink down on the porch railing and fixed her with a deeply annoyed stare. "Do you want to be assigned to more patrols?"

"That's not it," May said hastily. "I mean, um, with my powers. Because you know, if I could look more closely into what's causing the corruption—"

"It's an imprecise art." Augusta waved her hand dismissively. "Just focus on completing your patrols and reporting back to me, all right?"

"But people are still getting sick." Two more cases had been reported that morning, bringing the total number to five. May had assumed this would make her mother furious, but instead she seemed calm about the entire thing. Too calm, maybe.

Augusta looked sharply at her. Brutus, the larger of the mastiffs, raised his head, his black eyes blinking open. "You think I'm not aware of that?"

"I'm just saying," May said, eyeing Brutus nervously. She loved the dogs, but they were unquestionably her mother's. And they might not have been companions like Orpheus, but they knew when their master was upset. "I want to stop it. And I think I could."

"How?" Augusta sounded utterly uninterested. It was worse than if she'd yelled.

"Um." May shifted uncomfortably back and forth. She wasn't usually at a loss for words, but she had no idea how to say this correctly. Most likely her mother would dismiss her outright, and she would prove to Ezra that this had been a useless endeavor. "I guess I was just wondering. There are Hawthornes who have had the power to read the cards for generations. But has there ever been anyone who could alter a reading?"

Augusta's face, apathetic a moment before, changed instantly. Her jaw hardened; her gloves braced themselves on the arms of the chair as she leaned forward.

"Alter a reading?" she repeated. "You mean, change what will come to pass?"

May nodded. "Something like that."

"Then, yes," Augusta said quietly. "There was a Hawthorne who could do that. Our founder."

"Hetty Hawthorne could change the future?"

"Supposedly." Augusta pursed her lips. "May, don't tell me *this* is your grand idea."

"I'm just saying." Hurt welled up in her chest. "It could work."

"Hetty created the cards. No one else has ever been able to wield them the way she could."

"Have they tried?" May asked.

"As a matter of fact, they have." Augusta had a particular way of looking at her daughter that made May feel as if she was being measured for adequacy and had been found wanting. "The Gray swallowed them whole. Do you understand?"

Well, that made it clear. Even if May told her what she'd done, Augusta would never believe her. She could tell Augusta saw her as nothing more than a child full of silly ideas.

"I understand," May whispered.

"Your father was inordinately interested in her," Augusta continued, reaching for the whiskey. The ice cubes clinked together as she took a swig, seemingly unbothered by the chilly October air. "He was *endless* with his questions."

May's heart caught in her throat. *This* she had not been expecting. Augusta never spoke about her father. Perhaps this wasn't her first glass of liquor after all.

"Dad wanted to know . . . about Hetty?" She tried to ask the question as carefully as possible. She did not know if this chance would come again.

"He wanted to know about all of us." Augusta's smile was rueful. "You know, we only got together because of his research on occultism. I should've known then that all he cared about was studying us. Trying to figure out how I *worked* like I was some goddamn machine."

May had never heard this side of things before. "Why was he so curious?"

"I'm not sure." Augusta paused. "I don't know what he was looking for, I just know he never found it. No matter how many interviews he did. But that's all done now, anyway. Can't ask any questions when there's no one willing to answer them."

She looked at May, a little glassy-eyed, and shook her head, as if trying to dislodge something between her ears. "So. Do you still have a plan for how to fix the corruption?"

"No," May lied softly, stepping away from the porch. "Not anymore."

She'd come here for answers. Instead she'd found doubt and more questions. She let the door shut behind her and walked back up to her room, her mind racing.

How could she possibly have the same power as Hetty Hawthorne? And what, exactly, had her father been looking for that had upset Augusta so much?

CHAPTER TWELVE

Violet had come here for Justin Hawthorne's eighteenth birthday party, but so far it felt a lot more like a funeral. She and Harper stood at the edge of a clearing in the woods behind the Hawthorne house, deserted but for the logs set down in front of a tiny, crackling firepit and the birds chirping in the branches. Lanterns were strung through the trees, and staticky pop music blared from a portable speaker.

"Hey," she said, turning to Harper. "I thought you said this thing would be packed."

"It should be." Harper, standing beside her, looked absolutely unnerved. "I don't understand—where *is* everyone?"

"This is everyone." May stepped out from the trees. She was wearing a cropped pink sweatshirt, high-waisted jeans, and shiny platform sneakers the color of cotton candy. The look on her face suggested she would rather be anywhere but here, but then, May always looked like that.

"That's not possible," Harper said flatly. "Did he forget to send out invites or something?"

"The town knows he doesn't have powers." May tapped her phone and the song on the speakers changed, another upbeat tune that belonged at a crowded dance party instead of a nearly empty clearing. "Hence, consequences."

"But they aren't mad at us," Violet protested.

"No, not us," Harper agreed softly. "Just him."

Violet's stomach churned. She'd only agreed to go to this party because she knew Harper wanted to attend, even if she would never admit it. Violet had a lot on her mind lately—the evolving corruption sweeping through the forest, her own changing powers, and now Isaac. Something had been off with him earlier that day during their investigations, but she hadn't wanted to push him, as always. Maybe it was just his brother making him upset.

She didn't know what to make of this new Sullivan. Isaac had told her he was the one responsible for the scar on his neck, and it was clear that he believed it. Yet Gabriel's tattoos and muscles seemed like just as much of a defense mechanism to her as Isaac's high-necked shirts and his insistence on carrying around books like a security blanket. No matter how tough Gabriel looked, he didn't seem capable of attacking his younger brother. But that didn't mean anything either. Four Paths was full of good liars.

She'd found something in the Sullivan archives earlier that day. Part of a letter, ripped down the middle. She'd wanted to talk to Isaac about it, but it hadn't been the right time. The original was sitting on her desk at home right now, but she had a picture of it on her phone. She pulled it out now, frowning down at the screen as she read the words for the tenth time.

we must decline.
secret from the children,
the one they already carry as founders.

a secret that needs to die with us.
it would be the end of us all. If you tell them
there was nothing,
to keep.
another sunrise. But you will make

She'd searched and searched, but the other half of the letter was nowhere to be found. And the fragment she possessed was tantalizingly confusing.

In a place full of secrets, what was so terrible about this one?

Violet shook her thoughts away as Justin appeared at the edge of the clearing, toting a giant cooler with a spigot on the front.

"Hey." Justin's smile was plastered on a shade too tightly. He set the cooler down on a nearby stump and hurried over to them, looking so grateful that it made Violet's heart ache. She'd never expected to *pity* Justin Hawthorne. "So glad you two could make it."

"How could we miss it after such a riveting invitation?" Violet pulled out her phone and read the text aloud. "'Birthday party behind my house this Friday. The theme is "all my friends don't want to murder one another anymore." My mother won't be there, I promise.'"

Justin smiled, and Violet knew he'd seen what she was trying to do: pretend everything was normal and she could still make fun of him. Pretend the town hadn't turned on him even as it turned desperately to the other founders for the heroics he couldn't give them.

"Did you really send her that?" May asked, shaking her head. "You're ridiculous."

Justin shrugged. "I was just telling the truth."

"What's in there?" Harper asked softly, pointing to the cooler.

May's nose wrinkled. "You don't want to know."

"The Justin Shot," Justin said proudly. "My new signature drink."

Violet did not quite succeed in choking down an incredulous laugh. "Oh *no*."

"Oh yes." May shook her head. "He spent an hour raiding Augusta's liquor cabinet while she was at a meeting and put most of it in a cooler. She actually pretended to believe him when he told her it was just punch."

"Wanna try it?" Justin asked, gesturing at the cooler.

Violet looked at Harper. Harper looked at Violet.

"Fine," Violet said, already knowing in her gut that she would regret it.

A moment later, she and Harper were holding matching red Solo cups full of strangely murky liquid. Violet raised hers slowly to her lips, sipped it, and tried not to gag. It tasted like an electric shock.

Beside her, Harper let out an unpleasant cough. "Are you trying to murder us?" she gasped, glaring at Justin. "What the hell is in this?"

"Vodka and an energy drink... and a secret ingredient." Justin grinned at her. "Makes it impossible to get tired."

Violet rolled her eyes. "Is the secret ingredient rat poison?"

"Quite possibly," May said. Violet raised an eyebrow as the girl downed an entire cup, then stuck it under the spigot for a refill.

"Uh... rough day?"

May's smile was completely free of mirth. "You don't know the half of it."

A noise rustled in the underbrush behind the logs, a sharp *bang* and a crash.

"Who's there?" Justin called out, but there was no reply, just another loud cracking of branches. The mood in the clearing changed instantly. Solo cups were hastily set down on logs; Harper unsheathed a giant blade from the scabbard at her waist and brandished it at the woods.

"Show yourself!" she called out.

"You brought a *sword*?" Justin said, staring at her in obvious awe and a tiny bit of fear. Violet was pretty sure Harper liked it that way. She was also pretty sure Justin had consumed a significant amount of the cooler's contents already, considering he clearly hadn't noticed the giant scabbard Harper was wearing. "To my *birthday party*?"

"You're welcome!" Harper snapped.

"Are you seriously surprised?" Violet asked. "I'm pretty sure she sleeps with it. Like a stuffed animal."

Harper glared at both of them. "I'll stop arming myself for our social gatherings when you give me a good reason to believe I won't need a weapon."

"Calm down, everyone," May said tersely, gesturing at the woods. "It's just Isaac."

At the sight of his familiar dark curls emerging from the trees, Violet relaxed. But then the lantern light caught his face, and Violet's stomach sank. His eyes were glazed over, his cheeks slightly flushed. Violet understood why he'd been making so much noise: He was already drunk.

"What?" he asked, staring distantly at all of them. "I'm *here*— Hey, where is everybody?"

Justin flinched, while Harper looked deeply uncomfortable.

"I see you got a head start," May said, stepping forward and steering him into the clearing. "Maybe you should sit down."

"Don't tell me what to do." He shook her off and ambled toward the cooler. His eyes lit on the stumps at the other side of the clearing, nails half hammered in. "Hey—let's play Monster in the Gray."

Violet could feel the tension pulsating through the clearing, all of it centered on Isaac. He was wheeling out of control, a car screaming off the road, and yet she did not know how to stop him. She'd thought the Sullivans were dangerous because they destroyed the world around them. Now she understood the real danger was just how easily they destroyed themselves.

"Fuck it." Justin's voice was low and gravelly. "It's a party, isn't it? May, turn up the music. I'm getting a refill. Let's play."

Harper Carlisle had never really been drunk before. Once or twice, she'd stolen a little of her parents' whiskey just to try it, but that was it. She'd decided the moment Violet shoved a red Solo cup in her hand that she would pour most of it out on the grass and nurse the rest. She was vulnerable enough at Justin Hawthorne's birthday party as it was. Getting sloppy would only make this whole thing even more likely to end in disaster.

Although disaster seemed imminent anyway. It had been bad enough when she and Violet were the only party guests, but Isaac's presence had set her on edge. He was in no condition to play a drinking game. She didn't understand what Justin and Violet were thinking, enabling him like that, and she watched with apprehension as they herded him across the clearing, arguing loudly about the rules.

Harper was about to walk over and give them all a piece of

her mind when she felt May's spindly fingers close around her shoulder.

"Harper." Her voice was not hostile, but it was stern. "We should talk."

Harper turned, a tiny bit sad that she had set her sword down on a nearby log. May's hair shone white-blond in the lantern light, the veins in her neck standing out against her pale skin.

"Well, that's a first," she said shortly.

May clenched her perfectly manicured hand into a fist. "Excuse me?"

"Don't play nice." Harper shook her head. "You ignored me right up until I was a threat to you. All that time when Justin was trying to help Violet, and even Isaac was polite to me—you wouldn't even make eye contact."

May flushed. "I didn't think we could trust you. And I was right. You were working for the Church, which everyone else here seems to have conveniently forgotten."

Two could play at that line of logic. "The same way they've forgotten how you betrayed all of us for your mother?"

"You turned my tree to stone."

"You've allowed your mother to run this town into the ground."

"I didn't have any other choice." May's voice trembled, her hand unclenching, and Harper saw something she'd never expected: tears glimmering in the corners of the other girl's eyes. May tipped her cup to her mouth and took a long, emphatic swallow, then shook her head. Her next words were so soft, Harper could barely hear them. "You think my mother is hard on Justin? Please. Justin gets to misbehave. Justin gets to rebel. And he still gets to come back home, because he's always been her favorite. Some of us don't have the luxury of messing up."

"But you're the one with powers," Harper said.

"Doesn't matter," May said bitterly. "Augusta only pays attention to me now because she needs me. But she watches me in a way she's never watched Justin, and she always finds a way to blame me when something goes wrong."

"Then why listen to her at all, if you're never going to make her happy?"

May's gaze traveled above Harper's head to somewhere far away, and Harper knew she was remembering things she did not want to talk about.

"I don't," she said finally. "Not anymore."

"Oh." Harper paused. "What did you want to talk to me about?"

"The Gray." May's voice was soft, almost breathy. "Is it true the corruption is in there, too?"

Harper nodded. She was tired of telling the story over and over again, but perhaps the Justin Shot had loosened her tongue. "I don't think the Beast is causing it," she said. "It seemed like the corruption was attacking it, too, just as much as it's attacking the town."

May's brow furrowed. "That can't be right."

"I know what I saw," Harper said, tensing. But before either of them could say anything more, Justin's voice broke through the clearing.

"Hey!" Harper turned to see him just a few feet away, looking puzzled. "You two coming or what? We have a game to play."

"Just need to get a refill," May said, shaking her head and

heading toward the cooler. Whatever had just happened between her and Harper had passed, but Harper knew something had shifted between them.

She stared at the stump, at Isaac, who was swaying softly, at Justin's earnest face as he waited for her answer.

Saying yes was a bad idea. She nodded anyway.

The drinking game was called Monster in the Gray. Nails lined the edge of a tree stump in an uneven circle, their tips driven into the wood. The object of the game, Justin explained, was to take a hammer, throw it up in the air, catch it, and drive the nail deeper into the tree. If you didn't touch the nail, you drank.

"Well, that seems like a great way to send your friends to the hospital," Violet said, eyeing the stump with concern.

"I can't believe you made a big deal out of the sword and then wanted us to play *this*," said Harper.

"Isaac," May stage-whispered. "I think they're scared."

Isaac's grin was too wide. "I think they are." He grabbed the hammer, tossed it, caught it, and drove the nearest nail deep into the splintered wood in one quick, fluid motion. May and Justin nodded appreciatively. Even Harper had to admit that she was begrudgingly impressed.

"See?" he said, handing it to Violet. "You're the founders, guarding the town border, and if you drive all the nails in—"

"The Beast doesn't get out, yeah, yeah, I get it." Violet hefted the tool, looking anxious. "I'm not sure how to do this—"

"Here." Isaac reached over and adjusted Violet's fingers, shifting her grip. "So you don't hurt yourself." His hands lingered over hers, and Harper wondered if it was the alcohol or something entirely different that made them both pull away from each other a bit too slowly.

"Thanks," Violet said softly.

Harper glanced around at Justin and May to see that both of them were watching this, too, May still sober enough to look bored by it, Justin too drunk to pretend his focus was anywhere else.

"Okay," Violet said, tossing the hammer up in the air. She caught it, but her swing went wild, completely missing the nail, and her laughter washed the moment away.

The game went on and on. Harper tried it and realized her hand-eye coordination from sword training had made her very good at it, while Violet remained singularly terrible. They passed the hammer around, talking and laughing, until the bonfire was down to the embers and the sky above them was black. Harper stuck to her single cup of liquor. Everyone else had indulged far more, and it showed.

Still, she was having far more fun than she'd anticipated. It was her first party and it wasn't so bad, not when it meant she could forget for ten seconds that her dad had tried to kill her and there was an unstoppable corruption slowly infecting the entire town. Her foreboding from earlier had worn off—even Isaac seemed to be sobering up a little. Maybe this would be all right.

"How does it still taste so terrible?" Violet grumbled from beside her, shaking her cup accusatorially. They were sitting on the logs in front of the remnants of fire to combat the chilly fall air.

"I'm not sure," May said thoughtfully from the log next to her. "I think my taste buds have gone numb."

"Hey!" Isaac called out from the edge of the clearing. "Can somebody tell me which way the house is? I need water."

"Oh my god," May said, shaking her head. "How are you lost? It's literally right there."

"And I am literally wasted, thank you very much."

"All right, all right, I'll help you." She got up, and Violet followed her out of the clearing, saying something to May about finding a bathroom.

Which left Harper and Justin alone, a situation Harper had deliberately been trying to avoid. Harper set her now-empty cup on the ground, her heartbeat accelerating, and when she looked back up again, Justin had gotten up from his seat across the clearing.

"Hey," he said, gesturing at the log beside her. "Can I?"

She nodded. "I'm sorry nobody came to your party."

"That's not true." Justin's voice was quiet and earnest as he sat down. "You came."

Harper snorted. "Out of obligation."

But Justin was already shaking his head. "You never do anything you don't want to do." He set his drink down on the tree stump beside them and leaned forward. Harper had absolutely no idea what to do about the look on his face: solemn and serious, nothing at all like the drunk Justin she'd heard stories about. "Do you remember how we used to talk about this? How it would be after our rituals?"

Harper's throat burned. She could feel the alcohol coursing through her system, the cool autumn air against her face. "You used to promise you'd read my cards."

"And you would tell me that I wasn't allowed to lie to you,"

Justin said hoarsely. "That I had to tell you what was going to happen, even if it was terrible."

"And you'd say…" Harper paused, remembering the rest of it. The ache in her chest was suddenly unbearable, a deep, wordless longing that cut her to the core.

"That it wouldn't matter." Justin's voice trembled. "Because nothing that bad would ever happen to us."

Harper knew it wasn't funny, but the laugh spilled out of her anyway, a little bitter, a little sad. "You had to know even then that it was never going to be like that, Justin."

"I was trying to be optimistic."

"By telling yourself nice lies?"

"I get it, okay? I was naive and wrong and we're all fucked up now." Justin's eyes met hers, and Harper realized she could no longer pretend this was any kind of normal conversation. Not when she had to think through every word before she said it. Not when their knees were brushing and the lanterns in the trees had given everything around them a soft, hazy glow. "Happy fucking birthday, I guess."

She already knew this moment would become a memory that she would call upon more often than she was proud of, replaying each exquisite, agonizing word they had said until she knew them all by heart.

Harper reached her hand upward, cupping it around his cheek. Her fingers curled in the soft blond hair behind his ear as his eyes went wide.

"You could probably turn me to stone, huh?" he whispered. "If you really wanted to?"

"I probably could." Harper swept the curve of her palm down

to his neck. His heartbeat pulsed through her hand, so fast, so fragile. "But I wouldn't."

He leaned toward her, so handsome, so tentative. His eyes looked flat and unnatural in the darkness, and suddenly it all rushed through Harper—the Beast, the Gray, the corruption. She jerked back, nauseous, her hand returning to her lap.

"Sorry," Justin mumbled, looking horrified. "I didn't mean to overstep."

"That's not it." Harper shuddered. "I—I just— You know how I went into the Gray?"

Justin nodded solemnly. "Of course."

"Well, I didn't just see the corruption in there," she said heavily. "I also saw the Beast. And it's been, um . . . It's been haunting me."

Justin stared at her for a long, unbroken moment, the only sound the soft rustle of the leaves in the trees behind them and the crackle of the firelight. "What did it look like?"

It was a child's question—something they had asked each other dozens of times, when they were young and the Gray was a nightmare they could only dream about instead of one they had lived, when the monster inside it felt almost exciting. Because the idea of being necessary, the only people who could protect everyone, was intoxicating. It tugged at her even now, but the question it asked was different than the one she'd asked as a child. *What would we do*, it said, *if there was no monster for us to fight?*

Harper had pictured the monster in the Gray with a thousand eyes, with a spider's wiry legs, with great pointed teeth and slavering jaws. Now she stared at Justin's face and wondered why she'd even entertained the thought that the Beast could look like something else.

"You don't want to know," she whispered.

Justin frowned. "I can handle it."

The words hung in her throat, suspended.

"Well," she said at last. "I guess Violet saw Rosie for a reason. Because it shows you the person who'll hurt you the most."

She saw the moment he figured it out—the pain that cut through the flickering firelight, a raw, deep wound that she had needed no blade to inflict. And Harper understood in that moment that she should never have told him the truth. All it had done was make him look at her like he'd broken her and make her angry that he thought she needed to be fixed.

"Oh," he said quietly. "I see. I—I have to go."

He rose to his feet and stumbled off into the trees. Harper pulled her jacket around her shoulders and huddled closer to the fire, shivering. She'd thought not drinking much would help her handle this, but it wasn't about the alcohol. The problem was her and Justin.

She wanted to run her fingers through his soft blond hair—then close her hand into a fist and push him down to his knees. She wanted her lips on his throat in the same place she would put a blade. She wanted him to look at her the way he had when they had fought at the festival, with awe and fear and *want*, a want that matched hers. Neither of them knew exactly what to do about this wanting—and yet neither could bear to let it fade away.

She hadn't cried since she'd left home, but suddenly it was all too much: her father, the corruption, her siblings. Harper tucked her knees up to her forehead, her residual limb aching, and let the tears come.

CHAPTER THIRTEEN

Isaac could not remember the last time he'd been drunk like this. He'd started after he got home from the archives, with the dusty bottle of whiskey under the sink that he and Justin had paid a college student to buy for them. Just a shot to stop his hands from shaking and dull the knife's edge of his memory. But one shot had turned into three had turned into cradling the bottle like a baby while blaring music from his phone in a pitiful attempt to stop thinking.

The dagger at his throat. Gabriel's ambivalent stare. Blood dripping down his neck as he staggered through the woods, unable to scream for help.

The whiskey turned into a red Solo cup, the apartment turned into the forest, and finally Isaac reached a sort of intoxicated equilibrium. He floated outside his body still, but it was almost peaceful, as if he were watching himself play Monster in the Gray and down far too many Justin Shots from behind a movie screen. He was the eye of a storm of his own making.

He'd come to the Hawthorne house with May and Violet, but he'd lost them somehow on the way back. The clearing was close, he knew it was, if only he could find it. Unfortunately, all the trees looked the same at night and the world around him had started spinning a little while ago, blurring in and out of focus. Isaac knew he couldn't be lost. He'd lived in this shithole his entire life. Even wasted out of his mind, the forest was as familiar to him as his own bedroom.

The smell of charred flesh. Hot, thick panic in his chest. Gabriel's eyes like dark coals burning in the night—

A hand clamped down on his shoulder and Isaac whirled, heat buzzing in his palms.

Justin's blond hair shone ashen in the moonlight. Isaac blinked, trying to focus. Justin was speaking, he realized, but the words were fading in and out, disappearing beneath the shrill, distant sound of screaming.

He knew those noises weren't real. He knew because they were Isaiah's and Caleb's screams from the night they'd died, forever echoing in his memory.

"What?" he croaked.

Justin's grip tightened. "I said, are you all right?"

Isaac's palms fizzled. His Solo cup was half-melted, plastic and alcohol oozing between his fingers. He opened his hand and let it fall into the dead leaves.

"Yeah." The word did not feel like it was coming out of his mouth. "Just drunk."

"I've seen you drunk," Justin said, an urgency in his voice that Isaac had spent so many years latching on to as a form of affection. "This is different."

"Fine," Isaac drawled. "I'm *really* drunk."

"Isaac," Justin said softly. "You're shaking."

Justin's hand burned on Isaac's shoulder. Isaac's stomach twisted painfully. He wanted nothing more than to lean into his grip and tell his friend what was happening to him. It would be so easy to implode and let Justin put him back together. It had been that way ever since the first time Isaac had come to after his ritual, his wrists and ankles still manacled. Justin had been sitting next to him, two fingers pressed to his neck, his eyes wide open with shock.

"What happened?" he'd whispered, and Isaac had closed his eyes and pretended not to hear the question.

After his ritual, Isaac drew attention like a beacon wherever he went. But when Justin was there, the tone of that attention changed. And as the town grew used to seeing them together, Isaac grew used to it, too. Justin was always there when Isaac needed him, and it had all been fine and good until the day Isaac realized that he was completely in love with him.

He'd always known Justin didn't feel the same way about him. *Couldn't* feel the same way about him. So Isaac had done his best to get over his feelings with people who thought he was a bad boy, who wanted to do something thrilling and dangerous so they could whisper to their friends about it the next day.

None of it had worked, because the problem wasn't physical intimacy. It was all those different kinds of *need* twisted together, a dependency that had taken every ounce of Isaac's willpower to walk away from.

Now, drunk and exhausted, he wanted to take it all back. Instead, he forced himself to shrug Justin's grip away.

"I told you that I'm fine," he said brusquely. "So leave me *alone.*"

His hands buzzed with power again, and he felt something loosen in his mind. He'd lost focus. The memories were pressing in on him, his brothers' screams growing louder. The scar on his neck throbbed. He could feel his legs trembling beneath him, his heart thumping, and suddenly he was fourteen again. Lanterns flickered in the trees, his family's solemn faces moving in and out of focus. His bare back chafed against the altar's rough stone, and he could not move, not even when he saw the glint of the dagger in Gabriel's hand and understood it was for him.

S *for* sacrifice.

A surge of panic roared through Isaac, and he stumbled away from Justin, crashing through the underbrush as his power shuddered to life. And just as he had the night of his ritual, he surrendered to its crushing embrace.

It started as it always did, with a rush of pain Isaac could not fight and a rage he had to let free, and it ended as it always did, too. He was lying prone on the ground, coated in soot and ash, surrounded by the evidence of his destruction.

When Isaac had first come into his powers, the meltdowns had been far more frequent. He'd lost control in public a few times, but he had fought tooth and nail to keep his hands from shimmering, to keep the people around him from looking at him as if he were a time bomb instead of a boy trying desperately to keep it together.

Then there had been the Diner, where his reputation had gone from bad to worse.

Now there was this: Another disaster. Another mistake.

Isaac rolled over on his side and groaned. The last he could remember, he'd rushed into the woods—away from Justin.

Justin. *Shit.* There had been people nearby—had he hurt them? He felt for his phone, but it was gone, so he rose into a crouch, squinting into the darkness and hoping his eyes would adjust. Slowly, shapes loomed out of the darkness. Every tree within ten feet of him was dead, burned down to sooty stumps and scattered branches, but there were no bodies. Relief and nausea rushed through him, because he knew what Sullivan powers did to a human. The smell of roasted skin and burned hair, the bits of clothing and bone shards left behind. There was none of that here.

"Fuck," he whispered, guilt rushing through him. He might not have killed anyone, but he'd still charred an entire clearing into oblivion. He'd destroyed part of the forest for no other reason than his inability to keep his memories where they belonged, inside his head.

It was still night, but he wasn't drunk the way he'd been before. Time had passed; hours, maybe. Isaac's stomach twisted. He'd never come out of a meltdown alone before. Justin had always been there, waiting for him.

"Hello?" he called out, rising unsteadily to his feet. "Is anybody there?" His words echoed uselessly through the clearing. Isaac tried to think. Surely he couldn't be that far away from the Hawthorne house. He gazed up at the moon, mentally orienting himself—if he headed west, he'd either hit Justin and May's home or the main road.

He tried to walk, but only managed a single step before a wave of nausea roiled through him, so strong it forced him back to his knees. He was sweating and panting; the world spun, his palms digging into the ash on the ground. Using his powers always drained him, and combined with the alcohol still raging in his system, it was simply too much. Isaac groaned and dry-heaved in the general direction of the forest floor, but he was too dehydrated to even vomit properly.

He was a pathetic excuse for a founder. He deserved to rot here like one of the corrupted trees.

He did not know how long he knelt there, shuddering, before a light broke through the trees. He tipped his head up and realized it was bobbing and weaving, a flashlight beam.

"Hello?" he choked out, then cleared his throat and yelled, "Hey! I need help!"

The trees rustled, and a moment later Violet was standing in front of him. He squinted into the beam of her phone flashlight. As his eyes adjusted, he saw the dirt splotched across her velvet dress. Her tights were ripped; twigs poked out of her crimson hair.

"Isaac." Something happened to her face that he'd only seen once before—that day in her bedroom, when she had told him about Rosie. Like it pained her just to look at him, but she didn't want to stop. "Are you hurt?"

"Not more than I deserve."

"Good." She knelt down beside him, carelessly smearing dirt on her tights, and tipped her head up so that her eyes locked on his. Something stirred in his throat, in the core of his stomach, a different kind of heat, a different kind of fear. Then she held out a water bottle. "Here. Drink this."

He'd never tasted anything sweeter. When he looked up, the bottle drained, she was holding her phone up to her ear.

"Yeah," she said, sounding exhausted. "He's fine. You can go home—I'll handle this."

"Justin?" Isaac croaked.

Violet nodded. "He's had a bad night."

"Shit. Sorry."

"You think that's all you need to say sorry for?" Violet said, her tone leaving minimal room for interpretation.

Isaac felt something new—anger. Justin never would've talked to him like this. "I get it. You're pissed at me, I ruined everything, I've heard it all before."

"Is that the story you always tell yourself?" Violet asked him softly. "That you're just going to fuck everything up?"

"It's not a story," Isaac said. "It's the truth."

"You're more than this." Violet's jaw tightened. "Self-pity doesn't suit you."

"You don't know me well enough to say something like that."

The words hit Violet harder than Isaac had intended. She jerked backward, hurt spreading across her face.

"It took me two hours to find you, asshole," she said. "And I didn't know if you'd be *alive* when I did. Maybe I don't know everything about you, but I know how it feels to have powers that seem like they're taking you over, and, Isaac, I'm scared for you."

The last few words were said in a rushed, embarrassed whisper, and Violet dropped eye contact, sighing.

Two hours. Two hours of Violet walking through the forest that had taunted her for months, that had ripped her up and spat her out. Just for *him*. The thought made Isaac almost as nauseous as the alcohol. He didn't deserve that kind of loyalty.

"I'm sorry. I'm scared for me, too." It was the most honest thing Isaac had said since his confession to Justin, and the truth of it scorched his throat. "I just . . . My brother, my family . . . it's all too much. And what I said, about you not knowing me . . . the only reason you don't know is because I haven't told you. But you deserve the truth. You've deserved the truth for months."

He knew exactly how long he'd wanted to tell her. It had

started that night in Violet's bedroom, on the equinox, when he'd watched her rush into trouble to save Harper in the exact way he would have done for Justin. But Isaac had known even then that the truth would change things. What Justin had seen the night of Isaac's ritual had changed their relationship forever.

Isaac wanted her to know what had happened to him without it becoming a burden on them both. She deserved better than that. He had no idea how to do that, but he could not fathom keeping it a secret from her any longer, either.

And so there in the burned-out crater of destruction he had created, in the witching hour, Isaac Sullivan told Violet Saunders the truth about his ritual.

"The thing about the Sullivans," he began slowly, "is that we are taught, from when we are very young, that either our destiny will be to cause pain, or to stop it. And I never wanted to cause it."

"Who would?"

Isaac smiled grimly. "You'd be surprised. It's useful when you want people to take you seriously. And we did."

In elementary school, there had been a group of bullies, a few years older than him, who'd made a game out of stealing the book he'd always carried and forcing him to chase them around the playground.

"They thought it was funny," he explained, "because I was a Sullivan, and we were known for getting into fights, but I never did." Instead, he'd been the baby brother—scrawny and quiet, barely participating in class, always reading, always listening. "Anyway, when they stole the book, they'd always rough me up before they gave it back. Eventually, Isaiah figured out what was going on. Gabriel is five years older than me—Isaiah was seven years older, so he'd done his ritual, and he was *pissed*. He asked me to point out the bullies, and one day, after school, he pinned down their ringleader and threatened him. He made me watch."

Isaac paused, remembering the fear on the boy's face as Isaiah pinned him to the ground, his knee in the boy's back, and placed his hand on the nape of his neck. He'd never seen such raw, powerless terror before, and it made him sick inside to think of it even now.

"He didn't hurt him," he said. "But he terrified him, until he, um . . . he pissed himself. I begged Isaiah to stop—but he didn't listen."

And later, when they'd been home, Isaiah had gripped him by the shoulders and stared at him with wide, wild eyes. "He said, 'Pain is power,'" Isaac went on. "'You have to show the world that you can hurt it more than it can hurt you. That's the only way we survive.'"

"That's a terrible philosophy," said Violet.

"Yeah," said Isaac softly. "But it's kind of tough to unpack that when you're eight and your family is your whole world."

"Fair," said Violet. "So what happened next?"

Isaac didn't want to look at her for this part. He stared hopelessly at the destruction he'd wrought instead, dimly lit by Violet's phone flashlight. Charred stumps and piles of ash; the smell of burning, the smell of destruction. "I grew up. And every-thing changed."

Isaac hadn't known much about his family's ritual. They kept that a secret for as long as they could. But he had seen the scars: The lines that rose above his mother's shirts and lanced across her shoulders. The cuts across Gabriel's arms that he had taken great pains to tattoo over. They snaked down calves and across collarbones, in a slightly different place on all his aunts and uncles, but still scars, still there.

"We all give the Beast part of ourselves when we do our rituals," he continued. "You do it with your mind. The Hawthornes and the Carlisles have their conduits—the lake, the tree. But us Sullivans, we give it our blood."

Violet shuddered.

"I know," said Isaac. "Anyway...I knew my ritual would hurt. But I thought it would be worth it. I wanted to heal people like Gabriel did—he'd go on patrols and come back with all these grand stories about how he saved people who came out of the Gray. I realize now, of course, that they were bullshit. People don't come out of the Gray alive."

On his fourteenth birthday, the day of his ritual, Isaac had woken up early. Eaten his favorite breakfast, although he'd only picked at it, too excited, too nervous, to do much more than that. Found it only a little odd the way his family treated him, with far more affection than usual.

"I realize now," he continued, "that my mother tried to stop them. We went on a drive a few weeks before it happened—and we got off at this rest stop, right, and then my uncles were there, and we all acted like it was fine, oh, what a coincidence, but no. They knew she would try to run with me. And they were ready for it. So on my birthday, my mom was shut up in her room. They were guarding her."

"What about your dad?" asked Violet.

Isaac shrugged. "Never knew him. None of us did. Lots of single parents in the Sullivan family—we're sort of all raised together. I realize now that having an outsider parent involved makes it a whole lot harder when ritual day comes around. Anyway, dinner tasted a little funny that night. It wasn't until I was moments away from passing out that I realized I'd been drugged."

He had come to later in the night, chained to the altar in the woods behind the Sullivan house. His family gagged him. They chanted. There was a dagger, and Gabriel's face, and his neck hurt more than he had ever thought possible.

That was how it was supposed to go: the other Sullivans' rituals were mere precursors. They gave their blood to the earth, to the Beast. But to renew it, they needed to give it one of their own.

A sacrifice.

Isaac did not know why they had decided he would be the person from his generation to die. In the ensuing years, he had tormented himself trying to figure it out. Perhaps they had thought he was weak. Perhaps they had thought, out of all of them, he would simply be the easiest to kill.

They'd been wrong.

After they slit his throat, his mind slid into the Gray, and he heard the Beast's voice all around him, urging him to find the thing inside him that snarled and clawed and chafed against his rib cage.

And he had unleashed it.

His power had roared to life, wild and free, sparking its way through the woods around him. His family had panicked, because he was *not* dead—and then something else happened. Something that sent everything utterly off the rails. His mother and Caleb, rushing into the clearing to save him.

His family turned on one another after that. When they were done, Isaiah and Caleb were dead, his mother was unconscious, and everyone else had fled. Everyone but Gabriel, who had chased him deep into the woods until Isaac collapsed from sheer exhaustion, certain he would never wake up again. Until Justin Hawthorne found him, and one nightmare ended and another one began.

He finished talking—the sun peeking through the trees now, his heart heavy in his throat.

When he looked at Violet again, there were tears in her eyes.

"Thank you for telling me," she said hoarsely, and he didn't know which of them started it, but a moment later his arm was wrapped around her back and he was shuddering, dry sobs wracking his body to its very core.

"I'm sorry," he whispered into her velvet sleeve. "I hope this is okay—"

"It's okay," she said, her hand making small circles between his shoulder blades, and there was something in her voice that he hadn't heard from another person in a long time—tenderness without a single strand of pity. "Do you remember what you told me? How what happened to my aunt Daria wasn't my fault?"

Isaac pressed his forehead against her shoulder. "I remember."

"Well, this isn't your fault, either. I promise."

And so they stayed like that for a long time, holding each other. Something solid, something real, in the midst of everything he had destroyed, until Isaac was finally ready to stand.

It happened at dawn again. May thought at first that it was the alcohol tugging her from her bed, disrupting her sleep. But it wasn't. It was the hawthorn tree calling her, a cry of pain. A cry for help. A voice that twisted and screamed in the back of her head.

May didn't remember sliding on a sweater and her platform sneakers, but she must have, because it was only moments later that she was outside.

Frozen stone branches reached up, as if pushing the rising sun into the sky. They tugged at her chest and pulled her forward, the same physical sensation she'd felt the night Harper had turned the tree to stone. A tear slid down her cheek. She lifted her hand to her face; it came away scarlet.

"Harper promised," she whispered, rushing up to the tree and placing her palm against the stone that had once been bark. "Just hang on a little longer."

The voice in her mind stirred again, stronger this time, hissing panic at the edges of her thoughts. A deep *crack* rang through the dawn, and May saw it then, rippling out from the place where her outstretched hand had touched it: The stone was splintering. A deep, nauseating dread rolled through her as a familiar stench washed out from the tree: decay.

Something terrible is coming, she thought, but she knew that wasn't right. Because something terrible was already here, and it was just now getting ready to show itself.

The cracks in the tree snaked upward, stone flaking away like peeling skin. The patches they left behind were gray and oily, glimmering with a sickly glow that pulsated slowly in the night air. Iridescent liquid shot upward, oozing through the cracks and winding around the back of the tree like silver veins.

"No," May gasped as the branches creaked to life, buds lowering like extending hands. "*No.*"

She braced her other hand against the trunk, as if she could put the tree back together with the sheer power of her will, and grasped for the roots in her mind, for the future.

This won't happen. It won't.

She screwed her eyes shut, gasping, and when she opened them, Four Paths was gone.

Fog floated around her, misting in her hair and condensing on her eyelashes. Her hands were still outstretched, but the hawthorn had disappeared. Instead, she was standing on top of the founders' seal in the Gray.

The fog began to dissipate, revealing a canopy of intricately woven trees above her head. Something wrapped around her leg, and May realized that roots were spiraling below her feet, crawling over the seal and twining through her ankles. A voice echoed in her mind, tinny and hollow.

May knew she should have been terrified, and yet all around her was a powerful sense of calm, of familiarity. Roots wound across her wrists as if she was part of the forest itself, and when she opened her hands, her palms were bleeding, cut along her lifelines, the blood mixing with oily iridescence.

As soon as she saw the blood, the voice in her mind changed. It was a deep, clear sound that reverberated through the roots and branches embracing her.

Welcome home, Seven of Branches, it said, and then everything went black.

PART THREE
THE CRUSADER

CHAPTER FOURTEEN

Since she'd arrived in Four Paths, Violet had felt as if she had been slowly trusting people to hold parts of her. Harper had seen her long-buried grief for her father; Justin had seen her loneliness; Juniper had seen her grief for Rosie.

But Isaac had seen all three of them, and now at last she knew why he had understood it all so well. Violet had no illusions about the tragedy that had lurked around the edges of her life like some specter she could not name, even before she had come to Four Paths and realized it was a real monster, not just a run of bad luck—she knew it was not normal to have so little family left at seventeen. But Isaac's loss was something else entirely. It was frighteningly large; grief not just for those who had died that night, but for everything he'd believed, everything he'd been.

They were in a place beyond blame now, a place beyond words. So she had held him and waited until he was ready to leave the woods. They did not let go of each other the whole walk home, but their clasped hands didn't feel like a promise. They felt like a necessity, like the forest would swallow them whole if either of them let go.

The sun had risen by the time they reached the front door of his apartment in the town hall. Violet knew her mother would be furious that she hadn't come home. She turned to go face her wrath, but Isaac made a soft, scared noise in the back of his throat and whispered, "Stay?"

So she did.

Isaac's bedroom was cramped and cluttered. Books were strewn across the night table and the floor, mixed with clothes that spilled out of the small closet tucked into the corner. Isaac curled up on the twin mattress, eyes staring blankly across the room. Unsure of what else to do, Violet perched on the edge of his crumpled blue bedspread.

She sat on something strange and shifted to the side, frowning as she pulled out a copy of *The Hobbit* from beneath her. "How can you sleep with these in your bed?"

Isaac pulled his pillow aside, revealing a small library of paperbacks shoved beneath them. "I used to hide them here as a kid so I could read after lights-out. Now it's just a habit, I guess. Like how you carry around your binder full of sheet music."

Violet gaped at him. "You noticed that?"

"You spent the first few weeks of school staring at it instead of taking notes. There are, like, fifty people in our grade—it was tough not to notice."

Violet snorted. They fell silent for a moment, and she glanced around the rest of the room, trying to match up the pieces of Isaac that were here with the ones she'd already gathered. A few raggedy posters had been haphazardly tacked up on the walls, for the kind of indie bands Rosie had cheerfully called "sad-boy music," and beside them was a blown-up cover of *The Great Gatsby,* the famous blue one with a face in the center, with the eyes crossed out and JUSTICE FOR ZELDA written at the bottom.

Getting to know someone was something she was still adjusting to. Rosie had always been there—knowing her had been like breathing. But choosing to let someone into your life, letting them see the places where you were weak and the ones where you were strong—it was complicated. And exhausting. And rewarding, too. Because she and Rosie had never really had a choice. But here people did, and they had chosen her.

Violet's eyes fell on the photos taped just above the bed, next to the small nightstand lamp that was definitely a fire hazard. They looked like a photo-booth spread—Isaac was shoved between May's feathery blond hair and Justin's wide grin, looking progressively less miserable in every picture.

The photo at the very end captured most of Violet's attention, and made something drop in her stomach. Isaac was looking at Justin while Justin stared at the camera. The longing on Isaac's face was so transparent, so raw, that Violet turned her gaze away.

"Ugh," Isaac said quietly. "I should take those down."

Violet turned back toward him. She knew Isaac had fought with Justin. She also knew that Isaac was extremely into him. She had found out from the Four Paths rumor mill that Isaac had come out as bi in homeroom last spring, very casually, with a confidence Violet wished she could convey when discussing her own sexuality.

"We've already talked about enough tonight," she said. "We don't have to talk about you and Justin."

Isaac snorted. "There's nothing to talk about, anyway. I'm just a big bisexual disaster."

"Oh, same," Violet said, before she could think it all the way through.

Isaac's eyes widened, and Violet realized that she could walk this back or see it through. She thought about the conversation they had just had, about how good it had felt to tell Juniper the truth, and decided to commit. It was an exhausting feeling, to realize that she would have to come out to everyone in her life like this. She understood more now why Isaac had done it so publicly.

"Yeah, I'm bi, too," she said. "And I've totally had crushes on straight girls before. It sucks, liking someone who can't like you back."

"It really does," Isaac said. "But . . . hey. Thank you for telling me. I hope you know I would never out you or anything."

"I know," Violet said. "Especially since you did just unload a lot of stuff on me. I've got dirt on you, Sullivan."

"My life's a nightmare, I know."

"All of our lives are."

Isaac's laugh sounded like a cough. "Justin always said it was dangerous to try to play 'who's more messed up' with the founder kids. Everyone always loses."

"Is that game at least a little less dangerous than that drinking game we all played?"

"Monster in the Gray isn't dangerous," Isaac said, grinning a little. "Sure, you have to handle a hammer—"

"While chugging death juice!"

"It's a game of great skill, okay?" He paused. "You're distracting me, aren't you? That's what this is?"

"Depends," Violet said. "Is it working?"

"Maybe a little bit." Isaac was curled up on his side, his hair flopping across his forehead. The shaved part of the back of his head was growing back in, a messy, endearing thatch of dark brown hair. He looked vulnerable like this, younger, not like a boy who could disintegrate half the forest if he wanted to.

"I think the part I hate the most about the Justin thing," he said finally, "is that Justin understood when I told him. It hurt him, but like—he's not a homophobic jackass. He respected the boundary I set. He's listening to me."

Violet raised an eyebrow. "You're mad the guy you have a crush on treated you with respect?"

"*Had* a crush on," he said.

Her eyes met his, and she said, too carefully, "Had? As in past tense?"

"I mean, I'll always care about him," Isaac said. "But . . . it feels different now that I've taken a step back. I can see things I couldn't before. He found me right after everything happened, and I felt for so long like I was always trying to catch up to that moment. Like if I saved him enough times, we'd be even."

"I'm not exactly a relationship expert," said Violet, "but I don't think that's how it works. It doesn't have to be life and death all the time. And it doesn't have to be about keeping score."

"You're right," Isaac said. "Shit, Violet, I don't want you to feel like I'm putting too much on you. I feel like I've already asked you for too much."

"We're friends." Violet remembered in a rush just how recently Harper had said those same words to her. "Friends ask each other for help. Don't apologize for that."

His mouth quirked up at the corners. "Fine."

She could feel a tether stretching between the two of them. Not like the one that connected her to the Beast—something different. Something far more complex. A friendship was its own type of ritual, she realized, one where people bound themselves to one another not with blood but with words. And it had a power all its own, that *belonging*, that incalculable internal chemistry of choosing to let someone in.

So she stayed with him until his eyes fluttered shut and sleep claimed him, until she could tiptoe out the doorway and make her way home.

When May came to, she was faced with a corrupted hawthorn tree, a killer hangover, and an irate mother.

"You felt it, too," Augusta said. Not a question. May nodded, exhausted.

"Did you pass out?" she asked.

Augusta shook her head, curiosity lighting her eyes. "It affected you very . . . severely. I wonder why."

May thought about mentioning the fog, the voice, the blood seeping from her lifelines. But her mother had made it very clear that she did not care to think about the possibility that May might be stronger than her, so she kept her mouth shut.

Augusta coped with the damaged hawthorn tree by increasing patrols and spending even longer hours at the station. May coped by scheduling another meeting with her father as soon as possible. She wanted to talk through what she'd seen and ask about what Harper had told her—that she didn't think the corruption was the Beast's fault. That the Gray had seemed infected, too. May found Harper's theory almost impossible to believe. Whenever something went wrong in Four Paths, it could be traced back to the Beast.

Ezra was back in Syracuse again, trawling through the university's special collections library in person for more information that might help. But he'd traveled back at May's request. He wanted to see the tree in person, which proved difficult, but after a few days May found a morning when Justin was at a cross-country meet and her mother was tied up at the station.

The late-October air was harsh and blustery when May met Ezra outside the Hawthorne house. She stuffed her hands into her coat pockets as she led him around the side of the house, wishing she'd brought gloves. Ezra looked unbothered by the weather, professorial and unruffled in a tweed jacket and a plaid scarf. He adjusted his glasses and peered at the hawthorn tree from the edge of the woods, as close as May could justify bringing him to the site of the corruption. She didn't want him to get sick.

"The pictures you sent didn't do it justice," he said quietly. "The hawthorn is changing."

Her palms itched as she stared miserably at the silver veins snaking along the back of the tree, cutting sharply into its broad trunk. "It's not changing, it's dying. I watched it happen and I still couldn't stop it."

"You mentioned seeing something odd as the tree fell, some type of vision," Ezra said, the curiosity in his voice evident. "Tell me more about that."

May launched into what she could remember of the voice in her head, the fog, her bleeding palms. Since the initial outbreak, the veins had settled somewhat, the same buds she'd seen on the trees at the Sullivan ritual site, unopened but also refusing to go away.

"Interesting," Ezra said. "Do you think it's a vision brought on by your connection to the Deck of Omens?"

May hesitated. "I guess I didn't think about it like that."

"Perhaps you should. You're strong, May—your ritual has

allowed you a level of connection beyond that of the other founders."

"Yeah, about that." May had been thinking a lot about the conversation she'd had with Augusta right before the party. "I talked to my mom about my powers, like you asked me to. And she said nobody's been able to change the future since Hetty Hawthorne."

Ezra's eyes lit up with interest. "So that truly *is* a power that only the original Hawthorne ever possessed—until you."

"I'm not sure I do have that power, though," May said doubtfully. "I don't know. Maybe I imagined things when I changed the cards."

"No, you didn't. Don't sell yourself short." Ezra looked as if he could barely contain himself. "When I bound you to the Beast, I had hopes that it would re-create the process of the original founders' bindings. I was unsure what the effects of it would be, but if what your mother said is true about your ability, then it gave you the original founders' *powers*. Which means that perhaps you can succeed where the other founders have failed to make a difference in this fight."

A shock wave coursed through May as this sank in. The thought that she could be as powerful as the woman who had locked away the Beast itself was almost unfathomable. "Does that mean I might actually be able to change the future in a way that ensures we defeat the corruption?"

"Potentially." Ezra sighed thoughtfully. "It's risky. What you've described seeing when the hawthorn was corrupted distresses me. It means that, bound as you are, you could be killed if your efforts backfired. We can't mindlessly risk your life— we must find a way to proceed safely. I'll need to return to the university library, see if there's anything more there I can use to help you."

"They don't have a digital archive you can check?" May didn't like the idea of him leaving her again, alone with all of this worry to sort through.

"I'm afraid not," Ezra said. "But I *will* be back, May, I promise. In the meantime, I urge you not to do anything rash."

"All right," May said, although she itched to do *something*, anything. She hadn't known how to bring it up on the phone, but now that she was face-to-face with her father, there was something else she wanted to talk about. "Um. I also wanted to mention that when I talked to Mom . . . she said some things. About you."

"Ah." Ezra adjusted his glasses. "Allow me to guess—they were less than kind."

"You could say that."

"Well, I suppose I should have expected it." Ezra rapped his knuckles absently against the nearest tree trunk, as if contemplating what to say next. "Your mother is . . . quite set in her opinions of what happened between us."

"She said you studied us. Is that true?"

"Certainly." His lips pursed. "It's an old argument of ours. She felt that my interest in the founder mythology and customs was prying. I merely wished to find ways to help my family. It took me longer than I'm proud of to realize that her resistance came from the worry I would uncover the truth about her abilities."

May's stomach churned. "You mean about how she takes the town's memories?"

"Yes. I did not approve, and I made my concerns known. Which meant she no longer approved of *me*."

"Is that why you left?"

"That's part of it. But those are dark times, May, ones I don't particularly wish to relive."

"I understand." May paused. "I'm surprised she never tried to take your memories away."

"As am I. I suppose there are some lines she's still unwilling to cross."

"I just don't understand," May said quietly. "She seemed completely unwilling to even accept that I might be able to help her."

"That's because she's threatened by you." Ezra gestured at the back of the house, the gabled roofs, the hawthorn's dying branches. "She claims to want strong founders, but what she really wants is no one strong enough to challenge her. And because you can invert her powers, because you are capable of things she's only dreamed of, she has tried to stifle you instead of allowing you to grow."

"Just like what she did to Harper and Violet."

"Exactly." Ezra placed a gentle hand on her shoulder. "I don't think we need to look at this anymore. I'll be back in town soon. Meanwhile, you keep an eye on the corruption, all right?"

"Thanks," May said, exhausted. They parted ways, and she passed her dying tree, looking toward the home that did not feel like a home at all.

Usually, people met beneath the bleachers behind Four Paths High School to hook up or smoke up. Harper had something very different in mind. She cleared out the space in seconds, couples scattering and kids hastily putting out their joints before they realized that she was not in fact a teacher.

"You don't have to frighten them," Justin said from beside her, watching with concern as a group of freshmen scrambled back like startled mice. "They're just trying to enjoy their lunch period."

"Would you rather do this in front of half the school?" Harper asked dryly.

Justin's mouth twisted. "No."

"I figured." To be fair, this wasn't exactly Harper's first choice either, but the band practice rooms were taken. Slatted sunlight illuminated the graffiti scrawled beneath the bleachers, hearts and other body parts that Harper felt were an optimistic interpretation of reality. It smelled like gym socks and mold, but it was the only place they'd get a modicum of privacy during the school day to discuss what the hell was going on with the hawthorn tree. The meeting had been Justin's idea—he'd wanted to talk through the damage with her—but Harper wondered if he'd regretted asking her to do it as soon as possible as he gazed around at their classmates, his brow furrowed with dismay.

"Hey!" Harper said, frowning at the few brazen stragglers who remained. "Everybody out. We need this space for founder business."

"Dude," murmured some sophomore Harper knew hung around with her brother. "We should listen to her. You know what she did to that tree."

His friends nodded, their eyes wide as they crept out.

"Enjoying your newfound power, I see," Justin said once they had finally been left alone. Harper was sure *somebody* was still eavesdropping, so she kept her voice down, glancing around for nosy classmates and their phones. Harper could hear a twinge of jealousy in his voice, and she didn't blame him. A few months ago, he'd been the one who could empty a room just by clearing his throat.

"They don't know I can't control it," she said quietly.

"No, they don't," Justin said. "I'm sure they would have moved a lot more quickly if they did."

He paused for a moment, and an uncomfortable silence crept between them. Harper knew that it was more important for them to focus on the corruption than what had happened—or rather what *hadn't* happened—between them at his birthday party. But it had been a few days, and it still wouldn't leave her mind. How close he'd been, how sad he'd looked. How much the truth about what she'd seen in the Gray had hurt them both.

"So," she said at last. "The hawthorn. Has the corruption totally overtaken what I did to it?"

He nodded, looking relieved to have something to talk about. "The idea was floated that you could potentially try to turn it to stone again, to stop the spread of the damage."

"After weeks of you asking me to reverse it." Harper shook her head. The irony of how quickly things had been flipped around was not lost on her. "My power isn't reliable enough for that."

"That's what I said." Justin sighed. "You, Violet, and Isaac are strong, but even combined, it isn't enough to push back the corruption."

"So you brought me here to tell me I'm not good enough?"

"No." Justin reached into his backpack and pulled out a cheap pair of training swords. Harper recognized them immediately; the chipped paint on old wood. They were the same swords kids had used at the Founders' Day festival, the day she and Justin had squared off and she'd disarmed him. "I wanted to try something new to unlock your powers."

He held out a sword, and she took it automatically. It comforted her, as it always did—but for the first time, she wondered *why*. The power inside her was so much more dangerous than anything this blade could hold.

"Try something new?" she echoed hesitantly.

"I thought... maybe channeling your anger would help." Justin hesitated, the words emerging slowly and carefully. Harper could see how much he'd thought about this. "You saw the Beast as me. You've tried discipline, you've tried training. But when you were upset with us, you turned that tree to stone. Your anger makes you strong—so go ahead. Be angry with me. Let's fight the way you want to."

Harper stared at him, her mouth dry.

For years she'd dreamed of such a moment, where they could square off as equals and she could show him what she was capable of once and for all. But he *knew* what she was capable of, and the world had already punished Justin Hawthorne far more effectively than she ever could. He was lonely and frightened, stripped bare of all the things that had made her so furious with him. Harper could not hate the boy who was left behind. She wasn't sure what the answer to her power problems was, but she knew it wasn't *this*.

"I don't want to fight you," she said softly, letting the sword fall into the dirt. "Not anymore."

For better or for worse, Justin wasn't the only founder who had fixated on Harper's training. She got home from school that day to find Juniper waiting for her and Violet, whereupon Juniper led them up the stairs and through the trapdoor into the spire at the top of the Saunders manor. Harper's spine tingled as she took in the white circle on the floor, the heavy curtains on the windows. The shelf full of dusty old books.

"So that's where your family does their rituals," she said, turning to Juniper Saunders. The older woman stood beside the velvet curtain, staring out at the woods, the crow's-feet at the edges of her eyes crinkling with focus. She looked uneasy in here, which Harper supposed made sense. It had to be full of strange memories for her.

"It's supposed to be a secret," Juniper said. "But in light of the last few days, it feels like one you need to know." Harper didn't mention the fact that, though she'd never been up here before, Violet had already told her about it.

"Welcome!" Violet spread her arms wide. Orpheus's head peered up from the trapdoor, all ears and giant yellow eyes, before the gray tabby loped cautiously into the room, following Violet as she gestured emphatically. "Here you'll see the place where my entire family willingly traumatized ourselves for a hundred and fifty years. Please note the lovely aura of despair, as well as the circle that may or may not fling you into the Gray."

"You're being very flippant, Violet," Juniper said, a slight note of disapproval in her voice. "Harper is the first non-Saunders ever to set foot here—this is a big deal."

"You never took Augusta?" Violet drawled.

Juniper glared at her. "Absolutely not."

Harper cleared her throat. "Then why me?"

The two Saunderses paused, turning to look at her. Harper was struck for the thousandth time by how alike their movements were, even though neither of them seemed to see it.

"Because," Violet said finally, "I told Mom we could use your help."

"And I agreed with her." Juniper walked over to the bookshelf and pulled out a dusty wooden tube. "Your training has hit a bit of a wall, Harper. I'm sure you've noticed that."

Harper nodded. *Noticed* was an understatement. Training sessions with both Augusta and Juniper had shown her that turning things to stone was not the problem. The problem was *stopping*, or reversing the damage, and she had yet to come close to figuring out either.

"It's very clear that this block isn't about ability," Juniper continued. "It's mental. For some reason, you aren't ready to wield your powers. So today, I'll be giving you both a little bit of a history lesson that might help you understand the stakes we're dealing with here."

Juniper pulled a large sheet of rolled-up paper out of the tube and spread it out on the floor, piling books on the edges to keep it flat. Then she sat beside it and gestured for the girls to join her. Harper understood immediately what she was looking at: a map of Four Paths, almost identical to the one the Hawthornes possessed.

It was illustrated beautifully, green-and-brown etchings of trees interrupted by tiny drawings of town landmarks. But there was a key difference between this map and the one the Hawthornes had.

Drawn over it, in sharp black lines, was the founders' symbol: a circle with four lines cutting through it, not quite meeting at the center. The founders' symbol sliced perfectly through the four landmarks Augusta Hawthorne had talked about: Harper's family's lake, to the east. The Saunders manor to the north. The hawthorn tree to the south. And the Sullivan manor in the west.

"You should update the map," Violet said from beside her, tapping on the manor. "It's just ruins now."

"Not *just* ruins," Juniper said, looking up at them. "It's corrupted. Just like the hawthorn tree."

Harper shuddered, remembering the corrupted lake she'd seen in the Gray. She'd never seen anything so grotesque, so *wrong.*

"Something is off about all of this," Juniper continued. "I grew up in Four Paths. When the Beast acted on its own, its attacks were always random. But it's clear by now that there is nothing random about the way the corruption is spreading."

She tapped the map again, more meaningfully this time, and Harper understood.

"It's targeting the founders." It wasn't a question. "The hawthorn. The Sullivan ruins. The sheriff told me those are important places for us."

Juniper nodded. "That's why we brought you to the spire," she said solemnly.

"Because you think it's next?"

"Because I know it is. Our spire, your family's lake, and ..."

She pointed at the center of the map: the place where the four lines did not quite meet. Harper's heartbeat sped up. She knew exactly what was there, at the center of everything.

"The founders' seal," she said slowly. "Where the founders performed the ritual to trap the Beast in Four Paths."

"Exactly," Juniper said. "Augusta and I have a theory. You see, as of now, the corruption has not been able to spread outside the town borders. But we believe that if each of our ritual sites were to fall, it would destabilize those boundaries entirely. The Gray would collapse, and the corruption would spread beyond Four Paths. Which means we need to protect them at all costs. The sheriff and I have instituted a special patrol schedule for the rest of the founders that's related to proximity. The three of us will be responsible for the spire at all times. Mitzi and Seth Carlisle will guard the lake, while the Hawthornes and Isaac will watch the town seal. We need to be proactive about this."

"I understand." Harper gazed around the room. It looked very far removed from the forest. Now it was her responsibility to keep it that way.

"If we truly want to be proactive, we can't just patrol," Violet said. "These attacks are targeted at specific locations, which means there has to be a purpose behind them. Someone or something wants our ritual sites to fall."

"I agree." Juniper's brow furrowed. "It's possible someone is communicating with the Beast."

"I don't think the corruption is the Beast's doing." Harper hated the way they were both looking at her—with obvious disbelief. "I was in the Gray. I *know* what I saw—the corruption was hurting it, too."

Juniper's tone was not dismissive, exactly, but it was skeptical. "What else would target the places most important to our families?"

"I have an idea, actually," Violet said. "The Church of the Four Deities wanted to help the Beast before. They communicated with it more closely than anyone else I can think of. Maybe the corruption is tied to them, too, somehow."

Harper froze. Her mouth was dry, and she wanted a blade, a weapon, something to protect herself from what she could feel was coming next. "My dad doesn't remember," she said hoarsely. "None of them do. Even if they know what happened, they wouldn't be able to tell us."

"Unless someone gave them their memories back."

Violet's eyes locked on Harper's, and Harper understood in that moment what they were both thinking: *May Hawthorne.*

"She could do it," Harper said. "Do you think she *would* do it?"

"I don't know," Violet said. "And I'm not even sure that, if your dad *does* know something, he would tell us."

"He would tell me." He'd told Harper the truth about the Beast once before, after all, even though it had meant admitting to betraying her.

"Are you sure you could handle it?" Violet asked. "After everything..."

It would mean forcing herself to return to the home she'd been avoiding because of a mere hunch. It could all lead to nothing. But it could also stop the rest of their ritual sites from falling to the corruption. The thought of it made her residual limb ache, caused a swell of phantom pain. But just because she was frightened didn't mean it wasn't the right thing to do.

Harper met Violet's eyes. "I can handle it."

"You two have a plan," Juniper said from beside them, crossing her arms.

Violet nodded.

"Is it dangerous?"

"No comment."

"Could it help us?"

"Yes."

"Hmm." Juniper faced them both down, and Harper wondered if this was what it was like to have a parent who focused on you instead of asking you to either be a weapon or a babysitter. "You're both smart. You're both capable. But you're also seventeen. I know that I can't just keep you away from what's going on here—Four Paths has already demanded so much from you. But I want to make sure you're as safe as possible."

"None of us are safe," Violet said. "And none of us will be safe until this is over. The town's in danger—you have to trust us."

Juniper did the last thing Harper was expecting then: She smiled.

"Many years ago, I let this town defeat me. Perhaps it's high time we became the ones who do the defeating, instead. So tell me about this plan of yours."

CHAPTER FIFTEEN

Isaac had stood on the front porch of the Hawthorne house a thousand times, waiting impatiently for Justin to pull open the front door. But today, for the first time, he could not bring himself to ring the bell.

The more he thought about how he'd behaved at Justin's birthday party, the more ashamed he felt. He'd spent the past few days letting his humiliation eat away at him before his guilt finally drove him to his friend's front door.

A text or a call didn't feel right. He had to apologize in person. But when he finally got up the courage to ring the bell and Justin actually answered the door, Isaac realized he had no idea what to say.

"Hey," he muttered, addressing Justin's socks. "Can I come in?"

Justin's pause felt like it lasted a lifetime, but finally he nodded. "Yeah."

They wound up in his bedroom. It didn't smell great—Justin was a fan of Axe, which Isaac figured could double as a pesticide—but there was still something comforting about the line of wrecked running shoes along the wall, the faded posters tacked up above his unmade bed. A tower of unopened textbooks were stacked sloppily on the desk beside a laptop with a FOUR PATHS HIGH SCHOOL sticker in the middle.

Isaac stared glumly at the sticker, where a tree twined through the words. It was their mascot, the Mighty Oak, because how dare one thing in this town not be a reminder of the forest.

Trees don't run, he'd complained to Justin years ago. *It's a ridiculous symbol for any athletic team.*

What do you care? Justin had fired back. *You'd rather poke out your own eyes than join an organized sport.*

It had been so *easy* back then. Talking to Justin had felt effortless. But now there was so much more between them, and it was all Isaac's fault. He'd confessed his feelings; he'd lost it at Justin's birthday party. It was hard for him not to think about how he'd messed up a good thing—except it had never been good for him. Not really. It was just that Isaac hadn't brought up the problems, and now neither of them could pretend they didn't exist anymore.

"I'm sorry," he began, sitting in the desk chair after Justin plopped down on the bed. "For ruining your party. For losing control."

"Don't flatter yourself. You're not the only reason the party was ruined," Justin said wryly. "That thing was dead in the water the moment the entire town ghosted me."

"Right. About that. Are you okay?"

It was a ridiculous question. Justin didn't bother answering it.

"Are *you*?" he asked instead. "In the forest, Isaac ... you looked rough. Violet said you destroyed an entire clearing."

"It wasn't my finest moment." Isaac ran a hand along the side of the desk, trying not to think about the way those trees had crumbled beneath his palm. "But I'm not here to talk about me. I'm trying to apologize to you."

"I don't want an apology," Justin said. "I *hate* this. You're being so formal, showing up at my door, looking at me like you don't even know who I am anymore—"

"Of course I know who you are," Isaac snapped. "I just don't know how I'm supposed to talk to you."

"You open your mouth and the words come out, it's not that difficult—"

"It is when it's you." Isaac sighed. "Look, when I told you how I felt . . . I don't know if I weirded you out or made you angry, I don't even know why you invited me to your *party*—"

"Because you're still my best friend, you asshole."

The words hit Isaac like a sledgehammer. His chest burned from the weight of the pain in Justin's voice.

"Oh, fuck you," he whispered. "You know you're still my best friend, too."

Justin's voice shook. "Then why aren't we okay?"

Isaac hesitated. There were too many answers. Because they cared so much and they still couldn't get this right. Because there was so *much* they'd done wrong, and how did you make a friendship feel equal when it had started with one of them saving the other one?

Maybe the only way was to find a new foundation. To build it again. But he had no idea how to do that.

"Because it can't be the way it was before, Justin," he said at last. "Because I have to know that it's going to be different."

Justin's voice was suspiciously raspy. "It isn't *going* to be different. It already is, because you already are."

"What do you mean?"

"You don't need me anymore," Justin said softly. "Gabriel's back in town, and you never even asked us for help. You and Violet are always hanging out. Hell, you helped Harper of all people open the Gray and you didn't even *invite* me."

Justin was right, Isaac realized. He'd skulked behind the Hawthornes for years, a shadow, a protector, trying to pay them back for taking him in after he'd destroyed his home and his family. But all that dependency had meant that he'd always felt he had nowhere else to go. And it had left him afraid to fall—afraid deep down that if no one caught him, he'd crumble into ash just as easily as the trees. But Isaac was finally ready to look head-on at the thing he was most afraid of. Not Justin, not his mother, not his brother, not his powers. *Himself.*

"I don't know if I'm actually different," he said to Justin. "But I'm trying to be."

"So am I," Justin said. It struck Isaac how absolutely exhausted he looked. Dark circles, greasy blond hair, a cluster of zits budding on his nose. Justin had gone from Four Paths' de facto choice for future prom king to a total pariah because of a secret he had chosen to tell the whole town. And yet he still hadn't reached out to Isaac for help, or to whine. He'd respected his boundaries. He had only tried to come back into Isaac's life when he'd seen him falling apart.

Maybe the people they were turning into could be friends. Maybe the only way to find out was to give it a chance. But Isaac didn't know how to say any of that, so he settled for something easier.

"I know why you actually want to be friends again," he said aloud. "You just want me to do your homework."

Justin shot him a tired smile. "You got me."

"Unfortunately for you, I'm not doing *my* homework anymore either."

"Perfect," Justin said. "We can fail senior year together. Get held back."

Isaac snorted. "We can't graduate with May. She'll never let us live it down."

"You're right," Justin said, swinging down from the bed and sidling over to the dresser. He picked up their history textbook and swung it open, the spine cracking in a way that suggested he had never actually done so before. "Guess we'd better get started."

Isaac didn't leave the Hawthorne house for another two hours, and although the textbook was open between them that entire time, they didn't read a single word.

Harper had not been home in a long time. She'd known that this would hurt, but seeing the Carlisle cottage come into view for the first time in weeks was still unbearably painful. The sloping red-brown walls had once held her entire life inside them. Now they held far too many memories for comfort. Her eyes moved to the workshop behind the house, where her father's hands had closed around her throat, and she froze. Again, she felt that swell of phantom pain from her residual limb.

Maybe she wasn't ready for this. Maybe she would never be.

"Steady," Violet murmured gently from beside her. "You've got this."

It was enough to keep Harper walking. She forced her legs back into action, and together, they rounded the edge of the lake. Corruption laced through the trees around it, but it had yet to sink into the water the way it had in the Gray, and there were no buds on the trees like the ones extending from the hawthorn or hanging in the Sullivan ruins. Harper was grateful for that small mercy as they approached the statue garden in front of the house.

"Those are terrifying." May gestured at the watchful eyes of dozens of half-crumbled stone animals. She looked extraordinarily out of place in her fuzzy pink jacket and her shiny platform sneakers, like a flamingo that had wandered into a herd of geese.

"They're heirlooms," Harper said. True Carlisles were supposed to be able to control those animals, but Harper couldn't control *anything*. Maybe nobody would ever make them move again. She sighed and led the way up the front steps, her hand skimming the splintered wooden railing. A few of Nora's and Brett's toys were scattered across the porch.

The moment she knocked, she heard the familiar thump of running feet, and she knew who would be waiting for her when she pulled the door open. Not the father she had fled, but the siblings she had left behind.

"Harper!" Nora didn't wait for a hello before she rushed at her, wrapping her spindly arms around Harper's knees. Harper knelt in the front hallway and hugged Nora back, fighting down a sob. Her sister was so achingly familiar—the way she smelled like Play-Doh and soap, her wispy red pigtails, the freckles etched across her nose.

"Hey, kid," she said softly. "I missed you."

"Mom said you were sick," Brett piped up from beside her. It was her turn to hug him then. Harper was pretty sure he'd grown taller in the last few weeks. "Are you better now?"

"Mostly," Harper said. "I'm . . . working on it."

"Can you come home?" Nora asked hopefully. "Mitzi doesn't know how to make oatmeal the way I *like* it. And Seth taught me some new words that Mom says I'm not allowed to say—"

"Mom is probably right." Now that Harper was here, the thought of leaving again felt as if it would split her in two. It was why she'd stayed away in the first place. "I'll come home soon, okay? I promise."

It was a promise she had no idea if she could keep or not, but it seemed to make Brett and Nora happy. They were both clamoring for her to play with them when she saw a familiar pair of work boots appear in the far corner.

Harper rose to her feet as if in a dream. Her body stiffened on instinct; the man in front of her might not remember what he had done to her, but *she* did. His hands around her neck. The bruises on her throat. The pure, unrestrained violence in his eyes.

"I'm glad you're here," Maurice Carlisle said, his words ringing across a hallway that had suddenly gone silent. "We have a lot to talk about."

The Carlisle kitchen usually had at least five or six people in it at a time, but with the four of them it suddenly felt too small. Harper sat anxiously between Violet and May as her father pulled out the chair directly across from her.

"We understand that coming into your powers so late has been a shock to your system, Harper," he said. "We've given you time to come to terms with that. But it's been long enough, don't you think?"

Again, Harper was frozen. He was acting so *normal*. He didn't know the terrible things he'd done in the name of the Beast. He didn't know why she'd left. It hurt her more than she could articulate that her family believed her to be selfish and undisciplined, that they blamed her uncontrolled powers for her abandonment of them all.

She'd left for her own safety, but as she sat in her kitchen, Harper realized how messed up it was that she had been driven away from her own home by someone else's mistakes. She was not the one who deserved to be punished.

"I'm not here to talk about coming home," Harper choked out. "Can you please respect that?"

"All right." Maurice's brow furrowed. "Just know that we love you, Harper. No matter what."

Harper shuddered. Beside her, May and Violet looked deeply uncomfortable. She couldn't believe she had to do this in front of other people. In front of a *Hawthorne*.

"Uh, Mr. Carlisle." Violet's voice was the most formal Harper had ever heard it. "If we could switch the focus of this meeting to the matter at hand."

"Right, right." Harper's father knitted his hands together atop the table. "You said there was something you needed to discuss with me, about the corruption?"

"Yes." May reached into her quilted cream purse and pulled out a familiar wooden box with an all-seeing eye etched into the front. "We believe you may be able to help us provide clarity on a potential solution. Would it be all right if we did a reading with you?"

"I don't see why not," Maurice said hesitantly. "You really think this old man could help you?"

"Oh, I really do." May pulled out the Deck of Omens. Instantly, she looked much more relaxed. Harper envied the peace on her face as she clutched the cards. Her powers were part of her. She understood them, she *loved* them, while Harper could only think about the stone spreading from her fingers with a latent feeling of dread.

She began to shuffle them, the cards disappearing one by one. Maurice hesitated. "Aren't you supposed to ask them a question?"

"I have," May lied smoothly.

The cards disappeared until only a few were left, and then May held out her hands for Maurice's. "Go on."

He grasped them across the table, and Harper watched, her stomach twisting, as May shut her eyes and screwed up her face in concentration.

She saw the exact moment her father remembered. His jaw tightened, the veins in his neck sticking out, and then his eyes flew open, wide with horror as they locked on hers.

"No," he gasped, trying to pull away from May's grasp. "That can't be true."

"It's true." May didn't release her grip. "It's all real."

He stopped struggling then. His head drooped in defeat until May pulled her hands away. She was panting softly, sweat beading across her forehead.

"I've never done that before," she murmured.

"What do you mean?" Violet asked. "You've given me my memories back."

"You wanted them back." May jerked her head at Maurice. "He didn't."

Guilt and dread welled up in Harper's stomach, a deadly cocktail of emotion that threatened to overwhelm her. But she did not run from this. She'd done enough running already. Instead she watched her father as he tipped his head up and met her eyes.

"You remember?" she asked.

"I remember," he said. "Harper, I'm so—"

"Don't apologize." Harper barely recognized her voice. "You know that's not enough."

He nodded slowly. The horror on his face was bone-deep. "You left because of me."

"Yes," Harper said. "It wasn't safe."

"I see." There was so much packed into those words. They threatened to shatter Harper right there at the table, to take the tears she'd shoved down and force them to the surface. But she could not break, not yet. Right now she, May, and Violet had a job to do. And her father's distress and guilt was something they could use.

"We didn't give you back your memories for this." Harper kept her voice as even as she could. "We gave them back because we have some questions about the Church of the Four Deities. Are you willing to cooperate with us?"

"Yes, of course."

"Good." Harper cleared her throat. "The Church communicated with the Beast quite a bit, yes?"

"We did." Maurice looked at them all, shamefaced. "We used our ritual to contact it, to allow it deeper access into our heads. It was a bastardization of the Saunders ritual that Stephen taught us."

"And when you talked to the Beast, did it ever mention anything about this corruption?"

"I believe so, yes."

"Yes?" Violet leaned forward, and Harper gave her a look. This was *her* interrogation to direct.

"It talked about . . . a threat." Maurice hesitated. "Something that the Gray kept out. Something that would hurt everyone."

"So the Beast didn't create the corruption," Harper said, unable to stop the smugness that rose in her.

"No, I don't believe it did. It is older than any of us—its fear went back to the very beginning of Four Paths."

"So, then, why *now*?" Harper asked. "Why would this corruption be breaking through all of a sudden?"

"I'm afraid I don't know," Maurice said. Harper scowled and sat back in her chair, discouraged.

"Great," mumbled May. "This has been *super* helpful."

"I may not know," Maurice continued, "but the Church did have our own paperwork. There was a great deal of information in there. Some of it didn't make any sense to us, but perhaps you could make use of it now."

"My mother confiscated those papers," May said. "They didn't contain anything valuable."

"She didn't confiscate all of them." Maurice gestured to the kitchen door. "Our most important documents were hidden in my bedroom. I can show them to you."

Harper's heartbeat sped up. This might actually help them.

For so long, she had been scared to go home because it was the place where so much had been taken from her. But now she understood that it was also the place where, against all odds, she'd *survived*.

She was Harper Carlisle, betrayed and betrayer. She had endured the Gray, first by accident, then on purpose. She had won over the Hawthornes. She had made friends who would stand by her when she could not stand on her own.

Now, staring at her father, she finally understood why she was so frightened of the power she had fought so hard to gain. She'd looked up to Maurice Carlisle her entire life, and he had used his power to intimidate, to lie, to hurt others and threaten the safety of the town. Her attack on the hawthorn tree had done exactly that.

But that was one mistake. It did not define her or limit her unless she allowed it to. It was nothing like the guilt her father would carry for the rest of his life, the lengths he'd been pushed to by his own foolishness and greed.

She would never be like him. Not now, not ever. Which meant there was no longer anything in this house for her to be afraid of.

Harper pushed back her chair and rose to her feet.

"All right," she said. "Let's do this."

CHAPTER SIXTEEN

The archives Maurice Carlisle was talking about were a collection of notebooks and ancient accordion folders hidden beneath a false bottom in his bedframe. Violet carted them back to the Saunders manor, where she and May set to work spreading them out on the dining room table. Harper joined them at first, but Violet could tell the last few hours had shaken her up.

"I'm going to my room," she said finally. "I need a break from founder stuff for a little while. Tell me if you find anything good, okay?"

"We will," Violet said. "Get some rest."

Harper nodded gratefully. Her footsteps were slow and labored as she climbed the stairs. Violet had no idea how her friend had managed to deal with her father like that. After what he'd tried to do to her, it had taken all of Violet's willpower not to curse him out on Harper's behalf. But Harper had told Violet beforehand that she would handle it, and somehow she had.

"All right," she said, turning back to May. "I guess we should divide and conquer. It's not really that much stuff."

"I hope it's actually helpful." May looked doubtfully at the pile of papers in front of them. "This is the first day in ages I haven't had a patrol. I don't want to spend it wasting my time."

"Hey, you agreed to help us with Harper's dad." Violet turned to the first file and tugged out a sheet of paper. It was a blueprint of the library. "You could have said no."

"You know very well I couldn't have." May sighed and flipped open a yellowed newspaper clipping. "I consented to my mother taking the Church's memories away because it seemed easier. But I knew deep down that it was wrong. I know I can't fix everything she's messed up, but I'd be the frosty bitch you all think I am if I didn't try."

May said it very flippantly. Violet knew that meant she felt just the opposite.

"I don't think that," Violet said, and she meant it. May was deeply private in a way even Isaac wasn't. Maybe at first Violet had mistaken that for disinterest and even disdain. But she knew by now that it was a defense mechanism against a world that she did not trust.

"Sure you don't." May cast her a glance. "I've heard the shit people say about my mother when they think I'm not listening. They say it about me, too."

"They might. I don't." Violet looked away from the blueprints. "I know we've rarely been on the same side here. But I promise, we both want the same thing: for this town to be safe."

"I know," May said. "But I'm not so sure my family has *ever* kept it safe."

Violet had never heard May say something like that before. She certainly had her own doubts about the Hawthornes, about all the founders, but it was different to hear it from someone who was always so tightly wound. Her actions indicated that she didn't approve of her mother's conduct, but she was still helping Augusta. Or at least, Violet had thought she was.

"What do you mean?" She tried to keep her voice gentle.

"It's complicated." May's glossy lips were parted slightly, her eyes a little unfocused, like she was watching something that only she could see. "Being Augusta Hawthorne's daughter, I felt like I had something to prove—to show I was worthy of her consideration. Justin made our family look good, and she kept all our secrets hidden. I never really understood what she wanted from me, but I knew that if I wanted her to care about me I'd have to be an asset, too."

"But you read the cards. Doesn't that make you a major asset?"

"You'd think so." May frowned. "She still defended Justin, though. She still lied for him. Because he knows how to make people care about him, and I . . . I don't."

Violet remembered, in a rush, a part of Rosie that she did not like to think about. The girl who'd easily made friends while Violet ate lunch alone. The girl who let Violet tag along, sometimes out of pity. Rosie had been her best friend, her *only* friend, but Rosie had made a much bigger world for herself that Violet had never belonged in.

Violet still missed her sister terribly. But she knew what it was like to feel adjacent to the spotlight.

"Yeah, about that," Violet said. "Justin's my friend, but I have *never* understood Four Paths' infatuation with him."

May snorted. "Honestly, me neither. He can't even make toast without setting something on fire, he won't stop using Axe, and his room smells like something *died* in it."

"Forget the corruption. This is the real mystery in town."

May giggled, then paused, pain rushing over her face.

"Mystery solved, though," she said. "They don't like Justin anymore. And I don't know how to be confident like him or powerful like Augusta. I can't fill the holes they've left with their mistakes, but I keep trying anyway."

"So don't try to be them," Violet said. "Be *you*. Whoever you are, whatever strengths you have."

"You sound like a birthday card," May said, rolling her eyes, but Violet could tell from her tone and the slight smile on her face that her words had landed.

They fell into a silence that was a lot more comfortable than the one before as they went back to riffling through the archives. Violet knew that Harper and Justin thought this kind of thing was boring, but for her it was a welcome break from seemingly endless patrolling. Now that her powers had an offensive use, she'd spent a lot of time in the woods, charting the spread of the corruption. It was grueling and demoralizing work that left her physically exhausted, so exhausting her brain was a nice change.

"Huh," May murmured beside her. Violet turned and saw that she was examining a fragment of something—a piece of paper ripped down the center. It was ancient and yellowed, so fragile it looked as if it could crumble in her hands if not for the plastic sleeve someone had thought to store it in. "Where's the rest of it?"

Violet's entire body froze.

"Hey," she said, trying to stay calm. "Can I see that for a second?"

"Sure." May placed it carefully on the table. "It's a shame it's so torn up. Look…" She tapped the name and date in the corner. "They must have saved it because it's from Belinda Carlisle. She was one of Thomas Carlisle's kids—Harper's great-great-grandmother, I think. Although I guess it's a letter she never sent."

Violet stared at the scrawled script, the date. *October 24, 1910.*

It was unmistakable. The handwriting was exactly the same as the fragment she'd found in the Sullivan archives.

Her mind whirled. May Hawthorne was on her side for now, yes, but could she trust her with whatever this could be? Just a few weeks ago, the girl had been threatening to storm her house in order to yank Harper to the tree. Trust was a precious and fleeting thing in Four Paths.

But May had also given Violet her memories back. And she was starting to open up to her—their conversation was clear evidence of that. Violet didn't want the families to be divided the way they'd been for so many years, and that wouldn't change if she continued to keep her cards close to her chest.

"I have the rest of the letter," she said.

May's head shot up, her eyes wide. "What? How?"

"It's a long story."

Violet transported her half of the letter from her bedroom to the dining room as carefully as she could. The edges did not fit together perfectly, but it was close enough that Violet could clearly see that they were in fact two halves of the same letter. Pieces were missing from the middle, destroying the occasional word or phrase, but not so much that she couldn't decipher the general meaning.

Silas, my dear—

I regret to inform you that Millie, Clark, and I have discussed your proposal, and we must decline.

"Silas?" Violet turned to May.

"A Sullivan, I think." May frowned. "Millie is definitely Millie Hawthorne, and we know this is from a Carlisle—"

"So Clark probably has a creepy taxidermy dedicated to him somewhere."

"Probably, yeah."

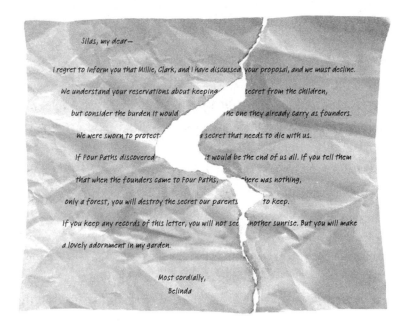

Silas, my dear—

I regret to inform you that Millie, Clark, and I have discussed your proposal, and we must decline.

We understand your reservations about keeping   secret from the children,

but consider the burden it would   the one they already carry as founders.

We were sworn to protect   a secret that needs to die with us.

If Four Paths discovered   it would be the end of us all. If you tell them

that when the founders came to Four Paths,   here was nothing,

only a forest, you will destroy the secret our parents   to keep.

If you keep any records of this letter, you will not see   nother sunrise. But you will make

a lovely adornment in my garden.

Most cordially,
Belinda

"What they're saying..." Violet stared at the note. "About the Beast. About the founders—"

"No," May whispered. "No, that can't be true."

"Can't it?" Violet asked. Behind them, the forest beckoned, trees that were slowly becoming tipped with silver. A world the founders had supposedly bound themselves to in order to protect it. But Violet thought suddenly of a phrase the Beast had taunted her with. It had stayed with her for weeks now—*Do you really think I was bound here out of altruism?*

"We draw our powers from the Beast. Our families trapped it. They use it. Why does it seem so impossible that they made it?"

May barely remembered going home. She was normally a cautious driver, but today she was careless with the silver family pickup, heedless of the fact that she'd only gotten her license a few months ago. She turned the radio up the highest it would go, pop music blaring through the speakers as she careened down the bumpy roads.

She didn't want to think about the letter she and Violet had found or the picture she'd taken of it, now stored in the phone stuffed in the cupholder. But the loud thumping of the music and her tires screeching on the road weren't enough to drown out the worries swimming in her mind.

If the Beast had been the founders' creation, then everything May knew about her family's purpose was a complete lie. They weren't heroes protecting their town—they were handling a mess they'd made, a mess that had cost countless people their lives.

She parked haphazardly in the driveway and rushed up the front steps, her only goal to make it to her bedroom without incident. It was a goal that was immediately thwarted by Justin emerging from the kitchen as soon as she slammed the front door.

"What happened?" he asked, his eyes widening. "Did the corruption get worse?"

May shook her head. The Hawthorne photographs on the walls of their front hallway glared at her, harsh and uncompromising. When she was a kid, she'd thought they all looked strong. Now she just thought they all looked miserable. Like they'd passed that down along with the ritual and the powers.

She was so tired of trying to handle this on her own.

"I have to show you something," she whispered, pulling her phone out of her pocket. "Something *bad*."

She explained what she, Violet, and Harper had dug up at

the Carlisle house. Justin peered at the letter on her phone, his face paling as he took it all in.

"Do you think it's true?" he asked her.

"I don't know. Violet seemed pretty convinced, but it's just one letter."

"If this *is* true, then we're frauds."

"I know."

"And our whole lives were for nothing."

"I know."

"Fuck!" The defeat in Justin's eyes was like nothing May had ever seen before. "We're not even *good* liars. We can't even solve a problem our ancestors might have created."

"That's not true."

Justin looked at her skeptically. "What?"

May hesitated. Her founder blood might just be blood on her hands. Her mother wouldn't listen to her. And it was true that her father had told her not to do anything rash, but she could not shake what Violet had said, either.

She knew who she was. She knew what she could do. And she needed to prove that she had been given those powers for a reason; that this disease infecting the town would *not* be her undoing.

"Justin," she said softly. "What if I told you there was something we could do about the corruption?"

The hawthorn tree was dying.

Silver-gray veins spread from the place where the stone bark had cracked, winding around the back of the trunk and up toward the branches. The stone was mostly crumbled away, and the bark beneath it was melting and morphing, gray and pulsating, with iridescent veins sinking deep beneath the surface of the tree and winding toward its heart. Buds hung from the trees, still closed, the smallest of mercies. The stench was overwhelming.

May could barely stand to look at it. This was so much worse than what Harper Carlisle had done. It was something far more insidious and dangerous, something that would swallow her whole world if she let it.

"You're sure we have to do this here?"

May turned. She knew her brother's expression, that tone of voice. Justin was *afraid*. Something stirred in her chest—a distant memory, clouded and foggy, of her brother standing in front of her, his face bearing that same expression. Behind them, drifting through the door, were the sounds of screams.

Don't go downstairs, May, he'd said. *Don't.*

"May?" Justin said softly, and she was back in the present, blinking. "Are you going to be okay?"

"Of course." May lowered herself into the last clear patch of grass she could find. "Let's hurry up, though. I don't know how much time we have."

She flipped open the wooden box and drew out the Deck of Omens. It was the only thing that felt right out here, a small tether to the world she wanted instead of the one she was living in.

"I need you to ask a question," she said to Justin. "About what you want me to change. Do you think you can do that?"

"Sure." Justin sat hesitantly beside her. "How can we fix this?"

The weight of the question surged through May's soul. A pathway opened, as it always did—but it was different from any pathway she'd ever felt before. These roots were not the normal ones she encountered in a reading, the ones that twined around Four Paths. They felt deeper—a kind of familiarity that made May wonder if they were her own, even though that wasn't possible. She couldn't do a reading for herself.

The Deck of Omens grew warm in her hands immediately, and May sensed something at the other end of the tether, something like fear. And when the roots began to vanish, one by one, it felt like they were running away instead of choosing which ones would show the correct path forward.

She focused her mind the same way she had before, beneath the stone tree. She thought of the corruption, tangling its way around the town. She thought of her fear, of her parents, of the world she thought she'd understood transforming into something utterly unknowable. And she felt it again—easier this time. One path spiraling more brightly than the others. A future that was *different*.

She grabbed it. She *pulled*. And as she pulled, an image swirled around her: endless fog just like what she'd seen when she touched the tree. But this time, something was different. A person was lying on the ground beside her, screaming and clawing at their bloated body. Roots rippled beneath their skin, wriggling up their arms and past their neck as a cloudy whiteness spread across the pupils, bleaching all the life out of them. Their spine gave a jerk, and then their body let out a horrible, sickening *crack*, the torso and legs winding in opposite directions, as if a hand had lifted them up and twisted them in two.

May gasped for breath and found herself beneath the tree again, shuddering. It was just a vision. It wasn't real, it *wasn't*.

"What happened?" Justin was kneeling beside her, looking concerned.

May shook him off. "Nothing."

There were bloody tears on her cheeks and three cards left in her hands. May found she had to work harder than usual to hold on to them. Stubbornly, she laid them on the ground, then stretched her hands out toward Justin's.

"Okay," she said slowly. "Let's see what happens."

His hands shook in hers, clammy and anxious. May pulled them away, dread coursing through her.

She flipped the first card over. It was blank.

"What?" The word bubbled out of her throat before she could think to hold it back. To pretend this was supposed to happen.

"What does that mean?" Justin asked from beside her.

May's stomach churned. "I don't know."

Never in her life had she heard of the Deck of Omens showing its chosen wielder *nothing*.

She flipped over the second card, then the third, but they were blank too.

"I don't understand," she whispered as blood dripped onto her collar. "What are you trying to tell me? What do you *want*?"

And then, above her, she heard it. The branches of the hawthorn tree groaned and creaked in a sudden gust of wind, and May raised her head, gasping.

The buds above her had opened all at once, dozens of hands unfurling. Fog poured from them, faster than she could comprehend, darkening the sky around them.

The corruption had gone airborne.

She met Justin's eyes and breathed, "Run."

CHAPTER SEVENTEEN

Isaac found his brother at the Pathways Inn, a cheap old house that had been partitioned off into motel rooms at some point and stayed open for business mostly out of sheer will.

Lia Raynes, whose family owned the place, was sitting behind the counter when Isaac walked in, texting and looking incredibly bored. She nearly dropped her phone in her lap when he approached the front desk.

"Don't know why you look so surprised," Isaac said tiredly. "You know who's staying here."

Lia gulped. "Yeah. I know. Did he come back to help with the corruption? Is the rest of your family coming back, too?"

Everybody always knew his business. It was one of his least favorite side effects of being a founder.

"Which room is he staying in?" Isaac asked, ignoring the question.

"Doesn't matter," said Lia, looking disappointed that he hadn't offered up more information. "He's out back. He likes to read on the porch."

"A man of culture, I see."

Lia's thumbs flew furiously across her phone screen as Isaac pushed open the back door and ascended onto the porch. In thirty seconds, the entirety of Four Paths High School would know all about the meeting between the Sullivan brothers. But Isaac didn't have it in him to care.

Facing things head-on didn't just mean apologizing to Justin. It meant confronting Gabriel about the role he'd played in Isaac's ritual and seeing what he had to say for himself.

As Isaac approached, his brother looked up from the rocking chair on the porch and flipped his tattered paperback shut, sliding it into the backpack he'd propped up against the railing. It was chilly, but he hadn't bothered with a jacket. His T-shirt showed off the tops of his tattoo sleeves—the trees that wound across his biceps, roots twisting around his arms that looked eerily like the one that had tried to burrow beneath his skin.

"Isaac." He scratched the back of his neck. "Is there another emergency you want my help with or something?"

"No." Isaac crossed the porch in two long strides. "I want the truth, Gabriel."

"Dramatic." Gabriel's mouth twisted. "You know the truth. I'm here about Mom."

"I'm not talking about that," Isaac said softly. "I'm talking about my ritual."

Gabriel paused, and for a long moment all Isaac could hear was the gentle rustling of the breeze in the forest behind them, the slight creaking of the porch's floorboards beneath his feet. Then, at last, he spoke.

"Took you long enough," he said. "Good thing I brought reinforcements."

He grabbed the backpack and raised it in the air, patting the side. Isaac recognized the sound of bottles clinking together.

"I don't need to drink," he said, his stomach churning at the memory of his meltdown.

"Oh, they're not for you." There was something dangerous in Gabriel's voice. "They're for me."

Isaac heard a noise and turned to see Lia's face peering through the upper window, her eyes wide with curiosity. At the sight of him, she hastily drew the curtains shut.

"I don't want the whole town to hear this," he said.

"Then let's go somewhere even they won't follow."

Gabriel drove them to the edge of the ruins. Neither had mentioned it as a destination, but Isaac had known exactly where they were going from the moment his brother started the car. It was late afternoon as they settled on a fallen tree behind the backyard. The autumn wind whipped at the edges of Isaac's jacket. Gabriel shrugged on a flannel and pulled two beers out of his backpack.

"You sure you don't want one?" he asked. "This stuff's basically water, anyway. Or at least that's how people treated it at Potsdam. College is wild."

Isaac inspected the red-and-white label. In another world, Gabriel would've bought him this beer for a party instead of trying to hand him one in front of the ashes of their family home.

"I'm sure," he said firmly. It was easy to forget about the rest of the world when you were in Four Paths. But unlike Justin and May, Isaac was determined to actually get out of here for college—if he could manage to get into a place that wouldn't send him into twenty years of student loan debt, anyway.

"So that's what college is like?" he asked, because it was easier than talking about anything else. "People drinking all the time?"

"Not all the time," said Gabriel. "Depends on where you go to school. And depends on who your friends are."

"What did you tell them?" asked Isaac.

"Tell who?"

"Your friends. About... this."

Gabriel looked out at the ashes, his mouth set in a grim line. His profile was sharp and gaunt, his stubble rough and uneven across his chin. "I lied. Told them my family was dead. Told them I didn't want to talk about it."

"That's not really a lie."

"It's not really the truth, either." Gabriel paused and took a long pull of his beer. "I only went to college because I'd applied before everything went to shit. And for the first semester or two, I was just... angry. I didn't go to class. I drank, I did whatever drugs people gave me, and I got into fights. I had a reputation."

"I was angry, too." Isaac was still angry—in a way that he was unsure how to handle, in a place inside of him that still felt too raw to touch. "But you don't seem out of control anymore."

Gabriel looked out at the ashes. "I'm not."

"So what changed?"

"I met a girl."

Isaac rolled his eyes. "There it is."

He couldn't help it—he felt a stab of envy. That his brother had been able to fall for someone who could care for him the same way he cared for her.

But when he turned to look at his brother, Gabriel did not look any happier. "We dated for two years," he continued. "I went to therapy. I got myself back on track. And then—after letting down my guard, after finally trusting her—I tried to tell her some of the truth. Left the weirdest stuff out, obviously."

"Did she believe you?"

Gabriel looked pained. "I almost wish she hadn't. It was too much for her to handle, she said, because she could see I hadn't actually dealt with it, and she left."

"Shit. I'm sorry."

"It's all right." Gabriel's tone clearly indicated otherwise. He finished his beer, placed the empty bottle carefully in his backpack, and pulled out another. "It made me realize that if I wanted to exist in the rest of this world, I had to come back. Mom needed help, but so did I. Your ritual never really leaves my head."

His words sparked a deep, unbridled fury in Isaac.

"Oh, fuck off," he said bitterly.

Gabriel blinked. "Excuse me? I'm just trying to explain my side of things to you. I thought that was what you wanted."

"Oh, yeah, I'm loving this," said Isaac. "It's great to hear about how traumatized you are from that time you tried to murder me in cold blood."

Gabriel froze. "Is that what you think happened?"

Isaac's throat went tight, and he swiveled his head around to look at Gabriel. "That *is* what happened."

"Let me tell you what I remember," Gabriel said. "About that day. About what happened."

Isaac realized his hands were beginning to shake, and he took a deep breath, knowing he was not ready to hear any of this, knowing already that there wasn't a chance in hell he could walk away.

"All right," he said, and Gabriel began.

"They didn't tell us," he said, "that someone would have to die. Not for a very long time. I did my ritual, and Caleb and Isaiah and Uncle Simon chained me up and bled me onto that altar, and it *hurt*. When it was over they told me that I had taken it well, and that I would carry on the Sullivan legacy. I assumed everyone's ritual was like that—I didn't ask too many questions, and they liked it that way. They told me specifically not to tell you, so whenever you asked about it I just shook my head. Because I was proud of being included.

"I'd always wanted to be like Caleb and Isaiah—it would've been cool to shatter things—and I was disappointed at first when I realized I could heal. But soon, I felt very useful. Everyone wanted me on their patrol because I was handy if there was an injury, or if a Sullivan lost control. And it was fine for years... until they told Mom it would be you.

"I don't know who made the decision. We're—we *were*— bigger than every other family, and the uncles were the ones who really called the shots, I don't know if you remember."

"I remember," said Isaac. "They never liked me very much."

They'd thought he was weak and strange, and they'd always encouraged him to hang out with his brothers and Justin, hoping they would be a good influence. Isaac had never wanted to be the type of man they were: men who drank too much and thought too little. His mother had called them out on their bullshit for a while, but it had started to wear on her, and eventually she'd given up on them entirely.

"They were assholes," Gabriel said matter-of-factly. "Anyway. I don't know if you remember Mom trying to run away with you before it happened."

"I remember," Isaac said quietly.

"I didn't understand what was going on," Gabriel said. "But I know what happened after they caught you two. She was put under constant surveillance, locked in her room like a prisoner. Caleb broke her out the night of the ritual because it was the only time they let down their guard, and they came to try to free you. But Caleb didn't tell me and Isaiah what was coming—I think he considered us in too deep—and so we didn't realize, neither of us did, that they were going to kill you until they'd already handed me the knife."

Gabriel's voice began to shake, and Isaac tried not to remember, tried to block it out, but it was there, it was all there. Right below the surface, churning through him, a loss too big to avoid, a pain too great to heal.

"They told—" His voice broke. "They told me that I wasn't just going to make you bleed, I was going to kill you. That it would make us stronger. I told them to go to hell. And then Uncle Si grabbed the knife out of my hands, and he was so quick—he pressed it against your throat; and there was blood everywhere, and I thought you were dying, we all did, we were screaming— and then your powers activated. Then Caleb and Mom showed up, and everything after that..." He trailed off. "It's blurry. Maybe it's better that way."

Isaac scar throbbed, and he felt bile rising in his throat. "It wasn't you," he whispered. "All those years...I thought you had chased me because you wanted to finish the job."

Gabriel shook his head. "No. I chased you because I wanted to heal you."

A puzzle piece clicked into place: Gabriel's medallion on the ground beside him when he'd come to. Isaac had thought he'd ripped it off his brother in the struggle, but that had never quite made sense. Isaac reached a hand up and touched the line at his throat, remembered what Justin had told him. That there was so much blood. That the wound had been too deep. But he'd lived anyway; he'd lived, and he'd never questioned why until now.

"Then why did you leave?" Isaac asked. "If you healed me... You left me in the woods."

"I went to get help," Gabriel said. "The Hawthornes found you before I could. And after it was all over, everything moved very quickly. Everyone who survived that night split in the next few days. They didn't want to be around when you got out of the hospital. They were ashamed of what they'd done. And I couldn't look at myself without thinking of how useless I'd been—I was supposed to be a healer, but I couldn't save Caleb, or Isaiah, or Mom. It felt better to leave you in the Hawthornes' care than to own up to everything I'd done."

"But you saved me," Isaac whispered, his heart pounding in his chest. All those years of running and hiding, and here it was: the truth. That Gabriel had never wanted to hurt him after all. "You saved me, and I never knew."

"Because I ran," said Gabriel. "Fuck it... I'm glad you destroyed the house. We weren't a family—we were a cult. And I've spent the past few years turning it over in my mind, trying to understand. Why our ritual asks for so much when the others don't. Why we did it for so many years. Why the rest of the town just let us kill children for hundreds of years. What the *fuck*? I mean—how did our uncles live with themselves? How could Mom have kids at all, knowing what might happen to us?"

"I don't understand it," Isaac said. "I don't think I ever will. Sometimes I have nightmares that they've come back. That's what I thought you were when I first saw you. A bad dream."

"It doesn't matter if they come back," said Gabriel. "This ends here. With us. No more sacrifices. No more bloody trades for power. I don't care what it gives us—it isn't worth it."

"Agreed," Isaac said, his words carried away on a sudden gust of wind. A weight tugged at his wrist: Gabriel's medallion. He hooked his fingers around it and unwound it from his wrist, the cracked red disc shining in the sun. "Hey. You should probably take this back."

"I don't think I deserve it."

"You're a founder." Isaac held it out: a gauntlet. "You earned it."

"All right. If you insist." But Isaac could see how much it meant to him as he gently tied it around his wrist.

All this time, he'd been wrong. He'd tried to stare at his fear head-on and found that there was no monster waiting for him, just someone who was as frightened as he was. The only person who could truly grasp the magnitude of betrayal he'd faced that night.

If he'd been brave enough, if Gabriel had been ready, they could have done this years ago. Isaac ached for all that wasted time where they had suffered separately, both unable to cope and struggling to heal. But against all odds, they had figured it out.

It wasn't too late. Not for him and not for Gabriel, either.

"About Mom," he said, thinking of Maya in her hospital bed. "You really think she's never going to wake up?"

The regret on Gabriel's face was palpable. "I really don't think she will, Isaac."

Isaac sat back, contemplating this. For the first time, he allowed himself to consider the possibility that maybe he'd been grieving her all along, that maybe, just like everything else in his family, he could not let her go.

And then something stirred in his peripheral vision.

"Hello?" He rose to his feet.

It stirred again, and he walked toward it, Gabriel following a step behind him. The moment they cleared the underbrush, Isaac understood.

The buds that hung above the Sullivan altar were blooming, terrible pulsating flowers in the shape of hands unfurling one by one.

And Isaac's newfound hope slipped away from him just as easily as the strands of smoke billowed from the flowers, iridescent flecks glimmering, and rose above the trees.

Violet was on watch in the spire when the attack came. She had been fretting about the letter she'd found, turning it over and over again in her mind as she tapped aimlessly at her phone. But a sudden noise made her bolt upright, her phone sliding carelessly off her lap and onto the attic floor. Beside her, Orpheus rose to his feet, mewling urgently. The red string around his ear twitched.

"Yeah, I know," Violet said, staring at the same place he was.

Roots surged from inside the circle a moment later, destroying the founders' symbol that had been painted inside.

She'd known this attack would come, but she hadn't anticipated it being such an aggressive assault. The roots wriggled across the floorboards more quickly than Violet could blink. Several strands clawed for purchase against the walls, tugging down the velvet curtains that shielded the windows. In the center of the circle, the roots *grew*, saplings sprouting from them that were utterly laden with those disgusting handlike buds. The smell made Violet's eyes water.

"Gross," Violet muttered as her sneaker made contact with

a puddle of silver goo leaking from the roots. She knelt down and pressed her palm against the iridescence, bracing herself as a familiar tether opened in the back of her mind.

"Don't even try it," she said, her hands outstretched, staring at the copse of trees attempting to invade her attic. Her *home*. Orpheus brushed reassuringly against her legs, hissing at the saplings as they shrank back against the wall.

The tether in her mind shivered and whined. Violet had noticed the sound before, but for the first time, she heard something else behind it. A voice, murmuring words she could not understand. But it wasn't the words that mattered; it was the tone. It was unmistakably *human*.

"I don't understand," she whispered. The saplings shifted and writhed, and for a split second she saw human bodies in the creases of their strange gray bark, arms and necks and torsos twisted in agony. The whining in the back of her mind intensified, shrill and panicked, and a tear brimmed in the corner of her eye. Violet knew it would be iridescent, just like the corruption.

Why was this happening so quickly? What had changed? Violet struggled to claw back her panic as the buds began to unfurl, smoke drifting from them and swirling together into a tiny tornado in the center of the spire.

Violet breathed in deeply, felt the rush of her power coursing through her. She tugged on this tether that she had not asked for, these powers she still did not fully understand, and with everything she had, she willed it all to *stop*.

That was how Juniper and Harper found her: arms outstretched, breathing heavily, sweat dripping from her brow as she held the corruption in place.

"It isn't going to work," she told them both, her mind

spinning, the trees moving in and out of focus. The voices were growing; first there had been one, then three, and now there was an entire chorus, whimpering like dying animals in the back of her head. "When I stop..."

"It'll spread," Juniper finished gently. "But you can't hold it forever, Violet. You have to let it go."

"*No.*"

"I can help." Harper appeared beside her. There was a ferocious look on her face. She knelt down, exhaled, and reached into the circle, closing her hand around a root.

Immediately, stone spread from her fingers. It snaked along the roots and up the saplings that had sprouted from them, petrifying the open buds into a dozen tiny, grotesque statues. When she stepped back, the entire thing was still and the screaming tether in Violet's head had shrunk to a whisper.

"Thank you," Violet said hoarsely, relief coursing through her as she collapsed to her knees, shuddering. The buds had released gray mist into the room, but it was already dissipating. Violet hoped their founder immunity would hold against this new development of the disease.

"No, thank *you*," Harper said. "You held it back."

"You stopped it." Violet grinned at her. "You got control of your powers!"

But Harper wasn't smiling back. "Not forever."

Already, Violet could see silver veins beginning to appear beneath the coating of red-brown stone.

"Oh," she whispered, dread coursing through her. "Oh no."

"It'll hold for at least a day, I think," Harper said. "But it's just temporary. The spire..."

"It's falling."

"Yeah."

Juniper had to help Violet back down the ladder. She didn't want to leave the corruption behind, but even she could admit that she needed to rest. Back in the living room, she wrapped a blanket around her shoulders and sipped anxiously from a hot mug of tea as Harper stared at her phone screen. Juniper had stayed behind to barricade the trapdoor.

"It's not just us," Harper said grimly. "Something's happening at the Hawthorne house. And the Sullivan ruins."

"Shit!" Violet groaned and tugged her blanket more tightly around her shoulders, shivering. "We have to go. We have to try to stop it—"

"We can't possibly be in three places at once." Harper's voice was gentle but firm. "Sit. Drink your tea."

Violet frowned at her. "Since when did you get so bossy?"

"I have four younger siblings," Harper said wryly. "I've always been bossy."

Harper's phone began to buzz, and her eyes widened. Violet leaned over, saw the name flashing on the screen, and choked back an incredulous laugh.

"You have Justin Hawthorne listed in your phone as *Ugh*?"

"You knew it was him, didn't you?" Harper asked, tapping the screen. A moment later his voice sounded through the speakers, crackly but clear.

"Harper?" he said.

"I'm here. What's going on?"

"I'm at the lake; I ran here—not important. The point is that the corruption is spreading here."

"*What?*"

"It's going to—it's—" He let out a panicked yell, and the call cut out abruptly.

"Justin?" Harper tapped frantically at her phone. "Justin! Are you kidding me? I'm going to *kill* him."

Again, Violet felt her own panic creeping up in her chest. If another ritual site was falling so close to this one, if those buds were unfurling, *something* had gone terribly wrong. An airborne strand of the corruption meant that anyone who breathed it in would get sick. They'd contained it in her attic, but if those flowers bloomed at the lake...

"I have to go home." Harper sounded calm, but Violet saw the urgency in her movements as she rose to her feet and went for the door. "He could be in danger."

"Won't your siblings be patrolling?"

"That doesn't mean they'll be enough to handle it, if what just happened in your attic is any indication."

Violet nodded. "Do you want me to come with you?"

"No. You need to keep an eye on the attic."

Violet understood. This was her home. Her turf to defend, just as the lake was Harper's.

"Be careful," she said fiercely.

Harper's smile was sharp around the edges. "You too," she said, and then she was gone.

In her absence, Violet paced back and forth in the living room, restless and uneasy. Her mother was watching the spire, had asked Violet to rest, but she had never felt less like relaxing. Dread squirmed in her stomach as she peered out the window—she could see a trail of smoke rising above the trees in the direction of the Carlisle cottage. Orpheus wound around her legs, his too-cold body somehow still comforting.

And then a knock sounded on the front door.

Violet didn't know who she was expecting. Isaac, maybe. Certainly not Augusta Hawthorne, flanked by her two giant dogs.

"Uh," she said. "I'll get my mom—"

"I'm here." Juniper appeared beside her a moment later, looking utterly exhausted. "August, I thought you were at your place—"

"June." Augusta's voice was utterly defeated. "The airborne corruption has begun to spread. We have to activate the emergency protocol."

Her mother's face collapsed, and Violet stared between the two of them, uncomprehending.

"What do you mean, emergency protocol?"

"She means it's time for the founders' last resort," Juniper said. "We've failed to protect this town. Which means we need to evacuate Four Paths."

CHAPTER EIGHTEEN

Harper followed the smoke rising above the trees, winding her way through a route she knew by heart: one that would take her home to her lake. She knew the corruption had spread again, but she was still unprepared for what she might find there. The horrors she'd seen in the Gray were merging with Four Paths in her mind the same way the Beast's face had merged with Justin's.

Justin.

The moment she'd heard the phone call cut out, something sharp and painful had crystallized in her chest. She'd remembered dropping that cheap wooden sword at his feet. The way his hair felt when she curled her fingers into it at his party. The conversation she'd had with Violet about how she didn't have to save him.

Harper knew how he felt about her. She had known for a long time. And in that moment, she was tired of pretending she did not feel the same way, tired of pushing him away from her when all she wanted to do was pull him closer. There were no more lies between them; their history was laid out neatly now, the betrayal on both sides, the hurt, the years of distance and quiet rage.

She needed to find him, and she needed to tell him. But as

she reached the trees that ringed the lake, Harper could not quell the fear that she had waited too long.

Just as he had said on the phone, it was changing.

Trees bent low over the water, their buds unfurled. They looked even more like hands than Harper remembered, fleshy and gray, five fingers twitching in time with the pulsating bark. Each emitted an endless stream of gray smoke, glimmering with iridescent flecks. Corruption was spreading steadily through the lake, the same iridescent liquid she'd seen in the Gray polluting the clear water.

Harper's heartbeat sped up. She stepped forward, her hand automatically reaching for her sword—and then she saw the body.

He was lying halfway in the lake, an arm limply outstretched, as if trying to crawl back to land. Water had soaked through his clothes, leaving them wet and clinging. His blond hair was darkened by red-brown dirt; his face was turned away from her. Roots from the nearest tree twined around his outstretched hand, crawling steadily down his arm.

"Justin!"

To her immense relief, he stirred. But her voice seemed to have sped up the encroaching trees. Harper's entire body went cold as one of the nearby buds swiveled, the branch bending toward his face. She knew the founders were immune to the corruption, but that didn't mean the forest couldn't hurt them.

She didn't think—instead she charged forward, each step a small eternity, and caught the branch in midair.

She had helped Violet inside the spire. She could do this again. Red-brown stone spread from her fingertips and engulfed

243

the branch, freezing it in place. Harper forced the stone to spread as far as she could manage, but it was physically difficult—like pushing a boulder up a hill. The corruption was strong and unwieldy; it tugged at the limits of her power. It was all she could do to turn that single tree to stone, but at least for the moment, it was not trying to hurt him anymore.

Harper knelt beside Justin, her breathing ragged, and peeled the stone root away from his arm. It disintegrated beneath her fingers as easily as dust, leaving behind a slimy residue on his skin. His eyes were locked on her, his lips slightly parted. He was staring at her with unabashed awe, and it kindled a great warmth inside her, made her forget that they were in the middle of a disaster, made her forget that the entire world was falling apart around them.

"Harper," he breathed.

"Yeah," she whispered. "I found you."

His hand cupped her cheek, and he grinned. "It's really you. Not the Gray."

"Of course it's me."

"I wasn't sure." He hesitated. "I didn't know if you would care enough to come help me."

The words hurt her more than she could say, because she understood exactly why he'd think them.

"Yes, I care enough," she said. "I care about you too much, Justin. That's always been my problem. Because I spent *years* trying to let you go, and I just...couldn't."

Something in his gaze changed, and for a moment Harper tensed with panic. But then he spoke.

"I couldn't let you go, either," he said softly. "I wanted you even when I wanted to forget you. I know I fucked it up. I know I didn't deserve all the chances I got. And maybe we've both been hurt too many times for this to ever work, you and me. But that hasn't made my feelings go away."

The moment after this seemed to stretch on for an eternity. Everything around them faded out—the smoke clouding the air around them, the corrupted trees at the edge of the lake, even the gentle sound of the lapping waves. All Harper could hear was her heartbeat ratcheting up in her chest, and all she saw was the look on Justin's face—fear and determination and desire all at once.

"It's okay if you don't feel the same way," Justin said, and Harper realized that she had waited too long to speak. "Seriously, Harper, I just needed to tell you—"

"I know," Harper said.

And then she kissed him.

It was a rough, impatient kiss that had been a long time in the making, and Justin's surprise only lasted for a moment before he wrapped an arm around her waist and brought her closer to him. His shirt was wet and cold. She slid her hand beneath the clinging fabric, heat flooding through her as he braced one hand against her back and used the other to carefully brush her curls away from her neck. His lips moved down her jawline, lingering at the edges of her collarbone, and when he reached her shoulder, she gasped and dragged her nails down his spine.

He shuddered and pulled away for a moment, and she hesitated, locking eyes with him.

"Is that okay?" she said. "I don't want to hurt you—"

He gasped out a laugh. "Fuck. Yes. Do it again."

Harper grinned and traced her nails down his back, a deep satisfaction stirring in her as he made a soft, eager noise and pulled her even closer to him.

The waves lapped around Harper, soaking her through, but she didn't notice. She was lost in the curve of Justin's shoulder, in his lips on the hollows of her throat, a different kind of drowning, where it felt as if any moment she spent coming up for air was wasted time.

And if this really was the beginning of the end, she thought, for Four Paths, for all of them, at least they had come together before it all broke apart.

It had taken less than twelve hours for the evacuation to be implemented throughout Four Paths. Technically it was optional, but Isaac had yet to see anybody protest. Although the founding families had quarantined the sites of the airborne corruption immediately, and no new buds had yet to open beyond the ritual sites, the clear and present danger could not be ignored.

The school had been shut down, houses shuttered and locked, stores temporarily closed. Isaac had woken up to a steady line of cars crawling down Main Street, all filled with people he'd known his entire life. It was surreal to watch them go. Surreal to think that after all these years of fighting back, Augusta had finally admitted that there was a problem the founders could not solve.

Or at least, a problem she wasn't *sure* the founders could solve. Because they weren't leaving. Not without a fight.

Which was how he found himself in the foyer of the Saunders manor, staring awkwardly around at the massive staircase that spiraled up to the second floor. Violet had crashed at the Pathways Inn with her mom the previous night, since the spire of the Saunders manor was compromised, and was supposed to be moving her stuff into the town hall that morning, but she hadn't shown and she wasn't responding to his texts. He couldn't help but worry that the corruption had spread again, so he went looking for her. His unease only intensified when he found the front door unlocked.

"Hello?" he called out. Isaac did not like the Saunders manor. It reminded him too much of his old house—a gloomy building filled with endless reminders of the dead. He eyed the taxidermy beside the coat rack—an owl—and shuddered.

A noise disturbed the dusty silence—a note, ringing out sharp and clear, and then a series of chords. Isaac followed the sound through the hallway and found an open doorway into an airy, spacious room that looked out on the woods behind the house. Violet was seated at the grand piano in the corner, lost in focus; her eyes were closed, her lips slightly parted, her hair glowing like autumn leaves in the sunlight.

For a moment, he was annoyed. This was where her priorities were when the entire town was in danger? But as Isaac raised a hand to knock on the side of the door frame, the music stopped him, held him in place as surely as if his hands had been bound.

It was like nothing he had ever heard before. A melody that crept through the corners of the room and wound around him, building slowly, her fingers extending across the keys in a way that was clearly as natural to her as breathing.

The music settled around him like a fog, plaintive and melancholy, and Isaac forgot about everything but his own memories, rumbling beneath those minor chords. The rough stone of the altar pressing against his back. His power swirling around his hands, uncontrolled and utterly wild. There was grief, sharp and furious; there was hope and fear and something deeper undercutting them all, engulfing him as she played faster. As the tempo of the piece sped up, Violet bent her head, her red hair falling across her face. And Isaac realized what he was feeling: Like this, his memories were an acknowledgment instead of an assault. A part of a bigger story instead of the entire book.

Isaac knew Violet played piano, that she was pretty good at it. But he hadn't known that she could do *this*—take feelings he'd never been able to articulate, ones she could not possibly understand, and give them shape and form. The melody had reached into his chest and turned him inside out, and when the final chord faded away, Isaac realized he was dangerously close to tears.

He cleared his throat, his arm brushing against the doorway, and that noise must have been enough to rouse her from her trance.

Her eyes flew open—and immediately widened with horror. "You." She gasped. "How long have you been standing there?"

Isaac felt a rush of guilt. Now that the music was gone, he realized how strange this truly was. But it had felt wrong to stop her, and he hadn't known how to walk away.

"Not long," he said quickly, and then, in a weak attempt to change the subject: "What piece is that?"

Violet hesitated, a hand curling protectively around the side of the sheet music. "It's ... mine. I'm working on it."

No wonder she had played with such passion, such fervor. No wonder she'd been angry with him for walking in on her.

"You *wrote* that?" He stepped forward hesitantly. "Holy shit."

"Yeah," she said. "I've been composing. I just have the first movement right now, and it's pretty rough...."

"It didn't sound rough to me."

She snorted. "Well, that just tells me you know nothing about classical piano."

Isaac hesitated. Behind her, the forest stretched down the hill and into the distance, disappearing into the faint, smudgy horizon.

"It feels like . . . that," he said, gesturing to the window. "Like the woods, like the corruption, like the rituals. Like you put this whole town into music."

Violet froze on the piano bench, her dark eyes locked on his. He could not read the look in them at all. "I call it the *Gray Sonata*."

"That's perfect." The words were soft, too soft, but she smiled at them, and that made him feel like he had gotten one tiny part of this whole interaction right.

"It's how I deal with everything," she said. "Rosie, Daria, this horrible cult town . . ."

"I wish I had a coping mechanism that good."

"I'm not sure it's very good," Violet said dryly. "I'm still extremely sad."

Isaac choked back a laugh. "Well, so am I. So it's not as if I've got anywhere to go but up."

Violet tipped her head to the side. "Do you ever worry that maybe you're sad because it's easy? Because you're good at it?"

"Are you saying that I *want* to feel like this?" Isaac felt a sudden swell of hurt. "Why would I ever—"

"I wasn't talking about you." Violet's voice had the same bite to it he'd heard the first time she'd spoken, when he'd seen the fire in her and thought that it was only a matter of time until Justin burned himself with it. "I was talking about *me*."

He swallowed. "Oh. Sorry." He'd been wrong about why Justin had tried so hard with her, when she'd first come to town. He'd been wrong about everything. He didn't want to get this wrong, too; whatever *this* was.

"I don't think either of us is sad because it's easy," he said slowly. "I think we're sad because life has been kind of shitty to us, and people we love keep dying, and it would be more messed up if we *weren't* sad sometimes."

"I guess. But I've started feeling guilty when I'm happy. Like it isn't allowed, after all of this."

"I feel guilty when I'm happy, too," he said. "And then I feel guilty about feeling guilty."

Violet snorted and lowered her gaze, her eyelashes casting dark, feathery shadows across her cheeks. "I wish I could turn it all off. Feel it all a little less."

"I don't," Isaac said, and realized to his own surprise that he meant it. "It happened, and I can't change that. The remembering doesn't have to break me. Forgetting would be worse."

She lifted her head. "I guess I feel that way about Rosie, too. Like . . . thinking about her isn't always painful. Sometimes it's actually really nice."

"I mean, of course it's nice sometimes," Isaac said, meeting her eyes. "You love her."

"I do." Violet paused. "I mean, grief is just another kind of love, right?"

Isaac nodded. "I think that's how your music felt. Or what it made me feel, anyway."

"Well, I'm glad," Violet said. "I wanted to play it one last time before I said goodbye. I guess I got carried away."

"About that." Isaac hesitated. "You should've been at the town hall by now. I was, um..."

"You were worried about me." Violet's mouth quirked upward at the corners, and he wondered if her smile had always looked like that, like they'd just shared a secret. "That's why you're here, isn't it?"

"Maybe." He hovered awkwardly at the edge of the bench. "I mean, your attic is kind of decaying. And you weren't answering your texts...."

"I can't believe people are scared of you," she said, a teasing edge in her voice. "You're soft, Sullivan."

"Yes, I think *soft* is the first word I'd use for someone trying to make sure everyone around them stays alive."

Violet snorted with laughter. "Fair enough," she said, rising from the piano bench and gesturing to a comically overstuffed duffel bag that sat on the couch. "Well, I guess I'd better get this loaded into the car."

"It'll take you hours to drive to the center of town," Isaac said grimly. "The roads are packed."

"Oh, *joy*." Violet paused, and then a smile lit up her face, far more mischievous than the one she'd been wearing before. "Well, since you're being so considerate today, how do you feel about carrying my stuff to the town hall?"

Isaac had no idea what Violet had packed, but it was obscenely, ridiculously heavy. He was sweating in the chilly November air long before the town square came into view. It was even busier now than it had been before he left, cars crowded everywhere. Augusta Hawthorne paced back and forth in front of the town seal, gesturing at the small army of deputies and volunteers in front of her. The seal itself looked completely free of corruption, at least for now. A sign that maybe they *could* turn all this around, if only they could figure out what the hell was causing the disease.

Isaac hated the feeling that they had half the puzzle put together. He knew they were missing something, he just wasn't sure *what*. And they were running out of time to solve the mystery.

"Did you know Augusta's calling this in as a flood warning?" Violet asked as Isaac heaved her bag through the town hall's back door and up the stairs to his apartment. The steps were absolute murder on his back, but at last he made it to his living room and set the duffel down. Isaac wasn't entirely certain how he'd wound up agreeing to let Violet and Harper crash in his apartment until further notice, but it had happened anyway. Saunders and Carlisle territory wasn't safe anymore. Neither was the Hawthorne house, but Isaac was utterly unsurprised by the family's refusal to leave their home behind. May had been born there, and it seemed like she had every intention of dying there too if necessary.

"You're *welcome*," he said, gesturing at the duffel. "I'm pretty sure that was my workout for the week. And no, I didn't. How do you know that?"

"Thanks for carrying it," Violet said, swinging her satchel-style backpack off her shoulder and setting it gently beside the duffel. Her cat jumped on Isaac's secondhand couch and surveyed his new territory, his whiskers twitching. "And I know because Augusta and Juniper were up till five a.m. holding a strategy meeting in the Pathways Inn. Talking about how to get the people who are sick into a hospital, how to cover all this up. Basically, they spent a million hours figuring out how to convincingly lie to the state of New York about the supernatural hellscape we live in."

"So she and your mom are still getting along?" Isaac had seen Violet's mother in passing on their way into the town hall. She'd been standing close to Augusta, tapping furiously away on a tablet.

"Mom's staying with the Hawthornes, so yeah, I guess so. She tried to get me to leave town, you know. As part of the evacuation."

Isaac turned his head sharply. "Really?"

"Yeah." She shrugged. "Only been here a few months, responsible parenting, protection, blah blah blah."

"And?"

Violet looked at him incredulously. "Are you kidding me? I can help fight this. I'm not going anywhere."

"Good." His voice was a little too raw for his liking.

A knock sounded at his door, and he went to swing it open, half expecting Harper asking him to carry something heavy, too. But it was Gabriel instead, far more disheveled than the last time Isaac had seen him. His clothes looked as if he'd slept in them, and his face was tired and worn.

"Hey," he said. "Can I talk to you? Alone?"

They wound up sitting on the couch. Isaac usually loved his apartment, but right now he saw it through Gabriel's eyes—the messy piles of books next to the overstuffed shelves, the unwashed dishes in the sink, the clothes spilling out of his closet and across his bedroom floor.

"So, you really live here by yourself," Gabriel mused, fishing out a worn paperback lodged between two couch cushions and tossing it onto the battered end table. "I'm surprised you can afford it."

"I can't," Isaac said shortly. "I live here for free. The sheriff and the mayor worked out an agreement."

"Four Paths sure does love its nepotism."

"And Augusta loves knowing I owe her family something."

"That checks out." Gabriel hesitated, his eyes darting around the room. Isaac wondered what he was looking for. "Listen, about the other day—I wanted to tell you that I meant what I said. I'm sorry about everything that's happened to us. I'm sorry I couldn't be the brother you needed."

"I'm sorry, too." Isaac couldn't put his finger on it, but there was something off here. He and Gabriel had covered all this already, and his brother wasn't really the type to keep picking the scabs off old wounds. "But at least you're here now."

"Yeah. About that." Gabriel's voice lowered. "You know how serious this situation in Four Paths is, right? I've been here for ten minutes, and even I can tell everything's crumbling."

"Everything's always crumbling," Isaac said, shrugging. "That's just how Four Paths is."

"This is different." Gabriel looked at Isaac, his expression deathly serious. "This isn't the Gray, Isaac. The more this corruption spreads, the more I see how different it is. How dangerous."

"Of course it's dangerous," Isaac said. "That's why we're evacuating the town. So we can fight without worrying about everyone else."

"I'm not staying," Gabriel said.

Isaac blinked at him. "What?"

"I'm evacuating with the rest of the town, Isaac, and I think you should come with me."

The words didn't register at first. They were nonsensical, foolish. Sullivans didn't hide from a fight—in fact, they were usually the ones who'd started the fight in the first place. And Isaac wasn't leaving his friends, his *home*, to fall to the corruption.

"I'm not running away," he said, his voice hoarse with disbelief. "And I can't believe you *are*. What about your healing powers? Our research?"

"All we've found are dead ends and proof of lies," Gabriel said. "We didn't ask for this fight, Isaac. It was forced on us, but we can turn it down. We can say no."

"You're a coward." The words came from deep in Isaac's gut. He watched them hit his brother like a blow, but he didn't regret them. "You're right that we didn't ask for this. But this is our life. Our family. Our responsibility."

"You don't understand," Gabriel said, leaning forward. "Something is coming, Isaac. The corruption is just a symptom. We haven't even seen the full disease yet."

Suspicion bloomed in Isaac's mind. A few days ago, Gabriel had been ready to stand by his side. A few *weeks* ago, Gabriel had a root crawling under his skin.

"Who told you this?" he asked.

Gabriel averted his eyes. "No one," he mumbled. "Common sense."

But Isaac knew he was lying. Something had happened, something to scare Gabriel away. And he wanted to know what.

"I thought you meant it when you said you regretted leaving me after the ritual," he said. "I was even thinking about why you came here. About letting Mom go. But if you're running now, then I guess you haven't changed at all. And I never should have listened to you in the first place."

Gabriel's face shuttered. "I'm not running. I'm trying to save your life."

"Oh, really?" Isaac's power surged furiously through him, begging for release, but he forced it back. Instead, he kept his words clipped and cold. "Get out of my house. And give me my medallion back. You don't deserve it."

Isaac was unsurprised by how quickly Gabriel listened to him. The door slammed shut, and the only proof that he'd ever come back at all was the cracked medallion sitting on the couch cushion. Isaac scooped it up, closed his hand around it, and let his power free, shuddering. In mere moments, it had crumbled to ash.

And now he was all alone again, the only Sullivan left to fight against the rising tide of disaster.

CHAPTER NINETEEN

The woods behind the Carlisle cottage were deathly silent. No birds sang in the branches; no animals rustled in the dying underbrush. It was a defeated, uneasy sort of quiet. Harper had to fight the urge to hold her breath, to make her footsteps as soft as possible.

The evacuation was nearly finished, and Harper could not shake the feeling that the lifeblood of the town was draining from it alongside most of its occupants. She tightened the bandanna over her mouth and gazed grimly out at the lake. The corrupted flowers that hung low over the water had done their job, turning the water entirely silvery and iridescent just like the lake she'd seen in the Gray.

Although it was a disturbing sight, the lake still kindled a warmth in her chest. It reminded her of the kiss—a kiss that Harper had held gently inside herself like a great candle burning in her rib cage. She and Justin had managed to get to the Carlisle cottage afterward, where they'd gotten a ride back to town from Seth. She'd woken up to the news of the evacuation, and from that moment onward it had consumed both of their focus.

Harper knew they would have to talk about it eventually,

but she didn't feel ready. It had only been a day, after all, and she wanted to keep this one good thing safe and untarnished for a little while longer.

For now, though, she needed to focus. She and Violet had spent the afternoon trying to keep the corruption as contained as they could, but their efforts could only slow it, not stop it. They'd started with the Sullivan ruins, then moved on to the Carlisle lake, where Harper touched trunk after trunk, strengthening the red-brown stone she'd used to cloak the trees while Violet protected her from stray flailing branches. But to Harper's dismay, her power was not working the way it had when she'd helped Justin. She had more control over it—that hadn't changed—but she could feel whatever energy lurked within the trees growing stronger.

Harper wasn't sure how much time they had left before all their efforts failed, but she knew it was coming soon. All they'd done was put a Band-Aid on a gaping wound. Violet had headed back to the town hall to regroup, but Harper hesitated, lingering at the edge of the trees.

She sighed, cast the lake a final glance, and walked over to the cottage. When she saw the cars in the driveway, her stomach sank.

She'd thought her family was already gone. But she'd timed it wrong, and instead she heard the telltale noise of children from inside the house. She was about to turn and hightail it back into the woods when the front door opened and Brett and Nora spilled out. They saw her immediately, of course, and rushed across the lawn, both bundled in their winter coats and clutching backpacks full of toys.

"Are you coming with us?" Nora asked, looking hopeful.

Harper shook her head, her heart heavy. "I have to stay. But I'm going to help make it so you can both come back soon, okay?"

"That's what Mitzi and Seth said." Brett's voice snaked up into a high-pitched whine. "And they said I'm too *young* to help protect everybody—"

"That's not true," Harper said quickly, placing her hand on his shoulder and looking him in the eyes. "You and Mom are going to protect Nora and baby Olly, aren't you?"

Brett sniffled. "Yeah. Yeah, I guess we are."

"Harper." The familiar sound of her father's voice made Harper stiffen, her heartbeat speeding up. They hadn't spoken since he'd gotten his memories back; he had called her a few times, but she hadn't responded. "Can we talk?"

Harper hesitated. Brett and Nora were looking at them both, visibly confused. "I . . . I don't know."

"Please."

The word was so soft, Harper thought for a moment that she hadn't heard it at all. This was him, begging her. Harper knew she could walk away if she wanted to. But it was the knowledge that it was her choice, that she was capable of saying no, that made her nod.

"All right."

They wound up standing awkwardly at the edge of the driveway. Brett and Nora had been sent inside, to "help" their mother finish packing. Harper didn't feel entirely comfortable alone with him, but she didn't want the kids to see this.

"So," Maurice began, "I've given all of this a lot of thought. What happened with the Church . . . what happened with us."

She could see the pain in Maurice's eyes, the devastation on his face. But she felt no regret or shame. He was her father, and he had tried to kill her. She'd thought that maybe once he got his memories back she'd feel as if there were some possibility for reconciliation, or healing. But now Harper realized that she did not want either of those things.

He had allowed the Church to turn him into a monster. There was no world in which she forgave him for that.

"I told your mother what happened," he continued. "We've both agreed that it's best I leave town. Not just for the evacuation—for good. It's not safe for me to be around you anymore."

Harper's throat went dry. Out of all the things she'd thought he might say, she'd never expected this. Maybe he wanted her to beg him to stay. Maybe he wanted her to promise that there was a chance for this, for things to heal.

Harper would not give him false hope.

"Good," she said softly. "I'm glad you understand that family is a privilege, not a right."

"Yes. It's a privilege I don't deserve anymore." Maurice's voice shook, but he continued on, the words hoarse. "I know you might think I'm a coward for doing this. But I love you, Harper. I'm sorry. And I will spend the rest of my life atoning for what I've done."

Then he turned and walked toward the car.

Harper understood that it was probably the last time she would ever see him. She didn't speak. She didn't move. The car pulled out of the driveway, exhaust drifting into the crisp fall air, and Harper felt grief and guilt and relief course through her all at once.

Then she took a deep breath, wiped away her tears, and walked back to the Carlisle cottage, pushing open the front door.

"Hey, Mom?" she called out, determined not to let the last few minutes overwhelm her. "I'm here to help you pack."

It took almost a half hour to get the younger Carlisles out the door. Harper bundled Brett and Nora into the car, kissed a babbling Olly on the forehead, then turned to her mother.

She had never had much to say to Laurie Carlisle. But today, she had two words.

"Thank you," she whispered, and her mother smiled, pain trembling at the edge of her face.

"You'll come home?" she asked. "When we're back?"

Harper nodded. "I will."

And then they were gone, too. Which left Harper, Seth, and Mitzi standing awkwardly on the porch. They were too powerful to be enticed into leaving. Harper had felt their gazes boring holes into her the entire time she'd been packing.

She braced herself for impact, just as she had back at the Saunders manor the month before.

"Well, go on," she said. "I know you've got shit to say."

"Why didn't you tell us about Dad?" Mitzi asked, yanking on a lock of her long red hair.

"I didn't know what to say," Harper said. "Or if you'd even believe me. You didn't seem to give a shit about Augusta."

"He tried to *kill* you." Seth glared at her. "That's pretty different from what the sheriff does with her powers."

"Seriously, Harper, did you think we wouldn't care?"

"Of course I thought you would care!" Harper hesitated. "There was just no good way to tell you."

"But your friends knew, didn't they?" Mitzi asked. "You let *them* in."

Harper caught the implication of Mitzi's words. Her siblings were right—she'd left them out. Kept the truth from them the same way so many truths had been kept from her. She hadn't intended to lie and run away, but that didn't matter. She'd done it anyway.

"I'm sorry," she said. "I should have told you the truth."

"Thank you," Seth said. "And we're sorry, too. That you felt like you couldn't."

"I just don't understand," Mitzi said. "Why did you leave us alone with him when you knew he was dangerous?"

Harper's chest ached at the betrayal in her sister's eyes.

"I know how messed up it sounds, but I think...even after everything Dad did, part of me still wanted to protect him. It felt cruel to punish him for a crime he couldn't remember committing."

So instead, she'd punished everyone *but* her father for his mistakes. The shame of it threatened to swallow her whole. But Harper knew she had to stare it down, because letting this go any further would only hurt them all more.

"Oh," Mitzi whispered, her brown eyes wide and watery.

"You deserved better," Harper continued, her voice wobbling. "I haven't exactly been the best sister, but I'm going to change that."

"I don't know if I'm ready for that," Mitzi murmured. "At least, not right now."

Seth nodded. "We need more time. To think about Dad. I know you've been sitting with this for months, but for us it's all new."

"Is this okay?" Mitzi asked anxiously.

"Yeah," Harper said. "That's okay."

She sat on the front stoop for a long while after they had both walked away. She had a patrol shift that evening. She needed to make sure her stuff was undisturbed at the town hall. But all she could think about was how *right* Seth and Mitzi were to be upset with her.

Harper's residual limb ached as she thought of how she'd shoved them both aside. She hadn't *let* them be part of her story; she hadn't told them the truth about their dad. She would give them the space they had asked for, but when they *were* ready, she hoped they would be able to heal their relationship.

Harper craved freedom, but she saw now that freedom did not mean solitude, nor did it mean avoiding responsibility and connection. It meant embracing the bonds that mattered. And it meant admitting to mistakes and regret, even when they asked her to look at the difficult, tangled pieces of herself.

She turned her gaze to the front lawn, where the statue garden stared back at her.

So far, her powers had only extended to turning things to stone. But she hadn't tested the other part. The ability that the most powerful Carlisles were known for above all else: the capability to control the stone creatures they created.

Harper saw in that moment that she'd been frightened of what might happen should she succeed, that once again her abilities might spiral out of control. But if she could make this power work, she could give them a better shot against the corruption. It was worth a try. So she shook the fear back, took a deep breath, and rose to her feet, scanning the statue garden.

There was a fox at the far edge of the lawn that seemed like a good candidate: almost perfectly preserved, eyes wide and alert. She knelt down, her heart racing, and stretched out her hand.

The stone was cool beneath her fingertips, and Harper felt her power hum through her, begging to be used, begging to show her what it could do.

For a moment she hesitated, that familiar fear threatening to overwhelm her. She didn't want this to be like when she'd run after May, or when she'd hurt the tree.

Other memories surfaced a moment later, though. Harper's hand shooting out to catch the root before it could hurt Justin. Rushing to the spire to help Violet. And at last, she understood. Her powers were only uncontrollable when she called on them from a place of rage. But she didn't want this to work because she was angry. She wanted this power to protect the people she loved.

Her palm tingled. Energy crackled through her palm and into the statue's forehead.

"Wake up," Harper whispered, and she knew before she was even finished speaking that it had worked. She watched, eyes wide, as its tail twitched, then its ears. She hesitantly removed her thumb from its forehead as the animal rose into a graceful stretch. Its sculpted, unblinking eyes were locked on her.

"I did it," she muttered, moving her hand away hesitantly from the guardian. And she *had* done it. She just wasn't sure what came next. This wasn't like the Saunderses' companions—she couldn't feel a tether like the one Violet had described.

And yet the stone fox was still gazing at her expectantly, the tip of its tail twitching.

"Hmm," she said quietly. "Will you ... guard the lake?"

The fox didn't move.

Harper pressed her fingers to its forehead and repeated the command. This time, the change was immediate. It bolted away, its stride quick and purposeful as it bounded through the maze of other statues until it was at the edge of the lake. Then it curled up in front of a tree, its eyes staring outward, and froze again.

"Whoa," Harper said. Then she turned, staring at the sea of half-disintegrated statues around her, a myriad of possibilities, an army all her own. And smiled.

Four Paths was deserted. No one loitered outside the grocer's or the bar; the general store was empty, a CLOSED sign flipped over in the window, and a deadbolt was lodged firmly across the front doors of the library. The shuttered windows gazed at them in the center of the town square like dozens of empty eye sockets.

The entire thing made Violet incredibly uneasy. It wasn't supposed to look like this. It was proof that they had lost a battle their families had been fighting for over a hundred and fifty years.

If *battle* was even the right word for it, based on what Violet had potentially discovered. Violet stared anxiously at Juniper, who was standing beside her, gazing at the photo of the letter on Violet's phone screen. Normally she would have died before willingly handing over her phone to her mother, but this patrol had been her first chance to be alone with Juniper since the announcement of the evacuation.

They'd been assigned to watch the founders' seal together, since it was clear by now that this was the most likely place the corruption would strike next. But Violet wasn't going to lose another opportunity to explain to her mother that she'd discovered something potentially important.

"Who have you shown this to?" Juniper asked sharply as soon as she was finished, lowering the screen.

"May," Violet said. "No one else. There's been so much going on—I didn't want to overwhelm them."

"Well, I appreciate you telling me that you uncovered this."
Juniper handed back the phone, her brow furrowed. "I assume
you're wondering about the validity of this potential claim?"

"Aren't you?" Violet asked hoarsely. She could not shake
the feeling that this was all tied together: the murky origins of
the Beast, the corruption invading the town's sacred places, the
humanity she sensed in her tether to the trees. She just couldn't
figure out *how*.

"I'm not wondering, I know," Juniper said softly. "Everything
you read in that letter is true."

Violet's entire body went cold. "What do you mean, you
know it's true?"

"I hoped I'd never have to tell you." Beside her, Juniper
looked utterly miserable. "But yes, Violet, it's true. Our ancestors created the Beast."

Violet's world rolled and spun frantically on its axis. Her legs
wobbled, her hands clammy with sweat. The mausoleum and the
town hall spun, all of it blurring together in her field of vision
until she thought she might pass out.

"How long?" she whispered. "How long have you known
this?"

"Oh, Violet." Juniper reached for her hand, but Violet
snatched it away.

"We said no more secrets. No more lies."

The words rang out across the deserted town square, accusatory and furious. Juniper winced beneath their weight.

"I'm sorry," she said.

"I don't want your apology." They had been through so much
together, and Juniper was still hiding things from her. After

they'd worked so hard to build trust. After Violet had finally started to feel as if she had a mother. "I want to know what you know."

Juniper's inclined head was a nod and a surrender. "It started when I was seventeen," she began. "At the time, I was tapped to be the future leader of the Saunders family. Back then, it meant being the mayor, and it came with certain knowledge in order to ensure the safety of the town, passed down from one mayor to the next."

"Knowledge like our entire family mythology being built on a *lie*?"

"It's not all a lie," Juniper said delicately. "But it *is* quite sensitive. Not even Augusta knows about this. When I regained my memories, I thought I was the only one left alive who knew the truth."

"Yeah, well, the Hawthornes have half the story now," Violet said quietly. "Secret's out, Mom. Might as well give me the rest of it."

Juniper's mouth twisted. "It is *not* a pleasant piece of information. You may not want to hear it—"

"Of course I want to hear it." Violet gaped at her. "I just learned how to trust you. Now I know I can't."

"You've made your point," Juniper said. In Violet's opinion, her mother had *not* earned the right to the wounded expression on her face. Dusk had fallen, swathing the town hall in a bluish shroud that winked iridescent in the slowly gathering mist. "And you have to understand that much of what you know *is* true. We are bound to the Beast. We draw our powers from it. It's trapped in the Gray, just as you've discovered, and we protect the town from it. Mayor Hiram—my uncle—had a saying about the story of the Beast we tell ourselves. That it's as true as most stories are, which is to say it is and it isn't."

"That just sounds like a convenient excuse for a lie."

"Perhaps." Juniper shrugged. "Regardless, the truth is messier, and it's passed down from mayor to mayor. It recounts how the founders discovered a power source when they arrived here, not a monster. When they figured out how to use it, however, it came with an unfortunate side effect."

"The Beast?"

"No." Juniper's lips thinned. "The same disease we're calling the corruption."

"So the corruption comes from *us*." The words felt like poison in Violet's throat. This disease, this nightmare—it *was* their fault after all.

"Well, yes." Juniper's footsteps sounded on the cobblestones as she came to stand beside Violet. "The founders made an attempt to stop the corruption, and it worked—but not fully."

"What exactly does that mean?"

"The founders died, which was obviously quite unintentional," Juniper said. "And the Gray was born, alongside the Beast. Again, their deaths creating the Gray is true, it's just that the *purpose* is not what you've been led to believe. It is a shield that keeps the corruption from spreading any further, and the Beast is an unfortunate side effect."

"An unfortunate side effect," Violet echoed hollowly. "How does an attempt to make a shield make a monster instead?"

"Well." Juniper sighed. "Something went wrong during the ritual, and the founders... melded with the power source. We draw our powers from the Beast because the Beast *is* an amalgamation of the founders, and their powers—the ones that corrupted Four Paths in the first place—are safe inside the Gray."

Juniper had known this back when she was a teenager, Violet realized, and on some level none of it surprised her. It made sense. More reason for her mother to run. More reason for Juniper's dread, for her insistence that she was uniquely suited to keeping Four Paths intact. She was the only one who had known what was truly going on.

"So this monster is an *accident*." Violet wanted to throw up. "So everything the people in this town look up to the founders for is just them trying to cover up a mistake."

"Perhaps that was true generations ago, but the secret died out with the founders' children. The founders now truly believe themselves to be heroes."

"I just can't believe you lied about all of this," Violet whispered. "I can't believe all of the mayors did."

Violet remembered the Beast's voice hissing in her ear: *Do you really think I was bound here out of altruism?*

She saw the founders for who they were now: people who had told themselves a story again and again until they believed it. They were cowards and liars with blood on their hands. This was the truth of her legacy, ugly and raw, ripping through her chest like a gaping wound.

"It's a lie that keeps us respected," Juniper said. "A lie that allows us to keep everyone else *safe*—"

"At what cost?" Violet shook her head. "I understand now. The founders have never really tried to destroy the Beast because the person in charge has always known it's our power source. Because they don't want their abilities taken away, and they're willing to pay for that selfishness with other peoples' *lives*."

"Or, Violet, because we don't know how to get rid of it, and this is the best we can do? Just because I know how something was broken doesn't mean I know how to fix it."

"Why should I believe you? Why should I ever believe anything you say again?"

Violet didn't know when she'd sunk to her knees. The world was still blurry, and she was still furious. The stone seal was rough beneath her jeans, but she couldn't bring herself to move.

"Listen, Violet," her mother said. "I know this is a lot to take in—"

Violet shuddered. "All this time, you could have helped us, and you stayed silent."

"That's not true," Juniper said. "I don't know why the Gray is failing now, or why the corruption is eating through it and hurting us. Something's changed, but I have no idea what."

"It still would have been helpful information to know." Violet had only been this angry at Rosie's funeral. It was an incandescent sort of rage that buoyed her even as it rooted her further in the ground. "I'm going to tell everyone in town exactly what you lied about. And I'm going to finish this fucking nightmare for good."

Juniper's face turned ashen, and Violet felt a sick rush of satisfaction that she'd finally gotten to her mother the way Juniper had gotten to her.

But then she realized that Juniper was staring not at her, but behind her.

She turned, her heart hammering in her chest.

All around her, roots were burrowing up from the seal. With them came the unmistakable stench of death.

CHAPTER TWENTY

May stared unhappily at the front of the Hawthorne house. Smoke wafted in curls above the gabled roof, but it wasn't coming from the chimney. It was coming from the tree.

The buds, once unfurled, could not be closed. Harper, Violet, and Isaac had done their best, but that was not enough to stop the air from changing. May blinked, her eyes watering in the thin film of mist that now hung around her home. It was a problem in all four of the founder territories, collected in the areas that had fallen to the corruption.

May hated it. It was a reminder of her failure. She'd tried to change the future and the cards had seized up on her. She'd been wrong about her capabilities, and the corruption had spread even farther as a result, leading to the evacuation of the town.

Which had left her with only one option: pooling her resources.

Ezra had seemed to view her inability to change the future as a mishap, not a catastrophic error, and he'd said he had another plan but it would take extra help. The time for respecting petty family rivalries was past. If Juniper Saunders could come to stay at their house, May figured she had nothing left to lose by inviting over her father. She was worried about his susceptibility to the airborne corruption, but he'd promised her that he was taking every precaution he could. May had to believe that would be enough.

His car pulled into the driveway, and she walked him to the front door, watching as he scanned the smoke rising behind the house.

"I'm so sorry," he said quietly. "The evacuation must have been hard on you."

"The evacuation was tough, but this is going to be worse," May said. "Mom's going to freak out when she sees you."

"You didn't warn her I was coming?"

"She would have told me no and grounded me until the corruption ate Four Paths alive."

"So she hasn't changed at all, then."

"Nope." May swung open the front door, took a deep breath, and gestured for her father to follow her inside.

She had known springing Ezra Bishop on the rest of her family would be an unpleasant experience. But she had not anticipated just how severely they would react when he appeared behind her in the doorway to the living room.

Augusta rose to her feet immediately, disbelief and anger mixing together on her face. Brutus and Cassius rose with her, their hackles raised defensively, while Justin remained seated, frozen.

He stared at Ezra as if he were seeing the Beast itself. It was like watching them both gaze into a mirror. Ezra had aged so well he barely looked in his thirties, let alone his fifties, and Justin had grown up in his absence. They had the same hair, the same eyes, the same wide, easy smile. But May knew already that neither of them would be smiling now, that this reunion wouldn't be anything like hers.

"What the fuck is he doing here?" Augusta asked, the words ricocheting off the wall like bullets. May rarely heard her mother swear. The word dropping out of her mouth so casually made May realize just how much she'd thrown into her family's path.

But things were desperate. She wasn't sure she'd had a choice.

"Helping," she said, meeting Augusta's eyes. "I know you're not going to be a huge fan of this idea, but he's been studying the corruption and he has a plan—"

"Studying the corruption?" Augusta snarled. "How long has he been here?"

"Augusta," Ezra said.

"I'm not talking to you." Augusta's gloved hands twitched with fury. "Ezra, sit. The dogs will keep you company. I need a word with my children."

Ezra sat nervously on the couch. Brutus and Cassius flanked him, still at full attention. A long string of drool dripped onto the floor from Brutus's gaping maw as he gazed at May's father like he was an afternoon snack. She hoped he'd still be in one piece whenever they came back.

Augusta herded Justin and May into the foyer. The moment the living room door was closed behind them, she rounded on May, her voice low but furious.

"May Elaine Hawthorne, how *long* has he *been here*?"

When Augusta was angry, she had a kind of terrifying focus. May had seen it in action many times, the way her mother could zero in on a target and immediately decide how best to eliminate it as a threat. Right now May was in the center of her mother's furious spotlight, and she knew there was only one way out: telling the truth.

"He's been in and out of town over the last few weeks," she said.

"And you didn't see fit to inform me that your father had decided to waltz back into Four Paths and make contact with you?"

"He didn't make contact with me. I invited him."

At this, Justin let out a sharp noise of disbelief.

Augusta's face twisted. "Why on earth would you do that?"

"Because we needed help." May was so tired of her family acting like any slight deviation from the Hawthornes' precious rules was a betrayal of the highest order. Following the rules had led them here, to a town on the verge of falling into a corrupted hell. As far as she was concerned, that meant the rules needed to be broken, or at least changed. "Help he's offering, if you would just be willing to *listen*—"

"You listen to me." Augusta leaned forward, tilting her head down until she was less than a foot away from her daughter. "You cannot trust that man. Any plan he wishes to put into motion will only benefit himself. It is not worth your time or consideration. So let me tell you what's going to happen: We are going to go back into the living room, and I will personally escort him out of town. He can evacuate, just like everyone else, and we will discuss your punishment for this transgression later."

"No."

May didn't even realize she'd spoken aloud until Augusta stepped back, as if she had been struck.

"No?" she repeated slowly.

"You heard me." May's heart was beating far too fast,

adrenaline coursing through her veins. She felt as if she might pass out, as if she was standing outside of her body. Never in her life had she spoken to Augusta this way. But she wasn't ready to stop. "Dad has a theory about my powers, about the corruption. About a way we might be able to stop it. I'm not giving up on that just because you told me to drop it."

"Wait." It was Justin's voice. He was staring at her with that same fearful expression May had seen as they knelt beneath the hawthorn tree. Again that memory stirred in her: his face, much younger. *Don't go downstairs, May*—but it slipped away before she could grasp it. "Is that why you said you could fix the corruption by changing the future? Because of *him*?"

"You *what*?" Augusta shook her head. "Of course. You came to me about your powers. I should have known that's where you got such a ridiculous idea."

"It isn't ridiculous!" Tears burned in the back of May's throat. Her voice had grown shrill, and she hated it—she *hated* it. "I did it before. I could do it again, if I had the right support. The right training."

"I told you, May. Some powers aren't meant for us."

"You mean *me*. Some powers aren't meant for *me*. Because it's not like you put those limits on yourself." May's voice rose. She was shaking; she was very close to screaming. "You've erased half this town's memories, but how dare I try to give any of them back. How *dare* I try to change the cards."

"When I was younger, May, I didn't know my limits. I'm trying to help you learn yours before you hurt someone you love. I don't know why you're so determined to let your father poison your mind, but I assure you that I know more about our family than he does."

"Oh, I see." May's voice was just as cruel as Augusta's. She knew how to use her anger, too. She knew how to make words hurt. "This isn't about Dad at all, is it? This is about my ritual. You *still* can't handle that the hawthorn tree chose me, not Justin. That's right, Mom, I'm powerful—more powerful than you. And it *terrifies* you, because you can't just take it away the same way you took it from Violet and Harper or control me the way you control Isaac."

"Be very careful, May," Augusta said softly. "You cannot take this back."

"Maybe I don't want to take it back." May stared at her. "Maybe you deserve to know that I see exactly what you've done to protect this town. And I think you've done a shitty job."

"I see you've made up your mind," Augusta said coldly. "If you're so determined to believe that you know everything, go on. Take him with you. Enact that brilliant plan of his and see just how well it goes for you. But if you think our family has done nothing but hurt this town, then surely you can protect us all without the gifts we've so generously given you."

She held out her hand expectantly. It took May a long, disbelieving moment to understand what she was asking for.

"The Deck of Omens doesn't belong to you," she whispered, her heart thumping painfully in her chest. "It chose me. It's *mine*."

"It belongs to the Hawthornes," Augusta said, a brutal smile flickering at the corners of her mouth. And May understood. This was her mother's trump card. If May refused to hand the deck over, she'd be a hypocrite. But if she did, she'd be powerless.

Slowly, she drew the cards from her pocket. Peeling her

fingers away and leaving them in her mother's hand felt like ripping out a vital organ with her fingernails.

"Take them, then," she said, proud of how her voice did not waver. She turned away, unable to bear even another second of watching Augusta clutch the cards triumphantly, and started toward the living room. But a hand closed around her wrist before she'd taken a single step.

"If you leave, you're betraying us." Justin's eyes were wide with panic, his hand clammy around her arm. He paused, gasping for breath, and May felt a stab of unease. He hadn't been running. Why was he so tired? "Just stay for a few minutes, all right? I want to talk to you about Dad. About your powers—"

May shook him off. She was done listening to her family's excuses.

"You've betrayed us for the so-called greater good a hundred times," she told him. "Seems right that I finally get a turn to save the day, don't you think?"

The forest was eerily silent. All sounds of life were absent except the rustling of May's footsteps in the dead leaves as the sun set around them. Before long, the ground grew soft and squishy beneath May's feet and the smell of corruption began to rise around her, stronger than she remembered. It was the smell of lost and ancient things, the smell of despair, the smell of death. But May headed deeper into the trees anyway. All she wanted to do was get as far away from her family as possible.

Well, *most* of her family.

"I must say," mused Ezra from beside her. "That was deeply unpleasant."

"I can't believe she threatened you with the dogs," May muttered angrily. "She had *no right—*"

"It is her choice to decide not to take my help," Ezra said. "I wish she were capable of changing her patterns, but both Augusta and your brother are unfortunately set in their ways."

"Yeah, tell me about it." May shoved down the awful things she'd said to them, the guilt she felt. She was tired of feeling like she would never be enough. There was someone who valued her abilities, who actually believed in nurturing her powers instead of suppressing them. That felt like a far healthier thing to focus on. "So. About this plan..."

"Ah. Yes." Ezra brightened up visibly behind his glasses. "As I said before, May, it would have been lovely to have their help, but they aren't necessary. The only part of this that's required is *you.*"

"But I failed," May said softly. "When I tried to change the future, the cards went blank. And the corruption got *worse.*"

Augusta taking the cards away stung more than anything else. She was disarmed. Declawed. But refusing would have been worse—would have felt like a different kind of loss.

"That's because we both miscalculated how strong the corruption would be," Ezra said. "You're strong too, but it will require more ability than you currently possess to destroy it. This ritual will grant you the power you need."

"But I don't have the cards. How can I—"

"Don't worry." Ezra's voice was soothing. "We won't need them."

The Sullivan ruins crested the horizon a moment later. May could barely see them through the haze of twilight and the smoke of the airborne corruption.

"Be careful," she told her father, handing him a cloth to wrap around his face. "I know you said you're safe, but I don't want you getting corrupted."

"Very thoughtful of you, May." He tied it around the bottom of his face and led her forward, into the thickening mist.

"Where are we going?" she said.

Ezra's gaze went solemn behind his glasses. Again, his words were muffled by the fabric. "In order to do this right, May, we must bind you more closely to the Beast. And we can only do that from inside the Gray."

Inside the Gray. May's heartbeat sped up at the thought, but they were out of other options. She would have to go through with this, however risky it was.

Whatever mist was pouring out of the corrupted flowers had thinned the walls between Four Paths and the Gray until it was as easily ripped apart as paper. Isaac had already warned them that it would be easy to stumble through at the founders' ritual sites, but May supposed that right now stumbling through was the plan. She stared, horrified, at the way the world shifted and changed between the trees, flickering back and forth between her world and the Beast's prison. All around her, flower petals twisted and twitched, a slight discoloration at their edges that reminded May of fingernails.

"Stick with me," she told Ezra, grasping for his arm in the darkness as they headed for the center of the churning fog. "Most humans don't do too well in the Gray."

May did her best to keep up the pretense of bravery as the fog engulfed them a moment later, but it wavered when a familiar voice rang out inside her head.

Fog rushed around them a moment later. *Seven of Branches,* it hissed, *Seven of Branches*—but May pushed it down. The fog thickened as they stumbled forward, and then May felt the world change around them in the matter of a single heartbeat. It was frightening to her, how easily they had stepped through a hole in the world. The fog cleared, and May blinked into the flat, surreal brightness of the Gray's staticky sky.

The first thing May noticed was that the corruption was even worse here than it was in Four Paths. They were near the Sullivan estate, which was still intact here, a small cabin that looked nothing like the mansion May had known before Isaac had destroyed it. May inspected the tree nearest to her, her stomach churning as she tracked the silvery veins running beneath the places where the bark had peeled back. The tree looked far too much like human skin, but skin leached of all color, gray and bloated as a corpse.

Seven of Branches, the voice snarled in the back of her mind. *Don't—*

She pushed it down.

"Where should we do the ritual?" she asked, turning to Ezra. Her voice rasped out a second later than her lips moved—it was disorienting. "Here?"

"No." To her surprise, he didn't seem frightened of the Gray at all. She supposed he'd probably heard a lot about it before— maybe he knew what to expect. "There's a place that's more important to the founders than this. It's a direct conduit to the Beast, and it will allow you to channel it more quickly."

May understood immediately. "The founders' seal."

"Exactly."

"Why didn't we just go into the Gray there?"

"The walls aren't thinned like they are here, in the places

where the corruption has already eaten them away," Ezra said, shrugging. "This was our gate. Now come on. Let's get going."

A copse of trees grew around the founders' seal. They were corrupted at a level May had not yet seen. Hanks of human hair grew from the branches in knotted, tangled clumps. Corrupted flowers bloomed across their branches, waving in a grotesque parody of human arms. And beneath their silver veins, pulsating gently inside each of the trees, was the thin, glowing outline of a human heart.

"Holy shit," May whispered, the words echoing a second too late as she watched the heart move.

She remembered with a sickening rush how many times she had felt the hawthorn tree's deep, steady heartbeat over the years. The dull thudding of these trees' heartbeats coursed through her, sluggish and strange. All of it was *wrong* on a level May could barely conceptualize: a forest of flesh, as if the trees were doing their best to become human but did not know how to put all the pieces together.

She needed to stop this *now*.

In the center of the founders' seal was a tree stump. Silvery veins radiated out from it, climbing over the seal. Inside the bark, spilling over the edges, was a boiling cauldron of iridescent gray liquid. Noxious smoke rose from it and wafted through the air. It was identical to the smoke pouring out of the flowers.

"What *is* this?" May gasped, turning to look at her father.

You know what it is, hissed the voice, so familiar, *too* familiar. *You know, you know, you know—*

"It's the center of town." Ezra was standing beside her now. May felt a slight rush of wooziness as she turned to look at him.

281

"This stump contains the closest thing Four Paths has to the glue that binds it together. It's the place the founders did their ritual to create the Gray and bind the beast. It will allow you to strengthen your own bond."

"How?"

"By drinking from it."

"You've got to be joking." May's stomach churned. "I am *not drinking that*."

"It will strengthen your bond," Ezra said calmly. "Desperate times call for—"

"No." May stared at him. He looked far too natural here. The voice screamed in her mind again, louder this time, and she could not tell anymore if it was hers or something else's. All she knew was that both her brain and the voice were saying the same thing: *Run*. "What do you want, Dad? What do you *really* want?"

"Would you truly like to know?"

May nodded, unease coursing through her. Something was wrong here. Something was *very* wrong.

Ezra reached forward and grabbed her hand in his, and suddenly, violently, they were somewhere else.

May knew immediately that it was a memory. She was *inside* Ezra's head somehow, the same way Augusta could sort through people's memories and pluck out the ones that displeased her. But how could he have founder powers? It simply wasn't possible.

Ezra's head turned, and May's heart stopped.

She was sitting in the center of Four Paths, but it was not the Four Paths she lived in now. Nor was it the one she'd seen in the Gray—not exactly, anyway. The buildings were old and barely buildings at all, the same dirt road branching out where Main

Street was now, the same trees covering the lot where there would one day be a mausoleum. But everything was in color, from the green, verdant leaves on the chestnut oaks to the deep blue sky above her head. She lowered her chin—*Ezra's chin*—and saw that he was sitting on the founders' seal, still made of stone. It was the only piece of all of this that remained unchanged.

"It is time," said a voice beside her, high and oddly familiar. "The power doesn't belong to us—we have to give it back."

She turned and saw a woman. The face was sharp and clever, angular and wild, with blond hair parted in the center and pulled back in elaborate, looping braids. May knew immediately that this memory was far older than humanly possible. There was the dress the woman wore, with closely fitted sleeves and a row of buttons that traced from the high neckline down to the gathered waist—something out of a history textbook. And there was also the matter of that face, because May recognized it.

It was Hetty Hawthorne's face.

She was staring at a founder.

May's shock only multiplied as she turned her head and realized that Hetty was not alone.

She had spent her entire life trying to live up to these people's legacy, and here were Hetty, Thomas Carlisle, and Lydia Saunders, all of them sitting on the town seal, in the same places the founder descendants now sat during the Founders' Day ceremony every year.

It didn't make sense that Ezra could show her this. It didn't make any sense at *all*.

"You're right that we have to end this," Ezra's voice said in the memory. May felt him pull the blade from his coat pocket. "But not the way you think we do."

He lunged ahead, a woman screamed, and suddenly time skipped forward. The founders' bodies lay at her feet—Ezra's feet—sprawled limply on the ground. There was blood, so much blood, dripping down the four lines that crossed toward the center of the seal. May had never seen so much in one place. And she had never seen blood *change* like this, foaming and steaming, slowly fading to gray.

Silvery veins began to spread from the center of the seal, cutting across the ground. And then the founders' bodies began to change, too. May watched them twist and writhe, their eyes turning bleach-white, their skin bloating and graying. Their bodies began to disintegrate into iridescent liquid, and then gray spread across the whole world, draining it of all color.

This will never be yours, hissed a voice, tinny and furious.

"No," Ezra's voice snarled. He reached out a bloodstained hand. "Where *are* you? Where have you gone?"

The scene faded out, then, and she was back in the Gray.

May stared at her father, her stomach churning, and said the last three words she ever would have dreamed of.

"You're Richard Sullivan."

Her father flourished his arm and bent down into a mock bow. "In the flesh."

"But . . ." she whispered. "How?"

"I took their powers as they died," he said, shrugging. "That Saunders immortality looks good on me, don't you think?"

It explained a lot. It explained too much. May knew that if she lived through this, it would take her a long, long time to sort through all of it, through the impossibility and ugliness of her very existence. But right now she had to think. She had to keep him talking, because he was telling her things that were actually useful. She could fall apart later.

"So then you *have* power," May said, frowning. "You have . . . everything. Why would you bring me here? Why would you tell me this?"

"Stop!" The voice rang out through the Gray, through the trees. May whirled around, her mind struggling to process the sight before her. Justin, bedraggled and sweaty, staring at them both with abject horror. May wanted to believe it was the Beast playing tricks on her, but she knew better. Her brother had followed them into the forest, into the Gray.

"Justin," she said. "What are you doing here?"

"I'm taking you home." Justin stared at her, determination written across his face.

"Well." Ezra—no, Richard—smiled slowly. "This is unexpected."

"Get out of here," May gasped. "He isn't who he says he is. Justin, I don't know how much of that you heard—"

"I heard enough," Justin said grimly. *"Richard."*

"You poor boy." Her father's voice was so soft, May barely heard the words. "You should not have followed us."

"Justin," May said again. "Run—"

But it was too late.

The roots around her moved, whipping into action. They bound Justin's arms and legs and forced him to his knees, his eyes wide with panic. He didn't even have time to scream before they slid across his mouth.

May rounded on her father. "Let him go!"

"No," Richard said hoarsely. "Not unless you drink."

May could not think, could not breathe. Her brother was here. Her brother was in terrible danger—they both were—and it was all her fault.

All she could think to do was keep Richard talking.

"Please," she said, extending a shaking hand. "Just explain why you even need *me* at all. Don't you have all the power you ever could have wanted?"

"No!" The word burst through his careful mask, and then Richard breathed, reeling his fury back in. It disturbed her to see how he could put his anger on and take it off again. "Their powers—our powers—are weak reflections of the true magic here. But the other founders were frightened of that power. It caused the corruption, and they wanted to stop it, even if it meant all of us losing our abilities. I couldn't let that happen."

"So you killed them." May's voice was hollow.

"I did what I had to do," Richard said. "But I didn't realize that their deaths meant I would be locked away from the source of our power. It took many years before I figured out that I would not be able to override their sacrifice in order to get my full powers back on my own. Someone else would have to do it."

"Someone else. You mean *me*."

Ezra—Richard—nodded. "You are the bridge between the Gray and Four Paths, May. You're a conduit, a mediator, and instead of keeping them apart"—he smiled—"you will bring them together, and you will give me the reward I've been chasing for a hundred and fifty years."

"I have no idea what you're talking about," May said, hot tears gathering in her throat. "I'm not capable of any of the things you just said."

"Yes, you are," Richard said, steepling his fingers thoughtfully beneath his chin. "When you use the Deck of Omens, May, you're asking a question. Who do you think is answering it?"

The voice. It had whispered at the edge of her consciousness for the past year, and she had tried to drown it out, push it back. But it had only grown stronger. May thought of all the words she had used for what she was communicating with when she used her powers. The roots. The tree. The town. None of them had ever been right. But they had all been so much safer than what she'd feared in the back of her mind, a truth that she could only face now that so many more terrifying truths had come to light.

"The Beast." May could barely choke the words out. And he nodded, and her world crumbled.

Her power wasn't seeing the future at all—it was talking to a monster.

"But it doesn't just answer you," Richard continued. "It *listens*, as it did when you changed the cards. It calls to you, even as you destroy it."

He raised a hand.

May hit the ground with a yell as roots twined around her legs and feet, anchoring her to the soft, loamy earth. Something slithered from the corner of her eye and down her cheek—a root, spiraling down her face like a wandering vein. It hooked on the inside of her lip. May snarled and bit it, spitting out bits of bark before they could make it down her throat. The sap inside it tasted rotten.

She struggled to no avail as the roots grabbed her wrists and yanked her forward, slamming her palm onto the nearest tree.

Dread surged through May's stomach. She snatched her hand away from the tree—the roots let her do that, at least—and gaped wordlessly. Her handprint was burned into the trunk. Spreading out from it were writhing silver roots, infecting the corrupted tree even further.

With a sudden, sickening lurch, May put it all together. She'd been trying to figure out what had changed in the town to start this, when *she* had been the one to change things. Which meant...

"It's me." She could barely get the words out. "You said our powers are weak reflections of the founder powers, but the founder powers are what cause the corruption, aren't they? And if I have Hetty's power...I started the corruption when I decided to mess with the future."

In front of her, Justin let out a horrified sound. She locked eyes with him and realized that he was no longer looking at her like she was something to save, but like something he would have to defeat.

It was a look that broke her heart, because she knew she deserved it.

"You did." Richard's voice was far too gentle, a feather when it should have been a razor's edge. "And you should be very proud. But you must grow stronger before you can use that corruption to destroy the Beast. Before you"—he gestured to the cauldron—"is the essence of the forest, the power of Four Paths itself, the power that runs through your veins. I wasn't lying. It *will* help you master your abilities."

"And it will help *you* hurt everyone I love."

"They don't love you." His voice broke on the last word, descending into a vicious growl. For a moment, the expression on his face flickered, and May saw the deep, unending fury beneath the mask he'd shown her.

"That's not true—"

"Look at how your brother fears you already." His voice was soft again. "Why are you resisting when you know there's nowhere for you to go home to, now that they know you're the one behind the corruption? That there's blood on your hands?"

He knelt beside her then, tucked a lock of blond hair behind her ear. Wiped a smudge of grime off her face as if she were a child who'd fallen.

"You have talent, May. Talent that none of them can appreciate. Talent I *gave* you. So use it."

May had grown up with the weight of the world on her shoulders—her father's strange expectations, her mother's eternal disappointment, and the town's perpetual disdain, no matter how well she performed the job she'd been born to do.

Maybe her father was right. Maybe it was too late for her to do anything but accept the fate she had so willingly led herself to.

"I'm losing patience," her father said above her.

He waved a hand in the air, and a tree root snaked across Justin's exposed throat. Justin let out a muffled noise of pain as it began to tighten.

It took everything May had—but she did not flinch. Did not shudder. The only way to make him stop this would be to pretend it didn't bother her.

"Is that what you think will do it?" she asked coolly. "Threatening Justin? You wouldn't kill your own son."

His grin in the light of the cauldron was ghoulish. "You have no idea what I'm capable of."

"That's not true," May said softly, as, behind them, the sounds of Justin choking began to echo through the clearing.

"You killed your friends. You had children because you thought we were *tools*. But you taught me to be just as cruel, just as ruthless, as you."

"You are weaker than you pretend to be," Richard said. The roots continued to tighten around Justin's throat. "And you cannot fool me, little Hawthorne. I'll let him die—but you won't."

The noises coming from her brother's throat were unimaginable; his face was turning blue, swelling. She could see the veins in his neck bulging out, the panic in his eyes.

Something unfurled in the back of her mind, the same doorway that opened whenever she did a reading. The voice was faint and hoarse, the quietest it had ever been, but she heard it anyway.

Drink, it said. *Drink and I will help you.*

May had nothing left to lose. Maybe this would kill her. Maybe it would make her Richard's puppet. But maybe—just maybe—the Beast was telling her the truth.

She lifted her head and made eye contact with her father.

"You win," she said, her stomach churning. "Let him go, and I'll drink."

He grinned, and immediately the vines around Justin's neck unfurled. For a moment, he remained dazed, his head drooping, and then he breathed deeply, his eyes locking on hers once more. May sagged with relief as Justin coughed and raised himself up.

"Good," she said, trying to force her voice not to shake. "Now promise me you'll let him leave unharmed."

Richard frowned at her. "I did not agree to that."

"Please," May said. "He's your *son*. I know you care about him, at least a little."

"You're wrong," said Richard. "I don't care about him." May's heart sank. "But . . . I care about you."

He turned to Justin. "Run, before I change my mind."

But Justin hesitated, and May knew why.

"Don't try to free me," she whispered.

"May—"

"*Don't*," she repeated. "He'll kill you. You need to go."

Justin looked at her one last time—and bolted. May sighed with relief as he disappeared from view. She hoped he could get out of the Gray on his own.

"Now, then," Richard said slowly. "Your end of the bargain. Or I could hunt him down and dispose of him right now, if you like."

"That won't be necessary," May said. "You can release me. I won't run—I give you my word."

"You can't run," he said lazily, but he waved a hand and obliged. May rose on her own two feet and closed the remaining distance between herself and the bubbling liquid.

Up close, the smell was overpowering. May gagged, shuddering, as her eyes traced the patterns left in the iridescent liquid. She swore that if she looked closely enough she could see entire stories playing out, figures living and dying in an endless cycle, an entire world inside this cauldron in the rotting, dying remnants of her home. It was harder than May liked to wrench her focus away.

"Drink," Richard said as the fumes made her eyes water, as the patterns swirled before her again and again. He dipped his own hands in the liquid and pulled them out, grinning, liquid pooling between his palms. "Go on."

May reached inside the stump and scooped out a handful of liquid, warm and steaming in her fingers, then held it reluctantly to her mouth. The liquid poured down her throat, thick and viscous. She gagged, coughing—but it was too late. She could feel it coursing through her, hot and strange.

Her body convulsed, and the door at the back of her mind swung wide open. A voice swirled around her, but it was three voices, not one, and she saw visions of skulls and daggers and melting trees dancing around her, hazy and iridescent.

Come home, the voices whispered. *Come home, Seven of Branches.*

And then there was nothing.

PART FOUR
THE BEAST

CHAPTER TWENTY-ONE

Harper's sword had never looked better. It was polished and buffed to perfection, the steel gleaming in the glow of Isaac's living room lamp.

"You really are always ready to fight, aren't you?"

Harper looked up to see Isaac standing in his bedroom door, his arms crossed, his mouth a thin line of unease.

"What?" Harper smiled at him. "Scared?"

He rolled his eyes. "Just keep your weapons away from my books."

Harper was well aware that polishing her weapons in the middle of Isaac Sullivan's apartment intimidated him. It was why she had absolutely no intention of stopping.

Crashing here hadn't exactly been her first choice, but she wasn't emotionally prepared to stay with her siblings at the Carlisle cottage—or Justin at the Hawthorne house. So Harper had chosen to join Violet at the town hall instead, even though it meant she had to be on Isaac's turf.

She had lost herself in the familiar rhythms of preparing for a fight when a knock sounded on the apartment door.

"Are you there?" Justin's voice drifted through the room, ragged and upset. "Isaac, open up—"

Harper and Isaac both rushed for the door. The surprise on Justin's face when he saw them standing beside each other was quickly eclipsed by distress. He looked awful, eyes red and puffy, panting and sweaty from a clear sprint over to the town hall.

And Harper didn't understand how, but in that moment she and Isaac somehow knew exactly what to do. Isaac shut the door behind Justin and rushed for his first-aid kit, while Harper guided him to the couch.

"What *happened*?" Harper asked as Isaac emerged with a towel. Justin accepted it wordlessly, wiping the sweat from his forehead. He looked horrible, clammy and pale, his skin drained of color and his hair glimmering with iridescent bits of slime.

"Water?" he croaked.

"Already on it," Isaac called from the kitchen. "Now tell us what the hell is going on."

"It's May." Justin's eyes locked on Harper's, wide with panic. "She's in terrible danger. We need to call Augusta—"

"Slow down." Now that the spaces between them had been closed once, it felt far too easy to do it again. Her hand fit automatically into his, where he curled his fingers around hers so tightly that it was almost painful. "We'll figure it out. Isaac?"

"My phone isn't working," he said. "Is yours?"

Harper spared a glance at hers, sitting screen-up on the table. "Huh. No service. Not even Wi-Fi."

Not that that was much of a loss. Isaac called his Wi-Fi network the Sanctum, which had made Harper roll her eyes so hard it actually hurt a little bit.

"Same here," Isaac said, reappearing in the living room with a mason jar full of ice water. His eyes flickered over their clasped hands, but he said nothing. "Do you think the corruption is messing with the signal?"

"I don't know," Harper said as Justin grabbed the water glass and drained it in a few quick swallows. "Justin, what's going on with May?"

Justin's brow furrowed. But before he could speak, the lamp beside them flickered. A second later, every light in the room went out, plunging them into pitch darkness.

"Shit!" Isaac swore, tripping over something and clattering into a wall. Harper sat stock-still, waiting impatiently for her eyes to adjust to the change in light. She could see something moving outside the window, shifting and slithering in the air. Smoke. The corruption had spread—again.

"Violet and her mom are supposed to be patrolling down there," Harper breathed. "Justin, did you see them? Did you see anything weird?"

"I went in through the back," Justin said hoarsely. "I wasn't really looking."

"Well, *something's* wrong," Isaac murmured from in front of the window. Harper joined him a moment later.

In the last vestiges of the fading twilight, she saw movement: saplings, their veins glowing silver in the night, weaving together in front of the founders' seal in the center of the town square. A mushroom cloud of dark gray smoke rose from their unfurling branches. Violet stood before it, her arms outstretched, red hair blown back from her face with the force of the whipping wind. There was no sign of Juniper at all.

"She's trying to hold it back." There was something like awe in Isaac's voice.

A great *crack* sounded through the sky above them. The clouds ripped open, dusk fading to off-white while the Gray poured through. Harper watched, horrified, as it cascaded out in a great wave, the trees at the edge of the town square transforming before her eyes from brown to gray. The world was warping far more quickly than she'd ever thought possible; with every breath, the fog rolled closer to them, creeping across the treetops like extending hands.

The founders' seal was falling, and Violet was still out there. Harper saw no hesitation in her stance, even as Orpheus's small form wound angrily around her ankles.

"She's not going to run." The words were heavy on Harper's tongue as she turned to Isaac and Justin.

"I know," Justin said.

"Come on," Isaac added. Something glinted in Harper's peripheral vision, and she realized what he was holding: her sword. "We need to get her inside."

Harper grabbed the weapon from his hand and nodded. Justin started to get up, but as one, they turned to him and glared.

"No," Harper said sharply. "You're not okay. Rest."

All this time she'd thought of herself and Isaac as opposites. He was pretentious and tormented, unable to handle the power that had been heaped on him, while she'd clawed her way to everything she had. Now, as she followed him down the stairs and through the foyer of the town hall, she realized that she'd had it all wrong.

They were both careful with their loyalties. Both emotionally hesitant because of how deeply they felt everything. And when they cared for someone, they would not hesitate to rush into the line of fire to save them.

Harper had experienced the equinox before, where the lines between the Gray and Four Paths blurred. But she had never seen anything like *this*. Iridescent ash fell from the cracks in the sky like rain, swirling in the wind. The trees that had grown around the founders' seal were grotesque, pulsating things—their roots snarled and knotted together like conjoined fingers. She could feel the spread of corruption through the town, the creep of a death rattle. She hoped Mitzi and Seth were safe, even though they were angry with her. She hoped everyone else had truly left Four Paths.

She didn't feel like she was in the real world anymore, and yet this did not feel like the Gray, either—it was both and neither, it was something outside of time, outside of space.

Violet was only a few yards away from the town hall, but it felt as if it had taken years to reach her by the time her thin frame came into view. Roots had wound around her ankles, and she was clutching Orpheus for dear life, the cat's head buried in her chest.

"What are you doing here?" she gasped at the sight of them.

"Helping you escape." Isaac's hands began to glow. He knelt down and set about disintegrating the roots holding Violet in place, while Harper used her sword to slash through the remaining bits of tree. But they were growing fast, faster than Harper had seen before. A root snaked beneath Isaac's foot, tripping him, while another one tried to yank her left leg out from under her. Harper kicked it away.

"Here," Violet gasped, shoving Orpheus into Isaac's arms. "Take him."

The cat squirmed for a moment, but settled almost immediately. Violet turned, a wild expression on her face, and stretched out her arms again.

"You can't fight this!" Isaac said desperately.

"I'm just trying to hold it back." Tears leaked from the corners of Violet's eyes, sliding down her cheeks. Harper felt a rush of relief as the roots attacking them slowed, then stilled. "We have a few seconds," Violet said. "Run."

They did, bolting back through the mist. Harper had no idea how Isaac knew what direction to go in, but she had never been so happy to see the steps of the town hall appear in front of her. A moment later, they had pushed open the door and collapsed in the foyer, all panting on the cold marble floor.

"Well, okay, then," Isaac mumbled from beside Harper. She turned and realized, to her great amusement, that Orpheus did not appear ready to let go of him. He'd tucked his entire body into Isaac's jacket, quivering. All that was visible was his gray-striped tail and the tips of his ears, one adorned as always with red yarn. "Uh, Violet? Do you want him back?"

But Violet didn't even seem to notice. She was already on her feet, riffling through her pockets. "Mom went to get the sheriff as soon as the seal fell," she said to Harper. "Is there still no service? We couldn't call anybody."

"Yeah, none of our phones are working."

Violet frowned. "I hope she's all right."

"You said she was going to find Augusta, yeah?" Isaac asked. "She's probably safe at the Hawthorne house."

"She'd better be," Violet murmured. "I should try to go find her."

"It's not safe out there," Harper said gently. "Your mom can protect herself. And she wouldn't want you running into danger."

Violet scowled at her, but Harper could tell she'd seen reason.

"Fine," she mumbled. "Well, I'm glad you two are here; I have something terrible to tell you—"

"So does Justin, apparently," Harper said, pushing open the door to Isaac's apartment. In their absence, Justin had lit candles, casting the room in a dim glow. At the sight of all three of them, the boy in question stepped forward, his face creased into a relieved smile.

"You're all okay," Justin said hoarsely, and then he turned to Isaac. "Huh. I guess you made a friend."

"He won't let go." Isaac attempted again to dislodge Orpheus, but the cat let out a hiss in protest. "Violet, can't you *do something* about this?"

"I don't control him." Violet's lips twitched with amusement. "Don't worry. He'll detach when he calms down."

"His claws are digging into my stomach."

"I think you'll live. Try scratching behind his ears; he likes that."

"Enough." Harper turned to all three of them. "Talk."

Violet's story was terrifying on its own, relaying the unpleasant truths of the secrets the founders had kept from their own flesh and blood. But Harper's horror only grew as Justin described who Ezra really was, the true nature of May's power, and the impossible decision that he'd forced upon her, with Justin's life on the line. After he was done, the room was silent for a long, unpleasant moment, until at last Isaac spoke.

"So you really believe he's Richard Sullivan?"

"I really do," Justin said grimly. "He used powers in a way I've never seen anyone do before."

"But what does that mean for you and May?" Violet asked.

Justin shrugged. "I've always known my dad was a scumbag. Now I just know he's an even bigger scumbag."

Isaac spoke then. "Do you think Augusta—"

"No." Justin looked haunted. "I don't think she did. Two founders make a dud, remember?" He gestured toward himself. "May only got the powers because he did something to her—bound her to the Beast the same way he bound himself."

"Shit," Isaac breathed.

Harper shuddered, thinking of Ezra Bishop—a Sullivan. *The* Sullivan. Of May in his clutches. May was tough, she knew that, but Harper had no idea what was happening to her, what unleashing the corruption on the town at this magnitude had done to her. Harper understood exactly how that kind of betrayal felt. The way it turned you inside out, made you into someone new, someone *worse.*

"So we're safe for as long as May can hold out against him," she said. "He can't finish this without her."

"May's strong," Isaac pointed out.

"We all are," Harper said. "But that's not the point. We shouldn't have to be."

She wanted a world where girls did not need to grow a spine of steel just to survive. Where they could be as soft and silly as they wanted. Where they could walk into a room full of new people and see endless possibilities instead of potential threats.

"No, we shouldn't," Violet said. "But we're cut off from everyone else, and we're the only four people with some idea of what's going on. That means we're the only ones who have a real chance of stopping Richard Sullivan before he gets even more powerful."

"How do we do that?" Isaac asked.

Violet twisted a lock of crimson hair around her finger, shadows flickering across her face in the candlelight. "The story Juniper told me was missing a piece. The founders' ritual to stop the corruption didn't fail because they did it wrong. It failed because Richard murdered them. Which means if we finish the job the founders tried to do, we can fix this."

"But how can we figure out what the founders did?" Isaac asked.

And then came a soft, gentle voice from the last person Harper expected.

"I have an idea," Justin said.

May woke up with the taste of guilt and bile in her mouth. Everything hurt; her limbs and torso ached in a way that felt soul-deep, as if she'd been ripped apart and sewn crudely back together.

She didn't want to open her eyes. She was too frightened of what she would see: the corrupted trees in the Gray, Justin's veins bulging out in his neck, the bubbling cauldron she'd been forced to drink from, or—worst of all—her father's sick, smiling face.

But when she finally forced herself to look, she was no longer in the Gray.

Instead, she was lying in the same place she'd seen at Justin's birthday party: fog drifting around her, branches knitting together above her head. Roots spiraled below her body like a bed, and through it all thumped a heartbeat, slow and steady, one May knew as well as her own. She rolled over and braced her hands against the roots, realizing as she sat up that she recognized where she was. Beneath the roots was the smooth gray stone of the founders' seal, but she was no longer here with her father, and that horrible cauldron of a tree stump was gone. Instead, she was alone in the center of another vision.

She should have been terrified. And yet on some bone-deep level she felt safe. No harm would come to her from this place. The only thing she had to fear was Ezra—*no,* Richard.

"What's going on?" she murmured, the words echoing through the drifting mist. And then came the last thing she expected: a response.

You asked for help, said a voice inside her mind, a little tinny and unfocused around the edges, like a radio with bad reception. *I'm afraid I could not protect you from Richard, but—* The words cut out and she heard hissing, spitting static instead.

"I'm sorry," she said, frowning. "I can't hear you."

The cards! cried the voice. *Use the cards—* And then it cut out again.

May had been forced to leave the Deck of Omens at home. And yet when she looked to her left, she saw a small box sitting on the roots with an all-seeing eye carved into the top.

A shiver ran down her spine.

She flipped open the box, drew out the cards. They felt real as ever between her fingers as she began to shuffle them, comforting and solid. Like home.

"What are you trying to tell me?" she asked aloud, and to her great relief she felt the question course through her, a tether of power that had come back to her once again. The cards began to disappear in her hands a moment later, until only five were left.

She laid out the first one—the Seven of Branches, her card— and felt the connection in her mind click back into place.

There you are, the voice whispered in her mind, sounding relieved. *Hello, Seven of Branches.*

"Hello," May said softly, feeling raw inside. "Beast."

So you've finally figured it out.

"Yes." Some part of her had known before her father had said it aloud, but it was undeniable now. With a surge of shame, May thought of all the things the Beast knew about her. It had seen so many of her ugliest, pettiest desires; in some ways, it understood her better than her own family did. "Is it true? That my power has just been . . . talking to you, all this time?"

Yes and no. The Beast's voice was deep and mournful. She could hear more clearly now that it was not one voice, but several speaking in unison. *Richard did not lie to you. He created you in an attempt to destroy me.*

"Destroy you?" May fought back a hysterical surge of laughter. *That* certainly would have solved a lot of Four Paths' problems. "I don't understand."

You will, it said. *Now that you're listening. Keep going, Seven of Branches.*

May flipped the second card over. It was the Six of Branches, her mother's card—and a moment later a vision of Augusta Hawthorne appeared in front of her, cross-legged and thoughtful, her eyes hooded with disapproval.

May gasped and scrambled backward. "Mom?"

My apologies. Augusta's head rose; her eyes met May's, and she realized that they were flat and lifeless instead of icy blue, that this Augusta was a little wispy and indistinct around the edges, like she was imperfectly formed. *I wasn't certain how I would appear to you, but I suppose this makes sense.*

"It's messed up." May forced her voice not to shake. "Talking to me through her like that."

Your mind chose her, the Beast said. *I do not pretend to understand the intricacies inherent in each of the founders' minds, only that you are all terribly unique and exhausting, and keeping up with your entanglements has frankly been impossible.*

"I feel the same way half the time." May sighed. And then she remembered what she was actually talking to, and she met her mother's lifeless gaze again. "What do you actually look like? What *are* you?"

That, the Beast said, *is rather complicated.*

"This isn't the time to be vague," she said as she flipped the third card over. "I need to understand." The art painted on the Deck of Omens revealed the Crusader. The sight of her father's card made her hands shake, her stomach churn.

Augusta's face twisted with regret. *When the founders came to Four Paths, they didn't find a monster. They found a forest with power, and they took it for their own. They did not understand then that they were never meant to bind themselves to this magic. They were not prepared for the way their humanity changed the forest, nor the way the forest changed their humanity. It created a grotesque problem—a plague, of sorts, spreading through the town and the trees.*

"So the picture Richard showed me wasn't a lie either," she said slowly. "The founders *did* know about the corruption. It goes back that far."

They did. And the more they used their powers, the worse it became. Desperate, they decided to try to give their powers back, to fix it.

"But Richard betrayed them?"

Yes. He believed he could sacrifice them to the forest and steal their powers. But the founders refused to yield to him as they died, and instead they created a shield, something that would lock Richard out. A world he could not access. Powers he could not reach.

"The Gray," May said slowly.

Not just the Gray, Augusta said. *They created me. I am the forest you live in, Seven of Branches, I am the town you love so much. I am your home. And I am the people who gave their lives so long ago, the gods you worshipped, and now the demon you wish to kill.*

May saw it suddenly, like a vision. The three founders' bodies melting into the ground and winding together. The way the forest felt like one great, gigantic organism to her, the way it was *alive* not just as all nature was, but a step beyond that. The hair and flesh on the trees. The roots burrowing beneath people's skin. All of it now made a sick sort of sense to May.

Violet had been right. The founders had made this monster, and their descendants were still paying for it. *She* was still paying for it.

Because of the ritual she'd done as a child, May's powers came from the Beast the same way the original founders had gotten their powers from the forest. Her strength had brought back the corruption they'd created, started this whole nightmare over again.

All this time, she'd believed that her father had seen something special in her. Now she knew that all he'd seen was the promise of death and destruction for his own personal gain.

"But why do you kill people, then?" May asked slowly, thinking of the body count the Beast left in its wake. "If you were created to protect the Gray from Richard..."

Blood is needed to keep the corruption from spreading further, to keep me strong. We have kept it at bay by taking from the town. But most people do not satiate us for long. It is founder blood we crave, founder blood we need.

May flipped the fourth card over, her stomach clenching.

A boy knelt in the center of a clearing, three swords hanging over his head. He was on his knees, arms outstretched; but he did not look like he was pleading. He looked defiant. He looked furious.

"Isaac," May breathed, understanding at last. "Is that why the Sullivans kill each other? Because Richard didn't die like the other founders?"

Yes, the voice hissed.

"That is so messed up," May mumbled. "That's why you tried to possess Violet—you wanted more."

Yes. The word coursed through her, laced with such *need*, May almost agreed with it—and then she pulled her mind back. The Beast might be trying to help her, but it was still dangerous. It was a monster that hadn't asked to be a monster, and May did not know what to do about that or how to fix it. And there was only one card left.

"There has to be a way to stop this," May said. "A way where you don't kill more people. A way where the corruption stops."

We thought so too, long ago, sang the voices in her ear. She knew who they belonged to now: Thomas Carlisle, Lydia Saunders, Hetty Hawthorne. *But Richard killed us before we could change anything.*

"So how do I stop him?"

You are stronger now, the voices mused. *And we are dying. You could destroy us and take the power he wants for yourself, if you wish. But that will not stop the corruption.*

"So if you die, the corruption spreads," May said slowly. "And if you live, I find some way to halt the corruption, and I defeat my dad, you'll still exist. You'll still kill people, because you need our deaths to keep going."

It is . . . not ideal. Augusta gestured toward the final card.

May flipped it over and stared into the cruel yellow eyes of the Beast, and she watched, her stomach sinking, as the blood-stained spires of the crown shifted before her eyes. The deck was changing to fit this nightmare she was living in, a threat—no, a warning. There were people on each of the spires now—people she recognized. Justin and Isaac and Harper and Violet, each of them dead. The sight made her want to vomit, want to cry.

"No," she whispered. "I won't let that happen."

You may not have a choice.

The roots below her shriveled and shrank, revealing the stone of the founders' seal. May saw a gap in the very center of the circle; light shone through it, a keyhole, an *idea.* And then the branches swam around her, and everything disintegrated into blackness once again.

But when May opened her eyes, she was no longer in her vision—or the Gray. Instead, she had somehow been transported back to Four Paths. She sat in the center of Main Street, on the real-life founders' seal that had been placed in the center of the town square. Trees surrounded her in a pulsating circle, their branches snarled and knotted together. The sky was open and screaming above her, gray and white bleeding together. And all around her, blanketing the ground, were iridescent bits of ash.

CHAPTER TWENTY-TWO

Justin's idea was utterly ridiculous, which Isaac suspected meant it might actually work.

"This is all too much," Violet said. They were in the lobby of the town hall, pulling down the storm shutters on the windows. Harper and Justin were doing the same in his apartment. Before they could do anything, Isaac wanted to be sure they were as safe as possible. But the town hall was a large building, and it was taking longer than he had anticipated to check everything. "How are you feeling about all of this? If what Justin's saying about his father is true..."

"Then he's my ancestor. Yeah, I know." Isaac slammed down a storm shutter with slightly more force than necessary as he thought of Richard Sullivan's burial slot in the mausoleum. Of the portrait hanging in the archives. Lies, all of it, and Isaac didn't know why that even surprised him anymore. "I mean, clearly he's some kind of founder. And my family always has been a bunch of assholes. Seems fitting that the guy responsible for all our problems would be one of us."

The only silver lining of all of this, Isaac reflected bitterly, was that the Sullivan bloodline was gigantic. All those disappearances had led to a vast, disconnected family network, which meant that he and Justin were probably only about as distantly related as anybody else in Four Paths. He'd dealt with enough tonight; finding out he'd once had a long-term crush on his cousin would have been the last straw.

"That doesn't seem like an entirely fair judgment," Violet said softly. "I mean, there's you, there's Gabriel..."

"Gabriel left."

Violet stared at him, her eyes wide. "What?"

"He ran away from this fight. Just like he ran before."

Isaac hadn't realized how much it was hurting him until he'd said it aloud.

"Shit," Violet said. "You're right. Most of your family *are* assholes."

Isaac couldn't help it—he laughed, and after a moment she joined in, both of them sounding slightly hysterical over the wind battering the storm shutters behind them.

"I can't believe any of this is happening," he confessed, tugging the latch closed on the window and turning toward her. "I can't believe Four Paths has turned into this. I can't believe we're stuck in here. And I can't believe the single real idea we have rests on the only one of us without any powers."

"Ah, Four Paths." Violet sighed. "Always finding new ways to ruin our lives."

"As if we can't do that all by ourselves."

Violet shook her head, still grinning. Her sweater had slid down over one of her shoulders. Isaac couldn't help but notice the smooth curve of her collarbone, the light of the candle she held aloft flickering across her exposed skin. There was a strange, heady feeling building inside him.

"What?" she said.

He shrugged. "It's just surreal to me that it's only been a few months since you moved here."

"I feel the same way." Violet tugged down the next storm shutter and latched it shut. "A year ago, my biggest problem was trying to perfect my audition program for conservatories. Now we might damn an entire town because our ancestors made some disastrously bad choices."

"Has it really been so bad here?"

She met his eyes. Smirked just a little. "It could've been worse."

Isaac still couldn't believe that Violet knew everything he had been through and didn't pity him. All his hopes, his fears, his dreams—she had borne witness to them without flinching, and he had done the same for her. Not because they needed something from each other, but because they'd wanted to. And after years of people looking at him like he was broken, it was a relief bigger than words to know someone else understood that healing did not mean going back to the way things had been before. It meant transforming into someone new and accepting that person, sharp edges and all.

He wanted to kiss her, he realized, and he'd never known that he could have romantic feelings for someone without the sadness, without the longing, without the *hurt*. He did not know how to tell her this; all he knew was that the knowledge of it was burning inside him like a newly lit flame, wild and unavoidable.

And he was trying to find the words to do this, to do it *right*, when Violet spoke again.

"Harper and Justin are done," she said, glancing over his shoulder.

Isaac turned to see that her cat had appeared at the end of the hallway, his tail twitching.

"He can tell you that?" he asked.

"Our tether can," Violet said, already halfway down the hallway. "It's sort of hard to explain."

Isaac watched her walk away for a moment. Then he sighed and trudged after her.

The four of them sat on the floor in the center of Isaac's living room, staring at the cards stacked in front of Justin's crossed legs. Harper couldn't help but feel a stab of unease as she gazed at the all-seeing eye etched into the back. The Carlisle abilities were straightforward and steady, while the Hawthornes dealt in the abstract: memories, fates, futures. It was a power she wasn't sure any human had the right to hold. Then again, that was how they'd gotten here in the first place: because their ancestors had been too greedy to know their limits.

"Okay," Violet said slowly. "So how, exactly, does this work?" She reached forward, but the second her fingers touched the cards, she gasped and pulled her hand back. "Shit. That *hurt.*"

"I probably should have warned you," Justin said from across the circle. "Touching the cards is a Hawthorne-only thing. That's why they're usually in the box."

He reached down and scooped up the cards. They clearly weren't bothering him, although Harper could tell how nervous he was. He looked pale and exhausted; all of this had obviously worn on him. He didn't hold the cards like May did, like they were an extension of her. He held them like a weapon he wasn't sure how to use.

"There's no guarantee this will work," he said. "But I heard most of May's confrontation with our father. The Deck of Omens *talks* to the Beast. And surely the Beast knows how to defeat Richard and give our powers back. So we're going to try asking it."

It sounded absolutely absurd, willingly talking to a monster. But Harper had to admit that none of them had a better idea.

"Aren't you supposed to ask a question to direct the reading?" Violet said.

"Someone else should," Justin said. "That's how May does it."

"You always promised you'd read my cards," Harper said softly.

"I did," Justin said. "So ask your question."

Harper smiled. "How can we defeat Richard?"

And Justin began to shuffle the deck.

For a few moments, there was only silence. The wind howled at the storm shutters, the candles flickered, and Justin's face registered rapt concentration. Then he spoke.

"Okay," Justin said. "I can feel something. . . . May always says it's like a path opens in the back of her mind, like she can see her way down to all of Four Paths' roots. . . ."

Soon Harper felt it, too. A presence stole into the room, making the candle flames shiver. And one by one, just like they did when May touched them, the cards began to disappear.

Justin was doing it. He was actually using the power he'd always wanted. Harper wondered how it felt for him, to know that after all this time he had finally been able to prove himself. His face was slightly flushed; sweat beaded along his forehead. But he kept at it, the presence growing stronger, until there were only a few cards left.

He laid them out on the floor, his hands trembling. Harper tried to remember what came next—May had to touch people for the power to work, she was pretty sure. She stretched out her hand, and Justin, looking grateful, took it. Their fingers twined together, his palm warm and gentle against hers.

And then the presence stirred again, and from the corner of the room, at the edge of Violet's peripheral vision, she saw the thin wisps of a humanoid figure forming.

Harper's heartbeat accelerated, and she braced herself for another Beast-Justin. But he never showed up.

Eight of... Branches...

The words rasped through Harper's mind, and she gasped. Across from her, Isaac clutched at his forehead and muttered a curse.

I have already told you, Two of Stones.... I have already warned you....

"Can you all hear that?" Harper whispered.

The others nodded.

"It's the Beast," Justin said hoarsely. "Aren't you?"

The form flickered weakly in the air.

You should not... have done this.... The words were laborious and carefully formed, as if each one had taken tremendous effort. *I... am weak... and your cards together are... too much... so tangled.... My control is... fading....*

"If you know how to help us," Justin said, "please. Tell us."

The Beast's form flickered in the air, and Harper wondered if it was too weak to materialize. The voice felt softer and weaker than she had ever heard it before.

I can tell you the ritual... the founders did.... They... we...

They ... met at the heart of things ... and renounced their titles as the deities. ... They gave their power back to the forest. ...

Harper struggled to keep up. "Can you tell us how to do it again?"

The Beast's form flickered again, and for a panicked moment Harper thought it was fading away. But then a sound drifted through the room like an ancient radio. It was the song the Church of the Four Deities had sung, but the lyrics were different. Harper had never heard these words before, soft and strange, and yet it felt as if she had always known them, the same way the voices that were singing them were new to her and yet just as familiar as her own name.

"Of course," she whispered, understanding surging through her.

Then she saw the tear glistening in the corner of Justin's eye—gray and iridescent. Harper followed it down his cheek— and then her throat clenched with dread. Because she could see something wriggling beneath the skin of his jawline. A root.

"I think ..." Justin began, reaching a hand toward his cheek. "I think I'm ..."

And then he shuddered and jolted backward, the staticky presence in the room fading away.

Harper lunged across the circle. Cards scattered everywhere as she gripped his shoulder, unable to hide her panic.

"Justin," she whispered. "Oh, Justin, what did you do?"

"Don't worry about me," he said, shaking his head. "You got what you needed."

Something was seeping through his shirt at the abdomen. Harper released his shoulder and yanked it upward, revealing his stomach. Gray veins pulsed beneath his skin.

"It's not supposed to hurt you," she whispered, horrified. "You're a founder."

"But I don't have powers," Justin said weakly, another iridescent tear sliding down his cheek. She could see the roots now, clustering beneath his skin. She had no idea how he'd hidden them for so long. "I've been corrupted since the lake. I figured it out when we got back. It's moving more slowly than it did for the rest of the people who got sick, but it's still spreading." He sighed. "So I thought I could give you all a fighting chance instead of being a total liability."

He locked eyes with her, and the determination in them surprised her: There was no hint of regret, no panic, only acceptance.

"You should have told us," Isaac said, looking perturbed as Justin turned back around. "If you've been corrupted this whole time..."

"I know." Justin looked at them all, shamefaced. "I just... I wanted to do something, okay? I wanted to matter, for once."

Harper's heart ached. She understood all too well what it was to feel powerless in a group of people who could do so much more than you. She knew he hadn't asked to be corrupted. But that didn't change the fact that he had just gone from an ally to a potential threat.

"Take off your shirt," she said quietly.

Justin grinned at her. "Okay—"

"Not like *that*." She glared at him. "We need to know how bad it is."

Dread coursed through her as he pulled his sweater over his head. He turned around, displaying his back, and her heart sank into her toes.

Silver veins snaked from his waistline up to his shoulders, the skin around them gray and iridescent. The roots had settled here, twitching slowly but not moving; they had joined together in a sort of spiral on his back, like a plant that had grown beneath his skin. There were far too many to cut out. Far too many to destroy.

"Harper." It was Violet's voice. She turned to see her friend crouched gently beside her, eyeing Justin with obvious trepidation. "Get back."

"He's our friend," Harper protested. "And he can't infect us—"

Violet gripped her shoulder and tugged her away. "He's still dangerous."

A convulsion ran through him, and his shoulders twitched, his eyes glazing over. He dropped to his knees, coughing, then wiped away gray slime. When he looked up, Harper blanched.

Once again, she was staring at the Beast as it wore Justin's face, as it stared back at her from those flat, dark eyes.

May didn't remember how she'd returned to her own bed, but she was warm and comfortable, and the room was dark. She rolled over, yawning, and stretched, wincing at the soreness in her joints as she sat up.

And gasped.

Dried blood was crusted at the tips of her fingers, rust-brown and flaky, and she could *feel* something on her cheeks—like a skincare mask left on too long. She swung out of bed and rushed to the vanity in the corner. At the sight of the tear tracks on her face, blood that had long since dried, it all came back to her.

Richard. Her power. The cauldron. The Beast.

She walked toward the window, dread pounding in her chest, and yanked up the storm shutters. Outside her bedroom was a world gone gray. Fog blanketed the woods beyond the backyard, rendering it nearly invisible, and ash coated the ground, bits of iridescence and bark mixing with the dead leaves. The tree itself looked worse than ever, veins standing out starkly against the thinning trunk, fleshy and bloated. The sight made May feel ill.

Four Paths was dying, and it was all her fault.

A knock sounded on the door, and May jumped, whirling around, scanning the room for anything she could use as a weapon.

"May?" It was her mother's voice. "Are you awake?"

May swallowed her panic and opened the door. "Mom?"

Half of her was expecting the Beast again. But she knew immediately that this was the real Augusta. It wasn't just her light blue eyes—it was the way she carried herself, the sharp expression on her face.

"So you've seen it," she said, gesturing toward the window.

May nodded. "Are we...in the Gray?"

That didn't quite feel right, but nothing outside *looked* right, either.

"No," Augusta said grimly. "The Gray seems to be bleeding into Four Paths instead."

"Good thing the evacuation happened," May said dully.

"Yes," Augusta said. "Good thing." She sat down on the bed and fixed May with an expectant stare. "Now—would you like to explain to me why I found you collapsed on the front porch several hours ago, covered in slime?"

May stared at her hands. "You won't like it."

Augusta's laugh sounded more like a bark. "Try me."

May's head spun, contemplating all she had learned, all the

Beast had told her, all she'd ever believed Augusta could tolerate before she told her to leave for good.

She had nothing left to lose anymore. So she explained everything, from the rituals she'd done as a child to those final moments in the Gray. It was like sucking out the poison Richard had pumped into her veins.

"I never wanted any of this to happen," May finished, aware as she said so of how false the words sounded. She'd wanted to be important, after all. She had asked for this, pushed aside red flags, deceived everyone in her life just to feel special. "I messed up. I ruined everything. I'm sorry."

She was staring down at her hands, trembling a little, when she heard her mother's voice.

"You didn't ruin everything." Augusta didn't sound furious, as May had feared. She sounded almost . . . gentle.

"I caused the corruption," May whispered, looking up at her. "People are dying because of me."

"This is not your fault," Augusta said hollowly. "It's mine."

"What?" May had never in her life heard those words come out of her mother's mouth.

"You heard me." Augusta sighed, looking deeply uncomfortable. "I miscalculated how far your father could reach. How talented he is at twisting minds and hearts."

"He didn't manipulate me. I *invited* him here." Shame burned through May as she thought of how easy it had been for him to talk her into pulling at the future more, spreading the corruption further. Her desperation for affection and validation had overridden her better judgment in favor of some foolish quest to save everyone. She'd been frustrated with Justin for constantly playing the hero, only to go and do the exact same thing—with far more disastrous results. "I worked with him. I trusted him."

"Yes, you invited him here," Augusta said. "But you only did so because I didn't know how to tell you the truth. There are some burdens I hoped you'd never have to bear. But I see now that keeping them from you has only hurt us both." She hesitated. "Remember what I told you before, May? About your father's interest in Four Paths? From the moment you were born, it was always centered on you and Justin. He explained to me that he had a theory about how to re-create the original ritual the founders did to imprison the Beast, but this time, the ritual would kill it. But there was a catch: It would require a different bonding process. And you two would be, effectively, his first experiments."

"So you knew about the ritual?" May's head swam. "Did you know that I actually did it?"

"No," Augusta said. "I was so horrified by the idea that I threw him out. But somehow, he always found a way back in. He'd send you two presents, or he'd make some ridiculous grand gesture, and I would relent."

May's stomach churned. She could remember Ezra flittering in and out of their lives, could remember the toys he'd bought them. She had always thought of Augusta as the harsh one for continuing to kick him out.

"You never told me any of this. Why?"

"Because you loved him," Augusta said simply. "Because he's your father, and even if our relationship wasn't going to work out, I thought you deserved to have one with him. And up until a few weeks ago, when you came to me with questions about changing the future, I thought he hadn't gone through with it."

"But you haven't let him back in for the last seven years," May said slowly. "What changed?"

Augusta's face paled.

"Something happened the day he left. We had a fight . . . but it went too far."

And May remembered then, that old memory swimming back into her brain. The screaming. *Don't go downstairs, May.* Justin standing in front of her, shielding her, and when she'd rushed into the front hallway—

There had been a red mark on her mother's cheek.

Nausea coursed through her.

"He hit you," she whispered.

Augusta blanched. "I thought you didn't see."

"I didn't." May's mind knitted it together then. She'd *heard* it happening. Justin had run up the stairs and told her not to go down there, and when she had, Ezra had been storming for the door, his bag in his hand. She couldn't imagine how painful it must have been, after that, for her mother to watch her rush after him, to beg her dad to take her with him. "But I should have figured it out. Of course you didn't want him to come back after that. I'm so sorry, I'm so sorry—" Her voice broke, and then there was nothing left but tears.

She was breaking, sliding into oblivion, struggling to reckon with a family that was stitched together by nothing more than the ways they'd hurt one another. No wonder Justin had chased her into the forest. He'd kept this secret all these years alongside her mother.

"You didn't know," Augusta whispered. May collapsed into her, and Augusta held her like she was a child again, stroking her hair as she sobbed.

"It doesn't matter," she choked out, clinging to her mother for dear life. "He won."

"No, he didn't." Augusta drew away from her, and May stared at her mother, her eyes wide. "He made a crucial mistake. He thought he could beat you down until you'd follow him anywhere. But that's not what happened, is it?"

For the first time, May did not see her mother as an obstacle or an enemy. She saw her for who she was. Selfish and corrupt, frightened and angry, yet still fighting with every breath she had to protect the people she loved.

May's father had been wrong about Augusta and Justin. Maybe he was wrong about her, too.

"No," she whispered. "It isn't."

"I've got a plan to end this," Augusta said gently. "All you have to do is listen to me."

Unease pricked at May's chest. Part of her wanted nothing more than to fold herself back into her mother's embrace and nod. But all that would do would be going from being one parent's tool to the other's. Her mother might not have been a monster, but May knew she couldn't fully be trusted.

"I'm the only one who's seen Dad in action these last few weeks," May said, "and I'm the only one strong enough to beat him. I need you to listen to *me* if we're going to take him down, okay?"

Her whole life she'd looked to someone else to give her validation, be it Augusta or Richard or the rest of Four Paths. But all that really mattered was that *she* knew what she was capable of.

She had the power to break this vicious cycle for good. She'd known that was true, but now at last she let herself believe it. Let herself trust that her own voice was enough, that she didn't need someone else to tell her so.

Augusta stared at her, and May stared back, unbroken, unbending.

"Okay, then," her mother said at last, the respect in her voice as sweet to May as honey. "What did you have in mind?"

CHAPTER TWENTY-THREE

They quarantined Justin in Isaac's bedroom. It was brutal work, and he writhed and wailed as roots pulsed down his back.

He didn't attack them as Violet had feared he might, but she was still worried enough about his mental state to remove everything from the room he could possibly use to hurt either himself or others. When they were done, there was hardly anything left besides the mattress he was lying on, wincing at the ceiling.

"It's not... going so well," he murmured. He was drifting in and out—sometimes it was the Beast in there, sometimes it was Justin. Violet was all too familiar with the feeling.

"You have to fight it," she said. "You're still *you*. It's still your mind. I promise."

"I'm... sorry," he croaked, locking eyes with her. "Wanted... to change things. But not like *this*."

"I know," Violet said. And she did know. "You saved me when the Church kidnapped me. Now we're going to save you, okay?"

Outside the room, she found herself pacing back and forth in the kitchen, wrecked with exhaustion. Orpheus rubbed against her legs in a futile attempt to comfort her, but she was far beyond that.

Things had moved so fast, she'd had very little time to process what Juniper had told her—or to worry about her. Now she let it all surge through her, utterly overwhelmed by its harshness. She had no idea where her mother was or if she was all right. And their last moments together before they'd been separated by the corruption had been a fight.

Violet was sad that Juniper hadn't told her the truth earlier, but she also understood the rationale behind her mother's lie. She had to believe for her own sanity that soon they'd get the chance to talk all this out in person.

For now, she had to focus. Justin was sick, and Richard had May in his clutches. They knew how to save them both, but the battle to come would not be easy.

She had the feeling that, one way or another, this fight would be her last.

Harper did not know how to say goodbye. She'd asked for a few minutes alone in the quarantine room, and it felt pathetic to spend them clutching her sword and choking back tears next to her not-quite-boyfriend. But the sight of him wincing with pain on Isaac's bare mattress was too much for her to bear. It had occurred to her many times that their lives were in danger. But never before had it felt so immediate. They were so fragile, all of them, and Harper hated that the feeling she'd had at the lake had come to pass. That she hadn't been able to save him after all.

Justin's blond hair was slicked back against his forehead, his skin sweaty and discolored from the corruption. Nobody had bothered to put his shirt back on, so Harper could see every root wriggling beneath his arms and burrowing deeper into his abdomen.

"You *asshole*," she whispered, staring at his slightly parted lips. "You should have told us you were sick. You should have let us try to help you—"

"Harper." His eyes fluttered open. His voice was weak, but unmistakably his own. "I thought I heard you insulting me."

Harper had walked into the quarantine room like it was a morgue, braced for a body that was already too far gone. Finding Justin instead, shuddering with pain but still *himself*, was almost worse.

"It worked," she said softly. "You woke up."

"It wasn't . . . easy." His eyes focused and unfocused. "But it's a little easier . . . when you're here."

"We're going to stop this," she said fiercely. "We're going to help you."

"Don't—" He coughed, then lifted a shaking hand to his mouth. It came away gray and glistening. "Don't make promises you can't keep."

Harper realized dimly that she had lost the battle against her tears, but these were neither iridescent nor crimson—they were ordinary, and that only made them all the more painful as they rolled down her cheeks.

"You're going to get better," she said, her voice rising in volume. "You're going to be *fine*."

"You're beautiful when you're stubborn," Justin murmured. "Have I ever told you that?"

Harper sniffled. "I think the corruption's reached your brain."

"Nah." Justin's mouth quirked up into a half smile. "I've thought that . . . for years."

Before she could respond, his eyes glazed over, a convulsion racking his body. When it finished, he wasn't Justin anymore. He rose in stiff, jerky motions until he was sitting, his eyes flat and lifeless.

Two of Stones, hissed the Beast's voice in her head. *You are running out of time.*

"Get out of his body," Harper hissed, drawing her sword.

It is . . . far safer here . . . than in the Gray. . . .

"Get the *fuck* out!" She swung the sword forward, bristling with rage, until the tip was pressed against Justin's throat. Roots bubbled beneath the skin, scattering away where the steel touched it. She wished she could carve them all out, but she knew doing so would only mean flaying Justin alive.

The Beast wailed in protest, its tinny voice trailing off, and the light returned to Justin's eyes. His face widened with surprise as his gaze locked onto hers.

"Well," he said weakly. "Trying to . . . finish me off, huh?"

Harper hastily yanked the blade away, slotting it back into her scabbard. "That's not funny, Justin. You know I don't want to hurt you."

"It's . . . a little funny." His lips twitched. "You wouldn't fight me under the bleachers, but you brought a sword to my sickbed."

"I thought I might need it."

"You're something else, Carlisle." He swayed slightly, coughing again, and Harper moved forward out of instinct, gripping his shoulder and helping prop him up against the headboard.

"Thanks," he said. "Now . . . shouldn't you . . . be going?"

"I should," Harper said softly. "But I have to say goodbye first."

She had thought that if they kissed again it would not be as urgent or raw as it had been at the lake. She was right—it was more, and it was messier. His lips were rough and careless against hers, his hands tight around her waist, pulling her onto the bed until she was in his lap. This was a horrible idea, Harper knew that, but she did not care. Instead she leaned into him, trailed her lips down his cheek, his neck, his ear. Her fingernails dug into his shoulder, and she shuddered at the roots that squirmed beneath them.

He smelled like Justin and something else, something musty and ancient, decay seeping from his very pores. She kissed him one last time, gentler now, and drew away. His hair was tousled; his earnest, perfect face was smeared with iridescent tear tracks.

"I understand why you hid the corruption from us," she said, disentangling herself from him and swinging her legs off the bed. "But if you die because of this, I'll never forgive you."

Then she walked out of the room, ready, at last, for war.

The walk through town was tense and quiet. Everything looked dormant and abandoned, storm shutters pulled down on most windows, cars gone, doors locked and barred. Ash coated the ground, shimmering in the cloudy, unnatural light of the off-white sky.

Isaac was struggling to shift his thoughts from the boy they'd left behind to the battle ahead. Abandoning Justin like that had felt dangerous, like they'd come back to a body. But they didn't really have a choice. If Gabriel hadn't left, he thought mutinously, maybe they could've done something about this, even though his healing had failed before. But his brother *had* run away. And it was hard for Isaac not to worry that the moment he'd stopped protecting Justin, Justin had completely disregarded his personal safety.

He knew this wasn't his fault, or his failure, but that old guilt was tough to completely ignore. Harper wasn't the only one who had taken this personally.

They were not in the Gray, and yet this felt worse somehow, knowing that it was no longer contained, that their home had been swallowed whole. None of them dared to break the strange, frightened silence—as if something would come running after them if they spoke too loudly—until they reached the outside of the Carlisle cottage.

The lake looked horrible. Isaac's stomach churned as he eyed the choppy, iridescent water; the pulsating trees hanging dangerously low over the lakebed. Harper, though, seemed utterly unbothered.

"Okay," she said softly, surveying the group of statues clustered outside the lakebed, red-brown stone coated in white and gray ash. "Stand back."

Harper stepped forward and knelt on the ground, pressing her hand to the nearest statue's head. Isaac's heartbeat sped up as he watched it stir, shaking away the detritus of the Gray and walking toward them. It was a fox, he realized, and although he could tell it was stone, it moved like something living.

Orpheus walked cautiously up to the statue and sniffed it, frowning. They circled each other as Harper moved slowly through the garden, waking the guardians up and murmuring quiet commands to each of them. When she was finally finished, looking exhausted but pleased, there were at least twenty stone creatures following in her wake.

"That's amazing," Violet said, grinning at her.

Isaac nodded in agreement. He'd heard stories about the Carlisles, but he'd never seen this power in action before.

It was incredible, and more than that—it gave them a fighting chance.

"Thanks," Harper said, flushing a little bit. She turned to face the guardians, and her voice rang out across the lake, strong and sure. "Remember: Follow me. And when I tell you who your target is, attack them without mercy."

They headed into the woods, flanked by the soft rustlings of Harper's stone army as they walked toward the town seal.

They had a plan, more or less, although in Isaac's opinion it was not a very good one. Their first priority was rescuing May. Justin had told them where Richard was in the Gray—perhaps it was naive to think he would still be there, but it was their best chance of finding him. She would be wherever he was, and then they'd have to see if the three of them were actually strong enough to take him down.

Isaac's palms burned in anticipation of what he was about to do as they reached the edge of the town square. The copse of trees here had grown wild and impassable, pulsating and writhing. Opening the Gray would be the easy part. The airborne corruption had thinned the veil to the point of rupture, and he could feel dozens of potential gateways all around him. All he had to do was find one and pull it open.

Isaac took a deep breath. His hands began to shimmer, and he opened them wide, ripping a hole in the world.

The guardians filed into the Gray at Harper's command. She walked through after them, looking fierce and unflappable with her sword. Violet went next, pausing at the edge of the portal for a moment.

"Hey," Isaac said softly. "You're not doing it alone this time."

She flashed him a grin. "I know."

And then she was gone.

Isaac followed a moment later. It was distressingly easy—no strain on his muscles or his powers the way it had always been before, as if he'd merely had to unlock a door this time instead of make it himself and pull it open.

When he entered the Gray, he landed in a standoff.

Richard Sullivan stood at the edge of the town square, his hands raised, roots coiling at his beck and call from the forest that stretched behind him. Above his head was a broken white-and-gray sky, clouds roiling and clashing together like a thunderstorm.

"Well," he said. "You three aren't what I was expecting. A splintered bone, a tarnished dagger, and a stone with a *sword* of all things."

Isaac realized, dread coursing through him, that his words had come out normally in the Gray, that the sound of their feet was not delayed a moment. If he looked to the horizon on all sides, he could see the world coming undone, the sharp outline of trees fading into mist. This place was falling apart at the seams, and they were at the center of its unraveling.

"Where's May?" he called out, trying to focus.

"Oh, so she didn't send you herself?" Richard said. "Disappointing."

Isaac didn't believe him. Richard wouldn't let her go that easily.

"Don't pretend," Violet snapped. "We know you have her."

"You're in such a rush to die," Richard said, sighing. "Well. Let's get on with it, then."

And the battle began.

Harper raised her hand, and her army of stone animals

rushed toward Richard. He countered with the ground itself. Corrupted roots sliced up from the dirt, coiling around red-brown stone. Isaac stared into the maelstrom, his mind churning.

This was the man all his troubles came from. His selfishness had created the cycle of brutality that had made Isaac's life a living hell. He was the reason why Caleb and Isaiah were dead, why his mother was dying, why he and Gabriel had been broken apart. All for this. All for power.

This was his chance to end this cycle once and for all.

He would make Richard Sullivan regret the day he'd turned on the other founders. And he would show him the boy who had survived his ancestor's brutal ritual. Heat burned through him as he focused on the trees nearest to him, and then his fury surged outward, his hand brushing against the nearest trunk, which disintegrated to ash. Roots coiled around his legs, but they sloughed off into ash wherever they touched bare skin. He was on fire; he was a Sullivan, through and through, and if he could only use his power to destroy, well, then he would destroy *this*.

"Not bad," Richard said, catching his eye from across the clearing. Beside him, Harper hacked off the edge of a root that was trying to snake around her limb. They froze when they touched her, too, in a different way—crystallizing into red-brown stone. "It's interesting to me that our kin chose you as a sacrifice. They must not have seen your potential."

"Nobody deserves to be sacrificed," Isaac said flatly, locking eyes with him.

He heard what happened next before he saw it. The ground began to shiver, stone animals jolting off-balance, and a great rushing sound emerged from behind him. Something was waking.

The roots Richard had been wielding went limp on the ground, and all around them, surging up from the dirt, came the desiccated remnants of the woods he had tried to destroy. Roots clawed their way free of the dirt and raced toward him, taking an entire tree with them. Its branches clawed at the air as they reached for Richard. Violet was in the center of it all, her red hair whipping across her face. Her arms were outstretched, her companion at her side.

She was radiant and terrifying, impossible to look away from. Isaac watched, his heart thumping in his chest, as she walked slowly toward Richard.

"You're not the only one who can handle the dead," she said, and Isaac felt it again, a pull so powerful that she might as well have twined those roots around him, too.

"All three of you are strong," Richard said thoughtfully as Violet advanced on him. "I'll give you that."

Violet flicked her wrist, and the tree branches whipped toward Richard's torso. His own palms shot out, and a moment before they could touch him, they froze.

"But," he continued, a vicious grin growing on his face, "I'm stronger."

He opened his arms wide, and the roots at his feet surged up again, faster than Isaac could process. They sped forward, slicing through the air, and impaled themselves in Violet's torso. Her body arched forward, and her scream split Isaac's world in two.

Suddenly Isaac was back on the altar again, listening to Caleb's and Isaiah's wails, his body convulsing as he struggled to burn through his restraints. Reality flickered in and out—he saw his feet moving; heard his voice roaring; saw a flash of Harper in his peripheral vision, her army swarming toward Richard in a red-brown wave.

He struggled forward, gasping for air, until he reached Violet's body. The roots had released her, dumped her carelessly on the ground. She lay on her side, too still, crimson leaking across her shirt. Orpheus meowed anxiously beside her, butting his head against her cheek.

"Violet," he breathed, kneeling beside her. "Violet, please—"

Her eyes fluttered open, and her hands moved weakly, scrabbling across the dirt until she could push herself up into a sitting position. He let out a deep sigh of relief to see her moving—and then he saw the blood trickling down her chin.

"Isaac," she croaked, lifting herself up. "It hurts."

"I know," he said. Behind them, Harper sent another wave of stone animals Richard's way, but he knew she couldn't hold him off forever. None of them were strong enough to do that on their own. "We're going to get you help, okay?"

Violet let out a choking sound. More blood dribbled from her lips, and Isaac realized she was trying to laugh.

"I know what death looks like," she said. "I'm not the only Saunders. You can still finish this—"

She shuddered and began to topple backward. He snaked an arm around her back on instinct, drew her close to him. There was so much blood; it smelled like copper and iron mixed with the decay of the world around them. Isaac's stomach churned as her eyes fluttered frantically, pupils glazed over.

"Rosie?" she whispered, and he knew in that moment that she was somewhere else. Beside her, Orpheus was curled up on the ground, his body growing limp.

Isaac stared at them both, struggling to comprehend what was happening. He cradled Violet in his arms, unable to breathe, unable to speak. He couldn't save her, the same way he hadn't been able to save his mom, his brothers. She would die here, and he was absolutely powerless to stop it.

He heard footsteps approaching and glanced up, expecting Richard's face. At least his suffering would be short-lived.

But it was not Richard waiting for him—it was Gabriel.

Gabriel was there, just as he had been there on the night of Isaac's ritual. But this time his brother did not hold a knife to his throat. Instead, he dropped to his knees and placed a hand on Isaac's shoulder.

"You came back," Isaac murmured.

"Yeah, well," Gabriel said. "I couldn't leave you to fight alone."

"Don't fight," Isaac choked out. "Help her."

Gabriel's gaze turned to Violet. Blood was still spreading from the wounds in her stomach. Her head turned slightly, a gasp of pain escaping as blood trickled down her chin.

"She's badly hurt," he said. "I'm not sure if I can—"

"*Please.* I can't lose her too."

The words came from somewhere raw and bloody, the part of Isaac that had spent the last few years screaming itself hoarse. It seemed to awaken something in Gabriel: a focus, a purpose.

"I will do everything in my power to keep her alive." He lifted her gently out of Isaac's arms. "But you'll need to distract that founder bastard."

Isaac nodded and rose to his feet, dazed. It had been a few minutes at most, but the world felt different. Violet's blood stained his forearms, his shirt, but there was nothing he could do for her now except keep Richard at bay and hope Gabriel would give her a fighting chance.

He could tell immediately that Harper was reaching the end of her rope. The remnants of stone animals were scattered everywhere, some still lurching forward pathetically, others deathly still. The girl herself was pale and panting, gasping for breath.

"Hey!" he called out. Harper turned, relief blooming on her face as Richard's focus shifted onto him.

"Here for seconds?" Richard asked.

Isaac didn't bother answering. He didn't give a shit about clever quips right now. All he cared about was that Richard had just tried to take away another person who mattered to him, and that meant he deserved no mercy whatsoever.

He knelt down, rage blooming inside him, and pressed his palms to the dirt.

A massive bubble of light rippled through the clearing, creating a shock wave that sent everyone but Isaac off-balance. Harper jolted; behind him, Gabriel yelled in protest, but Isaac didn't care. All around them, tree roots were disintegrating in a massive wave. He shuddered with effort as he pushed his power forward, but before it could touch Richard, it slammed into something invisible. Like a brick wall. He'd felt this before, with the Church of the Four Deities.

"You can't hurt me," Richard said softly.

Isaac snarled and lunged forward again, his hands burning with power, but Richard stretched out two palms and blocked him again. Behind him, Harper gasped in pain as roots twined around her legs, rooting her in place.

"You've lost," Richard said, advancing. "Just admit it."

And just as he was starting to panic, his eyes locked on the smug smile on Richard Sullivan's face, a familiar voice rang out from behind him.

"This isn't over," May Hawthorne said coldly. Behind her stood Juniper, Augusta, and Harper's siblings. All of them looked ready for war.

CHAPTER TWENTY-FOUR

May had never felt so simultaneously powerful and overwhelmed. She stared at her father from across the town square, the Gray swirling all around her, and tried to remember how to breathe. She'd asked for this responsibility, this fight. She needed to see it through.

For once, her mother had listened to her. So had Juniper Saunders. They'd banded together, found Mitzi and Seth Carlisle at their family home and gone looking for the group at the town hall, since everyone's phones were still malfunctioning, but had found a sick Justin instead. He'd filled them in and told them where to find everyone else.

Now May watched as the people she'd brought together rushed into action, just as she had asked them to. Mitzi and Seth ran to help their sister, while Juniper hurried over to Violet, who seemed to be injured. As for May, she stood beside her mother, both of them gazing grimly at Richard.

"Well, then," her father said. "This is a surprise."

He didn't sound particularly intimidated. May tried not to let that make her even more afraid of him. She looked around, taking note of everything she could about their surroundings.

They were standing in the middle of what should have been the town square. A copse of bloated gray trees had grown around the seal, completely blocking off their access.

"You go," Augusta said softly to her. "Get the others."

"Are you sure you can distract him?"

Augusta's smile was vicious. "I will *relish* it."

May rushed over to Harper as her mother stepped toward her father. The girl was surrounded by the remnants of stone animals, looking exhausted.

"You're controlling those?" May asked her.

Harper nodded proudly. "I thought your dad captured you," she told May. "We came here to rescue you."

"He did," May said, shoving down the burst of emotion she felt at that. This was not the time to get sappy. "It didn't stick. You're here to do the ritual, right? To give our powers back to the forest?"

Harper's eyes widened. "How do you know about that?"

"Long story," May said. "Let's just get to the seal and finish this."

They sprinted across the cobblestones to the place where Violet lay sprawled out on the ground. Juniper Saunders was sitting beside her daughter, her face drained of all color as she gripped her hand. Orpheus was curled up in Juniper's lap, while Gabriel was bent over Violet, his hands pressed to her torso, face screwed up in concentration. Green-and-gold light flowed around him.

"Is it working?" Harper asked.

Gabriel looked up, face flushed with sweat. "She'll live." May sagged with relief. "But she definitely can't fight. She needs to get out of here."

Violet's mouth moved. An indistinct mumble floated from her lips.

"Shh," Juniper hissed at them, and they all quieted, staring anxiously at her face. Behind May, the battle raged, Harper's siblings, her mother, and Isaac distracting Richard. She tried not to think about how strong he was, that four of them could only barely keep him occupied.

"I want to finish it," Violet croaked out, her eyes fluttering open. "Let me . . . do the ritual."

"No," Juniper said. "You can't."

"We do need someone from every family," May said. "And if she can't fight, she'll be safer in there than she is out here."

"See?" Violet pushed Gabriel's hands away, ignoring his noises of protest, and laboriously sat up. "I'll be *fine*."

May wasn't sure that was true, but they had no time to argue about it.

"Can you use your powers?" she asked.

Violet paused, then shook her head, panic dawning on her face.

"Not without hurting myself more," she said, looking even paler than usual.

"That's okay," May said, mentally readjusting her plan. They could still do this without Violet's Saunders abilities, but it would be a little tougher. "You won't need them, but you should probably leave your companion behind."

Violet nodded with understanding and gave Orpheus a quiet, knowing look.

"Keep Mom safe, all right?" she said to the cat, scratching him between the ears. "And, Mom—I promise, I'm coming back out."

May wasn't sure that was true either, for any of them, but she didn't say so. Instead, she reached out a hand and helped Violet to her feet.

Harper approached the trees growing thickly around the seal, her heart pounding in her chest. Behind them, the battle raged; she could hear Richard yelling and cursing at her siblings. Their goal, May explained, was to drive the girl's father away from the seal so that they could find a way through the trees to do the ritual inside. They had enough obstacles already without factoring in Richard's powers. It was working for now, but Harper had no idea how long they had until their reinforcements failed.

She turned around one final time and caught Mitzi's gaze. Her sister looked at her, fierce and determined, and Harper felt a tangled mixture of regret and pride for all they had endured. Her siblings were survivors, she realized, just like her. And if she could finish this, they *would* find a way to heal together.

Beside her, May and Isaac supported Violet as Harper walked up to the nearest tree trunk. All the trees were rippled and bloated, the clear outlines of iridescent hearts beating within their chests. Hair hung in great clumps from their branches, which crooked and wriggled like beckoning fingers. Human hands pounded against the trees from the inside out. It was an orchard of flesh, an image that Harper knew would be stamped indelibly on her brain for the rest of her life.

"This place radiates a deeply cursed energy," Violet murmured, her voice a little loopy.

"That's because it's literally cursed," May said, sighing. "Get it together, Saunders."

"That's no way to talk to a girl who almost died—"

"Stop it," Harper said quietly, drawing her sword. "Let's go."

The moment she swung the blade forward, branches shot out toward them, twisting, grasping. May jumped back, yanking Violet with her. Harper reacted on instinct, spinning and slicing through the branches. They fell to the ground, wriggling, as Isaac knelt down and pressed his hands into the dirt.

"Stand back," he growled, a moment before another shock wave emanated from him, just like the one he'd used to attack Richard earlier. The effect was immediate: a line of trees collapsed into a path, sinking, writhing, their trunks bubbling grotesquely as they disintegrated. Harper rushed forward, her sword at the ready. She sliced and hacked at branches as they reached for her, refusing to let her guard down. Every moment of her training had been for this: an army that she'd never expected yet knew exactly how to fight.

Together, they rushed through the tiny path they had made, one that was already closing behind them. Harper saw a great, writhing mass of roots over the town seal that extended up into a tree stump, a cauldron boiling with liquid. Already, the iridescent puddles they had left behind were writhing and foaming, new saplings rising from the ashes.

May walked toward the cauldron, her blond hair streaked with grime, and spread her arms wide.

"This is it," she whispered. "This is where we end it."

The founders' seal had grown markedly more corrupted since Richard had forced May to drink, the branches twining thickly above her head, nearly blocking out the light, the roots growing just as tightly along the ground.

All around them, the hearts illuminated in the trees beat in tandem, their *thump, thump, thump* loud enough to drown out the rhythm in May's own chest. May knew she should feel scared, but she felt strong instead. She could feel the Beast's presence swirling around her—what was left of it, anyway. Feel its panic pulsating at the edge of her consciousness, whining in the back of her mind. It was dying, but what power it had remaining was centered here.

The others looked just as disturbed as she did. May had no idea how Violet was even standing, her shirt caked in blood, her face flushed with the clear effort of every step she took. She swayed, then sank to her knees, panting. Isaac knelt gently beside her, gesturing for May to continue.

Beneath the membranous skin of the trees, forms stirred, vaguely humanoid. They pressed themselves against the edges of the trunks, reaching toward them but unable to break through. May gasped and stepped backward as a handprint appeared on the nearest chestnut oak, bulging outward. A familiar face appeared a moment later, then another, both of them baring iridescent teeth.

May's stomach dropped as she gazed at Caleb and Isaiah Sullivan.

Isaac's voice rang out a moment later. "No," he murmured. "No..."

Violet, who was leaning on his arm, let out a noise of recognition. May turned her head to see that Daria Saunders's wizened face had appeared across the clearing.

She whirled around, staring at faces she remembered from obituaries and so many others she did not. Each of these figures stirring in the forest was a life the Gray had taken to hold back the corruption, to satisfy its appetites. It didn't matter that she knew they were merely echoes, that the souls in each of them had long since departed the earth. They still shook her to her core.

May fell to her knees, her breaths coming too quickly, the world around her spinning. A moment later, a figure appeared in front of her—not an apparition or a grotesque reimagination of the dead, but Harper Carlisle, grime and iridescence smudged on her cheeks, her mouth a thin, determined slash.

May swallowed, tears brimming at the corners of her eyes. "It's all our fault," she whispered. "All of this...all of them..."

"Don't break on me, Hawthorne." Harper's voice was soft and steady. "Not now. Not when you *know* that this is his fault, not yours."

She held out her hand. May grasped it, and together, they rose to their feet. Across the clearing, Isaac and Violet still knelt together, transfixed and trembling. Wordlessly, they walked up to them; wordlessly, Isaac and Violet turned.

"We can't let him win," Harper said.

Violet snapped out of it first. She placed a hand on Isaac's shoulder, and he nodded, leaning into her touch, his eyes fluttering shut for one short, pained moment before they opened again, blazing with determination.

"Let's do this ritual, then," he said. "Now."

The roots grew wild and free, coiling across the founders' seal. May knelt in the center of the stone and yanked them away just as she had in her vision.

"It's like what we did on Founders' Day." Violet's voice was soft. "When they crowned us."

"You're right," May said, her eyes snapping up to the girl's disturbed expression. They had playacted this every year, she realized, glorifying something they did not understand. But they knew now.

Each of them sat in their place—May to the south, for the Hawthornes; Isaac to the west; Violet beside him at the north, still visibly shaky; and Harper in the final spot, in the east. The place where their ancestors had died. Where they would complete the ritual they had failed to finish all those years ago.

An iridescent liquid soaked through May's jeans. The cauldron bubbled and smoked between them as she pressed her hands to the cool stone, exhaling. A presence whistled through the air, a voice in the clearing, tinny and hollow.

Well done, Seven of Branches.

May could hear the voices twined together in it, now that she knew who they belonged to. They were the voices of three people who had found magic in the world and used it to make themselves stronger. They had twisted it and broken it until it could not survive on its own anymore, and all that remained was their blood, their legacy, their ugly, mutated sacrifice.

It was time at last for the monster they had become to find peace.

"If this works, our powers are gone," May said, staring around at all of them. "Are you sure that's really what you want?"

"Of course it is," Isaac said immediately.

"I didn't even know I could have these abilities until a few months ago," Violet said, shrugging. "I think I'll be okay."

Harper hesitated, though.

"It's the only way I can ever be free of this place," she said finally, locking eyes with May. "What about you? Are you ready?"

May nodded.

"All right," Harper said. "We know the song. You'll figure it out, I think—join in."

And she began, the tune as familiar to May as her own heartbeat. It was the "Founders' Lullaby" as she had never heard it sung before, and yet after only a few lines, she felt the forest's presence rushing through her. All their voices joined together, chanting the lines over and over again. It was a song and a promise and a story all in one.

Seekers in the woods, they say,
Found a forest, strange and gray,
Saw its power, found a way
To take it for their own.
Now we wish to give it back—
It was never ours to have.
Heed our plea, we beg, we pray:
Branches and stones, daggers and bones,
We wish it all away.

As they sang, May reached inside herself and *pushed*, surrendering her magic to the tree, energy moving through her and into the seal. And as she glanced around at the others, she saw that they were doing the same.

It was *working*, she realized. The ground beneath them was beginning to shake, the iridescent trees shivering, their fingerlike branches moving in an unseen wind.

And then a noise sounded through the clearing, a scream that seemed to tear through the fabric of reality itself. A figure appeared at the edge of the clearing, his hands braced against two dissolving tree trunks.

"Nice try," Richard Sullivan spat, stepping into the clearing. His coat was tattered, his hair windswept and wild, and blood and grime were smeared across his face. But he was here, and he was standing, and that alone was enough to make May's arms prickle with gooseflesh. "But this ends now."

Before any of them could move, he spread out his hands. The roots untwined from the ground again, easily incapacitating Isaac, Harper, and Violet. They were all yanked back, their arms and legs pinioned together by branches. They struggled and screamed, but he was too strong. The fight was over in mere moments, leaving only May to face Richard.

She rose slowly to her feet, her father's gaze tracking her every movement.

But he could not track her thoughts.

Are you there? she asked.

Yes. The voice was faint, but clear. *You've almost done it. Just one more push . . . just one more time . . .*

I'll do it. May set her jaw.

"Dad," she said. She couldn't think about whether or not he'd left bodies in his wake, and yet she couldn't imagine a world where the other founders let him pass while they could still move. But she could worry about that later; right now, this was all that mattered. The man before her and the ritual she'd promised to finish.

Richard looked at her, and she did not for a moment believe the regret she saw on his face. "It didn't need to come to this, May. If you'd only just cooperated . . ."

"Is that what you told the other founders?" May snapped. "Your *friends*?"

"I'm not here to argue about morality." Richard's voice was hollow. "I am here to take the powers I was promised when I made my sacrifice. There's still room for you to take that power, too. Do you understand that if you go through with this, all you've worked for will just . . . disappear? You're so talented, May. What a shame to throw that away."

May took a deep breath and tried to focus. Richard had raised her to believe that she was meant to be useful, not loved. That no one would notice her or care for her if she was ordinary.

But May knew better now.

She was more than her power. More than the Deck of Omens, more than the Gray. Strong enough to make a monster listen, and strong enough to know it wasn't right to command it at all. It was time to end this now, make it so that no child would have to go through this ever again. She would not let Four Paths do this to anyone else.

She'd come here to give all of this up, and she was not about to let her father stop her.

"But it isn't your power," May said, reaching for the roots in her mind. "It's never belonged to any of us."

As she exhaled, she let the hawthorn's endless pathways spiral through her. Her mind spun, visions dancing behind her eyes, and in that moment it was as if she held the entire forest inside her, as if she was at the heart of the whole town. Her mind spun as she felt the collective pain of all of those who had died here, their horror, their sadness and fear in their final moments.

She collapsed to the ground, her hands twining in the roots, and *pushed*.

The effect was instantaneous. The roots around her friends uncoiled, releasing them; they tumbled onto their sides, gasping for air, as the founders' symbol began to shake beneath them.

"Give it your power!" she called out to them. "Finish this."

Wordlessly, they pressed their hands to the roots as she had; May felt the collective hum of their power as it joined hers.

"What is this?" Richard snarled, stretching out his own hands. But nothing moved.

"You're too late to stop the ritual," May said, tipping her head up to meet his eyes. "I am not your tool. And you will *never* make another sacrifice."

As she spoke, gray mist poured out of the cracks in the founders' symbol. It hung in the air, coiling and uncoiling, and from it, three figures emerged.

At the sight of them, Richard blanched, and May gasped.

"You betrayed us," Lydia Saunders whispered. She was ethereal in gray, her braid dissolving into smoke at the ends.

"You destroyed us," Thomas Carlisle said, his eyes dark pits of despair.

"You have been running for a long time," Hetty Hawthorne snarled. "But not anymore, Richard. This ends here."

They advanced, and he ran, scrambling back toward the edge of the clearing. But they were far faster than anything living, and the moment they reached him, their hands grasping at his flesh, Richard began to scream.

He fell to his knees, writhing and twisting. May gasped as she realized that his hair was turning from blond to gray to snow-white, thinning across his scalp, his flesh puckering and changing as his magic seeped away.

His body turned ashen; his spine twisted and spasmed just as the founders' had in the memory Richard had shown May. Just as the body had in that vision the Beast had shown her.

Around her, the others bowed their heads, unable to watch.

But May did not look away as her father's flesh disintegrated. As roots spiraled down his arms and legs and his eyes faded to white. Soon there was nothing left of him but iridescent dust spread across the edge of the founders' seal.

May got to her feet, shuddering not with pity, but relief.

Richard Sullivan was the only real monster in Four Paths. And this death, at the hands of those he'd wronged, was exactly what he deserved.

She blinked again, and the founders were gone, their bodies dissolved into a mist that coiled in gray ropes around the seal. The Beast's voice murmured wordlessly in her ear, fading in and out of focus. Wind whipped through May's hair; the mist spun, and she tipped her head back, gasping as a great crack appeared in the center of the Gray's off-white sky.

A wave of light-headedness washed over her, and she beckoned the others. They crouched together at the edge of the shaking seal, their arms wrapped around one another as the world broke apart.

The Beast's voice sang inside her mind, and May knew with everything in her that this was the last time she would hear it.

Thank you, it whispered, and then a roar of screaming, howling wind swept it away.

When May opened her eyes again, the four of them were crouched in the center of the town square, their bodies braced against a storm that had finally passed.

They moved apart from one another, all staring with wide, silent eyes at the world around them.

The tree stump was gone. The sky was cloudy and beautiful above their heads, and the air was brisk and fresh, the smell of decay nowhere to be found.

May got to her feet and stared at the trees that still coiled around the seal, at the silver veins already beginning to wink out of view.

Something drifted down from the air above, a single fleck of white. May reached her hand out automatically to catch it, gasping as it dissolved on her palm, wet and cold. And then the relief came, the understanding that it was truly over, it was done.

Because it was not ash falling from the sky. It was snow.

CHAPTER TWENTY-FIVE

It surprised Violet more than anything else how quickly people came back. She'd wondered if the evacuation would be enough to turn Four Paths into a permanent ghost town, but it wasn't. People were stubborn about things like home, even when home was a place where the trees still looked a bit too much like flesh from the right angles and the smell of rot sometimes wafted mysteriously across the town square.

It surprised her, too, how much she missed her powers. They had only been part of her life for a few months, but she'd grown used to them, and although she'd never asked for them, she still felt their absence. Much like everything else in Four Paths, they'd grown on her.

Four Paths High School opened again within a week, as did all the businesses on Main Street. And the corrupted people got better, even Justin. Violet was well acquainted with everyone's progress due to her own elongated stay at the county hospital, where a seemingly endless string of medical professionals commented on how strange it was that two such brutal puncture wounds hadn't done more damage to her vital organs. Violet just smiled and nodded.

She had visitors—Justin, who was also in the hospital and extremely bored, and Harper, May, and Isaac, who all talked over each other to update her on what was happening in town.

But it was Juniper's visits that mattered the most. When Violet had awoken in the hospital for the first time, the sight of her mother sitting at her bedside, her face creased with concern, had been a massive relief.

"I'm sorry about our argument," Juniper said after she updated Violet on everyone else; Juniper, Augusta, Gabriel, and Harper's siblings had been incapacitated by Richard during the battle, but he had not done any lasting damage. Violet understood the thinly veiled panic in her mother's voice now. Their reconciliation was so recent—it was hard for her to fight with Juniper and not worry that it would return them to the way things had been before. "And I'm so glad you're safe. I nearly turned back from the Hawthorne house to go look for you when I realized how dangerous it was outside."

"The same thing happened to me," Violet said, remembering Harper and Isaac refusing to let her charge into danger. "I'm sorry, too. About the way I reacted. It was just hard, knowing there was something so massive you hadn't told me about Four Paths."

"I wish I had been brave enough to tell you the truth a little earlier," Juniper said. "But it's all done now."

Violet hesitated. "Not quite."

The hospital stay had given her time to think this through. The Beast was gone, and so was Richard. The truth Juniper had kept hidden for so long could fade away if they let it, crumble as easily as a bit of iridescent ash.

But Violet had learned by now that the most dangerous thing

in Four Paths had never been the Beast, or the Gray. It had been everyone's secrets.

"How?" Juniper asked.

"I want us to tell the town the truth they've always deserved," she said. "About what really happened with the founders."

"Violet." Juniper's lips pursed. "You know we can't do that."

"Why not?" Violet asked.

"Because someone else might try to do what our ancestors did," her mother said. "You four were altruistic enough to give it up. But the world isn't like that."

"I know it isn't," Violet said. "But we have to be. We've always been meant to guard the forest, right? I don't see why that has to change. But we can't guard it by lying about it. We guard it by being honest about how our ancestors messed up. Even if it makes us look bad. Even if they can't forgive us."

Because Juniper was right that there would be more people like Richard. More people like the Church of the Four Deities. But there would be more people like Violet and Isaac and May and Harper and Justin, too, she hoped. If they told the story right.

"It isn't going to be easy," Violet continued, squeezing her mother's hand. "But even if they hate us, if it means this never happens again, it's worth it."

"I don't know where you get that bravery from, Violet."

"I do," Violet said softly, the wounds in her stomach aching as she stared at the woman who had somehow walked through hell and come out the other side.

Violet spent three days being treated for her wounds and another night under observation before they let her go home. To her surprise, Augusta Hawthorne had taken to Violet's proposal more easily than Juniper had. By the time Violet went back to school, Augusta had issued a public statement describing the facts of what had occurred, then promptly tendered her resignation as sheriff of Four Paths.

With the announcement came endless unwanted attention—stares, rumors, and strange DMs. Violet did her best to ignore it all. She had other things to focus on, like her recovery. But it did not escape her notice how much time Augusta had started to spend at the Saunders manor.

And so she was radically unsurprised when her mother sat her down the week after she came home from the hospital and launched into an awkward speech about *changes.*

"I know it's been quite a year for us," Juniper said, "and I have promised you honesty, so in the interest of total transparency…"

"I know you and Augusta are dating again," Violet said, which earned her a sigh and a rather rueful look from Juniper. "What? You expected me *not* to notice that she's basically moved in here?"

"I just don't want you to be uncomfortable," Juniper said, wringing her hands. "I know that we have a lot of complicated history between us, and I know that the two of you haven't always gotten along."

Violet had been thinking about that a lot lately. May had shared the full truth of Augusta's past, and while it was not an excuse, it still felt like valuable perspective. Juniper and Augusta had both lost so much. She was glad on some level that they'd found each other. She was leaving for college in a few months anyway, and she would not get in the way of the happiness that they had fought so hard for. As long as Augusta behaved herself, anyway.

"Mom, it's cool," she said gently. "Just tell her to stop trying to cook for us, because she's really bad at it."

And that was that.

There was one more thing, though. Something Violet had been studiously avoiding, something she had grown immensely gifted at shoving into the back of her mind. But it would not disappear forever, and it found her shortly after she talked to Juniper about Augusta as she sat at the piano, fiddling with the final notes of the *Gray* Sonata. She had originally planned for the last movement to be loud and furious, emphasizing the minor key before fading into an uneasy silence. But Violet had decided, now that she knew the whole story, that it was better to include a key change. To resolve the chords back to major, just for one brief moment— and then bring the minor chord back in again.

She didn't want all of this to be forgotten. But she *did* hope that it could be forgiven.

Orpheus was curled up on the couch beside the piano bench, sleeping. She'd worried about him, but although the tether between them was gone, he seemed utterly fine. Whatever magic they had given back to the forest was clearly enough to sustain him—he belonged to Four Paths, and he seemed to enjoy the kind of second life it had given him, one where he was the permanent lord and master of the Saunders manor.

She was playing with the chord progression, thinking of those last few moments where the Gray had disintegrated around her, when Isaac walked into the music room. The wounds in her side ached as the November sunlight streamed in through the window behind her, emphasizing the sharpness of Isaac's nose, the curve of his cheekbones, the way his undercut had grown back into a messy nest of curls behind his ears.

"Hey," he said quietly. "I think we should talk."

Violet's heart stuttered in her chest.

She and Isaac had shared so much with each other over the last few months. But she'd mistaken human decency for romance before—she wouldn't do it again.

So Violet had decided to give herself some space. To get over him. She had thanked his brother profusely for saving her life, of course, and she was polite to Isaac in person. But she'd deliberately stayed distant. Because it was the only way for her to handle this that didn't end in humiliation.

"You could've called or something," she said.

"You're avoiding my calls. And my texts. I've been forced to resort to talking in person." Isaac walked over to the bench and peered over her shoulder. "You finished the sonata?"

"Sort of." Violet frowned at it. "It still needs a lot of work."

"Still better than anything I could do." He was so close to her. She could feel the edge of his flannel brushing her shoulder. "How's the recovery? Are you doing all right?"

"The doctors say the wounds will probably scar," Violet said, shrugging away from him and flipping the sheet music binder closed. "But I'll be okay."

"Scars aren't so bad," Isaac said, sitting on the piano bench beside her. She had noticed while trying very hard not to pay attention to Isaac that he'd started displaying his own scar. Not flaunting it, exactly, but not hiding it either. "Better than the alternative, anyway."

"You mean death," Violet said flatly. "You can just say it, Isaac. I think we're both familiar enough with it by now."

Isaac's smile was rueful. "This is kind of what I wanted to come here for, actually."

"To talk about death?"

"No. To thank you. You've made me think differently about the ways I've been handling my trauma over the last few months. It's changed me for the better, I think. And I also wanted to tell you that I get it. Why you're avoiding me, I mean."

Violet turned her head sharply, horrified. She could feel her cheeks flushing. "You do?"

"Yeah. I put so much on you. You handled it really well, but, like, of course you need a little while to process it. Everything that happened to me . . . it's a lot for people to deal with. I mean, I'm still figuring out how to deal with it myself. I found a therapist, and I'm talking to Gabriel about coming with me. But I have a long way to go. Anyway." He shrugged. "I'm rambling. The point is, I understand why you took a step back."

He was so off base, so adorably, absurdly off base that Violet couldn't help herself. A laugh slid up her throat.

"Holy shit, Isaac," she said. "You think I'm running away from you because of your *baggage?* Do you realize how much baggage I have, too? I'm glad you understand how intense the stuff you told me was, and you're getting outside help for it. But I also know what a big deal it was for you to tell me any of it at all."

"Oh," Isaac said. "I just thought . . . I mean, I didn't want to burden you."

"You are *not* a burden." Violet turned to face him. She hadn't meant to hurt him with this; she saw now that she had, that she'd miscalculated. "There is nothing you can say to me that will scare me away. I promise."

"Nothing?" he said softly, and suddenly he was looking at

her with a fresh intensity, with something that looked a lot like nerves.

"Nothing."

"Okay," said Isaac, the next words tumbling out of him in a rush, like a dam breaking. "Because I want to ask you out, but I don't know how. I just know that I want to do it right, and it freaks me out thinking how easily I could mess it all up."

The ache in Violet's chest transformed into a warm, incredulous rush of affection. Her mind rushed through the last few months, and for the first time, she told herself a different story. One where two people slowly let down their walls for each other, even though they'd been through enough heartache to last a lifetime. One where they figured out how to heal. One where they were both scared, but all that meant was that this *mattered* to both of them.

"I have an idea," she whispered, "for how you could do it right."

"Do you?"

"Yeah." Maybe someone else would have played it coy, but Violet had never been particularly subtle. And if Isaac was going to date her he would have to deal with that, so there was no point in trying to hide it. No point in trying to pretend to be anybody else. "You could stop freaking out and just kiss me."

Isaac's mouth widened into a sharp, incredulous grin. "Well. If you insist."

He leaned across the piano bench. The kiss was a slow, gentle thing at first; Violet felt the tension in both of them, the fear of doing it all wrong.

The past few months in Four Paths had been a time of

endings, of letting go. And in the wake of everything, Violet decided that she was tired of being scared. Of guarding herself from happiness.

So she gave herself permission to sink into the moment, his hands on her back, her arms curling gently around his neck, as, all around them, the room filled with the warm golden light of the sun setting behind the trees.

It was time, at last, to start building something new.

They met at the lake, which Harper supposed was fitting, even though it was early December and the weather was *not* cooperating. The water was beginning to freeze over, a thin crust of ice forming at the edges of the lakebed that wouldn't thaw until spring. But outside was preferable to the Carlisle cottage. Slowly but surely, things were improving with Harper's siblings, and she was overall glad she'd come back. However, one of the things Harper really hadn't missed about home was sharing a bedroom. Privacy was a complete impossibility in there, and she refused to have this talk with Justin in front of her siblings, who had a terrible habit of making kissing noises at them.

"Too important to text me, huh?" The tip of Justin's nose was already turning red from the cold, and a giant gray scarf was wrapped around his chin. Harper was still grateful, every time she looked at him, that the silver veins and iridescent tears were gone.

But today looking at him didn't make her feel relieved—it filled her with dread.

She took a deep breath and spat the words out. "I got in."

Harper hadn't been expecting it so soon, but when she'd

gotten home from school that afternoon it had been waiting in her inbox. Early admission to her top-choice SUNY—and a hefty merit aid package to boot.

Justin's face transformed immediately. He grinned, wrapping her in a hug. "That's amazing!"

"It is," Harper agreed, drawing back. "But I'm going to accept. And it means..."

His face changed. "It means you're leaving this summer."

She nodded.

It had been a strange few weeks. She and Justin had mutually agreed to simply focus on their own families in the immediate aftermath of the Gray dissolving. It had been necessary in order to survive the increased scrutiny of the town, and Harper had been determined to keep her promise to Seth and Mitzi to be an actual part of their lives.

The town knew what had happened now. She had braced herself for infamy again, but to her surprise they seemed more stunned than anything else. The fact that the original founders had lied sent shock waves through all of Four Paths, and Harper had noticed the changes not because of how they treated her and her friends, but how they treated the town itself.

The founder portraits in the town archives had been put in deep storage, the lobby placed under renovation. A new sheriff was appointed, one with no connection whatsoever to the founders. Mayor Storey had sponsored a cleanup effort where people helped clear the debris from the woods, now that it was no longer contagious. A copse of trees still grew around the founders' seal, their roots slowly breaking apart the stone. Everyone seemed too frightened to try to move them.

Harper had watched all of this with the full knowledge that

she was letting life happen around her, that she wasn't grasping the freedom she'd fought so hard to earn. And then Violet and Isaac decided to start dating, and college decisions happened, and she knew she couldn't put it off any longer.

"The thing is," she said now, "I know it feels like a long time away. But I also know that you're staying."

Justin nodded. "I can't leave May and my mom."

"I know," Harper said. And hesitated.

She wanted him and he wanted her. That much was clear; that much had *been* clear for a long time. But Harper was also very tired of Four Paths. She'd been thinking for the last few weeks about how good it would be to leave all of this behind, now that it was actually possible. It was over now, and she was ready to go. To find out who she was in a world without founders and beasts and blood.

She could not do that if she was dating Justin Hawthorne. He would always be as much a part of this town as the tree he'd been named after, and she would never ask him to be anything else. But she would not make herself someone different for him, either.

And although she knew they had an expiration date, that kissing him now would only force them to have this conversation in the not-so-distant future, part of her wanted to do it anyway.

She steadied herself and thought again of how much they'd both survived. It was better if they did this now, before it could hurt even more than it already would.

"We don't work as a couple," she whispered, her voice trembling. "Not like this."

She studied Justin's face, waiting desperately for a reaction, but it didn't change.

"I love you." The words rang out in the cold winter air,

through the tall, dark skeletons of the trees. "And I think we both know that you deserve to get out of here, without anyone holding you back."

Harper stared at him, tears freezing on the edges of her eyelashes. "I'm sorry. I wish—"

"No, you don't."

His smile made her break inside, gave her a massive twinge of phantom pain. And she understood that he'd been expecting this on some level. That he was willing to bear it. She hugged him, sniffling against his chest, and he held her as she cried, until at last, she was finally ready to let him go.

One day this would fade. They would grow up and move on and he would be a distant memory, or maybe even a friend.

But that did not stop the unbearable sadness she felt now. So she did not walk home after Justin left—instead, she took the familiar path through the woods and up the Saunderses' snow-covered front steps. When Violet opened the door and saw the tears on her face, she hugged her without speaking.

"Boys," Harper managed to choke out, and Violet yanked her up to the spare room where she had lived for a few weeks, a room that Violet had told her in no uncertain terms she would always be welcome in.

"You can cry as much as you want," Violet told her as they sat cross-legged on the floor, Orpheus prowling at the edges of the woolen rug, his stripy gray fur gleaming in the light of the candles Violet had lit. They were a reminder of those desperate few hours they'd all spent together at Isaac's apartment, a night where Harper thought the world might really end. "This is a no-judgment zone."

"I just hate this," Harper said. "That I know it's right, and it hurts anyway."

"Of course it hurts right now," Violet said as the candles flickered and the world around them flickered, too. "But it's not going to hurt you forever."

"You really think so?"

Violet smiled at her. "I *know* so. You were strong enough to turn him down. That means you're strong enough to get over him, too."

Harper leaned her head against Violet's shoulder, fighting back tears. But they were not the tears she'd come here to cry.

Violet was right, she realized. She was Harper Carlisle. The girl who'd raised a stone army. The girl who had helped save them all. The girl who could finally go home, the girl who was soft and strong and a little bit older than she'd been a few months ago.

And there was a future spiraling wide in front of her, filled to the brim with endless possibilities.

The mausoleum was quiet. Isaac stood in the shadow of his family's ashes, staring at the plaques that reached up to the ceiling, and felt the full weight of the last few years bear down upon his shoulders.

"I think it should be you," Gabriel said from beside him.

Isaac turned. They'd both dressed up for this, ties and sport coats that didn't fit either of them right, and it was hard not to feel like they were both wearing a costume. Kids playing at adulthood, grasping at something they were never quite going to be ready for. He'd left his collar open deliberately, the slash of his scar worn not proudly, but honestly.

"Are you sure?" Isaac asked, the words echoing off the walls. His hands no longer sparked with power now, and although he'd expected to feel nothing but relief when it was gone, the truth was that he missed it a little. But it had been worth giving it up for this, for peace. It was the only good sacrifice his family had ever made.

"Yeah," Gabriel said, handing him the small, unmarked urn that contained their mother's ashes. "I'm sure."

The decision to take Maya Sullivan off life support had not been an easy one. But it had been easier to make in the aftermath of all of this, with the full knowledge that no one would ever have to suffer the same way she had again. The truth was, she had died on Isaac's ritual day, but only now was he ready or able to admit that to himself. It hadn't been her in that hospital bed anymore, nor was it truly her inside that urn, and yet Isaac still grieved anyway.

One more loss for him to bear. But at least he did not need to bear it alone.

Isaac swallowed hard and lifted Maya's urn into the drawer beside his brothers, then slid it carefully shut. A shiny new plaque winked beside Caleb's and Isaiah's.

MAYA SULLIVAN

He'd wondered if it was right, burying her here, but it felt good to know they were all next to each other in some way. His eyes slid to the top of the mausoleum, where they'd removed Richard Sullivan's plaque.

"What an asshole," he muttered, staring at it.

"Tell me about it," Gabriel said grimly. Isaac had only found out after the dust had settled that Richard was the one behind Gabriel's sudden need to run away. He'd cornered him at the

Pathways Inn and told him that Juniper and Augusta were lying about the truth behind Four Paths, that there was no way to fix the corruption. Gabriel, panicked, had listened—he'd recognized Richard as Justin and May's father and figured he knew the truth. Isaac understood why Gabriel had bolted. Growth was hard. What mattered was that he'd come back.

It was Richard's bloodthirst that had started all of this. Isaac knew that now. But against all odds, they had ended it.

"I miss her." It was the only eulogy he could muster. "I miss all of them."

"So do I," Gabriel said. "But I think they'd be proud of us."

His brother's arm slid around his shoulder, and as they stood together, inside a monument to false gods and imaginary monsters, Isaac felt a bone-deep sense of relief.

All four of them were waiting for Isaac and Gabriel in his apartment. Harper nosing through his books, May organizing his kitchen, and Justin and Violet sitting on the couch, clearly in the middle of some kind of argument as he swung open the door.

"I told you this wasn't necessary," Isaac protested weakly, unsure which of them he was talking to. They'd understood when he explained that he just wanted the funeral to be him and Gabriel, but all of them had insisted they help out afterward, and they knew Isaac too well for him to effectively disagree. It was highly annoying.

"We're your *friends*," May said acridly, sticking her head out of the kitchen. "Now come on. We're kidnapping you both."

"I'm not sure it's kidnapping if you tell someone you're doing it first," Harper said mildly. "Or if they agreed to it beforehand."

"Also," Violet said, jabbing a thumb at Gabriel, "I'm pretty sure he could take all of us if he wanted to."

"Hey!" Justin said, while Gabriel simultaneously said, "I absolutely could."

"Semantics," May said, marching past them all and flinging open the door.

It was freezing cold outside—December in upstate New York was not exactly beach weather—but the exercise made it a little easier to bear. Perhaps it was overkill, to destroy the altar his family had kept in their backyard. But Isaac did not care. First they crushed it with a sledgehammer, smashing it one by one as the others cheered until there was nothing left but bits of crumbled stone. To celebrate, they carted over some kindling from the formerly corrupted trees and made a bonfire in the ashes of his family home. It was undoubtedly dangerous, but Isaac couldn't find it in him to be concerned.

He watched the flames crackling and exhaled slowly, his breath visible in the air for a brief moment before it vanished into the column of smoke heading up toward the sky.

"I kind of get it now," Violet said thoughtfully from beside him. "Property destruction is deeply cathartic."

Isaac couldn't hold back his laugh. "I can't do it with just my hands anymore, unfortunately."

"Somehow I think you'll endure," Violet said, knocking her shoulder against his.

Isaac snaked an arm around her back, and she leaned into him, her head nestled against his shoulder. "Somehow, I think I will."

"I can feel you smiling," her voice said, muffled. "You really are soft, huh?"

"You can't feel someone smiling."

"Aren't you, though?"

He laughed, and after a moment she joined in too.

Four Paths had done its best to break him, but he was still here. And he would make the most of this chance he'd been given. The brother who'd come back, the friends who'd stuck around, the girl beside him, just as warm and comforting as the bonfire that flickered around the ashes of his past.

He would never forget what had happened to him here. But it did not control him any longer.

He would heal, and he would grow, and he would *live*.

EPILOGUE

There is something in the forest.

It has been there for May Hawthorne's entire life, but things have changed. She and her family still guard it. Always have, always will. But what they guard it from now are people like Richard Sullivan. People like their ancestors.

People who would seek to take the forest's power and bend it to their will.

The story the founders tell is simple. There was a monster, and now there isn't anymore. Everyone is fine. Everyone is safe.

And it's as true as most stories are, which is to say that it is and it isn't.

It's true that there is no more Gray. No more bodies. No corrupted trees, apart from the ones that surface sometimes in her nightmares.

Instead, the magic is back where it has always belonged: In the rustle of the leaves as they fall from the trees. In the hawthorn tree's half-shut eye. In a brief moment when May turns her head and feels something watching her, feels that it is grateful—and then it's gone.

It lingers in the undead cat that lives inside the town boundaries, still prowling at Violet's side, in the ruins that Isaac and his brother have set about eradicating, burying their past selves in the dirt.

May knows that it will take a long time for trees to grow, but sometimes she goes out into the forest and helps them anyway. It feels good to get some dirt under her fingernails every once in a while. And it feels good when all five of them show up at parties and the town starts expecting them to arrive together, those founder kids always hanging out, because old habits die hard.

Augusta finds the whole family a therapist. May is skeptical at first, but it helps to talk to a stranger about her father, even though they skirt around some of the details. It allows the three of them to find the words they need to start healing.

She watches her friends get into college and wonders if they'll keep their promise to remember this once they leave. And then, in late spring, all four of them surprise her.

"It's everything we could find about the founders," Violet says, pulling a massive binder out of her tote bag and handing it to May. They're sitting in the forest, the five of them; reading or on their phones, it doesn't matter, because they all like to be there. It's where they feel safe.

May flips the binder open to the first page. It has papers from every family, all put together; it tells the truth, or at least as much of the truth as they can manage, through pictures and letters and handwritten stories and songs. And as May clutches the binder close to her chest, she understands why they have given it to her: because someone has to tell the story. Of the founders who became a monster, and the founders who finally laid it to rest.

She sits beneath the hawthorn tree that night, the Deck of Omens heavy in her hands. The tree itself is healed but scarred, deep divots in the trunk where the veins twisted through it. It will never be the same again, but it still lives, and that is all May could have hoped for.

She hasn't dared to touch the cards since her ritual all those months ago, not quite ready to think of how that connection between herself and the forest has flickered out.

But she is finally ready to let go.

May takes a deep breath and begins to shuffle as the branches wave above her head. The air smells of springtime and hope, of new beginnings.

And then she feels it: a door creaking open in her mind, something wordless surging through it. It sounds different from the voice she's heard before, and yet she still recognizes it immediately.

It is the forest she loves so much. It is her birthright. It is her home.

The hawthorn's slow heartbeat courses through her. And, one by one, the cards begin to disappear.

ACKNOWLEDGMENTS

The Deck of Omens was a challenging and personal book to write. I'm so grateful to everyone who supported me along the way.

Kelly Sonnack: Thank you for your tireless championing of the Devouring Gray duology and my career as a whole. You're an agenting superstar. Thanks as well to the entire rest of the team at Andrea Brown Lit, especially Maura Buckley, and to Taryn Fagerness for handling all things foreign sales.

Hannah Allaman: thank you, thank you, THANK YOU a thousand times over for being a complete dream of an editor. You make me a better writer, and you always seem to know exactly what my books need to take them to the next level. It's an honor to work with you.

Thank you as well to Emily Meehan, Christine Saunders and Seale Ballenger, Danielle DiMartino and Elke Villa, Dina Sherman, Jackie De Leo, Tyler Nevins, Melissa Lee, Guy Cunningham and Meredith Jones, Sara Liebling, and everyone else on the amazing Hyperion team. Special thanks to Mike Heath for the gorgeous cover, and to Shea Centore for the interior art. You've all been wonderful to work with.

On the UK side, a massive thank-you to the entire team at Titan Books, especially Lydia Gittins, Sam Matthews, George Sandison, Natasha MacKenzie, and Sarah Mathers.

Amanda Foody: You were there for all of it—and from endless texts and phone calls to crashing in each other's living rooms to panicked airport brainstorming sessions, you've never wavered. Thank you for helping me bring the TDG duology into the world, and for the gift of your incredible friendship.

Rory Power: Any amount of gratitude seems too small for how much you helped me unravel this book and put it back together, but thank you anyway. You are brilliant and kind and thoughtful, and I am deeply lucky that you're part of my life.

To the cult: Thank you for your tireless love and support. A good critique partner is hard to find—let alone nineteen. I'm so fortunate to have an entire crew of wonderful people in my corner.

To my writerly friends: Thank you for commiserating and hand-holding and sending appropriate memes at the perfect time. This industry is much brighter with all of you in it.

Kati Gardner: Thank you for your help on both TDG and TDO—it was invaluable and deeply appreciated.

Andrea, Louis, and Joanna: I'd make an ill-advised deal in the forest with you three any day. (Who's to say we haven't already?)

To the readers who found the woods kids out in the wild: Thank you so much for your support.

To Nova: Please continue taking long naps. You are an aspirational being. You're also a cat, so please stop jumping on my keyboard while I'm doing important things. (I know you won't.)

And to Trevor, who came home from work multiple times to find me lying on the floor, mumbling about plot holes and character arcs: You were right. I finished the book, and I love it. I think that means you get to say you told me so.